Peter Tremayne is the fiction pseudonym of a well-known authority on the ancient Celts, who utilises his knowledge of the Brehon law system and seventh-century Irish society to create a new concept in detective fiction.

All of Peter Tremayne's previous Sister Fidelma novels, most recently, *Smoke in the Wind*, *The Haunted Abbot* and *Badger's Moon* are available from Headline.

An International Sister Fidelma Society has been established with a journal entitled *The Brehon* appearing three times yearly. Details can be obtained either by writing to the Society at PO Box 1899, Little Rock, Arkansas 72203–1899, USA, or by logging onto the Society website at www.sisterfidelma.com.

'The Sister Fidelma books give the readers a rattling good yarn. But more than that, they bring vividly and viscerally to life the fascinating lost world of the Celtic Irish. I put down *The Spider's Web* with a sense of satisfaction at a good story well told, but also speculating on what modern life might have been like had that civilisation survived'   Ronan Bennett

'Definitely an Ellis Peters competitor . . . the background detail is marvellous'   *Evening Standard*

'A brilliant and beguiling heroine. Immensely appealing'
     Publishers Weekly

THE LEPER'S BELL

A Sister Fidelma Mystery

Peter Tremayne

headline

First published in Great Britain in 2004
by HEADLINE BOOK PUBLISHING

First published in paperback in 2005
by HEADLINE BOOK PUBLISHING

10 9 8 7 6 5 4 3 2 1

ISBN 0 7553 0226 5

Typeset in Times by Palimpsest Book Production Ltd,
Polmont, Stirlingshire

Printed and bound in Great Britain by Clays Ltd, St Ives plc

Headline's policy is to use papers that are natural, renewable
and recyclable products and made from wood grown in sustainable
forests. The logging and manufacturing processes are expected to
conform to the environmental regulations of the country of origin.

HEADLINE BOOK PUBLISHING
A division of Hodder Headline
338 Euston Road
London NW1 3BH

www.headline.co.uk
www.hodderheadline.com

For Pat and Andrew Broadbent:
the memories of Iona will not fade
nor the special festive hospitality
of 2003

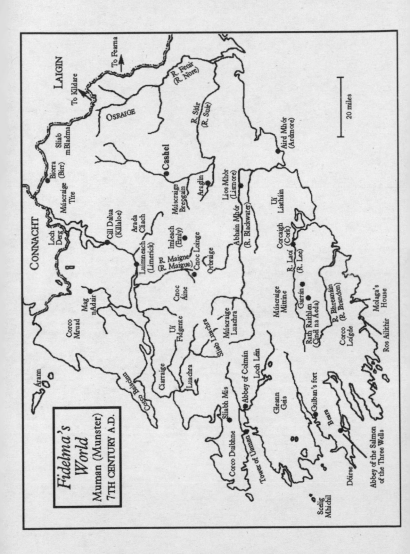

Fidelma's World
Muman (Munster)
7TH CENTURY A.D.

CONNACHT

LAIGIN

OSRAIGE

To Gildare
To Ferna

R. Feoir (R. Nore)
R. Siúir (R. Suir)

20 miles

Áram
Corco Mruad
Mag nÁdair
Loch Derg
Múscraige Tíre
Biorra (Birr)
Sliab mBladma
Cashel
Aird Mhór (Ardmore)

Cill Dalua (Killaloe)
Arada Cliach
Luimneach (Limerick)
R. Maigne (R. Maigue)
Imleach (Emly)
Cnoc Loinge
Ó'rtraige
Múscraige Breogáin
Aradin
Lios Mhór (Lismore)
Uí Liatháin

Corco Baiscinn
Ciarraige
Uí Fidgente
Cnoc Áine
Luachra
Sliab Luachra
Múscraige Luachra
Abhain Mhór (R. Blackwater)
Corcaigh (Cork)
R. Laoi (R. Lee)

Sliabh Mis
Abbey of Colmán
Loch Léin
Gleann Geis
Múscraige Mittine
Garráin
Ráth Raithlen (Cnú na Ada)
R. Bhreanáin (R. Brandon)
Corco Duibhne
Tower of Uaman
Gulban's fort
Corco Loígde
Molaga's House
Ros Ailithir

Béara
Déirse

Sceilg Mhichíl

Abbey of the Salmon of the Three Wells

. . . habebit vestimenta dissuta caput nudumos vesta contectum contaminatum ac sordidum se clamabit, omnu tempore quo leprosus est et immundus solus extra castra.

And the leper in whom the plague is, his clothes shall be rent, and his head bare, and he shall put a covering upon his upper lip, and shall cry, Unclean, unclean. As long as he has the infection he remains unclean. He must live alone: he must live outside the city.

Leviticus 13: 45–6

Principal Characters

Sister Fidelma of Cashel, a *dálaigh* or advocate of the law courts of seventh-century Ireland
Brother Eadulf of Seaxmund's Ham in the land of the South Folk, her companion

At Cashel

Colgú, king of Muman, Fidelma's brother
Finguine, his tanist or heir apparent, cousin to Colgú and Fidelma
Ségdae, bishop of Imleach
Brehon Dathal, chief judge of Muman
Cerball, bard to Colgú
Capa, commander of the king's bodyguard, Gobnat's husband
Gobnat, sister to the murdered nurse Sárait
Caol, a warrior of Cashel
Gormán, a warrior of Cashel
Conchoille, a woodsman
Della, a former prostitute or *bé-táide*
Bishop Petrán of Cashel
Brother Conchobar, an apothecary

Cuirgí
Cuán   three hostage chieftains of the Uí Fidgente
Crond

At Ara's Well

Aona, the innkeeper
Adag, his grandson
Cathalán, a former warrior

At the abbey of Imleach

Brother Madagan, the steward
Brother Buite of Magh Ghlas, leader of the pilgrims

At Cnoc Loinge

Fiachrae, the chieftain
Forindain, a dwarf and leader of the *crossan* or travelling players

At Rath na Drínne

Ferloga, the innkeeper

At the Well of the Oak Grove

Conrí, warlord of the Uí Fidgente

At Sliabh Mis

Corb, an itinerant herbalist
Corbnait, his wife
Uaman, lord of the passes of Sliabh Mis
Basil Nestorios, a Persian healer
Ganicca, an old man
Nessán, a shepherd of Gabhlán
Muirgen, his wife

Chapter One

୧୨

A mist was rolling down from the upper reaches of the mountains, cascading like a silent smoky-white tide towards the lower slopes, silently shrouding everything in its swift forward motion. Strangely, there appeared to be no wind disturbing the noiseless air, but the mist must have been activated by some cold, soft breath to start its avalanche-like movement.

The hungry vapour reached and enshrouded Nessán the shepherd as he moved swiftly down the rocky incline, following alongside the path of the frothy river, which rose in the now invisible high peaks above him. As the chilly fingers of the mist swept over him, he halted for a moment to adjust to the sudden change in visibility. Although he was no stranger to these mountains, he was thankful for the guidance of the river at his right hand side, for he knew that it flowed down to the lowlands, north into the sea, and he would not get lost. It had been a foolish thing to do: to venture into these mountains when the changeable weather could not be taken for granted. Many people had paid with their lives for such folly.

Yet had he really been foolish to ascend the mountains in

the first place? He shivered again, though this time not with cold. He had dared the climb, in spite of the condemnation of the New Faith, in order to make supplication to the old gods. He had told no one about his intention, not even his wife Muirgen, even though it was for her that he had taken such a dangerous step as to ignore the priests of Christ.

He had started his ascent of the mountains at dawn, climbing up by the foaming river and passing the lake, deep, black and still, in the speckled hollow. He had gone on up to the high ridges until he came to the spot where the river rose and then cascaded in a spectacular long waterfall as it began its descent through the lake and down the mountainside. This was the Top of the Three Hollows, *Barr Trí gCom*, where the ancients claimed that this world and the Otherworld met, where the fate of the five kingdoms had been decided by the gods.

Nessán the shepherd knew the stories well enough, for the old storytellers had passed them down to his people as they huddled round the flickering fires of their hearths. It was here that the sons of Milidh had fought with the ancient gods and goddesses of the Children of Danu and broken their power, driving them into the hills and relegating them from powerful deities to small, mischievous sprites. But before that had happened, on these same slopes, three goddesses of Danu – Banba, Fódhla and Éire – came to the sons of Milidh and each had made a plea, acknowledging the victory of the sons of Milidh, that their names be given to the land. So it came to pass. While poets often hailed the land of Banba and Fódhla, the ordinary people accepted that they lived in the land of Éire.

The slopes of these same mountains, according to the ancient storytellers, had been drenched with blood, for the victory of the sons of Milidh was not easily come by. Indeed,

2

on these very slopes fell Scota, daughter of the pharaoh Nectanebus, wife to Milidh, and her druid Uar; Fas, wife to the great hero Uige, who became ruler of Connacht, also perished with her druid Eithiar, and there fell three hundred of the greatest warriors who had followed the sons of Milidh. But in contrast, or so the stories went, there perished ten thousand followers of the Children of Danu, before the battle was conceded to Milidh's sons.

Indeed, these misty slopes had been fertilised by the ancient blood of the combatants. However, even that history was not the reason why these mountains were considered forbidding and often avoided by those who dwelt in their shadows.

It was said that in the time of Cormac the son of Art the Solitary, who was hailed as the 126th High King to rule at Tara, there was an attempt to invade the five kingdoms of Éireann by the army of Dáire Donn, who called himself King of the World. That formidable force landed on the very shores of the peninsula on which these same mountains rose. Cormac son of Art sent his great general, Fionn Mac Cumhail, and his élite warriors, the Fianna, to meet Dáire Donn. At a place called Fionntragha, the fair strand, by the shores of the sea, Fionn met the invaders and slaughtered every warrior of them.

Among the army was the daughter of Dáire Donn, a girl named Mis, who came upon her father's body on the battle-field. She began to drink the blood of his wounds and thus demented fled into the mountains, which took their name Sliabh Mis from her. Here she dwelt in her blood frenzy, killing every animal and human that passed her way and drinking their blood.

It required great courage for Nessán to brave these blood-stained mountains, but he felt desperate and desperation can give valour even to the most timid.

So he had ascended to the black waterfall, and, as he had heard his ancestors had done in the centuries before the New Faith arrived on these shores, he had snared a rabbit to make a sacrifice and called upon Dub Essa, the dark lady of the waterfall, to grant his wish. But not by a single sign did he receive an answer. He waited, trying not to show impatience, but he had no wish to spend a night on the upper reaches of the mountain. All was quiet, and eventually he saw the smoky mist rolling in from the sea. After a moment more of indecision, he reluctantly left the waterfall and began to follow the river downwards. He was on the lower slopes when the mist suddenly came down and engulfed him.

He continued determinedly along the path, hearing the gushing sounds of the river close by, oddly muffled by the mist that encompassed him. Beyond the length of a *fertach*, some three metres, the mist obscured everything and he concentrated his gaze on the ground immediately at his feet.

He was descending now to the level path at the foot of the mountains which he would take to the left, away from the river, around the base of the mountains towards his home. He was feeling a sense of relief that he had left the brooding, shrouded peaks behind him.

A hand bell jangled with a high, strident note in the mist ahead of him. It was a sharp sound even though it was somewhat muffled in the gloom.

He halted nervously.

There was a shadow seated by the dark rising trunk of a tree a short distance ahead. He could just make out the form in the swirling mist.

The hand bell jangled again.

'May the gods look down on you this day, Nessán the shepherd,' came a high-pitched and curiously singsong voice,

4

its quality not sounding quite human in the distortion of the murkiness.

Nessán screwed up his eyes to focus better, feeling the same chill as when the mist had first engulfed him.

'Who speaks?' he replied gruffly, trying to disguise his nervousness.

'I speak,' came the same voice, with what seemed a parody of a chuckle. The hand bell rang sharply again. '*Salach! Salach!*' The words were an automatic cry as the shepherd moved closer.

Nessán took an involuntary pace backwards. 'Are you a leper?'

He could not recognise the figure sitting at the bole of the tree because, from head to foot, it was covered in a hooded robe which did not reveal any features or show any flesh apart from one white – almost snow-white – claw that was the hand that held the small bell.

'I am,' came the response. 'I think that you know me, Nessán of Gabhlán.'

Nessán hesitated. A cold fear seized him as he realised who the leper was. Who had not heard of the Lord of the Passes, whose very name was a byword for terror and horror among the surrounding valleys?

'I know you, lord,' he whispered, 'but how do you know my name?'

This time the curious sound that came back through the mist was definitely a chuckle.

'I know many things, for are these not my lands and are you not of my people? Do I not know, Nessán, shepherd of Gabhlán, why you have been up to the Top of the Three Hollows? Do I not know why you have called on the dark lady of the waterfall even though it is forbidden by those who preach the New Faith?'

Nessán swallowed hard. 'How do you know these things?' He tried to sound defensive and demanding but only succeeded in sounding frightened.

'That is not for you to understand, Nessán.'

'What do you want of me, lord? I have done you no harm.'

This question brought another convulsion of mirth from the seated figure.

Nessán drew himself up. 'How do I know that you have the knowledge you claim?' He suddenly found a degree of defensive courage. 'You say that you know why I have been in the mountains. Anyone may guess reasons when they see a man descend from these peaks.'

The hand bell jangled again, as if to silence him.

'I have been sitting waiting for your return along this path, shepherd.' The voice had taken on a menacing tone. 'Why did you go and sacrifice a rabbit to the dark lady of the waterfall? I will tell you. A decade has passed since you wed your wife Muirgen. One child has recently been born to you and that stillborn. The midwife has told you that you will never be blessed with a child. Your wife Muirgen still has the milk destined for your dead infant. Muirgen is desperate in her desire for a child and, seeing her longing, witnessing her desperation, you in your turn have become desperate.'

Nessán stood rooted to the spot, listening to the recital with growing fear. The seated figure seemed to be penetrating his very thoughts.

'Last week, shepherd, you went to pray with Muirgen at the little chapel at the ford of the Imigh. You asked the visiting priest to intercede with the Christ and His Holy Mother. You knew that your supplications and prayers would go unanswered. That is why you have returned to the old ways, the Old Faith. You went to ask Dub Essa to grant that Muirgen would, by some miracle, have a child.'

6

Nessán's head lowered on his chest and his shoulders sagged. He felt like a boy who had been discovered in the act of some misdemeanour and now awaited the inevitable punishment.

'How . . . how do you know all this?' It was one last whispered attempt at regaining some self-respect.

'I have said, shepherd, that is not for you to understand. I am lord of these dark valleys and brooding peaks. I am here to tell you what you need to know. Return to your home. You will find that your supplication has fallen on favourable ears. The wish of Muirgen is now granted.'

Nessán raised his head sharply.

'You mean . . .?'

'Go home. Go back to Gabhlán. You will find a boy child on your doorstep. Do not ask from where or why he has come to you. Let no one know the way he came. Henceforth he shall be your child and you will name him Díoltas. You will raise him as a shepherd on these mountains.'

Nessán frowned, puzzled.

'Díoltas? Why should an innocent child be named "vengeance"?'

'Do not ask from where or why he has come to you,' repeated the figure with heavy emphasis. 'You will be observed and any transgression of these conditions shall be punished. Is this clear in your mind, shepherd?'

Nessán thought for a moment and then bowed his head again in acceptance. Who was he to argue with the ancient gods, who must surely have heard his prayers and sent this awesome leper as their messenger?

'It is clear,' he agreed quietly.

'Then go, but tell no one of our meeting. Forget that it was I who answered your prayers. Forget that it was I who bestowed this gift on you but simply remember that you owe me a debt. I may ask you to repay it by some favour one day that may or may not be forthcoming. Until then – go! Go swiftly!'

Nessán hesitated but a moment more and the figure raised an arm. He saw the dead white flesh and a skeletal finger that pointed into the gloom of the path before him. The shepherd uttered no further word but strode away from the seated figure. He went three or four paces and then some instinct made him glance back into the swirling mist. A breeze had come up and soon the vapour would be dispelled.

The tree was discernible to his eye but there was no one sitting under it. His mouth agape, Nessán glanced swiftly round. It seemed that he was alone on the track. A cold feeling tingled at the base of his neck. Turning, he began to move hurriedly along the path towards his home, his mouth dry, his face hot and sweaty with the fear that had come over him.

Chapter Two

❧

'Brother Eadulf, the king is expecting you.'

Capa, the warrior who commanded the king of Muman's bodyguard, greeted the Saxon monk as he entered the antechamber to the king's apartments in the ancient palace of Cashel. He was a tall, handsome man with fair hair and blue eyes and wore his golden necklet of office with an unconscious pride. But he did not smile in greeting as the sadfaced religieux made his way across the reception room. Neither did the several dignitaries who stood waiting in ones and twos to be called into the king's presence. They all knew Brother Eadulf but now they dropped their eyes and no one made any attempt to greet him. Eadulf seemed too preoccupied to notice them.

Capa moved to a tall oak door, tapped discreetly on it and then, without waiting for a response, threw it open.

'Go straight in, Brother Eadulf,' he instructed in a soft tone, as if he were issuing a condolence.

Brother Eadulf crossed the threshold and the door closed silently behind him.

Colgú, king of Muman, a young man with red, burnished hair, was standing before a great hearth in which a log fire crackled. He stood, feet apart, hands behind his back. His face was grave. As Brother Eadulf entered the room, the young man came forward with hands outstretched to greet him. There was anxiety on his features and his green eyes, which usually danced with merriment, appeared pale and dead.

'Come in, Eadulf,' he said, gripping the Saxon's hand in both his own. 'Come in, be seated. Do not stand on ceremony. How is my sister?' The words came out all in one breathless rush.

Brother Eadulf gestured a little helplessly by letting his shoulders slump as he took the seat indicated by the king.

'Thanks be to God, she is taking the first proper sleep that she has had in days,' he said. 'In truth, I feared for her health. She had not closed her eyes since we returned from Rath Raithlen and met your messenger outside the monastery of Finan the Leper.'

Colgú sighed deeply as he sank into a chair opposite.

'I worry for her. She is of a disposition that keeps a tight rein on her emotions. She tries to suppress them because she thinks it unseemly to allow others to see her real feelings. It is unnatural to do so.'

'Have no fear of that,' Eadulf said. 'Between ourselves, she has sobbed her heart out these last few nights until I believe she is unable to conjure up any more tears. Do not mention this to her for, as you say, she would prefer others to think she is in control.'

'Even her own brother?' Colgú grimaced. 'Well, at least she has displayed the emotion to you.' He paused for a moment and then said moodily: 'I feel that I am to blame for this grave misfortune which has fallen on our house.'

Eadulf raised a quizzical eyebrow. 'What blame can attach itself to you?'

'Did I not persuade Fidelma to go to Rath Raithlen, leaving her son in the care of the nurse Sárait? Now Sárait has been murdered and Alchú, my nephew, has been abducted.'

Brother Eadulf replied with a shake of his head. 'Unless you possessed some precognition of the event, what blame is there? You did not know, any more than we could know, what would happen in our absence. How could you tell that our son' – he emphasised the pronoun softly as an intended rebuke to Fidelma's brother – 'would be abducted?'

Colgú was not dissuaded from his personal anguish. He did not even respond to the subtle censure for ignoring Eadulf's position as father of Alchú.

'You say that Fidelma is now sleeping?'

Brother Eadulf made an affirmative gesture. 'With the help of a little sedative that I prepared – an infusion of heartsease, skullcap and lily-of-the-valley.'

'I know nothing of such apothecary's arts, Eadulf.'

Eadulf grimaced. 'What small healing art I have learnt is thanks to my study at Tuaim Drecain, in the kingdom of Breifne.'

Colgú forced a sad smile. 'Ah yes; I forget that you have spent time in our greatest medical school. So my sister sleeps? How is her state of mind?'

'As to be expected, she is in great agitation and anguish. At first she couldn't take in what had happened, but for the last two days she has been scouring the countryside questioning all in the vicinity of the place where Sárait was slain and the baby taken. Questioning but learning nothing. It is as if the earth has swallowed the child along with the person who committed this evil act.'

'Evil, indeed,' agreed Colgú in a soft voice.

He stood up abruptly and returned to stand before the fire in the same pose he had been in when Brother Eadulf entered,

11

back to the fire, feet apart, hands clasped behind him.

'Eadulf,' he said after a moment, as if he had been contemplating what he should say. 'I have sent for you because I have summoned my inner council, my closest advisers, to discuss this matter. I have seized this opportune time because I felt it wise to discuss this matter without my sister's presence.' He hesitated. 'My sister is too emotionally involved. During these last two days I have watched her wander in distraction, rushing hither and thither asking questions but not stopping to reflect on matters because her heart is in panic for her child.'

Brother Eadulf felt a surge of guilt. For two days he had been trying to persuade Fidelma to pause and take stock. It was true, as Colgú said, that she was in a state of frenzy. However, he said defensively: 'Fidelma is a trained and qualified *dálaigh*, Colgú. You know her reputation. If Fidelma cannot solve this conundrum, who can?'

The king gestured with his hand, half in defence, half in acknowledgement of what Eadulf said.

'My sister's reputation has spread through the five kingdoms of Éireann for the mastery of her investigations into mysteries and puzzles that no other minds can solve. And your own name, Eadulf, is firmly associated with that reputation. But this is her child of whom we speak.'

'And mine,' put in Brother Eadulf with quiet emphasis.

'Of course. But a mother – any mother – has emotions that sometimes prevent cold logic when it comes to a discussion of her baby. In sending men out to search, I had to rely on you to try to describe what baby clothes were missing, so that we might get an idea of what Sárait had dressed the child in before she took him out that night. Fidelma could not bring herself to examine his clothing to see what was missing.'

Eadulf silently agreed that it was true. He had had to

search through the little chest wherein they kept Alchú's baby clothes, trying to remember what had been there in order to recall what he might have been dressed in. Fidelma was too upset to do so.

'Well, Eadulf,' Colgú continued, 'you are the father of the child. That is true. But a man is more phlegmatic than a woman, and you especially, Eadulf, since I have known you, have been like a rock in a turbulent sea. Equable and self-controlled.'

Brother Eadulf sighed deeply. He did not feel cool-headed and balanced but he was inclined to agree with the young king that these last two days Fidelma had let her anxieties overwhelm her training as a clinical investigator of mysteries. However, his own emotional attachment to Fidelma made him feel as if he were betraying her by agreeing with Colgú.

'What are you proposing?' he asked quietly.

'That my council meet and we all – my advisers, you and I – sit down and discuss what we know of this matter. The facts first. Then what possibilities there are of discovering who might be responsible for the crime. The others stand ready outside. Do you agree on this course, Eadulf?'

Brother Eadulf thought for a moment more and then shrugged.

'We cannot continue without a plan,' he agreed. 'Nor should we do nothing at all. So the idea is acceptable to me.'

Colgú, without a further word, turned and reached for a small silver hand bell. Almost before its jangle had ceased, the door was thrown open and in came several men. Eadulf rose to his feet for, although he was the husband of Colgú's sister, his status in the kingdom of Muman was that of a stranger; a distinguished stranger, but still a foreigner to the kingdom, a visitor from the land of the South Folk, among the kingdoms of the Angles and Saxons.

13

They entered in order of precedence. The handsome young prince, Finguine, cousin to Colgú, was tanist or heir apparent to the kingship. Then came the elderly Brehon Dathal, chief legal adviser to the king, and with him was Cerball the Bard, the repository of all the genealogies and history of the kingdom, carrying a leather satchel. Ségdae came next, bishop of Imleach, *comarb* or successor of the Blessed Ailbe, who first brought Christianity to Muman. Behind them came Capa, chief warrior of Cashel as well as commander of the king's élite corps of bodyguards, each of whom was distinguished by the golden torque or collar that he wore round his neck. Moreover, Capa had been brother-in-law to the murdered nurse, Sárait. These were Colgú's closest advisers in the governing of the biggest of the five kingdoms of Éireann.

Colgú made his way to a round oak table on the far side of the room and sat down.

'There will be no ceremony. Seat yourselves and we will talk as equals, for in this council we are all equal. Eadulf – you will be seated next to me, here on my left.'

Eadulf hid his surprise at this intimate gesture before the members of the king's council. Yet no one seemed either shocked or put out by this honour shown to someone who was a stranger. If the truth were known, it was Eadulf's own insecurity that kept his status in the forefront of his mind. After all, although the father of Fidelma's son, he was only her *fer comtha*, not a 'full-husband'. The marriage laws of the five kingdoms were complicated and there were several definitions of what constituted proper wedlock. There were, in fact, nine different types of union, and while the status and rights of husband and wife between Eadulf and Fidelma were recognised under the law of the *Cáin Lánamnus*, it was still a trial marriage, lasting a year and a day. After that time, if unsuccessful, both sides could go their separate ways without incurring penalties or blame. Eadulf was well aware of the temporary nature of his position.

The members of the council took their seats round the table and there was an uncomfortable silence before Colgú, looking round to make sure they were all settled, spoke.

'You all know why you are summoned. Let us start off by recording the facts as we know them.'

Cerball, as bard and recorder, cleared his throat at once. 'The facts are simple. Sárait, a nurse, was slain and the child in her care was abducted. The child was the baby Alchú, son of Fidelma of Cashel and Eadulf of Seaxmund's Ham, a stranger to this kingdom. And this terrible event occurred four nights ago.'

There was a pause.

'Now let us add to those facts,' said Colgú. 'Sárait had served as a nurse in this palace of Cashel for nearly six months. My sister had chosen her when she needed a wet nurse on the birth of her child. Is this not so, Eadulf?'

Eadulf glanced up in surprise at being addressed in council by the king. Colgú smiled encouragingly as he correctly guessed the reason for the Saxon's hesitation.

'You have permission to speak freely at any time during these proceedings,' he added.

Eadulf inclined his head. 'It is true. Sárait was well regarded by both Fidelma and me. Fidelma trusted her to the extent that she made her wet nurse to our baby. When we were asked to journey to Rath Raithlen, we entrusted Alchú without qualms into her care.'

Colgú glanced at Capa. 'Sárait was sister to your wife, Capa. What would you add to this?'

The commander of the warriors pushed back his fair hair with a slightly vain gesture and leant back in his chair. His blue eyes were penetrating and serious. He looked sombre now.

'Sárait was a handsome woman, a mature woman,' he said slowly, clearly thinking about his choice of words. 'She was neither frivolous nor thoughtless and took her responsibilities seriously. She was a widow. Her husband Callada had been a warrior who gave his life defending this kingdom against the Uí Fidgente in the battle at Cnoc Áine. I can vouch for Sárait's probity. She had one relative and that was a sister called Gobnat, who, as everyone here knows, is my wife. We dwell in the township below the Rock. Sárait served at the palace, as Brother Eadulf has said. Her own baby had died and so the lady Fidelma took her to be wet nurse to their child.'

Colgú glanced round the table. 'When the news of the finding of Sárait's body was brought to me, I asked for the facts. I gathered that a child had come to the fortress with a message for Sárait. The message purported to come from her sister, Gobnat, asking Sárait to go to her immediately.'

'Was any reason given as to why Gobnat wanted to see her sister so urgently?' intervened Brehon Dathal. The old judge had a pedantic manner and took his position very seriously.

'The reason is not known,' replied Colgú. 'We presume that, not finding anyone to look after her charge, Sárait had no other course but to take the baby with her when she left the fortress. We also presume that she intended to go down to the township to see Gobnat in response to that message. An hour or so later, a woodsman, Conchoille, on his way home, discovered the body of Sárait in the woods outside the township. There was no sign of the baby.'

No one spoke. They had heard these facts before.

'And, for the record, Capa, what had your wife to say about this summons to Sárait?' prompted Brehon Dathal.

'That she did not send any summons at all to her sister. She and I knew nothing until we were told of Sárait's death,' answered Capa immediately.

'Which was how?' the old judge demanded.

'The first Gobnat and I knew that anything was amiss was when Conchoille, the woodsman, knocked on our door close on midnight and told us that he had found Sárait's body. I went back with him, but not before sending a message to the fortress to alert the guards. It was only later that we discovered that Sárait had left the palace with the baby.'

'And what of the child who came to the fortress with the message that purported to come from your wife?' queried Brehon Dathal.

Capa raised his arms in a gesture that indicated a lack of knowledge.

'The child has not been identified and inquiries in the township or immediate countryside have failed to find any such child.'

'Surely the guard who passed the child through . . .?' Eadulf began.

Capa was shaking his head.

'All that is remembered is that a small child, in a grey woollen robe on which the cowl had been drawn up, almost in the manner of a religious, came to the gates. The child appeared to be a mute for a piece of bark was handed to the guard on which was written "I am sent to see Sárait". The guard could not swear to any distinguishing features save that it was a thickset child who walked with a curious gait.'

'Such a child is surely not hard to find,' muttered Brethon Dathal.

'Nevertheless,' repeated Capa, 'the child has not been found.'

'And the piece of bark?' demanded Eadulf. 'Was that retained?'

'It was not.'

Eadulf shook his head with a sigh. All this was merely confirming what he already knew.

'All this happened in the evening . . .?' queried Cerball, who was keeping the record.

'It was already dark, for the sun sets early now that the feast of Samhain has passed,' replied Capa.

'Blame may be ascribed to Sárait for the lack of thought she displayed in taking the baby from the protection of the palace out into the winter evening.'

It was Brehon Dathal, the old judge, who made the comment. He was punctilious when it came to law and sometimes, it was said, he allowed for no human frailty.

Bishop Ségdae, the senior bishop and abbot of the kingdom, made a noise that sounded suspiciously like an ironic snort.

'In this situation, where she receives an urgent message from her sister, or is led to believe that she has, and can find no other to take care of the child, it would be natural for Sárait to take the baby with her,' he pointed out.

There was, as Eadulf had already picked up, a hint of rivalry between the two elderly men. Both were not averse to trying to score points against each other.

'Very well,' broke in Colgú. 'You are both right, but Sárait paid with her life for her mistake.'

'What of the woodsman who found the body?' asked Eadulf.

'Conchoille? He is known as a loyal man of Cashel,' Capa said immediately. 'He also fought against the Uí Fidgente at Cnoc Áine.'

'We should question him, though,' Bishop Ségdae said.

'Brehon Dathal has already done so,' Colgú replied. Indeed, Dathal, as Chief Brehon, had questioned everyone involved, from the guard who admitted the child messenger to the fortress to Gobnat, Sárait's sister.

'Even so, and with due respect to Brehon Dathal,' replied Bishop Ségdae in a pointed fashion, 'this council needs to make sure of its facts. So I have actually sent for Capa's wife, Gobnat, and for Conchoille and the guard who, I suspect, cannot add more to what has been said. But they all wait outside. I think we should all hear their stories in their own words.'

The Brehon Dathal was clearly irritated.

'A waste of time. I can tell you exactly what their evidence is.'

'It's not like hearing it for ourselves,' Bishop Ségdae replied. 'Then we can be sure it is not distorted.'

The Brehon Dathal's brows drew together.

'Are you suggesting . . .?' he began menacingly.

'There was a recent hearing at Lios Mhór,' broke in Bishop Ségdae softly, staring towards the ceiling as if in reflection, 'where the judge misunderstood some evidence and gave an erroneous judgement. The judgement was appealed and the judge had to pay compensation . . .'

Eadulf knew that Brehons could have their decisions appealed. If the judge was shown to have been biased, been bribed or issued a false judgement, as opposed to made a genuine error, then that judge could be deprived of his office and his honour-price. In other cases, fines were levied according to the extent of the error and its nature.

Brehon Dathal had grown crimson and he was making angry noises as he tried to find words to respond.

'At some stage we would have had to place this evidence on record,' Colgú said, trying to pacify the Brehon's wounded ego. 'So perhaps it is best if we hear all the witnesses now. Cerball will take down a record of their statements.'

'I have come prepared with my materials, lord,' the bard

agreed, drawing from his leather satchel some writing tablets, wooden frames in which there was soft clay, and a stylus.

Brehon Dathal glared at Bishop Ségdae with a look of hatred. Then he said: 'By all means, let us have the witnesses in one by one. Let us start with the guard.'

Capa glanced towards Colgú for confirmation of the procedure and the king nodded slightly. There was no need to upset the old judge further.

A moment later Capa had ushered in a warrior of medium height and sandy-coloured hair. He came to stand facing them at the table with an impassive expression.

'Your name, warrior?' demanded the Brehon Dathal.

'Caol, my lord. Fifteen years in the service of the kings of Muman.'

'I see, Caol, that you wear the golden necklet of the élite bodyguard of Cashel,' Colgú said.

The warrior was not sure if this was a question or simply a statement of fact, as his emblem was obvious.

'I do, lord,' he responded.

'We have heard, Caol, that you were on guard on the day Sárait was killed,' Colgú went on.

'I was on guard at the main gate of the palace, lord.'

'Tell us, in your own words, what happened.'

'It was just after darkness fell, late in the afternoon, that a child approached the gates. I did not recognise him for it was dark and even by the torchlight at the gates the manner of his clothing hid his features. But I doubt whether I have seen him before.'

Eadulf frowned. 'You say "him". Are you certain of the child's sex? In which case, presumably, you could see enough to tell whether the child was girl or boy?'

The warrior glanced at him and hesitated before replying.

'Speak up, man!' snapped Brehon Dathal.

'The child was clad in a robe from poll to ankle, a cowl being around its head. Yet I would say that it was male.'

'Why so? And why, not being able to perceive the features, did you also say that you doubt whether you had seen the child before?' Brehon Dathal said pointedly.

'The same answer applies to both questions. The child, in spite of the robes, seemed thickset in appearance and walked with a curious waddling gait. I believe that no girl would be so thickset, and that figure and gait would have been known to me if it were a child I had seen in the township or the palace. So I therefore concluded it was a stranger.'

Brehon Dathal sniffed irritably.

'It behoves you only to tell us the facts,' he rebuked the warrior. 'This is speculation.'

'Nevertheless,' intervened Bishop Ségdae with a smile, 'it is a logical conclusion to have drawn.'

'You told Capa that the child was mute,' went on Brehon Dathal, a tone of sarcasm entering his voice. 'How did you conclude that? Speculation again?'

'That is simple, learned Brehon. The child did not talk but handed me a piece of birch bark on which was written "I am sent to see Sárait". By signs and grunting noises the child indicated that he could not speak. I told him how to find her chamber.'

'And you didn't retain this piece of bark?' asked Eadulf.

The warrior shook his head. 'There was no reason for me to do so.'

'In what form was the writing?'

The warrior looked perplexed.

'Was it in the old form that you call ogham script or in the new script?' Eadulf explained.

'I cannot read the ogham,' replied the warrior. 'But I have been taught to read by the monks of Lios Mhór. The message was written in the new script that we now learn, and in bold letters.'

'Then what happened?' asked Brehon Dathal.

'A short while later, the child returned through the gate and did not respond to my salutation, from which I felt that he was not only dumb but hard of hearing. He disappeared into the night and I presumed at the time he was heading down the hill to the township. A short time elapsed and then Sárait came hurrying through the gates with a baby in her arms and told me that she had been called urgently to see her sister and would return shortly should anyone enquire after her or the child. She told me there was no one with whom she could safely leave the baby so she was taking it with her. That is all I know of these matters until someone came from the village on the orders of Capa to say Sárait's body had been discovered.'

'Which was when?' asked Eadulf.

'Towards the end of my period of duty, just before midnight.'

'Yet Sárait had told you that she would return shortly and she had not returned by midnight. Were you not worried for her?'

Caol shook his head. 'She had told me that she was visiting her sister. Everyone knows Gobnat. Her husband stands before you, the commander of the king's guards. Capa would have seen her safely back to the palace.'

There was a silence. Then Colgú dismissed the warrior and turned to Capa.

'You may bring in your wife.'

The woman who entered looked slightly awed by the company. She was an attractive woman, although no beauty. Her features were perhaps a little too sharp and angular for that. Eadulf could recognise something of Sárait in her sister.

22

Gobnat had a certain amount of strength in her features, almost a defiance, that was not possessed by the dead nurse. Sárait was softer, Eadulf thought, while Gobnat's mouth was firmly set. She exchanged a quick glance with her husband, as if seeking reassurance, then came to stand somewhat stiffly before the king.

'Do not be nervous, Gobnat.' Colgú smiled quickly. 'You know all of us and we have spoken with you severally during these last few days. You also know that we share your sorrow over the death of your sister.'

The woman bobbed as if performing a curtsey.

'I do, my lord. Thank you.'

The Brehon Dathal was sterner than the king.

'We want you to place in evidence your knowledge of the events of Sárait's death. We are told that she received a message telling her that you wanted to see her urgently. Not finding anyone to take care of the baby, she took him with her and went to see you.'

Gobnat shook her head. 'Not so, lord. All I know is that Conchoille, the woodsman, came to my door and told me that he had found my sister's body,' she said in a broken voice. 'I could not believe it as she lived and worked here, in the safety of the palace. Conchoille said that she was in the woods outside the village. My husband sent a message to the palace and went with Conchoille to recover the body. Between them they brought it to my house.'

'And you had not sent your sister a message that evening asking her to come to see you as a matter of urgency?' asked Bishop Ségdae in a more kindly voice than Brehon Dathal had employed.

'I had not.'

'You did not send a message by a child?' pressed Brehon Dathal, determined not to be left out.

'I have told you. I did not.' Gobnat stood twisting her hands together, clearly upset by the elderly judge's tone.

'You do not know any such child as is said to have delivered the message to Sárait?' Brehon Dathal seemed to wish to labour the matter.

'An improper question,' snapped Bishop Ségdae. 'The witness was not here when the description was given by Caol.'

Brehon Dathal flushed and Colgú hurriedly intervened again to keep the peace.

'This is not a court of law, so we do not have to be so formal. However, I think that we may accept Gobnat's word that she did not send any message to her sister at that time.'

'What time did the news come to you of the discovery of Sárait's body?' asked Eadulf.

'My husband and I were about to retire for the night. That was just before midnight.'

'And your husband had been with you since when?' asked Brehon Dathal.

Gobnat frowned quickly before answering.

'He had returned from the palace for the evening meal. That was a few hours after dusk had fallen. We had eaten, talked a little and were preparing for bed, as I have said.'

Bishop Ségdae was nodding sympathetically.

'It is as Capa says,' he said heavily for Brehon Dathal's benefit. Then he turned to the warrior. 'I suppose that you have asked throughout the township and surrounding countryside whether anyone recognised the description of the child given by Caol?'

'It was my first thought to make such inquiries, lord,' replied Capa.

'In that case,' Colgú intervened 'that is all, Gobnat. Thank you for attending.' He glanced at Capa. 'Would you bring in Conchoille?'

The woodsman who came to stand before them was of an indiscernible age, neither young nor elderly. He was muscular beneath his leather jerkin and his clear nut-brown skin demonstrated that he pursued an outdoor life. He displayed no awe at being confronted by the most prominent men of the kingdom.

'We just want to record the circumstances in which you found the body of Sárait,' Colgú said.

The man folded his arms across a broad chest and gazed thoughtfully at them.

'I have told the story several times.'

Brehon Dathal's brows gathered in an angry frown and he opened his mouth to speak but Bishop Ségdae, turning a broad smile on the man, spoke first.

'Indulge us by telling it one more time and we will try to make this the last.'

Conchoille shrugged indifferently. 'There is little to tell. I had been cutting wood by the place known as the rath of quarrels, south of here—'

'We know the place, Conchoille,' snapped Brehon Dathal testily. 'It is not much more than a mile south from here.'

'I had finished my day's work,' went on the woodsman, unperturbed. 'By the time I finished clearing up it was dark and so I set off for the township.'

Brehon Dathal leant forward quickly. 'It is dark in the late afternoon at this time of year. We have heard that it was shortly before midnight that you knocked on the door of Capa and Gobnat's cabin with news of your discovery. Now, estimating the time you finished work and set off for the township, and the time you spent presumably at the place where you found the body, even a slow walker would have been knocking at Capa's cabin many hours before you did so. Explain this anomaly?'

Conchoille looked in bemusement at the elderly judge. 'I do not understand such big words. Should I not be allowed to tell the tale in my own way?'

Brehon Dathal looked scandalised at the retort. Once more Colgú decided to intervene.

'We are interested in the truth but I can understand Brehon Dathal's question,' he said. 'Why did you take so long to get from your place of work, find the body and arrive at Capa's house?'

'Along the path before you enter the dark patch of woods is the inn of Ferloga. I no longer have a wife. It is my custom, therefore, at the end of my day's work to have my evening meal and a drink in Ferloga's inn if I am in that vicinity. So there I ate, and after I had exchanged a story or two with Ferloga I continued my journey to the village. I have told this story before.' He glanced with meaning at the elderly Brehon Dathal.

'Continue,' prompted Colgú.

'The path beyond the lantern that lights the sign of Ferloga's inn is dark, especially where it winds into the woods.'

'Did you not have a lantern?' queried Brehon Dathal pedantically.

The woodsman looked pained. 'Only a fool would not carry a lantern through the woods at that time. Remember that we have plenty of wolves roaming those woodlands.'

'I just want it made clear in the record,' snapped Brehon Dathal defensively.

'I had a lantern and it was lit,' returned Conchoille solemnly. 'I was coming to the outskirts of the township when I tripped over something on the path. I raised my lantern and saw that it was a shawl. A shawl of good quality, so I bent to pick it up. The first thing I realised was that it was bloodstained. Then the edge of the circle of light from the lantern caught something white on the ground. It was an arm.'

Then, as I moved nearer, I saw the body . . . it was Sárait. She was dead.'

'And you knew it was Sárait?' queried Bishop Ségdae.

Conchoille sighed deeply. 'Everyone in the village knew Sárait. She was a fine, comely woman and a widow. Many men would start counting how much they could afford by way of a *coibche* when their eyes fell on her.'

A *coibche* was the principal dowry paid by the prospective husband to the bride's family. After a year, the bride's father had to give one third to the girl who retained this as her personal property.

'Were you able to see how she had died?' asked Eadulf.

'Not then. Only that there was blood about the head.'

'What did you do then?' demanded Brehon Dathal.

'I ran to raise the alarm. I went directly to the house of Capa. I knew he was husband to Gobnat, Sárait's sister. Capa ordered his wife to remain in the cabin while he came with me, and along the way we saw someone making their way to the palace so Capa told him to raise the guard there. Capa and I carried the body back to his cabin. It was in the light of the cabin that we saw that the head had been battered and there were some stab wounds in the chest. Later, when Caol and his guards arrived, we heard that Sárait had left the fortress with the baby, Alchú. We returned to the woods and searched but there was no sign of the child.'

Capa was nodding slowly in agreement.

'This is true,' he intervened. 'I had no idea about the missing baby until Caol told me. Some neighbours, who had heard the commotion, joined us. It was clear that Sárait had not been killed by wild woodland animals, which is what we first thought when Conchoille told us that he had found her body. As he said, we went back to the spot and searched by lantern light but there was no sign of the baby. We searched again at first light but once more there was nothing to be found. Men were despatched the next day to spread the word, riding east to Gabrán, south to Lios Mhór, west to Cnoc Loinge and north to Durlas.'

Brother Eadulf had been sitting, head forward, listening to the evidence that he had already heard in emotional exchanges with Fidelma during the last two days. But now he felt more detached, as if he were hearing the facts for the first time. A thought occurred to him.

'Conchoille, you have said that you were working to the south of the township?'

'I did.'

'And you came across Sárait's body towards the edge of the woods, south of the township as you were returning to it?'

'That is what I said.'

Brother Eadulf rubbed his chin reflectively.

'What is it, Eadulf?' queried Colgú.

'I can confirm that Conchoille led us to a spot on the track south of the township,' Capa put in, looking curiously at the Saxon.

'We seem to be overlooking a curious puzzle here,' Eadulf said slowly.

'I don't see—' began Brehon Dathal officiously.

'This fortress stands to the north of the township, correct? You leave the gateway, as Sárait did with the baby, and walk down along the track which leads to the township, and she was found south of the township on the track beyond?'

Brehon Dathal exhaled impatiently. 'What is your point?'

It was Finguine, the tanist, who had said nothing so far in the council, who spoke. His voice was tinged with bewilderment.

'I understand the point. Sárait had been summoned

28

urgently to her sister, Gobnat. Gobnat lives in the township.'

'But Gobnat said she had not summoned her,' Brehon Dathal pointed out.

'True. But Sárait did not know that. Why, then, did she go through the township to be found murdered beyond it in the woods? Why take the child so far? What persuaded her to go past her sister's house?'

There was a silence. Then Brehon Dathal smiled as if explaining to an idiot.

'She must either have been forced to do so or she knew the message did not come from her sister.'

Eadulf leant forward quickly. 'Are we saying that Sárait told a lie to the guard? That she was really going to some other assignation?'

'Summon the woman Gobnat again,' ordered Brehon Dathal while they were considering the point.

'Have you done with me, my lords?' queried Conchoille. He had been waiting patiently during this discussion.

'You may wait outside,' Colgú told him absently.

Gobnat was ushered back into the chamber.

'We have a puzzle that you may help us with,' Brehon Dathal began. 'You say that you did not summon your sister to your house?'

'That is so, lord.' She nodded quickly.

'And did you see her at all that evening, any time after dusk in the afternoon, that is?'

'I did not summon her.'

'That is not what I said. Did you see her?'

'I did not. My sister and I are not very close and I cannot say that she is a frequent visitor to my house.'

Capa was frowning at her, and now he interrupted.

'My lords, we have already established that my wife did not send for her sister. I can confirm it.'

29

'But if Sárait believed that Gobnat had summoned her, she would have made her way directly to your house?' Finguine asked.

Gobnat shrugged indifferently.

'Where is your house situated?' pressed the tanist.

'Everyone knows that,' the woman replied. 'It is in the square near the smith's forge.'

'And to get to the path that leads south to Ferloga's inn and Rath na Drínne, one would have to pass through the township?'

'Of course, and—'

'And that is where your sister was found slaughtered,' Bishop Ségdae said softly, a frown crossing his face. It was not a question.

'And are you sure that your sister did not come to your house that evening before passing to the track beyond?' demanded Brehon Dathal. 'Is there a chance she might have come there and neither you nor Capa, if he was there at the time, heard her?'

'She did not. Capa and I heard nothing until Conchoille arrived.'

Capa was frowning.

'I do not understand this questioning of my wife, my lords. Do you doubt the truth of what she and I—'

It was Brother Eadulf who replied.

'A learned *dálaigh* once told me that a great legal philosopher, the Brehon Morann, said that thought is a human weapon by which reality is captured. During these last few days we have been endeavouring to find facts and we heard those facts but we did not think about them. We have been manacled by activity, but now our thoughts must set us free to find reality.'

While the others stared at him as if he were speaking a foreign language, Colgú grimaced ironically.

'I swear, Eadulf, that you are beginning to sound like my sister.'

Eadulf smiled wanly. 'That is a great compliment, Colgú, because she is the *dálaigh* that I am quoting.'

'I still do not understand what you mean, Brother Eadulf,' Capa said.

Eadulf leant back, his hands palm downward on the table before him.

'We should be trying to let our thoughts run with the facts we have. By thinking about them, ideas might come. Some we can dismiss, others might lead us to new paths. For example, if Sárait left the fortress, carrying the baby Alchú, in the belief that it was in answer to a summons from her sister, Gobnat, why did she not go to see Gobnat . . . make her way to Gobnat's house? Instead, she appears to skirt around the village and head away from her sister's home.'

'But, as we have been told, Gobnat never sent the message,' the Brehon Dathal pointed out irritably.

'So what caused Sárait to go in the opposite direction unless she knew that her sister had not sent the message and she lied to Caol? If so, who was she going to see and why take the child?'

'She could have been forced,' Capa pointed out.

'At what stage?' replied Eadulf. 'The child who had delivered the message had left the palace before her. Caol saw no one forcing her when she went.'

'She could have been forced once she came into the township and before she could reach our house,' Capa said. 'That is the simple explanation.'

'True enough,' agreed Eadulf. 'Although at that hour, even in the dark, there would still be people about in the main square. The occasional lantern or light would provide illumination. So whoever forced her, if she was so forced, would be taking a risk of being seen.'

'Such risk-taking is not unknown,' commented Bishop Ségdae.

'I point this out as something we should think about,' Eadulf replied. 'We have heard the facts and now, in thinking about them, we should be able to see before us a path of questions along which we must progress to the truth.'

Brehon Dathal's tone was disparaging as he looked at Eadulf.

'And do you feel that you are chosen to lead us along that path, Saxon?'

'That is unfair,' snapped Bishop Ségdae. 'Eadulf has a right to say what he feels as father of the missing child.'

'That is just my point,' returned Brehon Dathal with a sneer. 'Because he is the father, he is too emotionally blinded. He will see what he wants to see and it is no use quoting Brehon Morann's philosophies to justify himself. The same goes for Fidelma. She may be a *dálaigh* but any attempt by her to lead an inquiry into her own baby's kidnapping is doomed to failure. I will take charge of this case.'

'You will not.'

The words were spoken softly. A tall, red-haired woman in her late twenties had slipped into the chamber unnoticed and stood regarding Brehon Dathal with her green eyes flashing with a curious fire.

Eadulf rose hurriedly and in concern.

'Fidelma!'

Chapter Three

❧

Before anyone else could move, Fidelma had walked across and taken a vacant seat at the table without being asked. Not only was she sister to Colgú but being a *dálaigh*, qualified to the level of *anruth*, she could sit unbidden in the presence of provincial kings and even speak before they did. Eadulf dropped back into his seat looking worried. Was only he aware of her red-rimmed eyes and haggard features?

'I thought that you were sound asleep,' he muttered.

Fidelma grimaced. 'No thanks to your noxious brews that I am not,' she replied, but there was no bitterness in her voice. 'I know that you meant well, Eadulf. But I have slept enough. There is much to be done.'

Brehon Dathal was frowning in irritation. 'Certainly there is, but not by you. You must hand over to one who is not emotionally involved in this case.'

'Do you think that I have not the ability to investigate my own son's disappearance?' she replied coldly. 'And has Eadulf lost the capacity to follow logic because the subject of the inquiry is his child? Many times we have been entrusted with investigations on which the safety of this kingdom has hinged. Does that now count for nothing?'

Brehon Dathal's cheeks crimsoned at her challenge.

'You and the Saxon are too emotionally involved,' he protested again.

Fidelma smiled grimly. 'That only enhances our determination and resolve to find the culprits.'

'I am Chief Brehon of this kingdom and I—'

Colgú raised a hand to still him. 'Let us not quarrel at this stage, for we are being sidetracked. We are all involved in this matter. Brother Eadulf was making an interesting point when we interrupted him. We can at least hear what he has to say.'

Eadulf glanced at Fidelma but she was still regarding Brehon Dathal with ill-concealed anger.

'I was merely saying that considering the evidence we have heard, being able to reflect calmly on it, a path of questions should come to our minds,' he said.

'And does it?' prompted Bishop Ségdae. 'Do questions come to mind?'

'Well,' said Eadulf, 'let us start with the first assumption that came to all our minds when we first heard of this event. We immediately thought that someone wishing to kidnap Alchú attacked Sárait. We immediately thought that she was killed trying to prevent the kidnapping.'

'What other assumption is there?' demanded Brehon Dathal, still irritable.

'Let us take it step by step from what we have now heard,' continued Eadulf, ignoring him. 'A child is sent to the palace with a message for Sárait purporting to come from her sister, asking her to come to her urgently.'

'And you have heard from my wife Gobnat and myself that no such message was sent,' intervened Capa quickly.

'True,' agreed Eadulf.

'And we have also learnt that the child who delivered this

message is a stranger to us,' Colgú added. 'The description given by the guard, Caol, does not apply to anyone in the palace or the township.'

Again, Eadulf inclined his head in acknowledgement. 'Once the message is delivered, the child leaves the fortress. If we accept Caol's belief, it is a male child and his task is apparently done. A short while after, Sárait leaves the fortress with Alchú. She tells Caol where she is intending to go and explains that she is taking the baby, as she can find no one to leave it with. But that is—'

'That is the first mystery in this story,' Fidelma interrupted.

All eyes turned questioningly on her.

'Eadulf was about to say that there should be no logical reason for the nurse to take Alchú out into the darkness of the night, away from the safety of the palace.'

'How did you work that out?' demanded Brehon Dathal sceptically.

'How many women would you say dwelt within this palace? How many with children? Twenty? More? And how many would Sárait know well enough to call upon if she intended to leave for a short while? How many of them dwelt within a few steps of the chambers she occupied?'

Colgú said nothing but it was clear that the question had never occurred to him.

'Exactly,' Eadulf agreed. 'If Sárait was responding to an urgent message from her sister, there would be no reason why she should take the child. And, before anyone asks, I have questioned some of the women who were in the fortress that night. Sárait did not approach any of them to ask them to look after Alchú while she was gone. The first question, then, is why did Sárait take the baby?'

No one answered him.

'Let us examine another aspect.' Fidelma interrupted the

meditative silence as they considered possible explanations. 'Let us say that the child who came with the message purporting to be from Gobnat was part of some plan to lure Sárait and the baby from the fortress, the purpose of which was to seize Alchú. How could whoever planned this entrapment be sure that Sárait would leave the fortress with the infant?'

'In other words,' Eadulf added, 'if one received a message from one's sister asking them to come as a matter of urgency, it might be expected that they would leave their charge behind in the care of someone else. Yet Sárait, in spite of the nearby women with whom she could have safely left the baby, took it out into the cold night supposedly to hurry to her sister's side.'

Again there was silence as they thought about this.

'These questions merely endorse the fact that my wife did not send the message.' Capa cleared his throat. 'If she knew that the child did not come from Gobnat, the answer must be that Sárait lied to the guard, Caol, about the nature of the message?'

'That is a logical deduction,' Eadulf acceded.

'There is another mystery to consider,' Fidelma went on softly. She glanced at Eadulf and then towards her brother. 'Not being asked to be privy to your re-examination of the witnesses here, I am not sure if you have picked up on the point. Instead of going to her sister's home, as she informed the guard she was going to, Sárait took the baby, went round the village and along the track which leads through the woods beyond, where she met her death. Why?'

Brehon Dathal's tone was patronising. 'We have already recognised that point, Fidelma. It is a question we have considered.'

'But it was thanks to Brother Eadulf who pointed it out,' muttered Bishop Ségdae.

'And did you find an answer to the question?' asked Fidelma softly.

'The questions that are being proposed are unanswerable until we find the culprit,' Brehon Dathal snapped, irritated by the bishop's implied mockery. 'I cannot see any of these questions leading us to the guilty party.'

'At least the asking of the questions is a start along the path to a culprit,' Fidelma replied acidly. 'Or does the learned Brehon have another means of proceeding?'

'There are other aspects to consider.' Eadulf spoke quickly before the crimson-faced old man could respond.

They all turned back to him.

'Such as?' asked Cerball with interest, forgetting himself and glancing up from his tablet and stylus where he was still recording the council's words.

'There is a purpose behind every action,' replied Eadulf. 'Have we considered the purpose behind these actions?'

They stared blankly at him, with the exception of Fidelma who gave him an encouraging glance.

'Let us pose a question,' he continued. 'Was the purpose to entice Sárait out to the woods and kill her? Or was the purpose to entice her out with the baby and seize it to carry it away? Was the slaying of Sárait simply the inevitable result of the killer's attempting to kidnap the child?'

'Or, having killed Sárait, the intended victim all along, did the killer find himself left with the baby on his hands and have no option but to take it away?' Brehon Dathal ended.

Bishop Ségdae grimaced wryly. 'I can't see a killer, having just stabbed the nurse to death, having such solicitous feelings for a helpless baby that he takes it away with him to save it from the perils of the night.'

Fidelma raised an eyebrow quizzically. 'I notice that you all refer to the killer in masculine form. Do you have knowledge of the sex of the killer or is it that you do not believe a female capable of killing?'

The bishop stared at her. 'We presumed that—'

'I see.' Fidelma cut him short. She turned to the others. 'Presumption is a dangerous thing. We must keep an open mind on all things. Eadulf's questions are ones that have to be considered carefully.'

Brehon Dathal was shaking his head.

'There is a difference between someone's snatching a baby on the spur of the moment and abducting it by design. I have come across a case where a demented woman, having lost her own child, snatched a baby as some sort of replacement. But what is being suggested here is . . .'

'*Fúatach.*' Fidelma used the old legal term for an act of carrying off forcibly.

'For ransom?' Brehon Dathal's voice was incredulous and it seemed that he quite forgot to whom he spoke. 'No ransom demand has yet been made. If it were abduction we would have heard by now. I think we can dismiss such an ill-conceived notion . . .'

Colgú began to rise with a deep frown of annoyance. It was the tanist, Finguine, who reached out a hand and placed it as if in pacification on the king's arm to hold him in his seat.

'It is true,' Finguine said hurriedly, 'that we have had no demands made upon us that would warrant our coming to a belief in the idea that Alchú was kidnapped for a ransom. But we should not rule out the possibility altogether.'

'We have searched the surrounding countryside,' Capa pointed out. 'There is no sign of the child that Caol has described as coming to the palace and no sign of Alchú. Unless he and his abductors are well hidden, he must have been removed from the area.'

There was another silence. Eadulf sighed inwardly. It appeared that there was no path down which to proceed.

'I say that the baby must have been snatched by someone seeking a child,' Brehon Dathal announced. 'Any child and not necessarily the son of Fidelma. Whoever has him has moved on, passing through this territory. I see no other conclusion.'

Eadulf saw Fidelma's mouth tighten. Then, surprisingly, she relaxed in a smile, a sarcastic smile but a smile nevertheless. She turned to Capa.

'The Brehon Dathal has made a good point,' she said. Eadulf almost flinched waiting for the biting sarcasm that must surely follow, for he knew that she did not have too high an opinion of the pompous chief judge of Muman. But the sarcasm did not come. 'Cast your mind back three or four days – or to a period just before – and tell us what strangers passed through Cashel?'

Capa shook his head as he vainly tried to dredge his memories but it was Finguine the tanist who answered.

'I immediately thought of that possibility, Fidelma, and so I took it on myself to make a thorough check, but alas, cousin, it proved worthless. There were three boats that came up the River Suir, traders from the seaports. They unloaded their cargoes, waited to take on a return cargo and sailed back. My men searched those boats very thoroughly, and there were no children on board. Then there was a small group of pilgrims, a sad little group of disabled religious, who were taking the road to Imleach . . .'

Ségdae, the bishop of Imleach, gave swift confirmation. 'They had heard that I was staying here at Cashel, so they came here to ask a blessing before they passed to the holy shrine of the Blessed Ailbe. They sought a balm for their afflictions, some born malformed and others disabled by terrible wounds in the wars. There were neither children nor babies amongst them when they arrived.'

Finguine nodded agreement. 'I went to the inn in the township where the pilgrims slept that night, and questioned them as to whether they had seen or heard anything amiss. Poor creatures. I hope their prayers and supplications are rewarded.'

'I presume that they neither heard nor saw anything?' pressed Fidelma.

'Their leader, Brother Buite of Magh Ghlas, said he was disturbed by the noise of the guards and that must have been after the finding of Sárait. They could offer no information that would help us.'

'And this band of pilgrims have now passed on to Imleach?' queried Fidelma.

'They left on the morning after Sárait's body was found and would have reached Imleach some time ago,' agreed Bishop Ségdae.

'There were no women among them, no children and no babies,' confirmed Finguine. 'And they were the only strangers to pass through Cashel.'

Capa suddenly contradicted him as if with an afterthought.

'Apart from the northerner and the foreigner . . .' Then he hesitated and shrugged apologetically. 'But they passed here the day before Sárait was killed.'

'What foreigner? What northerner?' Fidelma quickly demanded.

'The foreigner called himself a religious and a healer. He said he was from some distant land to the east.'

'Persia,' Colgú confirmed. 'That was the land he said he came from.'

Eadulf and some of the others were looking blank.

Cerball, the bard, looked up from his transcription and smiled with the superiority of knowledge.

40

'It is an ancient land that borders on Scythia. Herodotus, in his fourth book, recounts how the Scythians repelled Darius, a king of Persia, who attempted to invade their land. And Justinian is likewise a witness to this history . . .'

Colgú interrupted the bard's lecture, waving him to silence.

'I had almost forgotten him in view of what has happened since then. He stayed as our guest on the night before Sárait's murder. A man of middle age, travelling, as he told me, in search of knowledge of these western lands. He spoke Greek and Latin and was accompanied by a young brother from Ard Macha who served him in the role of guide and interpreter during his travels. They travelled by horse and certainly had no child with them.'

'In what direction were they heading when they left here?' asked Eadulf curiously.

'West. I think they said their destination was the abbey of Colmán,' replied Colgú. 'Anyway, they left before Sárait was killed. The day before, as Capa said.'

Fidelma turned back to Capa. 'Just to clarify things in my own mind, what were you doing while Finguine was checking the religious travellers and merchants? As commander of the guard, was that not your role?'

Capa returned her gaze reproachfully for a moment or so. 'I was searching for your baby, lady. I and three companies of my guards spread from Cashel and made a day's travel in all directions but found no trace either alive or dead.'

'I intended no criticism, Capa. I merely wanted to get a complete picture of events.'

'It can only be some unknown traveller who took the opportunity to seize a child, any child.' Brehon Dathal's voice was heavy. 'That is my conclusion, and when Sárait, the

41

nurse, tried to defend the baby, they killed her and made off with it.'

Even Eadulf saw the flaws in his argument before Fidelma spoke. He caught her antagonistic movement out of the corner of his eye, and intervened quickly.

'With respect, Brehon Dathal, that is contradictory to the evidence that we have already discussed.'

Brehon Dathal's eyes narrowed. 'What do you mean, Saxon?' His voice held a degree of restrained belligerence.

'If Sárait had just chanced to be out at night with the baby, then your suggestion might have to be considered. But the evidence seems to point to Sárait's deliberately being lured from the palace to her death. If she was not lured, then – and we have posed the question – she went out knowing whom she was about to meet. In either situation, the identity of the child – the strange mute child who came to the palace – is crucial. The fact that this child, whose identity no one knows, came with a message for Sárait throws everything into confusion. That is one of the paths we must follow.'

'But there are no paths to follow now,' protested Brehon Dathal, spreading his hands and appealing to his fellow council members.

'When there are no logical paths to follow,' Fidelma observed in a tight voice, 'the only thing to do is follow the paths that are open, however illogical they may seem.'

Colgú glanced at her with a frown. 'What have you in mind, sister?'

'I will ride to Imleach and question those religious travellers. It may be that they heard or saw something on their travels.' She glanced towards Finguine and smiled apologetically. 'I am sure that you observed them well and questioned them diligently, but I would feel better if I did so as well.'

Finguine answered with a polite smile and the suggestion of a shrug. 'It is your prerogative, cousin.'

'I think it will be a wild goose chase,' Brehon Dathal asserted.

'It is the only goose there is to chase,' Fidelma returned shortly.

Colgú rose and, respectfully, they all rose with him.

'This council has ended. Finguine, you may dismiss the witnesses to their homes, but organise a company of our best warriors to search the countryside once more. Lead them yourself.'

Capa made to intervene indignantly, for the command of the warriors should rightly be his and he wanted to protest that he and his men had already scoured the countryside with no result. However, Colgú spoke before he could articulate his protest.

'I have a special task for you, Capa. Take the opportunity to tell your wife that you will be away for a few days and then choose two trusty men. You will accompany my sister.' He turned swiftly to Fidelma. 'Remain with me a moment. You as well, Eadulf. We will discuss this matter in private.'

The king waited in silence until the rest of them had left the chamber before returning his worried gaze to his sister and Eadulf.

'Come to the fire and sit down,' he instructed. 'Some mulled wine?'

They sat but neither felt in the mood to drink. Fidelma still had the sickly taste of Eadulf's sleeping brew in her mouth. Alcohol on that would surely make her nauseous.

'Are you absolutely determined to set out after these pilgrims?' Colgú began, helping himself to a goblet of wine and stretching before the blazing hearth.

'I have said as much,' Fidelma replied shortly.

43

'And you agree?' Colgú turned to Eadulf. 'You will go as well?'

'Of course,' Eadulf was about to add that he felt insulted that such a question should even be posed but compressed his lips. Colgú knew how he felt about Fidelma and must know how he felt about his lost child. 'We must take any opportunity, however slight, of tracking down those responsible for the disappearance of Alchú and returning him to our care.'

The king inclined his head in silence for a moment.

'Go then you must,' he sighed. He glanced quickly at Fidelma. 'You do not look well.'

The beginning of an angry frown crossed her face and then she carefully controlled her expression.

'There is nothing wrong that some sleep or simple relaxation will not cure. Have no concern for me, brother. I have vented my emotion and am now in control, and will remain in control until I have come to a resolution of this matter.' She looked quickly at Eadulf, almost in reproof, before turning back to her brother. 'Whatever you have heard, I am capable of investigating this matter. My mind is now clear and ordered. My feelings are restrained until such time as I can indulge them.'

Colgú hesitated and then shrugged.

'Very well. But there are many aspects of this matter that give me concern and you need a clear mind to consider them.'

Fidelma examined her brother with a frown.

'Then there is something worrying you? I do not simply mean your immediate concern for Alchú. Something else worries you.'

'I think Brehon Dathal can be a fool at times,' Colgú said unexpectedly.

Fidelma could not repress a quick grimace. 'Have you only just reached such a conclusion?'

Colgú almost smiled. 'I begin to think he is growing more eccentric as he ages. However, in truth, sister, I fear that this is some extraordinary plot either against you personally or against our house in general. Why, or who is behind it, I cannot guess at the moment. I think that you both share my feeling – this is neither an infant being randomly snatched by someone wanting a child, as Dathal fondly believes, nor, apparently, a means to some financial recompense.'

Fidelma looked thoughtfully at her brother. 'I thought that I was alone in that view.'

Eadulf compressed his lips in annoyance at being excluded. 'You will remember that I pointed this out when Brehon Dathal was—'

'The point is,' cut in Colgú, 'that you have both made enemies, both within and without this kingdom. There are many who might like to seek revenge on you.'

'I think we are well aware of it,' Eadulf said softly. 'I would say that anyone engaged in the enforcement of law is open to those who nurse grudges. You cannot gain the reputation that Fidelma has without creating enemies – and often in high places.'

'This is true,' agreed the king. 'But there are other areas from which danger might come, and not just from enemies that you have made in your pursuit of the law. Enemies with a personal grudge. You should consider these as well.'

Fidelma's eyes narrowed dangerously. 'I presume that you mean danger from those who object to my liaison with a foreigner?' she demanded.

Colgú shot an apologetic look at Eadulf and shrugged.

'Do not take this the wrong way, Eadulf, but we must examine all possibilities. Fidelma is of the royal house of the Eóghanacht, a daughter of a king and a sister of a king. Do you know what this means to us, Eadulf? Not just to our family, but to those of our culture?'

Eadulf's jaw rose a little. He spoke coldly.

'In my own land, Colgú, the lineage of our Saxon kings is held sacred. Each king of the Angles and the Saxons traces his descent from one or other of the seven sons of Woden. Many Angles and Saxons still believe in the divinity of Woden, chief of the raven clan, the All-Father of our people. My people have worshipped Woden from time immemorial, whereas the New Faith has only been accepted among us for a generation or so, far less in many places.'

Colgú smiled at the soft tone of belligerent pride in Eadulf's voice.

'Then you will appreciate it when I tell you that the Eóghanacht trace their lineage back to the beginning of time. Our bards, the Keepers of the Word, hail me as the ninety-sixth direct generation from the loins of Adam, the eightieth generation from Gaedheal Glas, son of Niul, who led the children of the Gael out of the Tower of Babel. I am the fifty-ninth generation from Eibhear Fionn son of Milidh who brought the children of the Gael to this land.'

'What is the point you are making, brother?' asked Fidelma softly.

'The point is that there are many, and many I suspect within our own family, who, as you say, object to you being the *ben charrthach* of a Saxon – and one of lower rank than you.' He held up his hand as Fidelma and Eadulf made to speak at once. 'I am merely pointing out a fact, not commenting upon it. It would not do to blind yourselves to this fact. Many would be outraged when you became mother to Eadulf's child.'

'You need not tell us that,' Eadulf replied quickly. 'It is

not something that I am liable to forget or be allowed to forget.'

Fidelma glanced at him, surprised at his tone. The words were spoken softly, and there was no obvious bitterness in them, but she felt the suppressed anger behind them. She was on the verge of saying something then closed her mouth firmly. Her face became a mask.

'I presume that these are just general observations, brother? You have no immediate suspicions?'

Colgú regarded her for a moment without expression and then shook his head.

'I cannot point to anyone and accuse them. I believe that everyone within our household behaves with proper etiquette but feelings can often be hidden, secret things. There may be some who think that a daughter of the Eóghanacht should be the mother of a son of Éireann and not a son of Saxony.'

'Alchú has . . . will have . . . a choice of cultures and lands,' replied Fidelma. 'His is the choice that will determine his own future. We will not presume to do that for him. And in this Alchú is in no way unique. Did not Oswy, king of Northumbria, have a child with Fína, daughter of the old High King Colmán Rímid? His name is Aldfrith and I hear he is a promising young scholar in Beannchar but is at home both in his mother's culture and in that of his father.'

The king smiled, a little sadly. 'You have good intentions. But again, I am not commenting, merely pointing out things that you should both be aware of. And there is something else.'

'Something else?' Eadulf mused cynically. 'I thought that we had enough to be meditating on.'

'It will not have escaped your notice that, apart from the considerations of nationality, you are both members of the religious. You have decided to pursue your talents primarily in the service of the New Faith. It was not so long ago that all our learned folk, whether judges, lawyers, bards or physicians, were accepted among the orders of druids. We accept that the New Faith has replaced the druids in most corners of the five kingdoms. Now, those following the New Faith do so without diminishing their personal lives. We accept that, like the druids before them, the religious of the New Faith can marry and bear children. There are mixed houses. You, Fidelma, were trained in the *conhospitae* of Kildare, the double-house founded by Abbess Brigid and Bishop Conlaed.'

Fidelma frowned. 'What are you trying to say, Colchú? Have you been converted by this new movement within the religious that argues that those who serve Christ should not be married nor consort with others of the opposite sex? Not even the Bishop of Rome has agreed that this should be a dogma of the Faith. It would be unnatural to forbid relationships between men and women. It is only small groups of ascetics here and there that argue thus. There have always been such people in all religions, who believe that they show faith and loyalty to the Deity by sublimating all human desires.'

'You may rest assured that I have not been converted, Fidelma. But several in the five kingdoms have,' Colgú said defensively. 'There are many who feel that they can best serve their Faith by the path of celibacy . . .'

'And they have my good wishes, even though I think it is unnatural. But it is one thing to follow one's own personal belief and another thing to force those ideas on everyone else as a dogma and the only path to take to serve God,' responded Fidelma.

'What I am trying to say, Fidelma,' went on Colgú patiently, 'is that there are now many religious within the five kingdoms who are taking vows of celibacy. Their movement is gathering strength and power. The fact that you, a princess of the Eóghanacht, have married a Saxon monk and given birth to a child, thus setting an example to your fellow religieuses, might be perceived as provocation by such groups. This might be another area where enemies may lurk.'

'Nonsense! It is—' began Fidelma, but Eadulf interrupted.

'I understand exactly, Colgú,' he said quietly but determinedly. 'Before we left for Rath Raithlen, I had an argument with Bishop Petrán on this very subject. And—' He stopped suddenly and his eyes widened. 'Where is Bishop Petrán? I have not seen him since we returned.'

Fidelma looked at Eadulf in surprise.

'Come, Eadulf. He is an old man with strong views but you don't suggest that he . . .? Why, I have known him since I was a child.'

Colgú leant forward with sudden suppressed excitement.

'But Eadulf's point is exactly that which I am making. Tell me more about this argument that you had with Bishop Petrán?'

'It was on the day that you asked us to meet your cousin, Becc of Rath Raithlen. You must remember that, Fidelma? It was nothing much but it irritated me. I have heard the arguments a hundred times before. He believes that we should follow the decision made at Whitby and accept the full authority of Rome in the matters of liturgy, tonsure and the dating of Easter. I believe that, too. I have never made a secret of it. Indeed, I supported the argument at the Council of Whitby. Yet Petrán goes further and argues that we should accept the principles laid out at the second Council of Tours – that clerics found in bed with their wives should be excommunicated for a year. He hopes that the next major council of the western bishops will decree that all clerics should take a vow of celibacy.'

There was a moment of silence.

'It would be best not to ignore Petrán,' Colgú finally observed in a soft voice. 'It is well known that he is a woman-hater as well as the leading advocate of the idea that the clergy of the New Faith should be celibate. When he heard that there were women in the hinterlands of the kingdom, as in Gaul and Britain, who were still being ordained as priests of the Faith, he demanded I lead a crusade to destroy the ungodly. I pointed out that who is ordained and who is not is a matter for the bishops of the New Faith and not for a secular authority such as myself.'

Eadulf raised an eyebrow in surprise. 'I thought that three centuries had passed since the Council of Laodicea decreed that women were not to be ordained as priests to conduct the Mass?'

'What is agreed in principle and what is done in practice are often two different things,' pointed out Fidelma. 'Brigid herself was not only ordained priest by Mel, son of Darerca, sister of Patrick, but had episcopal authority conferred on her. Hilda, whom you met at Whitby, was also ordained bishop. And there are still many women in Gaul who are ordained to conduct the Mass.'

'One should not ignore Bishop Petrán's rage. He may be old but he has influence and followers,' added Colgú.

'It is hard to ignore someone so pugnacious as Petrán,' Eadulf admitted ruefully. 'I openly admit that I am a supporter of the Petrine theory – I attended the Council of Whitby on behalf of the pro-Roman school. However, I do not support this group of ascetics who follow those who first gathered at the Council of Elvira and considered that celibacy should be enforced on all the clergy.'

Colgú frowned. 'Petrine theory?' he queried.

'It is the argument that the Bishops of Rome, Innocent and Celestine, first put forward two centuries ago: that it was the right of Rome to rule over all the Christian churches. That is why the Bishop of Rome is addressed as the Father of the Faithful, the Papa, as it is in Latin,' Fidelma explained.

'I support that idea for the very reasons accepted at Whitby,' added Eadulf. 'We are taught that Peter was the rock on which Christ placed the responsibility for His church on earth and it was in Rome that, we are told, Peter founded that church. Rome has the right . . .'

Fidelma did not suppress her exasperated sigh.

'This is no time for such theological arguments. My brother is stating that people like Bishop Petrán may have cause to hate us and hate our child because of their religious attitudes. Is that right?'

Colgú nodded. 'I hasten to say that I do not point the finger at Petrán but simply at people who think like him and might harbour hatred and take that hatred to extremes. There are always fanatics about.'

Eadulf grimaced morosely. 'Petrán is fanatic enough. Our argument nearly came to physical blows.'

'Why so?' Fidelma frowned, leaning forward suddenly. 'You did not mention that.'

'It was when he was declaiming on the piety of the Bishops of Rome in connection with his celibacy argument. I could not help but point out that if the Blessed Hormidas, Bishop of Rome, had not slept with his lady, then Rome would not have had his son the Blessed Silverius sitting, as his successor, on the throne of Peter. He was almost bursting with anger in attempting to deny that any Bishops of Rome married, let alone had children. Why,' Eadulf warmed to his theme, 'even Innocent, the first of his name to be Bishop of Rome, and who expounded the Petrine theory, was the son of Anastasius who had also been Bishop of Rome, and—'

'Is Bishop Petrán still at Cashel?' interrupted Fidelma, cutting Eadulf's enthusiastic argument short.

Colgú shook his head. 'Bishop Ségdae sent him on a tour of the western islands. He left over a week ago.'

'So that eliminates Petrán,' Fidelma said with satisfaction.

'But Petrán has followers, and it is precisely because he has strong views and leads a group who are fanatic about their ideas that such things should not be overlooked. I will ask Finguine to check the religious quarters of the palace as a matter of course.'

Fidelma shrugged. 'I doubt whether it will reveal anything, because, if such a plot was envisaged, exacting minds such as Petrán and those around him would not leave any evidence of it in their quarters,' she said, as if dismissing the matter.

'That is true, but even the most clever mind can sometimes overlook the obvious,' commented Colgú.

'I think we should set out before the day is older.' Fidelma rose abruptly from her chair.

'You still wish to catch up with the pilgrims at Imleach?' Colgú demanded.

'There is still no other path to follow.'

'Then, in view of what I have just said, I am sending Capa, my commander of the guard, with you. I told him to stand ready.'

Fidelma exchanged a glance with Eadulf.

'Are you concerned, brother, that we are really in some tangible danger?' she asked softly.

'For the very reasons that we have just been discussing, sister,' Colgú replied solemnly.

For a moment or two, Eadulf thought that Fidelma would argue with her brother. He knew she hated to be accompa- .

nied by armed warriors, even for her own protection. But Fidelma simply shrugged.

'Then make sure that Capa is at the gates within the hour, for Eadulf and I will depart for Imleach before the noonday bell has finished striking.'

They left the king's apartments, passing Capa as he entered to receive his instructions. They were passing down the corridor back to their own chambers when a young warrior halted them by the simple expedient of standing in their way in the narrow corridor.

'Forgive me, lady,' he began awkwardly.

He was a youthful man with a shock of raven-black hair, a fair skin and eyes to match the colour of his hair. He was well muscled, and a scar on his arm showed that he had already served in combat. In spite of his youth, he wore the golden torque of the élite bodyguard of the king and his clothes were well cared for. His features were pleasant and seemed vaguely familiar to Fidelma. She presumed that she must have seen him about the palace. His eyes held a look of anxiety, and she controlled her impatience at being waylaid.

'Well, warrior? You wish to speak to me?'

The young man swallowed. 'Lady, my name is Gormán.'

'Well, Gormán?' Her voice was frosty and not encouraging.

'Lady, I have heard that Capa, our captain, is looking for a couple of warriors to accompany him. The rumour says that he is to escort you to Imleach in search of Sárait's murderer, the kidnapper of your child. Capa has already chosen Caol for this task.'

'And?' snapped Fidelma, angry that the news had spread so rapidly.

'I would like very much to go with you, lady.'

Fidelma's annoyance increased. 'It is no concern of mine what choice Capa makes. You must speak to him.'

The young warrior shook his head. 'Capa has taken a dislike to me, lady, although I have done him no wrong. But I must, I must go with you.'

Fidelma stared at him in surprise for a moment.

'Must? Why?'

The young man shrugged awkwardly.

'I . . . I knew the lady Sárait. I feel . . . feel . . .'

Fidelma's forbidding features softened as the young man stood with reddening face.

'I presume that you were in love with her?'

The young warrior coloured hotly, dropping his gaze as if he were confessing to some heinous crime.

'I am . . . was.'

'Why does Capa dislike you that you need my intervention with him to ensure you come on this journey?'

'My youth, I suppose. I think that is why Capa ignores me.'

He hesitated and Fidelma felt that he was holding something back.

'That is not the real reason, is it?' she pressed.

The young man blushed. 'I am baseborn. My mother was a prostitute.'

'But you wear the golden torque,' Eadulf pointed out. 'I thought that . . .' He hesitated, feeling awkward. 'I thought that only nobles could join the élite bodyguard?'

'Donndubháin, who was heir apparent to Colgú before Finguine, promoted me to the élite bodyguard when I was instrumental in turning back an Uí Fidgente attack at the battle of Cnoc Áine. Capa thinks only sons of nobles should serve in the *Nasc Niadh* – the bodyguard. I want a chance to prove myself to him.'

Eadulf sniffed in dismissive fashion. 'A young man wanting vengeance to prove himself with his commander disliking him . . .' He shook his head. 'That sounds a recipe for disaster to me.'

Gormán turned pleading eyes on Fidelma.

'Please, lady . . .'

'Gormán!'

It was the stern voice of Capa, who appeared behind them on his way back from Colgú's chambers. The commander of the guard raised his hand in salute as he recognised Fidelma and Eadulf.

'I beg your pardon, lady. I wanted a word with young Gormán here.' He glanced at the warrior, now stiffening to attention. 'You will be ready to accompany Caol and me within the hour. We are to be escort to the lady Fidelma and Brother Eadulf.'

The young man dropped his jaw in surprise at the announcement. Capa inclined his head in salute again and turned down the corridor.

Fidelma smiled at the confused young man.

'There, you did not need to ask for my intercession. Have you heard of the saying *si finis bonus est, totum bonum erit*?'

The young man shook his head.

'If the end is good, everything will be good.' Eadulf smiled. 'We will see you at the main gate within the hour.'

Chapter Four

✆

It was just before midday when Fidelma and Eadulf,
followed by Capa, with Gormán and Caol riding behind,
reached the dark flowing waters of the River Suir, west of
Cashel, at the point where a bridge crossed to a small island
in the middle before continuing on to the far bank. On the
island stood a small fortification which served to protect the
approaches to Cashel in times of war. Dense woodland grew
on either side of the broad waters.

Eadulf recalled the last time he had ridden along this highway with Fidelma. He shivered slightly, for then they had been
held up by warriors of the Uí Fidgente when they had been on
a journey to Imleach to investigate the mysterious disappearance of the holy relics of St Ailbe and Brother Mochta, Keeper
of the Holy Relics. Eadulf glanced nervously about him as they
rode up to the bridge. They had been waylaid by enemy warriors
at this very spot and he had been forced to swim with his horse,
gasping for breath as the icy river clutched at him.

The brooding waters were beginning to reflect the spreading dark clouds coming from the west, which reared up into
a flattened anvil shape dominating the sky. Fidelma glanced
up.

'Thunder clouds,' she muttered. 'We might have to seek shelter before we reach Imleach.'

Eadulf recalled that beyond the bridge there was a settlement called the Well of Ara where they had stayed before. A man called Aona who had once commanded the bodyguard of the king of Cashel ran the inn there.

He started nervously.

'What is it?' whispered Fidelma, catching his movement.

'I think that there is someone hidden in the fortress on the island. There is someone watching us.'

Capa edged his horse forward, overhearing Eadulf's alarm.

'They should be our warriors, lady. Men were sent out to patrol the roads soon after we discovered the body of Sárait and realised the child was missing. I posted three of my men to check all travellers crossing the bridge.'

He urged his mount forward and led the way across the bridge. Eadulf watched anxiously as a warrior emerged from the small rath ahead of them and made his way to greet them. He saluted Capa and his eyes widened a little as he recognised Fidelma and Eadulf.

'What news?' Capa demanded.

'Little to tell, lord,' the man replied. 'There has been nothing out of the ordinary along the road. Soon after we arrived, a band of pilgrims crossed here. Apart from those, only local folk have crossed about their business and they have been well known to us. That is all. No sign of anyone with a baby . . .' He cast a look at Fidelma and dropped his eyes awkwardly.

'Have you watched both day and night?' Capa said sharply, demanding the man's attention.

'My comrades and I have done so most diligently. From the morning that Finguine sent us here, the morning when the alarm was raised, we have maintained a constant watch.

We have taken turns on watch – one to watch while the others slept. But no one has ever attempted to cross the bridge at night.'

Eadulf pursed his lips with cynicism. 'Why cross this bridge at all? There are fords further upstream. Besides, whoever did this deed could have crossed in the hours of darkness on the very night that Sárait was slain and the baby taken,' he pointed out. 'This might be a matter of closing the stable door after the horse has bolted.'

'You may be right, Brother Eadulf,' Capa agreed with reluctance. 'But the alarm was raised and patrols sent into the countryside as soon as the facts were learnt. It was better to do something than nothing.'

'Tell me more about the pilgrims,' Fidelma queried, leaning forward slightly to give emphasis to her interest.

The man frowned as if gathering his thoughts, pausing for a moment before replying.

'Little to tell, lady. We passed them on the road, for they were on foot and we were on horseback. We came here and eventually they caught up with us. There were about six of them. I have seen their sort many times en route to holy sanctuaries in search of cures for their ailments. There was nothing to distinguish them, one from another. Each one of them was clad in robes, and they had their heads covered in cowls so that we could not tell age or even sex. There were no children with them; any babies, that is.'

Fidelma examined him with a frown.

'What makes you qualify your statement?'

The man hesitated and shrugged.

'I thought one of them might have been a child, a short, almost misshapen poor soul.'

Fidelma raised an eyebrow. 'A misshapen child?' Her voice was sharp.

The warrior shrugged as he considered how best to describe what he had seen.

'The pilgrim was not what I would call a child. The figure was quite stocky. And about so high . . .' He was a tall man and raised a hand to the level of his waistband.

Capa was looking on with disapproval. 'You did not check the identities of these travellers, I gather? You surely know that we are looking for the misshapen child who brought the message to Cashel? You should have stopped this pilgrim.'

The man looked unhappy. 'I was not told about a misshapen child, Capa, only about the baby, Alchú. That is all. Anyway, when we went closer to the pilgrims to question them, this small figure produced a bell – a leper's bell – and rang it. I noticed the other pilgrims tended to keep their distance. Therefore we did not venture nearer but let them pass on to Imleach.'

Fidelma exhaled slowly. It was her only sign of exasperation. The warrior turned to her with an expression that was almost woeful.

'Truly, lady,' he said, speaking directly to her, 'we were not told to search for a misshapen child – only for a baby.'

Capa looked irritable. 'Who gave you your orders, warrior?'

'Why, my lord Finguine did so.'

'Well, now you know, although I fear it is too late,' Capa replied. 'A misshapen child brought the message to Cashel that lured Sárait to her death. Keep a careful watch from now on.'

The warrior nodded glumly.

Low down behind the distant western mountains came a rumble of thunder. Fidelma stirred reluctantly.

'We should press on to the Well of Ara before the storm breaks.'

Capa turned and led the way across the bridge with Fidelma and Eadulf following and their escort of Caol and Gormán bringing up the rear.

The warrior on the bridge watched their going with a glum face. Then he seemed to relax and pulled himself up with a disdainful gesture of his shoulders. Capa was mad if he expected the men to start searching passing lepers too closely.

The rain was just starting to fall in heavy droplets and the rumble of thunder was growing more prevalent as, some kilometres further on, the party came to a small rise beyond which the road dipped towards another substantial river. On both banks of this river, and connected by a series of easily fordable shallows, lay the settlement of Ara's Well. In fact, the waters barely came up to the fetlocks of the horses as they splashed through the crossing and halted before a tavern situated exactly by the ford.

A youth, scarcely out of his boyhood, certainly no more than fourteen, opened the door of the inn and came forward to greet them.

'Welcome, travellers. You are welcome to . . .'

His eyes suddenly fell on Fidelma and then on Eadulf and a broad urchin grin lit up his features.

'Greetings to you, Adag.' Fidelma smiled as she swung down from her horse. 'Are you well?'

'Well, indeed, lady. Welcome. Brother Eadulf, welcome. You are both most welcome.'

Eadulf smiled and ruffled the boy's already tousled hair.

'Good to see you again, Adag. You have grown since I last laid eyes on you.'

The boy drew himself up. He looked different from the small eleven-year-old whom Eadulf had first seen sitting by the river bank, casting his line into the waters and trying to lift the wild brown trout for the pot.

'How is your grandfather, Adag?' asked Fidelma, as the boy took her horse's reins. The boy paused before he turned to gather the reins of the other mounts.

'He is inside, lady. He will be happy to see you. I will take your horses to the stable and attend to them. But my grandfather will take care of your wants. Will you be staying? I can look after your horses, if so?'

Fidelma glanced at the sky, just as a lightning flash lit it. She blinked and silently counted, reaching four before the thunder reverberated in the air.

'It is near enough,' she observed in resignation. 'We will wait out the storm.' With a smile, she added: 'How long do you think that will be, Adag?'

The boy tilted his head to one side with a serious expression as he surveyed the sky.

'It will be gone before the hour is up, but there is time enough to take a bowl of stew and a mug of my grandfather's *corma*. I will feed and rub down the horses.'

Capa, who had been silent during this exchange, frowned.

'My men are capable of tending to their own mounts . . .'

Fidelma raised a hand. 'Adag can take care of all our mounts, Capa. He is capable enough. Come inside and leave him to do his job.'

She turned and pushed into the interior of the tavern. It was dark inside but a dancing fire provided a curious light, where flames ate hungrily into a pile of crackling logs. There was an aroma of mutton stew simmering in its large pot from a hook above the fire.

An elderly man was placing drinking vessels on the table. He turned as they entered and opened his mouth to welcome them, then halted as he recognised them.

61

'Hello, Aona. Are you well?'

'I am the better for seeing you, my lady. And with our good Saxon friend, Eadulf. Life has been quiet in my tavern since last you visited us.'

'Ah, I pray that it may continue to be so, Aona,' replied Fidelma in solemn humour. 'Better peace than conflict, eh?'

Capa looked irritated at being excluded from this friendly exchange. His handsome features seemed disdainful of the intimacy between Fidelma and the innkeeper.

'Landlord, fetch us food and drink,' he said officiously.

Fidelma turned to him and only Eadulf saw the swift look of annoyance cross her features before it was gone.

'Aona, let me present Capa. Capa now holds the position that you once held.'

Capa frowned, not understanding, colouring at the implied rebuke. Then he peered at the old innkeeper with an expression of surprise as memory came to him.

'Are you Aona who was commander of the guard of Cashel in the days of my grandfather? Aona whose deeds and combats are still spoken of?'

Behind Capa, Caol and Gormán were regarding the old innkeeper with something approaching awe. They were both young men, full of pride at being chosen to wear the golden necklet of the élite bodyguard of Cashel. But over their fires, at night, they had also heard of the deeds and valour of the great warriors who had gone before them and whose image they wanted to live up to.

The old innkeeper chuckled at their expressions.

'I am Aona who once served as commander of the guard,' he replied. 'But you make me sound positively ancient, my young warrior.' His grey eyes glinted like steel as he regarded the younger man. 'So you are now commander of the guard, eh? Well, command is not merely in the strength of one's muscles, young friend. Let us hope your mind is as agile as your body.'

Capa's chin came up defensively.

'I pride myself that Colgú has no cause to complain of me,' he retorted.

'I am glad to hear it,' Aona assured him calmly. Then he glanced swiftly to Fidelma and winked. 'You are fond of quoting Publilius Syrus, lady. Didn't he say that there is but a step between a proud man's glory and his disgrace?'

He gave the quotation in the original Latin and Capa apparently did not understand it. Fidelma restrained a smile for she knew that Aona had also spotted what she felt was Capa's weakness – his arrogance. She turned and indicated that Capa and his men should seat themselves and order something to drink. She and Eadulf moved towards the fire while Aona, in answer to their request, placed a jug of reddish-coloured ale called *leann*, distilled from rye, and some pottery drinking vessels before the three warriors. They fell to with unconcealed eagerness. Fidelma motioned Aona to join them.

'Before we sample your stew and your famous *corma*, Aona, have you heard or seen anything unusual on this road? You see . . .'

Aona interrupted with a shake of his head.

'You do not have to explain, lady. I have heard of your distress. If there is anything I can do, you have only to command. There have been only a few travellers on the road from Cashel.'

Fidelma's features expressed silent gratitude.

'We are trying to pick up some lead,' she explained. 'Something to give us a clue to where my baby has been taken. I want to question some pilgrims who will have taken this road.'

Aona raised a hand and pushed back his hair, letting it run through his fingers.

'Pilgrims? They did not venture near my tavern for which mercy, in truth, I uttered a prayer of thanks.'

'Why would that be?' Fidelma asked in surprise.

'The pilgrims took the western road to Imleach but one of them, who walked in the rear, rang a leper's bell to warn of his approach. I watched them cross the ford and pass through the settlement without stopping and, I would say, much to everyone's relief.' He held up a hand. 'Do not lecture me on charity, lady. I have charity as much as the next man but even so I could not help feeling gratitude when they passed on, with the leper, without asking for alms or hospitality.'

'But you saw them pass by?' Eadulf pressed quickly. 'Was one short in stature – perhaps a child or a youth?'

'I only saw them from a distance. Even then they were clad from poll to foot in their robes. They wore cowls. I think that the one with the bell might have been shorter than the others. It was hard to tell. No one was carrying a baby, though.' He frowned, tugging at his ear. 'During this week it has been quiet on this road, lady. I've scarcely seen a dozen travellers and half of those are known to me. From some of them, I learnt about your baby's disappearance. Of the strangers with babies . . . there was an itinerant herbalist with his wife and two babies in a wagon. I was fishing on the river so noticed their arrival. They came from the north, though, along the road from Cappagh, and joined the Cashel road just by the bridge.'

'When was that?' asked Eadulf.

'Four or five days ago.'

Fidelma shook her head. 'They had two babies with them, you say?'

Aona nodded.

'No matter,' Fidelma assured him. 'Has anyone else passed here? Any other strangers?'

'Two more only. A short time before the apothecary and his wife, two religious passed here. One was from the northern kingdom, travelling with a stranger from beyond the seas. They rode good horses. The stranger from beyond the seas was unlike any foreign religious that I have seen. At first, I thought him to be a Greek, because I have encountered several of those who have passed on their way to Imleach. Yet he was not quite the same as a Greek . . .'

'That was probably the Persian,' Eadulf intervened by way of explanation. 'Was the one who came from the north a brother from the abbey at Ard Macha?'

Aona grimaced indifferently. 'He could well have been, Brother Eadulf. He was a proud young man and mentioned with pride his king, Blathmac mac Máel Cobo . . .'

'Of the Dál Fiatach of Ulaidh,' confirmed Fidelma. 'How long did they stay here?'

'Long enough for a meal. They said that they were passing on to Colmán's abbey on the western coast.' Aona paused and glanced at the warriors. 'If you will excuse me, lady, I'd better attend to the food. I presume young Adag is looking after your horses?'

On learning this was the case Aona disappeared, to quickly reappear with bread, freshly baked, and hot bowls of savoury mutton stew.

Eadulf joined the others as they fell to the bowls of steaming soup. While they were so engaged, Aona went round filling pottery mugs with *corma*, the fiery barley distilled alcohol that he personally brewed on the premises. Eadulf remembered the first time he had been at Aona's inn and how he had nearly choked as the fiery liquid left him gasping for breath. He asked for a jug of water and met with Aona's knowing grin.

'I see you remember my *corma* well, Brother Eadulf.'

Fidelma sat on a window seat, watching the rain splattering down and nibbling pensively on a dish of fruit that Aona had tempted her with.

Presently, when they were all more relaxed and oblivious of the thunderstorm raging outside, Fidelma and Eadulf drew their chairs before the fire and settled down with Aona to talk more about old times. Adag, having fed and settled the horses, came in then, pausing to shake the rain off his heavy woollen cloak.

'Do you still reckon on an hour until the storm passes, youngster?' Capa called cynically.

Adag grinned, unembarrassed. 'Not much more than an hour, warrior. The mountain hid the full extent of the storm clouds from me. But already there is blue showing behind the clouds, so it will soon pass,' he added confidently.

Amid the soft conversation of the warriors and the crackle of the fire there appeared a lull in the exchange of the old comrades. Then Aona said sadly: 'I was unhappy to hear that it was Sárait who had been murdered. A sad family.'

'Sad?' queried Eadulf sharply. 'Did you know her family?'

'Rather I knew the family of her husband,' Aona amended. 'I knew her husband's father, Cathchern, very well indeed. He was one of my men and came from the Well of Ara. I watched his son Callada grow up and was not surprised when he followed his father into the bodyguard of the kings of Cashel. Callada and Sárait married here – yes, it was here in this very room that we had the feasting. That was three or four years ago.'

'I did not know Callada well,' admitted Fidelma.

'He would have been about ten years older than you, lady.'

'But why did you say the family was sad?' Eadulf was puzzled.

'Well, my old comrade Cathchern was killed in a battle against the Uí Néill when Callada had hardly reached the age of choice. Cathchern's wife died of the Yellow Plague. Then Callada . . . he was killed at the battle of Cnoc Áine scarce two years ago.'

'That I knew,' Fidelma said. 'And because of that, Sárait was given work at my brother's palace when I returned there for my confinement. She became my nurse and nurse to my baby.'

'I presume that Cathchern and his son Callada both freely chose life as warriors?' asked Eadulf. 'If so, death must be recognised as a constant companion, and many people died in the Yellow Plague. Yet you say they were a sad family?'

'There were ugly stories.'

'Ugly stories?'

Aona made an awkward gesture with his hands as if trying to dismiss what he had said. 'Maybe it is not right to repeat them now.'

Eadulf snorted in annoyance. 'The time to have hesitated was before you hinted at some intrigue. Continue your tale now.'

Aona hesitated, shrugged and bent forward with lowered voice.

'I heard from a couple of warriors who were at the battle of Cnoc Áine that Callada was slain not by the enemy – the Uí Fidgente – but by one of his own men.'

Eadulf was not shocked. He had heard similar tales about deaths in battles.

'You mean that he turned coward on the field? I have heard enough stories of battles to know that often a man has been slain when he showed cowardice and endangered the lives of his comrades.'

'That I know. But Callada was no coward. He was a good warrior and descended from a line of great warriors. Yet these stories have persisted. However he died, he was slain at Cnoc Áine. Now Sárait has come by a violent death as well. It is a sad, sad family in which death comes in violent ways and no one is left to sing the praises of the deeds of the past generations.'

Fidelma said nothing for a moment. Then she grimaced.

'Well, Aona, we have seen our fair share of violence. It would be pleasing now if we could take ourselves off to some isolated valley high up in the mountains and begin to live in peace with ourselves and our surroundings.'

Aona's face was sad.

'There is no permanent sanctuary against the violence of mankind. It is a permanent condition, I fear, lady.'

Fidelma stood up and gazed through the window at the lightening sky.

'I think Adag is being proved correct. The sky is brighter. The storm is passing. We must soon be on our way to Imleach.'

The old innkeeper rose in response.

'I wish you well in your quest, lady. May you have all success in finding your child and bringing the murderer of Sárait to justice.'

Capa and his men had also risen.

'Are we continuing the journey to Imleach, lady?' Capa asked. At Fidelma's affirmative, he went on: 'We will go and prepare the horses, then. No need to trouble the young lad, innkeeper.' Adag had gone to the brewery at the side of the inn to carry out some jobs for Aona.

The warriors had just left when the door opened again and a thickset, middle-aged man entered. His features showed good humour and he seemed to have a commanding presence.

'Greetings, Adag. I see your guests are just leaving, warriors by the look of them . . .'

His eyes suddenly fell on Fidelma and Eadulf and he halted in confusion. Aona turned to Fidelma with a smile.

'On the very subject of which we have been speaking – this is Cathalán. He fought at Cnoc Áine. Cathalán, this . . .'

The newcomer had crossed the room and bowed his head in respect.

'Lady, I had the honour to serve your brother at Cnoc Áine. I recognise you and have heard of your trouble, for which I am sorry.'

Fidelma inclined her head in acknowledgement.

'Cathalán, we were speaking a short time ago of Sárait's husband and the manner of his death.'

'Were you a witness to how he died?' Eadulf asked.

Cathalán shook his head at once.

'Not a witness, no. I merely heard stories. In battle, Brother Eadulf, one hears a story from someone. When you question them, they say they heard it from someone else and that someone saw it happen. When you ask that person, then they, too, have heard it from someone who, they say, saw it happen. But the story that Callada was killed by one of our own warriors came from two separate sources. One was an Uí Fidgente and the other was one of our own men. I doubt it not. But we have not been able to discover anything further for we have found no one who could be claimed as a true witness.'

'Was the matter reported to a Brehon?' queried Fidelma.

'It was. Brehon Dathal said he had examined the matter but found nothing over which action could be taken.'

'I see. So you were one of the warriors who were merely repeating what others told you.'

Cathalán hesitated for a moment.

'There is something else?' prompted Fidelma.

'I was Callada's *cenn-feadhna*.' Eadulf took a moment to remember that the military structures of Éireann were well organised and a *cenn-feadhna* was the captain of a *buden* or company of one hundred warriors. 'We lost sight of one another in the heat of the battle on Cnoc Áine. In fact, several of my company – fourteen men in all – perished that day because we were one of the first to be ordered forward into the centre of the Uí Fidgente.' He paused. 'I knew that there was something troubling Callada on the evening before the battle, as we sat round the fire. I asked him what ailed him and he was reluctant to say anything at first. But as he was troubled and I pressed the matter, he finally told me that he had good reason to believe that his wife Sárait was unfaithful to him.'

'That she was having an affair with another man?' Eadulf asked, making sure he understood.

'That she *might* have been having an affair with another.' The former warrior corrected the emphasis with a grave expression.

'Who else knew of this?' It was Fidelma who posed the question.

'He spoke to me reluctantly. I do not think that he had told his suspicions to anyone else . . .' He suddenly frowned. 'You think there is some connection with Sárait's death?' He shook his head immediately. 'But no, she was nursing your child and the baby has been kidnapped. There is surely no relation?'

'Yet all possibilities must be considered,' Fidelma said softly. 'Sárait is now dead. She was enticed from the palace to her death. Was it a means to kidnap my child? If so, then—'

She suddenly snapped her mouth shut, realising that she

was thinking aloud. She focused her green-blue eyes on Cathalán.

'Did Callada say whom he suspected of having an affair with his wife?'

'Alas, he did not.'

'And hearing this rumour, how he met his death, you are presuming . . . what exactly?'

Cathalán shrugged. 'I was not made a *cenn-feadhna* for presuming things, lady. I merely reported the facts to old Brehon Dathal. Those facts may be connected and thus they pose a question. That is all I am saying.'

Gormán put his head round the inn door without observing the newcomer.

'The horses are ready, lady.'

Fidelma paused a moment and then smiled at the former warrior.

'I am grateful for this information, Cathalán. Do not think that I am not. It may or may not be of relevance. Probably not. But all information is of help.' She turned back to Aona. 'Once more we are indebted for your welcome hospitality, Aona.' She pressed some coins into his reluctant hand.

'I am always pleased to serve you, lady.' The old innkeeper smiled. 'There is no person in this kingdom, having heard of your plight, who does not wish you success in tracking down the culprit.'

Eadulf pursed his lips cynically. 'Surely one would have to accept there must be at least one person in this kingdom who does not, Aona,' he said dryly as he turned and followed Fidelma from the inn. It took Aona a moment or two before he understood what Eadulf meant, by which time the door had closed behind him.

Within a short time they were following the north bank of the River Ara while, to the south, the long wooded ridge of Slievenamuck stood framed against the lighter sky. The heavy storm clouds had passed over to the east and it looked as though the late afternoon was going to be fine. The sun was in the western sky but not low as yet. Eadulf was trying to remember the name of the hills to the north of them, some miles distant. Fidelma had told him when they had first made their journey along this road.

Fidelma, as though she had read his thoughts, at that moment leant over and touched him on the arm.

'The Slieve Felim mountains,' she said, pointing. 'Beyond those are the lands of the Uí Fidgente. Not a place to go wandering without protection.'

When they emerged from the woodland and into an open hilly area, Eadulf recognised his surroundings immediately.

Imleach Iubhair: 'the borderland of yew trees'. The great stone walls surrounded the abbey of St Ailbe, who had first preached Christianity in Muman. They dominated the little township that stretched before them. He found it hard to accept that it was here that he and Fidelma had nearly lost their lives. He felt very much at home as he looked on the stretches of grazing land, edged with forests of yew trees, tall and round-headed.

The first time he had seen Imleach it was deserted, but now the market place, directly in front of the abbey, was bustling. People were thronging the stalls and pens in which cattle patiently stood waiting to be sold, and goats, pigs and sheep moved impatiently in their confines. Traders were shouting their wares; cheesemakers, blacksmiths, bakers and a hundred and one others trying to attract customers.

'Not like the last time I came here,' Eadulf remarked humorously.

'Life has returned to normal,' observed Fidelma shortly as she led the way through the market square towards the sad-looking, burnt-out remains of a massive yew tree that had once dominated even the great walls of the abbey. Once it had risen nearly twenty-two metres in height. Fidelma, with Capa and the other warriors, halted her horse before it and bowed her head. Eadulf remembered that this was once the sacred totem of the Eóghanacht, their 'Tree of Life', which was said to have been planted by the hand of Eibhear Foinn, son of Milidh, from whom the Eóghanacht claimed to have descended. Eadulf remembered the time when the enemies of the Eóghanacht had attacked and tried to destroy it. He and Fidelma had been sheltering in the abbey and impotent to halt the destruction. Yet halted it had been.

'In spite of our enemies,' Gormán smiled proudly, pointing to some green shoots on some of the higher branches, 'our tree still thrives.'

Eadulf was surprised that the ancient tree was still living. It remained the symbol of Eóghanacht power. It was an ancient belief that the tree was a symbol of the vitality of the Eóghanacht dynasty and if the tree flourished, they flourished. If it were destroyed . . . then the dynasty would fall and be no more. But the dynasty, like the tree, had survived; survived, if the ancient bards were to be trusted, for fifty-nine generations since Eibhear Foinn established it.

They turned from the tree and moved on to the abbey. The gatekeeper had already spotted their approach and the great oak doors stood open. A familiar figure stood ready to receive them. It was Brother Madagan, the *rechtaire* or steward of the abbey.

Chapter Five

❧

They sat in Brother Madagan's chamber, from where the
steward administered the great abbey of Imleach. As
rechtaire, he assumed control in the absence of Bishop
Ségdae, who was not only bishop but also abbot of Imleach.
The mood was sombre. Brother Madagan had sat silently
while Fidelma had explained the reason for their visit to the
abbey. During the course of her explanation he continually
raised a hand to finger the scar on his forehead. Both Fidelma
and Eadulf knew well how he had received the wound during
the attack on Imleach.

When Fidelma had finished telling Brother Madagan what
had brought them to the abbey again, they sat sombrely in
front of the crackling fire. The steward was filled with concern
at the news and offered to give what help he could. Fidelma
had told him about the pilgrims and the other travellers who
had passed through Cashel.

'So you are wishing to question the pilgrims who have
come to pray in the chapel of the Blessed Ailbe?'

'I am indeed,' Fidelma affirmed. 'I hope they are still
here?'

Brother Madagan nodded. 'But the others you mentioned

. . . Brother Tanaide, and the stranger from beyond the seas, are no longer here. They have already continued their journey westward after one night of hospitality.'

'Who is Brother Tanaide?' asked Eadulf.

'The young monk who was guide and interpreter for the stranger from Persia.'

'What did this stranger from Persia want here?'

'He calls himself Brother Basil Nestorios and speaks Greek and Latin as well as his native tongue. He has a lively discourse and spoke much about his homeland and beliefs. I felt sad that he could only spend a night here before travelling on to the abbey of Colmán. You surely don't need to speak to them?' Brother Madagan hesitated and then shook his head. 'I am sure that neither of these brothers of the Faith could have had anything to do with the matter that brings you hither.'

Fidelma smiled tiredly. 'I am sure you are right. It is merely a matter of questioning to hear if they observed anything that might help us. What may be seen and discarded as unimportant by a bystander, when collected, like a piece of a puzzle, and compared to other accounts might create a complete picture.'

'Where is this abbey of Colmán?' asked Eadulf.

'To the west, standing by the sea at the mouth of the River Maighin, the river of the plain,' explained the steward. 'It is at least one day's journey from here if one rode a fast horse.'

'It stands at the beginning of the lands of the Corco Duibhne, the land of Duibhne's people,' added Fidelma. 'To get there it means crossing Uí Fidgente territory.'

'Are the Corco Duibhne part of your brother's kingdom?'

'Their sub-king Slébéne pays tribute to Cashel. However, they are a fierce and independent people who still claim a pagan goddess named Duinech as their foster-mother. She was said to have regenerated herself into seven periods of youth so that she became mother to the widely scattered tribes of the Múscraige. The abbey of Colmán lies on the edge of his territory, which is guarded by a vicious Uí Fidgente warlord who, so reports tell us, claims to be lord of the passes through the mountains there. I, for one, would prefer to avoid Slébéne's petty kingdom.'

Brother Madagan, seeing Eadulf's puzzled look, leant forward in agreement.

'His kingdom is not what we would call Christian. The land is a long peninsula, mountainous and wild, and Slébéne's capital is so isolated, at the end of the peninsula, that few venture to it. It is said to be an evil place.'

Eadulf smiled wryly. 'I think I have enough experience dealing with non-Christians to worry little about them. Christian or not, people do not vary one from another simply because of religion. When I was in Rome, I went to see a play called *Asinaria*. The lesson was that pride and avarice are the causes of man's evil to man, not religion. Man is a wolf to man.'

Fidelma was bitter.

'*Lupus est homo homini*,' she murmured. 'Yet the author, Titus Plautus, mistook the main point – wolves do not attack one another. Only man attacks his own kind without cause.' Then she rose abruptly. 'Let us see the leader of the pilgrim band, Brother Madagan.'

Apparently the pilgrims from Cashel were, at that moment, praying in the chapel that housed the relics of the Blessed Ailbe. The steward suggested that Fidelma and Eadulf remain in his chambers while he went to fetch their leader, Brother Buite.

Eadulf expressed his surprise. 'Praying in the chapel? You don't mind a poor body afflicted with leprosy wandering freely about the abbey?'

76

It was Brother Madagan's turn to look surprised.

'What makes you think that any of these pilgrims have leprosy?' he queried.

Fidelma turned sharply to him.

'Among the band of pilgrims that came from Cashel there was supposed to be one that looked like a misshapen child who rang a leper's bell. Is he not among this band?'

Brother Madagan shook his head. 'No such misshapen pilgrim was among them. Certainly no leper came with them. But Brother Buite did say that they had come through Cashel recently.'

Fidelma pursed her lips thoughtfully and glanced towards Eadulf. Then she shrugged and turned back to Brother Madagan.

'We will hear what Brother Buite has to tell us.'

Fidelma and Eadulf sat together in silence for a while, Fidelma leaning back in the comfortable wooden chair of the steward while only her tapping fingers, drumming a strange but rhythmic tattoo, showed her agitation. It was the first time they had been entirely alone for some time

'At some stage, we must talk,' Eadulf finally said.

Fidelma closed her eyes momentarily and Eadulf waited for some outburst.

'About what?' Her voice was equally soft.

'About ourselves. There is much left unsaid.'

She turned round and he was surprised at the sad smile that broke on her features.

'You are right, Eadulf. Much has been left unsaid between us since we returned from Rath Raithlen. That is my fault. But be patient for a little while longer. At this time, I need your strength. We will speak soon. I promise.'

Eadulf turned his gaze to the fire and fell silent.

Fidelma was grateful for his sensitivity. She felt enough

of a sense of guilt already not only because of the missing child but because, for the last several months, she had been questioning her relationship with Eadulf. Since little Alchú had been born she had been in a constant state of depression. It had taken her a long time to agree to become Eadulf's *ben charrthach*, his wife for a year and a day. It was one of the nine forms of recognised marital relationship in which the woman's status and rights were acknowledged under the law of the *Cáin Lánamnus*.

Fidelma had long avoided the inevitable outcome of her attraction to Eadulf. She had already experienced one unhappy affair with a warrior named Cian and thought that she would never undergo the agony of falling in love again. But some inner spark had ignited when she first met Eadulf at the great Council of Whitby, even though he was a Saxon and an advocate for the acceptance of the teachings of Rome. She had tried to argue that she cared too much for Eadulf to rush into easy decisions; that she had tried to avoid any close relation because, under the laws of the five kingdoms, it would be a marriage of unequal persons. Fidelma was of royal rank and Eadulf, as a stranger in the land and not even of royal status, would not have equal property rights with his wife.

Then it seemed that all was well. She had made the decision. During the trial marriage she had become pregnant and their son Alchú was born. Had she resented the birth of Alchú? Her mind had dwelt on the freedom she had lost and she had begun to resent Eadulf and the idea of a life confined to Cashel. The request of her brother, Colgú the king, to go to Rath Raithlen and solve the mystery of the slaughtered young women had been a godsend to her. She had been dwelling on her personal problems as she and Eadulf had ridden back to Cashel having been successful in resolving the mystery. She had been considering whether she should end the trial marriage now, for the year and a day would soon be over. Then she had learnt the news about her baby son.

She gave a sharp intake of breath as the pain of the news struck her once again.

'What is it?' demanded Eadulf, concern on his features.

She glanced at him and grimaced.

'I was just thinking of something Publilius Syrus once wrote . . .'

At another time Eadulf might have made some humorous aside, for Fidelma was always ready to quote a moral axiom of the former slave of Rome. She seemed to know them all by heart. Instead he just said: 'Yes?'

'How unhappy are they who cannot forgive themselves,' she replied sadly.

Eadulf was about to respond when the door opened and Brother Madagan entered, then stood aside to usher in a medium-sized man in long brown woollen robes who walked with a distinctive limp. His left arm dangled uselessly at his side. He was not elderly but his features were deeply marked by experience rather than age. His long dark hair had white streaks in it and his dark eyes seemed to glow as if reflecting the horrors he had seen. His was the face of a man marred by his vicissitudes.

'This is Brother Buite of Magh Ghlas,' announced the steward.

Brother Buite limped forward and bowed briefly to Fidelma.

'How can I help you, lady?'

Fidelma returned his gaze for a moment. 'You know me?'

Brother Buite inclined his head. 'I served in the army of your brother at Cnoc Áine. That was where I . . .'

79

He reached unconsciously with his right hand across his chest towards his useless left arm, and then his hand dropped back and he shrugged.

'I know you, lady, and I know of your sorrow. I was in Cashel with my brothers on the night it happened. If there is anything I can do to relieve the pain you have but to ask.'

'You are generous in spirit, Brother Buite,' replied Fidelma solemnly. 'This is Brother Eadulf. Take a seat and speak with us a while.'

The man limped to an indicated seat and sat awkwardly while Brother Madagan, at a glance from Fidelma, went to resume his seat.

'I understand that you and your companions were in Cashel when my nurse was murdered and my baby taken. Tell me about your companions.'

Brother Buite flushed a little.

'I will speak of myself but you must question my companions about themselves. Sufficient to say that we all met on the road not far outside Cashel and I, knowing of the shrine of Ailbe, offered to guide them here to the abbey. We spent a night at the inn in the township below your brother's palace. I was told the following morning of the death of a nurse and the disappearance of your child, lady. But as it was clear that we had no baby with us, the noble prince Finguine allowed us to continue the journey here.'

'Ah yes. It was Finguine who came to the inn to question your party the next morning, I believe?'

'Just so, lady.'

'And then you brought your companions here?'

'I did.'

'But not all of them?'

Brother Buite looked startled.

'I believe that you travelled with a leper? But we are told

that when you arrived here a leper was not in your company.'

'Ah.' It was a soft breath. 'A leper did come with us.'

'Where did this companion leave you?'

'Just before we reached the abbey here. Five of us, the original party, proceeded to the abbey but our sixth traveller went on towards the west.'

'This sixth companion was small and carried a leper's bell?'

'That is so. He was a dwarf. Because of his illness we kept slightly apart from him but he did not seem to mind.'

'A dwarf?' Fidelma's eyes sparkled at the information. 'And he was a male?'

'The name he gave us was Forindain.'

'He spoke?' Eadulf asked the question with a note of surprise. Caol had said the misshapen child who came to the palace was mute. It had not occurred to him until that moment that the pilgrim Brother Buite was describing might be possessed of speech.

Brother Buite glanced at him. 'Why wouldn't he speak?'

Fidelma glanced warningly at Eadulf and shook her head slightly.

'And where did Forindain join your band?' she asked.

'At Cashel itself.'

'Was he staying at the inn there?'

'Not exactly. I had the impression that he slept in a barn.'

'Why was that?'

'I saw him eating in the inn before we retired for the night. He did not indicate by his bell that he was a leper then. That is contrary to the rules of the Faith. It was only when we were leaving in the morning and I found him in the yard with straw on his clothing and a leper's bell that I realised he was so afflicted. Have I transgressed some law, lady, by allowing him to accompany us?'

Fidelma leant back and examined Brother Buite's features keenly.

'You are troubled by my questions, Brother Buite. Let me tell you why I ask them. Sárait the nurse was apparently lured from the safety of my brother's palace when, according to the guard on duty, a child came with a message saying that her sister needed to see her urgently. The message was false. The messenger was said to be thickset and misshapen. It was dark. The guard, Caol, thought he saw a child. I suspect that he saw the dwarf who has been travelling with you. If so, we need to speak to this Forindain.'

Brother Buite blinked rapidly. 'Was Sárait the nurse who was killed?' he asked in surprise. 'Sárait who was the wife to Callada?'

'You knew her?' Eadulf pressed quickly.

Brother Buite inclined his head. 'I met her only once. It was Callada, her husband, that I knew. He was a popular fellow. He fought at Cnoc Áine and died there. I saw Sárait when she came in search of his body. I did not realise that she was the nurse who had been killed.'

'As a matter of interest, do you know how this Callada died?'

Brother Buite glanced suspiciously at Eadulf, who had asked the question.

'You mean, have I heard of the rumours that spread after the battle? Rumours that he had been found with an Eóghanacht spear in his back? I heard them. Indeed, it was Cathalán who commanded us and who pointed out that a spear has no allegiance – it is the man who wields the spear. Any one – Uí Fidgente or Eóghanacht – could have picked up the spear that transfixed Callada. But I know the rumours persisted.'

'We are more concerned to hear about your pilgrims and

how they fell in with this dwarf who gave his name as Forindain,' Fidelma interrupted.

'I will tell you what I know, lady,' replied the former warrior. 'My fellow pilgrims and I had reached Cashel, and hearing Bishop Ségdae was there we went to the palace and asked a blessing and permission to continue our pilgrimage to see the holy relics of Ailbe. Then we went to the inn to eat before taking a room there. As I have said, that was when I first saw the dwarf, but there was no indication then that he was a leper. In the morning, Prince Finguine came to the inn and asked if we had been disturbed during the night. Some of us had been awoken by the sounds of warriors moving about. He told us that there had been a killing and that a child was missing.

'After he left, I went into the yard and found the dwarf. He was, as you say, small and misshapen and clad from poll to toe in his robes. He told me his name was Forindain and that he was also on the road to Imleach. When I told him that was where we were heading, he asked if he could join us. But then he warned me not to come close for he carried the curse of leprosy as well as being malformed from childhood. I said that he was welcome to join us for we are equal under God.'

He paused, as if remembering something else.

'The dwarf asked us when we were departing for Imleach. When I said after we had broken our fast, he replied with satisfaction that this was well for he had something to see. When we were ready to depart, he was in the yard and walked some paces behind us. In this fashion, we came to Imleach.'

'Did this Forindain tell you where he came from?' asked Eadulf. 'Did he tell you anything at all about himself?'

Brother Buite shook his head. 'All I could tell was that he was originally from the kingdom of Laigin.'

'You learnt nothing else about him?'

'He kept himself to himself. Whenever anyone came too near, he would jangle that little bell of his as warning. We had our own cares and left him well alone. He followed behind us, always keeping a distance away.'

'What manner of person was he?' Fidelma pressed. 'Happy, outgoing, sad, morose, good-tempered or ill-tempered?'

Brother Buite shrugged. 'Hard to say. He was not loquacious, that is for sure. He kept his head cowled. I do not think I saw his face once. He was always in shadows. He moved agilely enough, in spite of jerking motions when he walked. He had thick, stubby hands – strong hands. Oh . . . I had almost forgotten. When he spoke, he spoke with a lisp as if his tongue was too large for his head.'

'How did this Forindain come to leave you?' she asked.

The leader of the pilgrims passed his good hand across his chin, as though to brush away an annoying insect.

'I suppose I assumed that when Forindain said he was on the road to Imleach, he meant that he was coming to the abbey. Outside the township here, he simply bade us farewell. I did ask where he was going. He said that his road now took him further to the west. So we left him at the crossroads outside the town. That was the last we saw of him and that was where our interest in him stopped.'

'And when did you part company?'

'About three days ago.'

Fidelma was quiet for a while, nodding silently. Then she suddenly smiled.

'You have been most helpful, Buite. I need not detain you or your companions.'

Brother Buite hesitated. 'Do you believe that this Forindain was involved with the murder of Sárait and the kidnapping of . . .?' His voice trailed off and he raised a shoulder and let it fall.

Fidelma's voice was emotionless. 'Belief is to regard what has been told one as being true. It is to be persuaded without final proof. That is not the task of a *dálaigh*, Brother Buite of Magh Ghlas. One seeks out truth through fact and not through opinion.'

Brother Buite flushed a little. Eadulf at once felt contrite, and hurried into speech.

'We are following all leads, however obscure and faint, and hope that somewhere along the way they will turn into those facts that we are looking for. We have questions that this Forindain can answer, that is all. Thank you for being so helpful.'

He smiled reassuringly at him and Brother Buite returned the smile before Brother Madagan ushered him from the chamber. Eadulf turned to Fidelma.

'Well, at least we know that the dwarf Forindain is not the so-called child seen by Caol, the guard at the palace,' he said emphatically.

Fidelma raised an eyebrow in query.

'How so?'

'Because Forindain had the power of speech, even though Brother Buite claims he spoke strangely, with a lisp. The child who came to the palace was mute. Caol said so.'

'And how did Caol know?'

Eadulf was impatient, not understanding her point.

'Because the child produced a note which said it could not speak?' Fidelma went on. 'And we must believe this because a note was produced? Belief is not fact, as I have just told Brother Buite.'

Eadulf considered the point. 'Do you have reason to believe that the child was lying to Caol?'

She shook her head. 'If the child or the dwarf were part of a plot to kill Sárait or abduct our baby, of course it would be lying. Anyway, nothing should ever be accepted on face value without checking. That is the rule of the Brehon.'

'An axiom of Brehon Morann?' replied Eadulf, a little sharply. 'I know. Well, that does not get us anywhere. This leper has disappeared taking the western road. He might be anywhere now. He might or might not have been the person who delivered the note to Sárait and even if he did he might or might not have been involved in the murder and kidnapping. There are too many ifs and buts. Where do we go from here?'

There was a dry cough from the shadows. They had forgotten Brother Madagan.

'If I might make a suggestion . . .?' The steward came forward smiling. 'I think your first priority is to refresh yourselves and, as the sky is darkening, to spend the night here before you travel on.'

Fidelma smiled tiredly.

'A good idea, Brother Madagan. We are too tired to think logically tonight. We will seek refreshment in food and contemplation.'

Brother Madagan turned towards the door.

'I will order a chamber to be prepared for you,' he said over his shoulder. 'Your warrior companions can sleep in the guests' dormitory. Would you like to wash? It will not be long before the bell sounds for the evening meal.' At the door, he hesitated and turned back. 'I could not help but hear that you were interested in a dwarf.'

'A particular dwarf,' Fidelma said sharply. 'Why?'

Brother Madagan made a gesture with his shoulder that was not quite a shrug.

'Only that there was a group of *drúth* passing through the

town a few days ago and there were dwarfs among them.'

'*Drui*?' queried Eadulf, not quite hearing the pronunciation and thinking the steward had mentioned druids.

Brother Madagan shook his head and corrected him.

'No, *drúth* – jesters, jugglers and gleemen. Those who travel the country to entertain and amuse with music, songs, stories and acrobatics.'

'When did they pass through here?' asked Fidelma. 'Before or after the pilgrims arrived?'

'Oh, the day before, I think. They entertained in the town for one night and then moved on. One of our brethren attended the entertainment and told me that they played the story of Bebo and Iubdán, which seemed much suited to their talents.'

'It would be a good choice of story,' Fidelma agreed. 'But the little person whom we seek was, according to accounts, a leper and a religieux.'

Brother Madagan shrugged. 'It was a thought. They said that they were going on to the Hill of the Ship. There is a fair there tomorrow. It is not very far west from here.'

'I know it. The chieftain is a distant cousin of mine. I'll bear it in mind, Brother Madagan. Thank you.'

Later, in their chamber, Eadulf asked: 'What did you mean when you said that the story of Bebo and Iubdán was a good choice of story? I do not understand.'

Fidelma was combing her hair and paused.

'A good choice for little people to play? It is one of the ancient tales. Iubdán was king of the Faylinn—'

'I've heard of many people in these kingdoms but not the Faylinn,' interrupted Eadulf.

'They are what we call the little people. A diminutive race that live in a parallel world. The story goes that Iubdán is able to travel to Emain Macha, the capital of the kingdom of Ulaidh. His wife Bebo comes with him. Iubdán clumsily falls into the porridge, which has been prepared for the breakfast of the king of Ulaidh, Fergus mac Léide. He cannot get out of the porridge bowl and is captured by Fergus. However, Fergus falls in love with Bebo, who comes to plead for her husband's life. Bebo is very beautiful, and they have an affair while he keeps her husband locked up. Bebo and Iubdán were his prisoners for a year and a day before he offered them freedom in exchange for Iubdán's most prized possession.'

'Which was . . .?' demanded Eadulf when she paused.

'A pair of enchanted shoes which enabled the king to travel over water as easily as over dry land.'

'And did they get their freedom?'

'They did so, after a year and a day . . .'

Fidelma's voice trailed off. A year and a day. She stirred uneasily at her thoughts about her marriage. Her own year and a day, which marked the time when she must decide her future with Eadulf, was rapidly nearing and yet how could she make any decision in the current situation? Her mind was already confused about her relationship and even now more confused by the tragedy of Alchú.

Eadulf had not noticed her sudden melancholy. He was continuing to talk.

'I have noticed here that dwarfs are not usually treated as figures of fun. It is different in other lands.'

Fidelma stirred herself and continued combing her red tresses. She tried to turn her mind away from her dark thoughts and concentrate on what Eadulf was saying.

'Why should they be regarded as other than people? Are they so different? In the days before the New Faith, two of the old gods, the children of Danu, were dwarfs. Luchta was one of the three great wrights who crafted shields and spear-shafts. Abcán, whose very name means "little dwarf", was a poet to the gods and goddesses and used to sail a curious metal boat on the waters of Eas Ruadh, the red cataract, which lies in a great river to the north of here. And you will find that little folk are often employed as poets and musicians at the great courts. Even Fionn Mac Cumhail had a harpist named Cnú Deireóil who was a dwarf. He was very handsome, with golden hair and such a sweet voice that he could lull you to sleep by the sound of his singing. Those who are small in stature are not necessarily small in mind.'

Eadulf was silent for a moment.

'I noticed that when you speak of them you always use the term *abacc*, while some people use the terms *droich* and *drochcumtha*. Which is the proper term for a small person?'

'*Abacc* is the better word for them, for it carries no connotation of anything bad or misshapen about a person,' she said. 'That implies an arrogance on the part of the speaker which is unworthy.'

Eadulf moved to the window and looked out at the dark cloistered courtyard beyond. One of the abbey's brethren was going round lighting the torches that hung in their iron braziers on the walls. Eadulf peered up at the patch of blackness above the courtyard and sighed.

'The month of Cet Gaimred,' he used the Irish name, 'and the clouds are so thick and dark that we cannot see this first of the winter moons.' He shivered abruptly. 'I am never happy at this time of year,' he said.

Fidelma glanced across at him.

'You cannot deny the natural order of things. Before rebirth there is always a period of darkness. That is why we consider our year begins with the darkness of winter. It is a time when we can rest and contemplate as Nature does before springing forth anew into light and growth.'

Eadulf turned and smiled softly.

'I never knew why your festival of Samhain should be considered as marking the start of the year.'

'Isn't it natural to sit, rest and meditate before one rises up into action? The crops rest, the trees rest, the people rest in their houses awaiting the first sign of the spring. As a baby rests in the darkness of its mother's womb, gaining strength, before plunging into the world.'

'You cannot be advocating that we should be doing nothing but waiting for the start of spring.' Eadulf leant back against the window and brushed a hand against the hair hanging over his forehead. 'Are we to do nothing until the feast that marks the ewes' coming into milk? There are times, such as this, when we must eschew contemplation and deny ourselves that rest.'

Almost as he said it, he realised it was not a good thing to say in the circumstances. Fidelma seemed to wince for a moment, as if struck by a physical pain, and he stepped quickly across to her with his hands held out. She did not take them, but turned her head away, leaving him frozen for a moment in the gesture. Then she sniffed and rose, brushing by him.

'You are right, Eadulf. Now is not the time for doing nothing.'

'I did not mean—'

'The refectory bell will sound in a moment,' she went on, ignoring his hurt and guilty look. 'Time to make a decision on what we should do now.'

Eadulf cleared his throat, wondering whether to challenge her behaviour, then he dropped his hands to his side and shrugged.

'As I see it, we can move west hoping that we might catch up with the little leper,' Fidelma said.

'I would agree that we could do so,' Eadulf replied.

'However, do we really know where he was heading, even if we accept that he was the strange figure seen by Caol, bringing the message to Sárait? What hope have we of finding this Forindain if we only know a general direction? He could go anywhere, not necessarily to the fair. It might be like looking for a needle in a stack of hay. What if he only said he was going west to Brother Buite? What if he went south, or north, or even returned east? I agree that we should perhaps follow any lead, however fragile and faint, but we might waste valuable time on this course of action.'

Fidelma looked thoughtful. 'Is there an alternative?'

'I think we could admit that this trail has gone cold.'

Fidelma sniffed slightly. 'There is always an alternative to any action in life. Life is governed by the fact that when a decision is made there are always two paths to choose from.'

'What else, then?' Eadulf pressed, perhaps a little aggressive now in his feeling of irritated hurt.

The refectory bell began to toll, summoning the brethren to the evening meal. Fidelma turned towards the door without answering.

'A moment!' snapped Eadulf.

Fidelma turned back to him, surprised at the sudden anger in his voice.

'I think,' Eadulf said, his voice suddenly cold, his tone measured, 'that you should tell me what you intend to do before we join the others. You should tell me, even if you have no respect for me as your husband, for the sake of the fact that I am the father of Alchú, who is my son as well as yours.'

Fidelma flushed in annoyance. For a moment she said nothing as a strange combination of guilt and anger welled in her, rose up until her tongue was ready to articulate it.

Then something seemed to spread like a cooling tide through her mind. Her guilt suddenly outweighed her impulse to anger.

She realised that the fault lay with her. She had taken Eadulf for granted and she had used arrogance to disguise her feelings of guilt for fear of showing them. Eadulf was right. Had she pushed the good nature of the Saxon too far? She stared at his resolute features. They seemed so alien now, so cold and impassive. She had never seen him look so controlled and distant before.

'Eadulf . . .' she began, but found her lips suddenly dry.

He waited a moment.

'Well?' he demanded harshly. 'What do you intend? Am I to be told or do you prefer to make decisions without informing me? Don't let it concern you. I am used to those at Cashel nudging one another, smirking and treating me with disrespect. There goes the foreigner! It is right that he is treated like a servant for he is not worthy of marriage to our princess.'

Fidelma stared at him, shocked.

'Who says this about you?' she demanded after a pause.

Eadulf's features formed into a sneer. She had never seen him like this before.

'Are you claiming that you are blind to what happens at Cashel? Are you deaf to the whispers in the corridors of your brother's palace? It is obvious that I am not thought worthy of you and you have often demonstrated that you share that opinion. I am considered . . .'

The angry words faded away as he failed to find suitable ones to express the months of built-up frustration and anger that lay within him.

Fidelma stood still, watching him. She suddenly felt that he had become a stranger to her. She was shocked by his suppressed passion. He stared back, his mouth a thin line, waiting for her to react. Finally, she sighed deeply.

'I was going to suggest that we continue west until we reach Cnoc Loinge, the Hill of the Ship, to see if we can learn anything further about the dwarf Forindain,' she said quietly.

'That,' replied Eadulf in a tight voice, 'is acceptable to me.'

He brushed quickly by her and left her staring in confusion after him.

Chapter Six

The next morning, Fidelma turned her horse westward. She had hardly spoken to Eadulf since their harsh words of the night before and a long, uncomfortable silence hung between them. To Capa she had merely said: 'I am in a mind to go to Cnoc Loinge, the Hill of the Ship. It will take us a few hours out of our journey, that is all.'

Capa had protested.

'There is nothing there, lady.'

'Except a fair that I have a mind to see.'

Capa raised his eyebrows in surprise but said nothing further. After a while, Fidelma decided to unbend and confided in Capa and his men what the purpose of going to Cnoc Loinge was.

Capa was clearly not enthusiastic.

'You say that this dwarf, Forindain, might be the messenger that lured my sister-in-law from the palace? A leper? And we are going to Cnoc Loinge to see a band of travelling players among whom this Forindain might be hiding? It sounds a waste of time to me.'

'Nevertheless,' Fidelma assured him, 'that is why we are going there.'

Capa glanced at Eadulf, who had remained silent. It was clear that he recognised the unease between them. He regarded them with a troubled expression but said no more.

The distinctively shaped hill lay scarcely five kilometres from the abbey of Imleach. It was a pleasant and easy ride through wooded countryside until they came to the settlement nestling under the long, narrow hill. But just before they reached their destination, Eadulf saw that several travellers were joining the road. Soon the track was crowded and they had to pick their way among all manner of pedestrians, riders and those driving carts drawn by sturdy donkeys. It was clear that they were all heading for the fair, and when they reached the settlement they became aware of festivities taking place.

Apart from the wooden buildings of the village, there were stalls and tents erected on the main green, an area called the *faithche* that was set aside for the purpose. Fidelma knew that the smaller fairs throughout the country were presided over by the local chieftain, who assigned certain people to clear away the brambles and rubbish from the area on which the fair was to be held. Fences and mounds marked out the ground on which stalls were erected, and there was also an area set aside for sports such as jumping and running, and displays of weaponry and wrestling. To one side, she could see a *cluichi mag* had been prepared. This was a grassy level, where the ancient game of *camán* or hurling would be played. A local fair like this was called an *oirecht* as opposed to the major festivals of the *Féis*.

However, for such a small fair, there were a lot of people attending. It was probable that most of the population of the outlying areas had come to attend or participate in the sports or be entertained by the travelling players.

The stalls were crowded with people selling their wares,

from farmers selling goats and pigs to those selling fruits and baked produce such as pies. Above the hubbub and shouting of the crowds came the sound of music. Here and there an *airfidig* or solitary minstrel wandered, singing ballads and reciting poetry, while in one corner a group of musicians, including a *cruit* or harp player, a *cnamh-fhir* or bone man who played bone castanets, and a drummer, entertained a crowd, with *cuirsig*, pipes and flutes.

Fidelma's sharp eye caught a small stage. It was empty but had obviously been erected for an entertainment. A notice attached to a pole read, 'The Love of Bebo of the Faylinn to be played here.' So the dwarfs were still here, she noted with satisfaction. Of course, it did not mean that the leper, Forindain, was with them, but she felt intuitively that she would find him.

She drew her horse to a halt and called to a man, who looked like a local, who was standing by a stream that meandered along the edge of the fairground where people could water their horses. This man, however, held a great wolfhound on a lead, and it was lapping at the waters.

'Greetings, my friend. Where is the *suide-dála*, the convention seat, and will your chieftain be there?'

The man, tall with ginger hair and the look of a smith rather than a farmer, glanced quickly at her with bright blue eyes, his gaze travelling from her attire to the golden necklets of her companions announcing them to be the élite of the king of Cashel's warriors. He inclined his head in obeisance.

'You are welcome to Cnoc Loinge, lady.' He had obviously deduced that she was no mere religieuse but someone of importance. 'If you follow this stream here you will come to the convention seat by the *camán* field, the large blue tent, where our chieftain, Fiachrae, takes his rest before the game starts.'

'Thank you.' Fidelma turned towards the tent the man had indicated. They had not gone far when Capa called to her.

'Lady, do you want us to set about finding the dwarfs and discovering if they know the religieux leper?'

Fidelma drew rein.

'I am going to talk to the chieftain here. He is Fiachrae, a distant cousin of mine – one of the Eóghanacht. But we can save time. Make your search and inquiries. See if you can find Forindain. You know his description: a dwarf in religious robes and doubtless carrying a leper's bell.'

Gormán's face took on a concerned look.

'How should we approach a leper?'

Fidelma regarded him with amusement.

'Like anyone else. Inform him that a *dálaigh* wishes to speak to him. He has a legal obligation to comply. As soon as I have made myself known to the chieftain, I will join you in the search.'

Eadulf, concentrating on what was being said, did not know exactly what happened. One minute he was seated easily on his horse, next to Fidelma, and the next his mount was rearing and whinnying as if something had startled it. Eadulf was not the best of horsemen and clung on for dear life. His powerful beast kicked out and caught Fidelma's mount, which also reared unexpectedly, and lost its footing, its hind legs splashing back into the stream. Caught by surprise, Fidelma was catapulted backwards into the muddy waters.

Capa reached forward and grasped her horse's head while Gormán caught at Eadulf's mount. A moment later, both animals stood still and trembling. Eadulf and Capa immediately slid from their horses and moved hurriedly to where Fidelma still sat spluttering in the muddy waters, gasping and choking.

'Are you all right?' demanded Eadulf anxiously, reaching forward.

Her cheeks were bright pink with anger. She glared up at him.

'Haven't you learnt to control a horse yet?' she demanded angrily.

He stepped back as if she had slapped him. Then her anger seemed to evaporate.

'Sorry. I am bruised and muddy and soaked but doubtless my pride is more hurt than my body. Help me up out of this.'

Eadulf and Capa leant forward and drew her upright. She looked down at her muddy clothes ruefully.

'Hardly dressed to greet my cousin,' she murmured.

'Your dress does not matter, Cousin Fidelma,' came a deep, sonorous voice. A stout, round-faced, middle-aged man had approached unnoticed with some attendants. He was richly dressed and wore a gold chain of office.

Fidelma blinked. 'Fiachrae?'

'You are welcome to my *oirechtas*, cousin. But come, let one of my attendants lead you to my bathhouse and bring you dry clothes before you catch your death of cold. Then come and join me for some refreshment in my tent. Plenty of time to tell me what brings you to my little village.'

Fidelma glanced down at herself again. There was not much to argue about. She indicated Eadulf.

'First, I must introduce you to . . . to my *fer comtha*, Eadulf of Seaxmund's Ham.'

The chieftain gazed with round pale eyes on Eadulf. A *fer comtha* indicated Eadulf's status as husband on a temporary basis.

'I have heard much of you,' he said hesitantly, then glanced back to Fidelma. 'I will take Eadulf under my care and you will find us in my tent.'

Fidelma nodded, turning to Capa and his men.

'My mishap does not alter my plan. You may look at the fair.'

'Understood, lady,' agreed Capa, raising his hand in salute.

Eadulf picked up the feeling that Fidelma had not wanted Fiachrae to be informed of the purpose of their visit until later. The chieftain signalled to one of his attendants to take the horses of Fidelma and Eadulf and then led the way towards the large blue tent that served as his seat during the period of the fair.

The crowds that had gathered round to see what entertainment was offered by the arrival of the newcomers, realising it was no entertainment at all, began to drift away. The chieftain turned and summoned a female servant from the crowd.

'Follow my attendant that way, Cousin Fidelma.' The rotund chieftain indicated a group of buildings behind the tent. 'She will see to all your wants.' Fidelma went without another word. The chieftain had become quite friendly to Eadulf, talking non-stop of trivialities. He tucked his arm under Eadulf's in intimate fashion and propelled him smilingly into the tent. An iron brazier, in which a fire smouldered to give warmth on the chill day, was placed in the centre of the tent, its smoke curling up through an aperture by the main pole.

'Now, my Saxon friend – or should I say cousin by marriage – let us have a mug of honey mead to keep out the winter cold.'

Eadulf smiled wearily and sank into a seat that the chieftain indicated.

'That would be most welcome.'

Within a few minutes, Eadulf had realised that the chieftain was a loquacious fellow who seemed to talk for the sake of talking. He was a teller of tales whether his audience was appreciative or not.

Fiachrae passed a mug of mead to Eadulf.

'Have you visited Cnoc Loinge before, my Saxon friend? I do not recall you and, of course, it is a long time since I last saw my cousin.'

Eadulf shook his head as he sipped the sweet mead.

'The closest I have come to Cnoc Loinge is to Imleach,' he replied.

'Ah, I heard of that occasion. It was when Brother Mochta and the holy relics of Ailbe went missing.'

Eadulf simply inclined his head in confirmation.

'Well, you will find that my little rath has a great history. It was here that the ancestor of the Eóghanacht kings asserted their independence from any unjust demands of the High King.'

It was clear that the rotund chieftain wanted to tell the story and Eadulf thought it better to assuage his pride than to make Fidelma's task the more difficult by rudeness. Fiachrae was seated comfortably in his chair, a mug of mead in his hand, and smiling almost meditatively.

'The lady Moncha gave birth to a son some months after her lord, Eóghan, ancestor of all the Eóghanacht, was slain in battle. The son was Fiachrae Muilleathan, and justly was he named "king of battles".'

Eadulf smiled. 'While I know that Fiachrae, which is your own name, means "king of battles", as you say, I thought Muilleathan meant broad-crowned.'

The chieftain sniffed, not liking his tale to be interrupted.

'An astrologer predicted that if the child were born on a certain day he would be chief jester of the five kingdoms of Éireann. If he was born on the following day, then the position of the stars would be more auspicious and he would become the most powerful king in the country. So when Moncha felt the birth pangs and the day of the better prediction had not yet come, she left the palace at Cnoc Rafoan and walked into the shallows of the nearby River Suir. She sat on a flat stone to delay the baby's coming. So that day passed, and the baby came on the day when it was predicted that the child, if born then, would be a great king. But Moncha died from her efforts to delay the birth. When the infant emerged, the force of being pressed against the stone had flattened his forehead and hence he bore thereafter the sobriquet of Muilleathan or broad-crowned.'

The chieftain spoke in all seriousness and Eadulf controlled his features, which were about to give way to mirth, and merely nodded.

'Go on.'

'Fiachrae, or Fiacha, for he was also known by the diminutive form as a token of affection by his people, became a great king. He ruled here during the time when the great Cormac mac Art held the high kingship, which was about four centuries ago. The Uí Néill, of the sept of the Dál Riada, expelled Cormac for a time from Tara, but Fiachrae came forward and fought in his support, and Cormac regained the high kingship. For a time, all was well between the two kings, but Cormac was ill advised. An ambitious administrator told him that this kingdom of Muman, being the largest of the five kingdoms, should pay double the tribute to the High King of any other of the kingdoms. When this was demanded, Fiachrae refused.

'Then Cormac did a very unwise thing, spurred on by the ambitions of his bad adviser. He came with an army into Muman. Fiachrae's own army gathered here at this very spot, on this very hill which is shaped like a ship, and here it was that Cormac's army surrounded Fiachrae's men. Again

101

Cormac was ill advised. His generals told him to burn out the army of Fiachrae and they set fire to the trees and bushes, but Fiachrae's druid Mag Ruith caused a great wind to arise and the smoke was blown on to Cormac's warriors, suffocating them and causing them to flee. Then Fiachrae gave the order for his warriors to pursue and punish Cormac's army. Cormac had to pay reparation to Fiachrae.'

Eadulf smothered a yawn, doing his best to hide his boredom.

'And everyone lived in happiness thereafter?' he said.

The chieftain shook his head.

'Life is not like a fairy story in this land, Saxon,' he rebuked his guest, not picking up on Eadulf's sarcasm. 'Cormac had his revenge.'

Eadulf had glanced quickly round, wondering why Fidelma was so long in rejoining them. He realised that he should say something, and asked: 'How?'

'Cormac had a fosterling named Connla, son of Tadhg, lord of Éile, a rival to the Muman throne, and cousin of Fiachrae. Connla had contracted leprosy while at Tara . . .'

Eadulf stirred uneasily as he was reminded of the purpose in coming to Cnoc Loinge. 'Leprosy?'

'Indeed. And Cormac played a subtle game for his revenge. He persuaded Connla that a cure could be found if he bathed in the blood of a king who was kin to him. Connla went south and was welcomed at the court at Cnoc Rafoan and treated well by Fiachrae. Connla bided his time and one day he and Fiachrae went swimming in the Suir at Áth Aiseal, the ford of the ass. When the opportunity arose, he drove his sword into Fiachrae . . .'

'And was cured of leprosy?' Eadulf smiled.

The chieftain frowned at his flippancy.

'Of course not,' he snapped. 'Connla was taken by

Fiachrae's guards but the dying king, showing his nobility, told them to spare his life and sent him to the house of the lepers in the land of the Corco Duibhne. The king died and was succeeded by his tanist Ailill Flann Bec from whose noble line descends our present king, Colgú ... and, of course, your wife Fidelma.'

The chieftain suddenly smiled and cast a sideways glance at Eadulf.

'But I hear that Fidelma is now mother to a son. How is the child? I believe his name is Alchú, is it not?'

Eadulf seized the opportunity to tell Fiachrae what had brought them to his small settlement. The chieftain's garrulousness vanished.

'But ... but this is terrible. You should have told me immediately,' he said. 'This is catastrophic. A tragedy. Awful.'

Eadulf had the impression that Fiachrae's words lacked sincerity. He felt a compulsion to point out that he had had little opportunity to tell the chieftain anything. It was only after he had told the story about the dwarf leper that he remembered Fidelma's reticence about revealing the reason for their presence to Fiachrae earlier.

'Well,' Fiachrae said after a moment or two, putting down his mug, 'there have been no reports of itinerants or lepers of any shape or size passing through here.'

'Fidelma thought that he might have joined the dwarfs who are here ...'

Fiachrae shook his head immediately. 'These dwarfs are *crossan*. I hardly think that a leper, or a religious of any sort, would join them.'

'*Crossan?*'

'*Crossan* or *drúth* – gleemen or players. They are performing some play and the word has spread so that many people are coming to the fair from the surrounding countryside. I

103

am told that they come from the Féis Tailltenn where they had great success in the entertainment of the High King.'

'And none of them has been seen with a baby?'

Fiachrae was frowning. 'You have reason to suspect these performers of the abduction of your child?'

'There is reason to suppose that a dwarf was involved,' Eadulf said shortly, for he was not entirely sure he agreed with Fidelma's intuition on the matter.

'Well, they do not have any babies with them. Nor have they come from Cashel. I am told that they came from Cluain Mic Nois and Tír dhá Ghlas, the territory of the two streams, directly north of Imleach.'

'You seem well apprised of their movements.'

Fiachrae smiled thinly. 'I have to be, my friend. I can take you to the top of the hill behind us and show you where the territory of the Uí Fidgente commences.'

'So close?' Eadulf had always associated the Uí Fidgente with a territory well to the west and slightly to the north.

'Cnoc Áine, where we defeated the Uí Fidgente last year, is only five kilometres north of here. We are on the borderlands of the fractious clan that is always plotting against the rule of the Eóghanacht. That is why I have to take an interest in all the travellers passing through here. My people know this and have orders to tell me of any strangers passing into the country of the Uí Fidgente.'

Eadulf leant forward with interest. 'So you would know what travellers have come this way in the last few days?'

Fiachrae smiled complacently. 'I do. I can tell you of a very strange person, for example, travelling with a religieux from the northern Uí Néill kingdom. He hardly knew our language, although he spoke several including the tongues of the Greek and the Roman.'

'Ah, I have heard of them,' agreed Eadulf. However, the chieftain was disposed to continue.

'Brother Basil Nestorios was his name,' he went on. 'His companion, whose name was Brother Tanaide, told me that this Basil Nestorios was a healer from lands in the east. He boasted, or rather Brother Tanaide boasted on his behalf, that he could cure leprosy by his potions and herbs. He was probably a madman, but most foreigners are . . .'

He suddenly realised what he had said and glanced at Eadulf to see if he had taken offence.

'Anyone else?' pressed Eadulf, ignoring the remark. 'We are particularly interested in anyone who carried a baby with them.'

Fiachrae shook his head. 'No one has passed here carrying a solitary baby.'

Eadulf sat back, disappointed.

There was a movement at the door. Fidelma entered, having washed and changed into dry clothing.

'I am sorry to be so long, Fiachrae,' she said, coming to the fire and taking her seat before Fiachrae could rise from his chair.

'Do not worry, cousin. I have been entertaining our Saxon friend with stories of our history, and how it is that this small spot ensured the prosperity of the Eóghanacht.'

Fidelma grimaced. 'The story of our ancestor Fiachrae son of Eóghan? The story of Cnoc Loinge and the siege is one of the sagas of our kingdom. I remember that you are fond of telling it.' There was a sense of weariness in her voice as if Fiachrae and his storytelling were well known to her and not really appreciated.

The chieftain beamed a little and rose, moving to the side table.

'Mead to keep out the cold after your immersion in the stream?' he offered.

'I do not wish to seem an ungracious guest, Fiachrae, but I had expected Capa and the others to have returned by now. Surely, the fair is not so large?'

'It gets larger each year as our prosperity grows. But three pairs of eyes should have accomplished the task of finding a leper.' His grin broadened as he saw her frown. 'We have had a long talk, Eadulf and I. He has told me of your quest. You have but to instruct me and if it is in my power, I will accomplish the task.'

Fidelma glanced towards Eadulf and then seemed to relax.

'You are gracious, Fiachrae.'

'As I was telling Eadulf here, I know of every stranger who has come to the fair. It is my duty. Your brother, our king, charged me with it after the victory at Cnoc Áine. No lepers are in attendance at the fair today. And the dwarfs are only *crossan*.'

The corners of Fidelma's mouth turned down and she glanced disapprovingly at Eadulf.

'Doubtless my *fer comtha* has been asking what strangers have been passing through your settlement and whether any carried babies.'

Fiachrae suppressed a chuckle.

'Sharp as ever, cousin. He has.'

He had poured a second mug of mead for Eadulf without asking him and thrust it into his hand. Eadulf took it automatically.

'And what was your answer?' Fidelma asked coldly.

'No one has passed through with a single baby that was not theirs.'

She was about to rise when one of Fiachrae's men entered unannounced into the tent and hurried up to him. He seemed slightly breathless.

'Fiachrae, there has been a killing,' he said without preamble.

The chieftain's brows drew together in surprise.

'What? Who? Speak up, man.'

'The Cashel warrior, Capa, sent me to inform you and the lady Fidelma that she should come at once. They have found a body on the far side of the fair ground.'

'Capa? Is he hurt? Is he or one of his men involved?' demanded Fidelma, rising immediately with Eadulf and Fiachrae.

The messenger shook his head. 'No, lady, he and his men were not involved, other than that they found the body and now ask me to take you to them.'

'Lead on, then.'

The messenger hurried forward with the three of them close behind, moving swiftly between the stalls and across a wooden plank bridge spanning the stream that acted as a border to the fair ground. After a short distance, on the far side, the forest of dark yews, holly and leafless blackthorns began. One of Capa's men, Caol, stood on the edge of the wood and waved to them immediately.

'This way, lady,' he called.

It was only a short distance along a narrow path before they came across Capa and Gormán, who was looking unnaturally pale.

By the side of the path was a small area where bushes of dogwood, still in its autumnal blood-red shoots and crimson leaves, grew among a number of ashwood stumps. Someone had obviously cut the ash trees in the past, for the stumps were old and covered with black crampballs of inedible fungus.

Capa pointed dramatically downwards.

'We have found him, lady,' he said simply.

107

There was no need to ask whom.

The body of a very short man with a large head, clad in a religious robe, lay flat on its back surrounded by a mass of orange peel fungus which seemed to lend a surreal quality to the image, making a bright frame for the dead little body.

There was no need to ask how the dwarf had met his death. The cord which had fastened his robe at the waist was still knotted in garrotte fashion round his neck. The features were distorted, the skin mottled and almost blackened, and the tongue protruding between the teeth.

Chapter Seven

'Quiet!' snapped Fidelma, as several voices began to speak at once.

She moved forward and knelt by the side of the body. The dwarf had a young face in spite of the distortion of the garrotting. He had dark hair and there was no sign of a religious tonsure. The body was still warm to the touch. Not long dead. She noticed a piece of metal half hidden by the body and reached for it. It came away with a musical chime. It was a small bronze bell with a wooden handle. She looked at it for a few minutes before placing it on the ground beside her and then she carefully examined the hands and face of the body. As she did so a puzzled frown began to crease her brow.

To the surprise of the watchers, she began to pull open the robes, slowly and carefully, to reveal the flesh of the body. In silence they watched her make her examination, and then she replaced the robe over the little body and stood up.

'Is there a physician here in Cnoc Loinge?' she asked Fiachrae.

The chieftain had been watching her in bewilderment and now shook his head.

'There is a herbalist and there is the man who dresses

109

corpses for burial. The nearest physician resides in the abbey of Imleach.'

'Have the herbalist take the body to a place where he can examine it thoroughly. I want his report within the hour.'

'What is he to look for?'

'He is to report whether this man had any afflictions.'

Fiachrae turned to the attendant who had brought them hither and repeated the order. The man went off at a trot.

Fidelma had turned back to the warriors.

'Now, how was this body discovered?'

Gormán shuffled his feet awkwardly.

'I discovered it, lady.'

'How was that?' asked Fidelma sharply. 'This spot is well away from the fair ground, where you were asked to search. The body is hidden in this wood.'

'Indeed. When you left us, Capa told us to separate to complete our search more quickly. I had been wandering through the fair for some time when Capa came to me and told me that a woman had reported that she had seen a dwarf in religious robes with a leper's bell lurking in the woods in this direction. He sent me to see if there was truth in the report.'

Capa made to intervene but Fidelma raised her hand to silence him.

'Go on, Gormán.'

'I came here and began to look round. The body was not exactly hidden and so I came upon it quite easily.'

'And was it in the position that I first saw it?'

'Exactly so, lady. I touched nothing, but, ascertaining the little man was dead, and certainly not wishing to touch a leper, I ran back and found Capa who was still searching the fair with Caol. We came here and then Capa returned to the fair for a moment. He said that he had told a man to go to fetch you.'

Caol moved forward. 'Capa and Gormán remained with the body while I waited on the edge of the wood for you.'

'And so, Gormán, when you came upon the body, there was no sign of anyone else nearby?'

'No, lady. As soon as I saw in what manner the little man had died, I looked quickly round, so far as my eyes could penetrate the wood, but saw no one nor any sign of anyone.'

Fidelma nodded slowly and turned her gaze on Capa.

'I need to be clear in my own mind about the sequence of events. How did the woman know you were looking for a dwarf in religious clothing with a leper's bell? If the woman told you that she had seen the dwarf lurking at the edge of the woods here, why did you not come to investigate yourself?'

Capa's smile was disarming.

'I was asking some people if they had seen signs of the dwarf. I thought it might quicken our search if I did so. No one had seen him except this woman. I would estimate that she was some farmer's daughter. She told me that she had seen this strange fellow while she was at the stream drawing water for her animals. Almost immediately, I saw Gormán,' he indicated the raven-haired young warrior, 'and told him to investigate. I went on asking people . . . and, shortly after, Gormán returned. The rest was as he narrated it, lady.'

Fidelma sighed deeply.

'Let us return to your tent, Fiachrae. Wait here,' she added to Capa and his men, 'for the coming of the herbalist. Impress upon him that I want a thorough examination of the body for sign of any affliction that he may have suffered from, and when it is done, one of you come to Fiachrae's tent to report to me. Then I will come and speak to him. Make sure he is thorough in his examination.'

Capa raised a hand in acknowledgement and Fidelma, with Fiachrae and Eadulf at her side, walked back towards the tent of the chieftain.

'I don't understand, cousin,' protested Fiachrae. 'I don't follow any of this.'

'No reason why you should,' Fidelma replied shortly.

Eadulf cleared his throat meaningfully. After all, this was Fiachrae's village over which he had jurisdiction. Fidelma unbent a little.

'I think this is the dwarf we were looking for. But I do not believe the dwarf was a leper.'

Eadulf's eyes rounded a little. 'He did carry a leper's bell.'

'That is why I have asked that the body be examined by someone who can confirm my suspicion.'

Back in the chieftain's tent, Fiachrae went immediately to the jug of mead, pouring himself a large measure. Then he remembered his manners and turned, jug in hand, to Fidelma and Eadulf.

'Will you join me?'

This time Eadulf shook his head while Fidelma accepted.

'A small measure,' she added when she saw that her cousin was prepared to be generous with his liquor.

'This has put a black cloud in the sky of our fair, cousin,' muttered Fiachrae. 'Who is this little religieux and who killed him? The slaughter was done in my territory and I am responsible for finding the evildoer.'

'As a *dálaigh*, even though just visiting your territory, I take responsibility in that matter, cousin,' Fidelma assured him.

'But who is he?' demanded Fiachrae. His eyes widened as if a thought had suddenly struck him. 'I nearly overlooked something. I'd better inform the *crossan*, the little gleemen, just in case they know this dwarf.'

'Good for you!' exclaimed Fidelma. 'I was nearly forgetting . . . ask them to gather at the place where the herbalist is making his examination. But on no account let them enter until I have seen the herbalist.'

When Fiachrae left, Eadulf leant quickly forward to Fidelma.

'I have formed a theory. The young warrior, Gormán – he had the ideal opportunity to kill the dwarf.'

She returned his gaze evenly.

'Why would you think that, Eadulf?'

'He was more than keen to accompany us. He admitted he was in love with Sárait and wanted vengeance. Those are good reasons.' His eyes widened suddenly. 'If Aona is right, why, Gormán might even have been responsible for the death of Sárait's husband Callada, and—'

Fidelma interrupted him. 'I think we are racing ahead without evidence. It is fascinating to speculate but as I have often told you, Eadulf, speculation without facts will take us nowhere. Why would he kill the dwarf? We have no knowledge that the dwarf killed Sárait, only that a figure, which Caol deemed a misshapen child, brought a message to her and she went out of the palace in answer to it. We are working on supposition.'

Eadulf looked glum. 'I had forgotten it was Caol who saw the misshapen child that night. Perhaps he recognised the dwarf and . . .'

Fidelma shook her head. 'Let's stop speculating until we hear further,' she said.

It was not long before Caol summoned them to the herbalist's shop. It was a wooden hut hung with dried herbs and flowers and a fire smouldered in a hearth at one end, enhancing the thick aromatic atmosphere to the point where Eadulf started to cough and even Fidelma had to catch her breath.

Even though it was still daylight, the interior was lit with lamps as the small windows let in hardly any light.

The herbalist was old and querulous.

'Well, the dwarf is dead,' he snapped as they entered, peering in short-sighted fashion at them. 'Dead,' he repeated. 'Why am I bothered further?'

Fidelma moved forward to face the old man.

'A fool can tell that he is dead. I instructed that you look for signs of any affliction.'

The herbalist stared myopically at her.

'Of course he was afflicted,' he snapped. 'He was a dwarf, wasn't he?'

'Again that is obvious,' replied Fidelma sharply. 'Did he suffer from leprosy?'

'Did he . . . what?' The herbalist was even more irritable. 'I am being asked to teach a class in basic medicine?'

Fiachrae had joined them and moved close to the herbalist.

'This is the sister of King Colgú, a *dálaigh* of the courts. Answer her questions in civil fashion or you may find that you will no longer be practising your art here,' he said quietly.

The herbalist blinked, peering once again at Fidelma.

'The dwarf did not suffer from leprosy,' he said shortly.

'So far as you could tell, has he ever done so?'

'He has never done so. You do not, so far as I have knowledge, recover from such a pestilence, even though some strangers claim such miraculous cures.'

Fidelma compressed her lips.

'That is exactly what I wanted to confirm.' Then she frowned. 'What do you mean about strangers claiming cures?'

The old man sniffed in deprecation.

'A day or so ago, a stranger came through here . . . his

114

companion translated his words as he did not have much of our language. His companion told me that he was a healer in his own land. He claimed he knew of various herbs which might cure the disease. I knew none of them except burdock, but that I only know as a plant whose juices can be used to treat burns and sores.'

'And we eat the young stalks in salads,' added Eadulf, who, having spent some time studying the apothecary's art, knew a little of such matters. 'But what were the others that this stranger spoke of?'

The herbalist glanced at him in disfavour.

'Things with strange foreign names. Not even the blessed Fintan of Teach Munna in Laigin was able to cure himself once he contracted the disease. I heard Bishop Petrán once argue that Fintan was cursed with the affliction because, during the great Synod of Magh Lene that was held when I was a young man some thirty-five years old, Fintan had argued against Rome's authority. He went so far as to criticise some of the pronouncements of the Bishops of Rome, such as their approval of the Edict of Lyons when it was decreed that lepers should be cast out of society and go about ringing bells to warn others of their coming.'

Fidelma gave an intake of breath showing her impatience.

'I am sure we are not interested in curses, apothecary, nor, at this moment, in the rights and wrongs of our culture and our church.' She glanced to where the body lay on the table on which the apothecary had conducted his investigation. It was now clothed in the robe again and laid out in a manner ready for burial. The small child-like form was a pathetic sight.

'Very well,' she said. 'Herbalist, we need to take over your shop for a few minutes. Will you wait outside with my guard?

Fiachrae, remain with me. Eadulf, ask Capa to tell the *crossan* to come in.'

Eadulf escorted the disgruntled herbalist to the door and looking out saw Capa and his men standing with a group of half a dozen small people in garish clothing who were obviously the gleemen.

'Let them come in now,' he called to Capa.

The warrior nodded and the gleemen moved forward curiously, passing Eadulf into the apothecary's hut and peering about.

They had hardly set foot inside the door when a wail suddenly came from one of them, who had pointed towards the body on the table. A great outcry arose from the others, anguish and despair rending the air. Fidelma had no need to ask if they recognised the dead man.

One of them ran forward, tugging at the body as if to ascertain whether it was alive or not. Fidelma saw a strong likeness between his face and that of the corpse. Of the gleemen, he seemed the most distraught, and it was pitiful to see his distress.

She moved forward and laid a hand on his shoulder.

'I am sorry to have done this without forewarning. I just wanted to know if you or any of your companions would recognise the body.'

The dwarf, blinking back tears, gazed up at her. His grief was plain.

'Of course I recognise him. He was my brother and one of our company.' He spoke as many of his companions did with a slight lisp in his speech.

'And his name was Forindain?'

The dwarf stared at her for a moment and then shook his head.

'His name was Iubdán. Forindain was a part that I played.'

Fidelma hid her bewilderment. 'Your name is Forindain?'

'I am known as such,' replied the dwarf. 'None of these are our real names. We use the names of the characters we play. I play Forindain in our little love tale of Bebo.'

'You are not a religious, Forindain?'

'That is the part of my character – Brother Forindain the Leper who betrays the Faylinn in the story. Why do you ask this . . .?' The little man's eyes wandered to the body of his brother, taking in the costume he wore. 'Ah, I see.'

Fidelma pursed her lips for a moment.

'Which is more than I do. Forindain, I am sorry for the death of your brother. Believe me. But I am a *dálaigh*, and I am concerned to find out how and why he was killed . . .'

'Was he murdered?' demanded the dwarf, suddenly noticing the mark of the ligature round his brother's neck. 'Who would kill a *crossan*, a travelling player, who had no enemy in the world?'

'That is what I must find out. Come with me to Fiachrae's tent and let me discuss this with you and then, I promise, I will let you and your fellows mourn in peace.'

The *crossan* hesitated, glanced again at his brother's body, and turned to his companions.

'We must contain our grief for a moment. One of you must go and inform the people that we must cancel our play. Another must ask that the body of our friend, my brother, be wrapped in a *recholl*, a shroud, and we need someone to prepare the *fuat*, the bier, to bear him to his grave. I also need to speak to the chieftain, Fiachrae, and find out where he can be buried. Do these things, my friends, that I ask of you while I go and speak with this learned *dálaigh*. When they are done, then we, together, may start on the time of watching and make this coming night into day with the blaze of our torches while we raise our voices in the traditional *caoine*.'

Fidelma was surprised by the intense cadences of his voice, the articulate phrases of his speech, until she realised that she had been overlooking the fact that the little man was a player, one of the *crossan*.

Fiachrae led the small party back to the convention seat. Fidelma had despatched Capa and his men to refresh themselves until such time as they were called for. In the tent, Fiachrae indicated that everyone should sit, and called for an attendant to bring *corma*. To his obvious surprise everyone else refused it while he, himself, poured a liberal measure of the fiery alcohol into his mug.

'You are in charge here, cousin,' he said. 'Handle it in your way.'

'Thank you, Fiachrae,' Fidelma replied solemnly. She had been prepared to do so anyway. She turned to the dwarf. 'Now, how shall I address you? As Forindain?'

The *crossan* inclined his head. 'Since I joined the travelling players, it has become my name, Sister. My parents cast me out as soon as they could legally dispose of me . . . my brother and I, that is. We were fostered by an *obláire*, the chief of a company of players, and taught his skills so that we could use those attributes nature endowed us with for the entertainment of our fellows. You may call me Forindain as, after such a passage of time, I can answer to no other name.'

'Thank you. You know this is Fiachrae, the chieftain of Cnoc Loinge, and this is Brother Eadulf of Seaxmund's Ham, in the land of the South Folk beyond the seas.'

Forindain's gaze swept them all before returning to Fidelma.

'And you are a *dálaigh*, you say?'

'My name is Fidelma, Fidelma of Cashel.'

Forindain blinked in recognition. 'Are you sister to Colgú, king of Muman?' he asked quietly.

'I am. And you know of me?'

'I have heard that you are a great *dálaigh*.'

'Nothing else?'

The dwarf frowned. 'Is there anything else that I should know?' he countered.

Fidelma was silent for a moment. Then she said: 'Let us speak of your brother, Iubdán. Tell me about him.'

'Little to tell. His life paralleled mine until it was cruelly taken away. Since we were fostered by the *obláire* we have been among the same *crossan*. We ran our small company of players together.'

'And when did Iubdán join you here at Cnoc Loinge?'

Forindain frowned momentarily. 'Join us? He came with the company. I joined the company here and—'

He paused abruptly and stared at her. Then his face went pale and a hand came up to his throat.

'What troubles you, Forindain?' Fidelma asked, trying to read what he was thinking by the expression in his amber-coloured eyes. Then she suddenly made an intuitive leap.

'You were the one who came here from Cashel and not your brother, weren't you?'

'I will tell you my story, Fidelma of Cashel,' Forindain said slowly, 'and now I should like that drink of *corma*, Fiachrae.'

Bewildered, Fiachrae rose and poured the drink. The dwarf swallowed it in one quick mouthful.

'We were performing in Tailltenn, before the High King himself,' he began reflectively. 'We had planned a tour which took in the township by the abbey of Cluain Mic Nois and then that of Tír dhá Ghlas before we came here. We also planned to go to the town of Ros Cairbre and others, working our way east along the coast to Ard Mhór and then up to Cluain Meala and Cashel the capital itself.'

Fidelma sat back, regarding him thoughtfully.

'And why tell us this itinerary?'

'Our company set out from Tailltenn all together, but at Tír dhá Ghlas, the land of the two streams, where we played before the settlement around the monastery there, I left the company.'

'Why?'

'We have never played in Cashel and so I decided to visit it before the company went there. I wanted to know whether it was a suitable place. Unfortunately, I was late reaching there. It was late afternoon and already dark. I knew that I could only spare a short time the following morning to look at the township. There was some disturbance going on and I felt it better to leave with a band of pilgrims who were heading west. I merely glanced round the main area of the township and then joined them at the inn.'

'And you travelled to Cashel in your guise of Brother Forindain the Leper?'

Forindain grimaced. 'I often find it a useful method of travelling. It keeps people at a distance, as there are many in the land who think they can take advantage of one of my size. We do not dwell in a perfect world.'

'True enough,' agreed Eadulf, seeing the logic of the explanation.

'Why was your brother clad in your costume?' Fidelma asked the question with sudden sharpness.

Forindain blinked.

'We were preparing for the performance later this afternoon,' he replied after a moment's hesitation. 'We always perform stories of the Faylinn, the little people, as it suits the whimsy of our presentation. I always play Brother Forindain the Leper. Iubdán often likes to try his hand at other parts and, in this manner, we can ensure that if one or other of our company is ill there is always someone who can step into his or her part. So, this morning, Iubdán took my robe and bell and went off into the woods to rehearse.'

'And he paid with his life,' Fidelma said quietly. 'He was mistaken for you.'

Eadulf looked shocked. He had not reached that conclusion at all.

'You have a quick mind, Sister . . . I mean, lady,' the dwarf said slowly. It was obvious that the thought had occurred to him. 'But I do not understand why he was killed – or, rather, why anyone would want to kill me.'

'It was for something you did at Cashel,' replied Fidelma.

The dwarf looked puzzled. 'Nothing happened at Cashel.'

'Think back. Something happened to you,' pressed Fidelma.

'Little of consequence, except that I earned myself a *screpall* and then slept in a barn before joining the pilgrims who were going to Imleach. I prefer to travel on my own but, as I said, with the fuss going on, I could become anonymous among the pilgrims. I utilised their company on the road to Imleach. Company, I should say, in the broadest sense for I walked a distance behind them with my bell to serve as warning should they come too close. It is amazing how quickly one can travel as a leper.'

'Very well,' Fidelma said. 'Let us return to Cashel. How did you earn the *screpall*?'

The dwarf shrugged. 'I was simply asked to take a message to the palace – that would be the palace of your brother, lady. I was to find a woman called Sárait and convey the message that her sister needed to see her urgently. That was all.'

'How was it that you were chosen to take this message?'

'I was walking through the square of the township, it was dusk, and I had barely arrived in the place. There was little to see, so I went straight to the inn. I was approaching it when a hound bounded out at me.' The dwarf sounded bitter. 'It frequently happens. Often it is no accident. People can be cruel. They will release their hounds on purpose. Anyway, a woman called it off. She was standing in the shadows by the inn. Then she spoke to me. She offered me a *screpall* if I would take a message to the palace. I was to ask for a nurse-maid called Sárait and tell her that Gobnat wanted to see her at once and urgently. I think it was her way of compensating me for the action of her hound. Well, it was too early for sleep, and I did not want to draw comment on myself by going into the inn at that time. Above all a *screpall* was a *screpall*.'

'Did the woman see you were dressed as a leper?'

'I'd given up that part for the moment as I wanted to eat in comfort in the inn.'

'You say this woman was in the shadows of the inn?'

'By the inn. Just outside.'

'Did she tell you why she was unable to go herself to the palace with the message?'

'I did not ask when money was offered.'

'How did you deliver this message?'

'She told me that the guards at the palace would ask too many questions. I should pretend that I was a mute. Well, I have acted mutes before. But I asked her how I could tell the guards who I wanted to see if I was to be a mute. It seems that she was already prepared. She pulled a piece of bark from her *marsupium* and handed it to me. It had writing on it.'

'What did it say exactly?'

'It said, "I am sent to see Sárait." Something like that. I can't swear to the exact words.'

'And the guard passed you through the gate when you showed it to him?'

'He did.'

'How did you convey the idea that you were mute?'

The dwarf laughed. 'How does any player convey concepts but with mime?'

'How did you find Sárait?'

'I had been instructed by the guard how to find her chamber. No one bothered me and I found it. She was alone so I was able to tell her the message.'

'Which was?'

'As I have said, that she should not delay but go at once to her sister for she needed to see her urgently.'

'That was all?'

'That was the message.'

'How would you have delivered the message had you found that Sárait was not alone?' Eadulf interrupted. 'And you pretending that you were mute?'

Forindain grimaced wearily. 'Then I had to use my own judgement. But she was alone and so I told her. I can also read and write, you know.' His voice was slightly patronising. 'We players are quite literate.'

'Did you wait to accompany the woman, Sárait, back to the village?' Fidelma asked.

Forindain shook his head immediately. 'I had earned my *screpall* and went back to the inn. I was tempted to use it for a good room there but I didn't.'

Fidelma sighed deeply. 'So you went back to the inn after delivering the message?'

'I had *corma* and a bowl of soup. I saw some pilgrims, and heard them talking about walking to Imleach. Then I left and went to one of the barns. It was less expensive than the inn. I found a warm place among the straw. I did not wake until I heard the noise of people in the yard. I saw some warriors speaking with the pilgrims. They left. I spoke to the

123

leader of the pilgrims and he accepted me as a travelling companion. I had a short time to look round the township and then I joined them as they set off on the highway. At that stage, I decided to play the leper's part again as it is fine for travelling on the road but not so good in getting accommodation and food.'

'But you heard nothing? There was no outcry?'

'Outcry?' The dwarf rubbed his chin. 'There was, as I say, some fuss and some warriors seem to be searching for someone. I did not inquire too closely what it was about. I was into my leper's role at the time so did not really speak to anyone. What am I supposed to have done?'

There was a pause and then Fidelma nodded to Eadulf who answered: 'When Sárait left the palace, she walked to meet her murderer.'

Forindain blinked rapidly.

'I did not kill her. I did not know her. What I said is true,' he said.

'There is more,' interrupted Fidelma. 'She was nurse to my baby and, finding no one to look after it, she carried the child with her. Since then, my baby has vanished.'

The little dwarf moaned a little.

'I . . . I was not involved in this. I simply carried a message, lady. I was not part of it . . .'

Fidelma did not bother to reassure him.

'I am concerned with the woman who gave you the message to take to Sárait.'

'I told you, she was Sárait's sister. It is she that you should be questioning.'

Fidelma regarded him thoughtfully.

'Sarait's sister has denied that she sent any such message. Describe this woman, so that I may compare the description.'

'I have said, it was nearly dusk and she kept herself in the shadow of the inn.'

'She kept in the shadows the entire time?'

Forindain considered.

'She did come nearly into the circle of light once. That was when she gave me the note. But she had a cloak with a hood covering her features. I had the impression that she was shapely, small of stature . . . for a woman of normal growth, that is,' he corrected himself. 'Her voice was not that of a young girl. I remember . . .' Forindain was suddenly excited. 'In the light of the lantern I had a momentary glimpse of the colours of her cloak, which I thought unusual for someone to wear in such a time and at such a place.'

'Unusual?' queried Eadulf. 'How so?'

'It was a long mantle of green silk with a hood that covered her features, as I have said. And the green silk was enriched with red embroidery. The cloak was fastened with a clasp that seemed to be silver and bejewelled. I noticed she had rings on her fingers when she handed me the money but I felt those by touch and did not see them.'

Eadulf glanced questioningly at Fidelma but she seemed lost in thought.

'Well,' he said, 'that certainly is not a description of Sárait's sister. She is rather dowdy in her dress.'

Fidelma looked up from her reverie, returning his gaze for a moment.

'Did you expect that it would be?' she asked.

'It merely eliminates her from involvement, that is all,' he protested.

'I had nothing to do with any murder, lady,' Forindain was saying again. He was nervous and kept clutching his hands together in front of him.

'This woman was waiting in the shadows to get someone

to take a message to the palace,' Fidelma mused. 'It seems that it was fortuitous that you happened to come along and be willing to take the message.'

'Fortuitous? What do you mean?'

'How would she know that you would be there?'

The dwarf grimaced sourly. 'Maybe she was a fortune teller,' he snapped. 'How would I know that?'

Suddenly Fidelma gently smiled at him.

'Will your band of players, the *crossan*, continue on your travels?' she asked, apparently changing the subject. 'Will you now go on to Cashel?'

Forindain sighed. 'My brother was a good player but we must go on. There is no other means for us to make a living. We have only the play and the fairs. We will follow our original plan.'

'So we may expect you to return to Cashel?' she pressed.

'There is a fair at Cashel at the end of next week. We shall be there, lady, unless we are forbidden because of what has happened.'

'You are not forbidden.' Fidelma rose from her seat. 'In fact, I would welcome you there. You may return to your comrades, Forindain, and please accept that I am sorry for your loss.'

Forindain rose uncertainly. 'And my brother Iubdán? Will he have justice, lady?'

'I would advise you to adopt another name, another character. Your brother was clearly mistaken for you. Keep the fact a secret. Though I believe you might be clear of danger now that you have spoken to me. I believe it was your information that the killer wanted to suppress. Still, take no chances. Be Iubdán from now until you come to see me at Cashel.'

The dwarf hesitated. Then he gave a little bow and left the tent.

Fiachrae was shaking his head.

'I understand nothing of this, cousin.'

'That is best, cousin,' replied Fidelma solemnly. 'Nothing of what has passed here must leave this tent. I will keep you informed as I find out more. Now, as it is approaching midday, perhaps we can trouble you for some refreshment . . . er, of the edible kind,' she added as Fiachrae's gaze went to the table on which the jug of *corma* sat. 'After we have eaten, we will be on our way back to Cashel.'

Fiachrae looked puzzled.

'But the killer of the dwarf . . .?' he protested. 'Won't you want to stay in order to find him?'

'The person behind the killing of Iubdán will not be in Cnoc Loinge but will be found in Cashel. Do not worry, cousin. I will inform you when I have caught him.'

After Fiachrae had left to organise a meal for them, Eadulf turned with a puzzled look to Fidelma.

'What did you mean by that?'

Fidelma looked at him with a bland expression. 'By what, exactly?'

'That the killer of Iubdán will be found in Cashel.'

Her lips thinned a moment. 'I said the person behind the killing would be found in Cashel.'

Eadulf exhaled sharply. 'So far as I can see, we have come to a dead end. Someone went to great lengths to disguise themselves and send the innocent dwarf up to the palace to inveigle Sárait out into the night to meet her killer. But at least we now learn that it was not the intention to kidnap Alchú, otherwise the message he was sent to deliver would have requested her to bring the child. It was pure chance that she could not find anyone to look after our baby and had to take him with her.'

Fidelma looked thoughtfully at him.

'It is a good point and one that could be overlooked,' she observed.

'But there is now no lead. No lead at all.'

'On the contrary,' Fidelma contradicted. 'I believe the description of those clothes will lead me directly to the person who wears such distinctive garments.'

Chapter Eight

❧

Fidelma and Eadulf rode the entire way back to Cashel without exchanging more than a few words. Although they had been more at ease at Cnoc Loinge, the underlying tension between them remained. In addition, Fidelma had not been open with Eadulf about who it was in Cashel who wore such distinctive clothing as had been described by Forindain the dwarf. The knowledge had made her reel inside for she had counted that person as a friend. She felt she could not reveal this knowledge to anyone as yet, least of all to Eadulf. That made her feel doubly guilty about the argument they had had at Imleach. She glanced at him once or twice in surreptitious fashion as they rode along. Eadulf, his brow drawn in a permanent frown, appeared to have sunk deep into his own thoughts. Apart from her astonishment at hearing Forindain's description of the woman who had sent the dwarf to the palace to persuade Sárait to meet her killer, Fidelma was still feeling slightly shocked at Eadulf's outburst. Perhaps she had taken his placidity too much for granted. She had long ago realised that she was too used to having her own way, exerting authority not simply thanks to her privileged background but more to her own hard-won status as a *dálaigh*. The very thing that she had liked most about Eadulf was that he had accepted her faults. He seemed to absorb snappishness and outbursts of temper. That he had suddenly turned in such a fashion had astonished her, almost driving her preoccupation with her lost child momentarily from her mind.

She realised, as if it were a sudden revelation, that she needed to question herself more rigorously.

She had never really looked on herself as a religieuse. Her passion was law. It was a distant cousin, Abbot Laisran of Durrow, who had persuaded her to join the double-house of St Brigid at Kildare, for practically everyone involved in the professions and arts was to be found among the religious as had, a few generations before, their predecessors been part of the druid orders. She had not been long in learning that life in an abbey was not for her, and when the abbess of Kildare placed herself above the law Fidelma had left and returned to her brother's capital of Cashel.

She was a *dálaigh* first and foremost, a princess of the Eóghanacht, and then a religieuse. She suddenly compressed her lips, for she had left wife and mother out of that equation. Her knowledge of scripture, of theology and philosophy, could scarcely be attained by many who promoted the New Faith. She knew Latin and Greek almost as well as she knew her native tongue, and she had fluency in the language of the Britons as well as a working command of the tongue of the Saxons, thanks mainly to Eadulf. But it was law that always demanded her attention. She had no problems in her life in identifying what she should be doing in that respect.

But what of being a wife and mother?

Eadulf had not been her first love. That had been Cian and he had betrayed her trust. Well, she had sorted that out, although the final strands had not come together until her recent and curious voyage to Iberia where she had gone on a pilgrimage to the tomb of the Blessed James in order to sort out her feelings about Eadulf and her commitment to the religious life. She had not reached the object of the pilgrimage in physical terms but she had realised that her feelings about Eadulf could not be dismissed as easily as she had come to the decision that being a member of the religious was simply a means to an end for her to pursue her commitment to law.

Now she had to sort out her feelings as a wife, albeit a *ben charrthach*. And she was also a mother. Mother! A sudden pang went through her as she realised how selfish she was being. She knew now that she had not bonded with little Alchú. It had been a painful birth and she had begun to resent the child for keeping her confined in her brother's palace, instead of pursuing her passion for law. She knew that Eadulf suspected that she resented the birth of their baby. That made her more angry with him.

Eadulf had tried to make her drink some noxious brew made from *brachlais* – St John's Wort as he called it in his own tongue. Fidelma was not stupid. She knew that the apothecaries of Éireann applied it to women who became dispirited and despondent after giving birth.

Her child had been kidnapped or worse, his nurse had been killed, and now she was trying to form some logical analysis of her thoughts and fears. Whereas other women might be tearing their hair and prostrate in grief, Fidelma remained calm and logical. It was her gift, or was it a curse? What was it that her mentor, the Brehon Morann, once told her? 'You have a gift for logic, Fidelma, especially when it comes to your personal affairs. Try to develop your intuitive qualities, for logic can sometimes be like a dagger without a handle. It may cut the person who tries to use it.'

Deep within her she knew that she felt like screaming as any other mother would when their baby was taken from them. It was her logic that kept her from doing so, not her lack of feeling for her child. What good was there in giving way to emotion in these circumstances? It would not bring her one step nearer to discovering the truth of this mystery. There would be plenty of time for emotion later.

A line from Euripides came into her mind: 'Logic can challenge and overthrow terror itself.'

Her features suddenly relaxed as she gave an inward sigh.

Yes, plenty of time to give way to emotion later.

Colgú had come to the gates of the palace as they rode up the slope to the great complex of Cashel. Finguine, the heir apparent, was at his side. It would have been obvious even to an inexperienced eye that there was some important news they were waiting to impart. Her heart began to beat faster.

'You have returned in time, sister,' called Colgú as she halted her horse.

'In time for what? What is it?' demanded Fidelma, quickly dismounting and facing her brother with an anxious expression. 'Is there news? News of Alchú?'

'There is,' Colgú replied quickly, reaching out a hand to lay reassuring fingers on his sister's arm. 'The baby is alive. We have just received a note demanding ransom for him.'

Behind her, Fidelma heard Capa exclaim: 'Then we should have waited here instead of setting off on a wild goose chase.' She did not turn but continued to gaze apprehensively at her brother, trying to work out this new development and not succeeding.

'A ransom note? Where is it?'

'It is in my chambers.' He motioned the servants forward to take the horses and then began to lead the way to the main

132

building with Fidelma at his side. Eadulf fell in step beside Finguine and Capa brought up the rear, having dismissed Caol and Gormán to the stables.

'So it was a kidnapping, after all?' Capa made the statement into a question.

'It would seem so,' Finguine replied, his words flung back over his shoulder.

'What manner of note is it? How was it delivered? What are its demands?' Fidelma's questions came out almost in a breathless rush.

'As to the note, you will see it soon enough.' Colgú's voice was quiet. 'The manner of its delivery was that it was found attached to the door of the local inn with instructions for it to be delivered here, to me. Its demands are simple. As you know, after the battle of Cnoc Áine, we took several Uí Fidgente as prisoners. Among them were three prominent chieftains, cousins of the former petty king, Eoganán. We made them hostages for the good behaviour of their people.'

Fidelma frowned impatiently. 'And?' she prompted. 'What is the connection?'

'The note demands their release,' he replied. 'When they are freed then Alchú will be returned to us safe and sound.'

There was a brief silence.

'So it was some new Uí Fidgente plot.' Capa sounded almost triumphant.

'It looks that way,' admitted Finguine.

Colgú led them straight to his private chambers. On the table lay a single piece of bark. Fidelma picked it up at once and scrutinised it carefully.

'Bark, as was the material on which the note was written that was given to the dwarf, Forindain, to bring to Cashel,' she said quietly to Eadulf.

Colgú opened his mouth to ask a question but then closed it. His sister would explain in her own time.

Bark was a fairly common material for writing. The white epidermis of birch bark had been found by ancient scribes to be separable into thin layers which, when flattened and dried, could be written on. Fidelma examined it carefully.

'It does not appear to be written in a hand that is used to the forming of letters. They are almost childish in the way they have been shaped, as if the person was copying some unfamiliar forms.'

Capa laughed cynically. 'Who said the Uí Fidgente are literate?'

Fidelma ignored him. It was Eadulf who, leaning forward, pointed out that the formation of the letters might simply be a means to disguise the authorship.

'Why disguise it?' Finguine seemed amused by the idea. 'The authorship is clear: it is a message on behalf of the Uí Fidgente. That cannot be disguised.'

Fidelma replaced the note on the table and looked round. 'Before we can accept this note as genuine,' she said quietly, 'what proof do we have to support that conclusion?'

They stared at her in surprise.

'You doubt that it is genuine?' Colgú asked, puzzled.

'It is no secret that my baby has been stolen,' Fidelma replied. 'Why wait nearly a week before issuing such a demand? It could well be someone trying to take advantage from the situation.'

Finguine was shaking his head in disagreement.

'Had it been a demand for financial reward, then that might be a matter for consideration. But this is a political demand. Why would anyone demand the release of the Uí Fidgente chieftains if they were not in possession of the baby?'

'It would be dangerous to dismiss the note as not genuine,' added Capa. 'The child's life is at stake.'

'I am the mother of the child in question,' snapped Fidelma, angered by the implication that she did not care about Alchú. Then she added with firmness: 'We must proceed logically.' At the word 'logically' she felt a spasm of guilt but pressed on. She raised the note again and scrutinised the text. 'It demands that the three chieftains of the Uí Fidgente should be released . . .' She counted briefly. 'From the time stipulated, they are to be released before the end of two more days . . .'

'And they are then to be allowed time to cross the border into the territory of the Dál gCais at which time Alchú will be released and not before,' finished Colgú.

'It seems a curious gamble,' Eadulf commented with a frown. 'I am inclined to agree with Fidelma that we need some proof of the child's well-being. If someone could be dishonest and take the opportunity to make a demand for financial gain, we should consider that someone could be dishonest enough to make an equivalent demand for political gain. Power and money are not dissimilar motives.'

Fidelma glanced across at him in appreciation. Eadulf could be trusted to accept logic when confronted with it.

'It is also a gamble whether the Uí Fidgente are to be relied upon to fulfil their part of the bargain,' she said.

'In that matter, I agree with you,' Finguine rejoined.

'It is my opinion that, whoever "they" are, they should provide some proof that they hold Alchú before we release these chieftains.'

Everyone turned to Eadulf, who had spoken quietly.

'Come, man, it is your own son about whom we are talking,' Capa admonished, his handsome face flushed. 'We should be making every effort to free him and return him to Cashel.'

Eadulf turned to face Capa directly. He spoke slowly and softly.

'Do you think that I am not aware that I speak of my own son? I hope everyone present concedes the fact that I am as much concerned in his welfare as anyone else.' Fidelma coloured a little and there was an uncomfortable silence. She had automatically opened her mouth to explain that, under law, Eadulf was wrong. While the welfare and rearing of a child in normal circumstances was the responsibility of both parents, if the father was a *cúl glas*, a foreigner, a stranger to the mother's people, the full responsibility for how the child should be raised fell on the mother. But this was a time for such facts to remain unexpressed. Eadulf was continuing: 'But this note, as Fidelma has said, is not proof that the person who wrote it has possession of the child, nor are any guarantees offered for his release. That is, in itself, strange when demanding a ransom. We need more information before acting.'

'You would jeopardise your own son's life?' asked Capa, aghast. There was a murmur of support for Capa's protest. Fidelma held up a hand to still it.

'Eadulf is absolutely right,' she said firmly. 'A note appears out of nowhere with demands; demands that might eventually lead to endangering the kingdom, for these particular Uí Fidgente chieftains are bitter and remorseless enemies who were kin to their leader Eoganán who tried to overthrown my brother from the kingship and died in that attempt. We need proof that they hold Alchú.'

Finguine's jaw was thrust out pugnaciously.

'And just how do we get in touch with the anonymous writer of this demand, cousin?' he asked with a tone of sarcasm. 'There is neither name nor location on it. There is no way that we can send a return note.'

Fidelma regarded him with equal sarcasm.

'What you say is true, cousin,' she replied. 'But a little imagination will work wonders. I suspect that the writer of this note will have good communications in or around Cashel and will soon pick up our response.'

Colgú pursed his lips thoughtfully.

'We can make an announcement in the square of the town demanding that some proof must be furnished before we contemplate releasing the three chieftains.'

Fidelma nodded agreement.

'I would also suggest that a herald be sent to place a similar message in every inn between here and the border of the Uí Fidgente country,' added Finguine. 'And that the message be sent to the current chieftain of the Uí Fidgente. In that way, the word will certainly get back to the writer of this demand.'

'But what proof could be furnished?' Capa frowned. 'What proof short of producing the baby himself?'

'No difficulty in that,' Eadulf replied immediately. 'Perhaps some item of clothing could be shown, something Alchú was wearing when he was taken. I am sure that Fidelma and I would recognise any such thing.'

He glanced towards Fidelma who nodded quickly. 'Let it be done at once.'

'Who shall I order to ride to the country of the Uí Fidgente?' demanded Capa uneasily.

'Perhaps you will volunteer?' smiled Finguine. There was a quiet sarcasm in his voice and Fidelma had a feeling that there was no love lost between the two men.

The handsome commander seemed affronted. 'I am commander of the guard here and not a *techtaire* – a herald.

137

Moreover, I command the *Nasc Niadh*, the élite guard of the Cashel kings.'

Finguine smiled broadly. 'I admit, it may be too dangerous for you to go among the Uí Fidgente.'

Colgú was shaking his head in disapproval at both men.

'You both know well enough that the safety of a herald is sacred and inviolable – even the most bitter enemies treat a *techtaire* with the utmost respect. It is not merely the law but a matter of honour that any herald has a guarantee of safe passage even through enemy territory. Capa, it is because you are my guard commander that I send you on this task. I will ask Cerball the scribe to write several copies of our demand that you may take with you. Make sure one is posted on the door of the inn here and thence all inns between here and the country of the Uí Fidgente.' He looked towards his sister, who indicated her approval of his action.

Capa was clearly not happy at the order. He appeared to think that the role of a *techtaire* was beneath him. But he said nothing further, bowing his head in reluctant obedience towards the king.

'I am sure that by this means we will find whoever wrote this ransom demand,' Fidelma said in satisfaction. 'And we will soon know whether it is a genuine demand or a means of tricking us into releasing our enemies.'

'I'll find Cerball and tell him to come here,' Finguine offered.

Colgú agreed, adding: 'While we wait for Cerball to draw up the notices requesting proof, Capa, you'd better fetch my standard, which you will carry as a *techtaire*. You will find it in the chamber at the end of the corridor where my sister's chambers are situated.'

Fidelma and Eadulf stayed with Colgú awhile to bring him up to date with the results of their trip to Imleach and Cnoc Loinge before returning to their own chambers. As they were passing along a cloistered walkway by an open courtyard, Eadulf suddenly paused by an arch and looked across the stone quadrangle. Frowning, Fidelma paused also, glancing across Eadulf's shoulder.

'We weren't told that he was back in Cashel,' Eadulf said softly.

The object of his scrutiny was the tall, gaunt figure of a religieux, standing talking with an elderly member of the cloth.

'Bishop Petrán,' Fidelma observed. 'You don't like him very much, do you?'

Eadulf admitted as much. 'I remember what your brother suggested about enemies within. Do you think that Petrán or any of his followers are capable of kidnapping?'

'He is a human being, and once fanaticism takes over as our faith we are capable of anything, Eadulf,' she pointed out. 'But I doubt whether Petrán would have conspired to release the Uí Fidgente chieftains. He has always been loyal to the Eóghanacht and not to the Dál gCais. But I thought my brother said that Petrán had been sent on a tour of the western islands about a week ago? He could not have completed such a task already. So what has brought him back to Cashel?'

As if he had heard her whispered question, Bishop Petrán had turned and spotted them. He said something to his companion, then walked across the quadrangle towards them. He halted in front of the archway under which they stood.

'God be with you, Fidelma, and with you, Brother Eadulf.' The elderly bishop greeted them in a manner that sounded more suited to intoning the last rites. It was a hollow voice of mourning.

Eadulf's eyes narrowed in dislike but Fidelma replied in formal manner.

'God and Mary be your guide, Bishop Petrán. What brings you back to Cashel so soon? I was told that you had only recently departed to the western islands.'

The bishop sniffed dismissively.

'An unexpected matter arose and I proceeded no further than the abbey of Colmán on the coast. I did not even set foot on shipboard.'

'Nothing serious, I trust?'

The bishop shook his head. Obviously he did not feel the necessity to speak further on the subject. He cleared his throat hesitantly.

'I have just heard of your loss. My . . . er, my condolences. I will say a mass for the repose of the soul of Sárait, who was an obedient daughter of the Faith . . .' he hesitated again, 'and I will pray for the safe return of the child.'

Eadulf grimaced sourly.

'You will pray for *our* son, Alchú?' he asked with emphasis. 'My wife is most appreciative of such a gesture.'

Bishop Petrán blinked at the quiet belligerence in his voice.

'It is not a gesture but my duty as a servant of the Faith.'

'But I thought you disapproved of *our* son? Indeed, you do not even approve of our marital union,' Eadulf continued, without disguising the sneer in his voice. Fidelma tried to give him a warning glance but he was not looking.

Bishop Petrán's pale cheeks had reddened a little.

'I have my beliefs, Eadulf of Seaxmund's Ham,' he replied irritably. 'It does not prevent me from being concerned with the fate of the son of the sister of my temporal king.'

'Or *my* son?' snapped Eadulf. 'You surprise me. I thought you condemned all marital unions between the members of the religious as inspired by evil, especially those unions wrought between women of your land and the men of my country?'

Fidelma stirred uncomfortably at his side. She had been shocked into silence by Eadulf's verbal attack on the elderly bishop. Once again, she was dumbfounded at seeing this new, angry side to Eadulf's nature. It both astonished and concerned her.

'This is not the time to speak of theological differences, Eadulf,' she admonished. 'We should thank the bishop for his spiritual concern.'

Eadulf snorted in disgust.

'I have spoken of your appreciation. Yet I do not give thanks for that which should be a natural reaction. Petrán and I both know well that we hold differences that are irreconcilable. I have to say, however, that I find his words sanctimonious and lacking in sincerity.'

Bishop Petrán took a step backward, his eyes wide. The flush deepened as his expression hardened into dislike.

'I have no knowledge of how your people treat their bishops, Saxon,' he said coldly. 'Indeed, I know that only a generation or so ago they had not even heard the Word of the True Faith, let alone had bishops to guide them. My people had to teach them, so maybe you are still in the process of learning. However, in this land, the bishops are treated with respect.'

Eadulf's eyes were like pinpricks of fire. His face, too, was flushed with anger.

'Respect is something that a Saxon, whether bishop or king, has to earn, Petrán. It is not given as a right. I have spent enough time in Rome and Gaul to know that you hold a very narrow view of the Faith. I upheld Rome at the great Council of Whitby and not even the Bishop of Rome, who is the Father of the Faith, preaches or condones those things that you teach.'

Bishop Petrán actually smiled, albeit a grimace without warmth.

'I presume that you mean my teaching that for the religious only celibacy is the true path to God?' he demanded. 'In that case, I should remind you what the great Gregory of Rome said – that all sexual desire is sinful in itself.'

Eadulf uttered a short sharp bark of laughter.

'Then he must mean that desire itself is intrinsically evil. How can that be? Did God not create men and women and the means to procreate? Do you say that God created something that is fundamentally evil? Something that is sinful?'

Bishop Petrán's face darkened for a moment.

'Do not question the word of a great saint. Gregory the Great is God's infallible word. He is not to be challenged.'

'Then you must condemn the great abbot and missionary Columbanus who defied him? Columbanus adhered to the ecclesiastical customs and teachings of the five kingdoms of Éireann, and when challenged by Gregory he wrote in defence of those teachings. Do you argue that the Faith is closed to such challenge and debate?'

'Columbanus was a Laigin man who should have been content to remain abbot of Bangor in the northern kingdom. His pride in arguing with Gregory was sinful.'

Eadulf shook his head sadly. 'You are prejudiced in your beliefs. That makes you a bigot.'

Bishop Petrán twisted his lips into an ugly sneer. 'Heraclitus wrote that bigotry was a sacred disease.'

'And that prejudice is the child of ignorance,' riposted Eadulf.

'And Aristotle pointed out that some men are just as sure of the truth of their opinions as are others of what they know,' intervened Fidelma, raising her voice sharply as she tried to mediate in the argument.

'When I travelled in Rome,' went on Eadulf, ignoring her, as did Bishop Petrán, 'I learnt that even Christ's own people in Judaea believed that marriage was the prominent symbol for the relationship of God to his people, that marriage and family were in the centre of life and celibacy was not recognised as having any religious value. Very few Bishops of Rome have so far argued that the only route to God would come through celibacy.'

Bishop Petrán scowled as he replied.

'The Faith, the congregation of bishops, is moving slowly to an acceptance of the teaching that the way of achieving greater devotion to God and victory over the world's evils is to live the celibate life. For those religious who achieve it, it is to achieve a place in the hereafter as great as martyrdom.'

'And I have no intention of achieving either martyrdom or celibacy,' replied Eadulf. 'Nowhere is it decreed by God or Christ that those who follow the Faith must abandon a normal life. Even those who a few centuries ago started to practise sexual abstinence as though it was a possible vocation did so in the belief that it was a transitory ritual during the brief time they thought they had to wait while the form of this world was passing away before the Kingdom of Christ arrived.'

The bishop shook his head in exasperation.

'I have my belief, Saxon. I know I am right. I am fighting to keep the truth safe.' He suddenly held out his hands, each balled into a fist. 'I grasp that truth tight in these hands for protection.'

'And your grip might kill it, Petrán,' interposed Fidelma softly, speaking again in an attempt to end the argument. 'Let each of you have his own truth for the time being. We have other matters of more immediate concern. I thank you, Petrán, for your prayers and good wishes.'

She turned, with a meaningful look at Eadulf, and began to walk away. After a second's hesitation, Eadulf reluctantly followed after her.

'What are you doing, verbally and outrageously attacking Bishop Petrán?' she hissed as they turned into the corridor leading to their chambers. A shadow was standing near their door. It was the tall warrior, Gormán.

'Are you look for us, Gormán?' asked Fidelma.

The warrior looked embarrassed.

'No, lady. I was looking for Capa. He went to fetch the herald's standard. I think the king is awaiting his return.'

Fidelma indicated further along the corridor.

'The room of the *techtaire*, the herald's room with the standards, is at the end of this corridor. The door to your left. That is where Capa should be.'

'Thank you, lady,' grunted the warrior, raising a hand in salute before moving off.

Eadulf paused to open the door to their chambers and stood aside while Fidelma entered. He was still truculent about his argument.

'That hypocrite!' he muttered, referring to Bishop Petrán. 'If he has been behind the kidnapping of Alchú, I want him to know that I will not pander to his insincerity.'

'And if he is behind it, you have certainly alerted him to your dislike,' Fidelma admonished irritably.

A female servant, piling logs on the fire, rose in haste with a quick bob towards Fidelma.

'I was just tidying your chambers. Is there anything you need, lady?' she asked breathlessly.

'A jug of wine,' snapped Eadulf before Fidelma had a chance to respond.

The servant looked at Fidelma, who made a neutral gesture that the servant took as an affirmative. When she had disappeared, Eadulf flung himself into the seat before the fire and glared moodily at the flames.

'I would, at times, give much to live the Faith as Bishop Petrán argues it,' he muttered.

Fidelma stared at him in surprise.

'What do you mean, Eadulf? I swear your reasoning is beyond me at times.'

Eadulf scowled back.

'Bishop Petrán is known to believe in the literal word of scripture – would he not argue that we must obey the epistles of Paul? That to Ephesians, perhaps? "Wives, be subject to your husbands as to the Lord; for the man is the master of the woman, just as Christ is the head of the church. Christ is, indeed, the Saviour of the body; but just as the church is subject to Christ, so must women be subject to their husbands in everything." Yet it seems your laws deny Holy Scripture. Here women are not subject to their husbands but husbands seem subject to their women.'

Fidelma's brows came together in anger.

'I swear that you can be boorish at times, Eadulf. Here, no woman is subject in her own home nor is any man her master. And no man is subject to his wife.'

Eadulf chuckled sardonically.

'Except when a woman takes a foreigner as husband. Then he remains on sufferance of the woman and her family, without rights, without even respect. I cannot even ask wine from a servant without her looking at you for approval.'

Fidelma coloured a little. There was some truth in what Eadulf said. She knew it. Yet it was the way of her people. How was it growing into the problem that was causing Eadulf to behave so belligerently?

'Eadulf, you have never talked this way before,' she said defensively.

'Perhaps I have been too compliant. It is, indeed, my great fault that I have not done so before now.'

'You do not believe what you are saying, Eadulf. I know you too well to accept that you believe in the dictums of Paul of Tarsus on the obedience of women to men.'

Eadulf's truculent features suddenly dissolved into an expression of sadness.

'Fidelma, I am a Saxon, not an Éireannach. I was taught that my ancestors sprang from the loins of Woden, that no one was as great as we were and no other Saxon was as great as those of the South Folk. People trembled at our word. Were we not of the race of Wegdaeg, son of Woden, and of Uffa, who drove the Britons from the land we then took as our own?'

Fidelma gazed at him in astonishment.

She had heard such diatribes from Saxon princelings and warriors about the glories of their people but she had never heard it from the lips of Eadulf before. She did not know how to answer him.

Eadulf gazed at her with an agonised look.

'What I am trying to say, Fidelma, is that imbued with such spirit I have tried to accept the mantle of charity and brotherhood that is the mark of the Faith. Fursa, a wandering monk of your own race, taught me, when I had scarcely reached manhood. I was not brought up in the Faith but I forsook and forswore the old gods of the South Folk on my twentieth birthday. I was hereditary *gerefa*, magistrate, of the thane of Seaxmund's Ham. I have pride, Fidelma. I have self-esteem. I have the vanity of my race. It is sometimes hard for me to find myself here. I am a stranger in a strange land.'

Fidelma felt the bewildered misery in his voice.

'I thought that you liked this country,' she said, trying to formulate her thoughts.

'I do, otherwise I would not have spent so much time here. I came here to learn the canons of the Faith long before I met you. But it is hard to completely turn one's back on one's homeland and one's culture. During this last year, I have especially been reminded of what it is that I miss.'

'This last year? Since we married? Since we had little Alchú?'

Eadulf gestured helplessly with his arms.

'You want to return to your own land?'

'I don't know. I think so.'

'I could never live in that country, Eadulf. That is why I tried to keep our relationship at a distance.'

'I know.'

She hesitated and then took a step towards him.

'Eadulf . . .' she began.

There was a knock on the door and the servant came back with a jug of Gaulish wine and pottery mugs. The moment of intimacy had gone.

'Do you want me to continue cleaning, lady?' the woman asked. 'I had only just come to the chamber when you entered.'

Fidelma shook her head. She was turning aside when her eye was caught by a garment hanging out of a small wooden chest, not properly folded away. The chest stood near Alchú's cot. She shivered slightly, not wishing to go near it.

'Just tuck that in before you go,' she instructed the servant. 'I do not like to see things left untidy. If you are to clean these chambers, make sure that such things are put away.'

The servant seemed about to speak but then she shrugged and went to carry out the instruction. There was silence until she left the room.

Eadulf was helping himself liberally to the wine. His movements still implied suppressed anger.

Fidelma spoke with a considered calm.

'Eadulf, we are both in a state of emotional uncertainty. We have a crisis confronting us. There must be peace between us if we are to overcome this matter.'

Eadulf glanced at her. His expression did not change. He shrugged.

'I cannot continue like this, Fidelma,' he said simply. 'When we did not have any formal marriage between us, I did not feel the antipathy that I am now subjected to by the people who surround you. What I cannot stand is the way that your actions and attitude to me now seem to condone the antagonism that is ranged against me.'

Fidelma considered for a while before responding.

'I cannot change my character, Eadulf. For a long while, as you well know, I refused to make any decision about a resolution of the feelings we had for one another. I knew that, if you settled here in Cashel with me, you would be classed as a foreigner in our law, a landless foreigner with restricted rights. There are decisions that I have to make under our law which you cannot make.'

'Your law is not my law, Fidelma. There is much we must consider about the future.'

'Shall it be peace between us until we have regained our son?' she asked quietly.

Eadulf pursed his lips and thought for a moment.

'Let it be peace,' he finally said. 'As soon as Alchú is returned safely to us and those responsible are discovered, then we shall talk. *Absit invidia*,' he added. Let ill will be absent.

Fidelma smiled sadly. '*Mox nox in rem*,' she said solemnly, using the Latin phrase to answer his. Soon night, to the business.

'What can we do until there is an answer to our request for some proof that the ransom note is genuine?'

'I have some inquiries to make about a certain green silk cloak, remember?' Fidelma reminded him. 'And that I am about to do now.' Eadulf made a move to join her but she shook her head quickly. 'This time, I shall have to go alone. The matter is . . . personal.'

Eadulf was worried. 'Where are you going? I should know if there is danger beyond these walls.'

'I do not think there is danger for me, Eadulf. Otherwise I would tell you. In this matter, I have to keep my own counsel in case I am making a mistake. But I can assure you of this: I am not going beyond the confines of the township below and I will be back soon.'

Eadulf was reluctant to let it go at that.

'I swear, Eadulf,' she went on, 'as soon as I return, we will eat and I will tell you where my suspicions have taken me.'

Eadulf knew when to accept the inevitable.

Chapter Nine

❧

Fidelma left the palace alone, in spite of the protests of the guards on duty at the gate who wanted to send a warrior with her as escort, in view of the perceived threat from the Uí Fidgente. She rode down the hill into the township below. Dusk was settling across the buildings and a thin mist was just rising, making everything seem gloomy and chill. She made her way across the nearly deserted square. At the far end was the inn on whose door she could see the demand for proof that the abductors had Alchú. It was tacked to the doorpost, illuminated by the lantern light, for every inn, whether in the country or in the town, was required by law to hang a lantern outside during the hours of darkness. She presumed that Cerball had finished his work and that Capa had now set off to get these notices set up as instructed.

The noise of music and laughter came from the inn. It sounded carefree and boisterous. The thought crossed her mind that perhaps she should have let Eadulf know where she was going. She became aware of a group of children outside the inn; two or three older children who she guessed were awaiting one or other of their parents who were inside. They seemed engrossed in some game by the light of the lantern. She made a sudden decision and called to them.

'Would one of you like to earn a *pingín* by taking a message up to the palace?'

The tallest child, a boy, looked up at her.

'Only a *pingín*?' he protested. 'It was worth a *screpall* last time.'

Fidelma gazed at him in surprised silence for a moment. Then she said: 'Last time?'

'You asked me if I would take a message to the palace before, and you promised to pay me a *screpall*. Last week, it was.'

'Are you sure it was me?' asked Fidelma.

'Well,' the boy hesitated, head to one side, 'it was a woman in a fine cloak. Can't be sure. She was in the shadows by the corner of the inn there.'

'But you didn't accept her offer?'

'I didn't. I was about to when my dad came out of the inn. That's where he is now. I had to take him home. Too much *corma*.'

His companions were chuckling but apparently the boy did not mind.

Fidelma experienced a feeling of both excitement and satisfaction. The question that had been irritating her for a while was answered. How was it that the woman had chosen the dwarf to take the message? She had just learnt the answer. It was an accident. The mysterious woman had been waiting to choose someone who would not question her. She had deliberately kept in the shadows so as not to be recognised. She had tried to get this boy to take it and he could not. Then the dwarf had come along.

'Anyway,' the boy was still speaking, 'I'm not running errands for less than you promised before.'

Fidelma did not bother to reply but tossed the youth a

little bronze *pingín* coin. Deep in thought, she let her horse walk on. She was still pensive when she came to a house on the edge of the township. The building stood a little way apart from the others; a medium-sized structure with its own outhouse and barn. Dark had descended now but the warmth of the township kept the rising mist at bay.

A short distance from the house Fidelma came out of her reverie and suddenly reined in her mount. Outside the very house that was her destination, she saw the dark shape of a tethered horse. Even as she was wondering whether to go on, the door opened. A lantern hung over the porch and by its light she recognised the tall, broad-shouldered warrior with black hair. It was Gormán. He stood for a moment holding the hand of the woman who remained on the threshold.

'Take care of yourself, Gormán,' came the woman's voice. 'Do nothing precipitous.'

The warrior replied in a low voice but Fidelma could not hear the words. Then he bent forward with an intimate embrace before he mounted his horse and was gone into the night. Thankfully he did not come towards the township along the road where Fidelma had halted. After waiting a few moments, she continued on to the house. She slid from her horse and slipped the reins over the post by the door.

Her footsteps creaked on the wooden plank of the porch and at once the door was flung open.

'Gormán, have you—'

The woman who stood there allowed her voice to fade away as her eyes fell on Fidelma. She suddenly seemed embarrassed.

'Good evening, Della.'

A woman of short stature stood framed in the doorway. Her look of dismay quickly changed into a smile of welcome. She was in her forties, yet maturity had not dimmed the youthfulness of her features or the golden abundance of her hair. She was clad in a close-fitting dress that emphasised a good figure whose hips had not broadened and whose limbs were still shapely.

Fidelma took the hands that the older woman held out in greeting to her.

'Fidelma! It is good to see you.'

'It has been a long time, Della,' Fidelma returned.

The woman looked deeply into Fidelma's eyes. Her expression was one of deep sympathy.

'I have heard of your sorrow. Is there any further news of Alchú?'

Fidelma shook her head and Della stood aside, motioning her to enter the house.

'Take a seat, lady. There, that seat close by the fire, for the day is chill. A drink? There is *corma* or I have a sweet drink made from the flowers of *trom*, the elder tree.'

Fidelma seated herself and opted for a drink of elder-flower wine. Della brought the drink and sat down opposite her.

'I am sad for you, and also sad that my friend has lost her life in this tragedy.'

Fidelma did not hide her surprise. 'Your friend?'

'Sárait.'

'I did not know that you knew Sárait.'

Della frowned for a moment. 'I thought that was why you had come to see me.'

Fidelma shook her head. 'The reason can wait for a moment. Tell me more about you and Sárait. When did you become friends?'

'Oh, after her husband was slain . . . or rather murdered.'

'So you have heard the rumours about his death at Cnoc Áine? From whom?'

'From the mouth of Sárait herself.'

'She knew that he had been murdered?'

'She would not say much but . . . well, let me tell you what I know. Sárait was always pleasant to me, even when I was a *bé-táide*, a prostitute. Her sister, Gobnat, was too prim and proper. She would always ignore me and she still does. But Sárait was a kindly and a friendly soul. Some months after her husband was killed she came to me and she was in a state of anguish. It looked as if she had been beaten.'

Fidelma leaned forward with a frown.

'You mean that she was physically beaten?'

'There were bruises on her body. She came to me because she wanted advice from someone who knew the worst as well as the best of a man's capability.'

'Did she tell you who had assaulted her?'

'Alas, she did not. It was someone who was in love with her but she felt repelled by him. She believed that he was the man who had killed her husband, Callada. He was trying to force his attentions on her. Indeed, he had raped her. She had fought back but he was too strong.'

Fidelma sat back with wide eyes.

'If the man killed her husband at Cnoc Áine, he could only have been a warrior known to Cashel.'

'She did not say who he was,' repeated Della. 'But the rape was forceful.'

'*Forcor* is a heinous crime against a woman.'

There were two types of rape recognised by the law. *Forcor* was forceful rape using physical violence while *sleth* covered all other situations. *Sleth* was especially associated with drunkenness, and sexual intercourse with a woman who was too drunk to consent was regarded as just as serious an offence as forcible rape.

'She would not tell me the identity of the man but she

wanted someone she could talk to without recrimination or condemnation. That was when we became friends and from then on she often used to call here to drink sweet mead and talk. But what is it that I can do for you, lady? You do not visit me often. Is it something you would speak of concerning your child?'

Fidelma felt embarrassment. There was a curious bond between the two women but it was true that Fidelma did not visit often, even though Della lived no more than ten minutes from the palace of Cashel. Fidelma had once represented Della when she had been raped, so it did not surprise her that Sárait had sought Della out when she was in similar straits. Fidelma suddenly found herself thinking of Eadulf's reaction when she had told him the story of Della. His response had been prompted by the fact that Della had been a prostitute, a *bé-táide*, or woman of secrets as it was euphemistically called in the language of the Éireannach. Fidelma had been irritated by Eadulf's sarcasm at the idea of a prostitute's being raped. She had snapped at him: 'Cannot a woman be raped simply because she is a prostitute?' The laws of the five kingdoms allowed that, even if a woman was a *bé-táide*, if rape was proved then she could be compensated by half of her honour price. After Fidelma had won the case, Della had rejected her previous life and was reinstated fully in society, inheriting this little house in Cashel from her father. However, Fidelma knew that many people in the township still treated her with contempt and she had more or less become a recluse in her own home. Fidelma closed her eyes for a moment. She felt a little guilty that she did not visit more often and when she came to Della's house it was usually at night and in secret.

'Can you recall our last meeting?' Della prompted suddenly.

'I can,' Fidelma confirmed.

The older woman sighed. 'You were kind in ensuring that I was compensated when my house was smashed by the warriors of Donennach while I was hiding Brother Mochta and the holy relics of Ailbe.'

'But do you remember what you said as we parted?'

'That I also remember well. I said that solitude was the best society and a short abstinence from solitude urges the sweet return to it.'

Fidelma nodded, having remembered the words well. 'And I replied that we are all of us condemned to solitude but some of our sheltering walls are merely our own skins and thus there is no door to exit from solitude into life.'

Della was regarding her with sympathy.

'You have felt solitude since your baby was stolen?'

Fidelma felt a sudden anguish, like a pain in her stomach. She did her best to disguise it; to ignore it.

'I need to ask you a question, Della.'

'You do not need my permission to ask it.'

'Then let me remind you of an unpleasant time, for it is necessary to my question. Do you recall when I represented you when you sought compensation—'

'I remember how you defended me, yes,' replied Della shortly.

'You came to the court wearing a green silk cloak with a hood. It was enriched with red embroidery and fastened by a clasp of bejewelled silver. It was quite beautiful.'

Della looked at her thoughtfully and nodded.

'Do you still have that robe?'

Della hesitated a moment and then bowed her head in affirmation. 'I have not worn it since I gave up being . . . gave up being a *bé-táide*.'

'But you still have it?'

'I have.'

'Will you show it to me?'

Again Della hesitated and then shrugged. She stood up and went to a wooden chest in the corner of the room and bent down to open it. It seemed to be full of clothes and she began to take them out and lay them on the ground. They were rich garments and Fidelma did not have to ask how Della had accumulated them. They were the memories of her past life.

Suddenly she heard Della's sharp intake of breath.

'What is it?' she demanded.

'I don't know. I think someone has been looking through this chest. One of the dresses is torn, the sewing ripped at the seam. It was not like that when I packed these clothes away.'

'Which was when?'

'Just after the case in which you defended me. I have not wanted these garments of my past life since then.'

'Find the green silk cloak.'

Fidelma's voice was suddenly harsh. Della glanced questioningly at her and then bent again to the trunk. When she had turned everything out she sat back on the floor with a puzzled expression.

'It is not here.'

Fidelma sighed deeply. 'I rather suspected that it might not be.'

Della looked at her with a deepening frown.

'What do you mean? I think you owe me some explanation,' she demanded.

'Della, where were you on the night that Sárait was killed?'

The woman's lips trembled a little.

'Am I being accused of something?'

'Please, Della.' Fidelma's voice was now soft and coaxing. In other circumstances she would have been harsh, demanding, but she knew Della too well. 'I will explain if you answer a couple of questions.'

'So far as I recall, I was here. I am usually here.'

'Can anyone vouch for that?'

Della seemed to hesitate a moment and then shook her head. 'I was alone.'

Something made Fidelma feel that her friend was not being truthful. She decided to let it pass for the moment.

'When was the last time that you saw your green cloak?'

'As I have said, I put it away in this chest when I ceased to be a *bé-táide*, which was, as you know, three years ago. I have not bothered to look at it since.'

'Why keep it, then? You could have sold it. It is a very valuable cloak.'

Della shrugged. 'We do many things in life that are not logical, lady. You have seen these clothes that I have kept. They are a reminder of times past . . . to remind myself of what I was.'

'You are not aware of anyone breaking into your house? Perhaps the cloak could have been stolen?'

Della shook her head. 'There is no reason why anyone should break in here. I never keep a locked door – it is open to anyone to come and go as they please.'

'And you have left the house with the door unlocked?'

Fidelma well knew that locking doors was not a custom among the local people. However, the doors of nobles and professionals were secured on either side by a bolt or more usually by an iron lock – a *glais iarnaidhi*. When the Blessed Colmcille went to preach to the pagan King Brude of the Picts, he found that the king had caused all the doors of his fortress to be locked against him. Colmcille uttered a prayer which caused the iron locks to be miraculously opened. Why she suddenly thought of the story, she did not know.

'I always leave my door unlocked. Only at night, I draw the bolt shut.'

'So anyone might have come in at any time and taken the cloak?'

'I suppose so. Now, are you going to tell me what this is all about?'

Fidelma compressed her lips for a moment.

'On the night Sárait died and my baby was taken, she was lured from the palace by a false message. A dwarf went to her and told her that her sister wanted to see her urgently.'

'Gobnat? She hardly spoke to her sister.'

'You know her that well?'

'Everyone in the township knows her. Gobnat is one of those righteous women who still refuse to acknowledge my existence. She is supposed to be very moral, a pillar of the Faith.'

Fidelma stretched before the fire.

'You sound as if you do not like her?'

'I am merely irritated by her attitude. But then many people are.'

Fidelma looked at Della curiously. 'What do you mean?'

Della shrugged quickly. 'I mean her inflated self-esteem as if she is far better than other women here. Her conceit has grown immensely now that her husband, Capa, is captain of the élite warriors that guard your brother.'

'My mentor, the Brehon Morann, used to say that pride is but a mask covering one's own faults.'

Della smiled humorously. 'If anyone has a true reason for pride, it is you, Fidelma. You are wise and learned and your deeds are known in all five kingdoms of Éireann.'

Fidelma shook her head. 'When I went to attend the law

159

school of Brehon Morann, the first thing I had to do was part with self-conceit. Admitting one knew nothing and would never know more than a fraction even if one spent an entire life in contemplation and study, was the start of learning. Otherwise it would have been impossible to learn even what I thought I already knew.'

Della tried to bring Fidelma's mind back to the matter in hand.

'You mentioned that a dwarf went to the palace. Are you trying to track down this dwarf?'

Fidelma smiled thinly. 'I have already done so. He told me a story that I believe. I believe it because the poor creature's brother paid for its veracity with his life.'

'And that story is?'

'That the dwarf was passing through Cashel on that night and was asked to deliver the message to Sárait by a woman – a woman dressed in a green silk cloak, enriched with red embroidery.'

She was watching Della's face carefully. She was surprised to see a look of relief relax her features.

'Then the dwarf will be able to identify the wearer of this garment and prove who it was.'

'Not exactly,' replied Fidelma. 'You see, while the light of a lamp fell on the woman's clothing, it did not reveal her features. All he could see was that she was not youthful but had a good figure. The woman paid him to take the message to Sárait.'

Della began to look a little strained and pale again.

'I see now why you have come to me with your questions,' she said. 'You think that I am that woman. However, other women could have cloaks of green silk with red embroidery.'

Fidelma indicated the chest of clothes.

'The fact that you cannot produce your cloak seems to indicate that it was the cloak in question.'

'It does not mean that I was wearing it.'

'True. Can you add anything to your explanation of where you were that night?'

Della hesitated.

'Fidelma, you have befriended me when others shunned my company. You defended me when others would have condemned me. By that friendship I swear this, that I am not the woman whom you seek. I know nothing of the matter other than that I once possessed a green silk cloak and now it is gone.'

Fidelma looked intently at her for a moment or two.

'Speaking as your friend, Della, I believe you. But in this matter, I have to speak as a *dálaigh*. I have to try to find out when this cloak was stolen from you and have some corroboration of where you were on the night Sárait was killed.'

Della raised her arms in a helpless gesture.

'I know nothing of law, lady. You must do as you must. I will answer your questions so far as I am able but I can tell you nothing further that will help you in this matter.'

'You cannot tell me where you were on that night or provide me with the name of anyone who would vouch for you?' she pressed.

'I can say nothing more on that subject,' Della replied firmly.

Fidelma sighed deeply.

'Very well. I do believe you, Della, but I must do what I must to find my child. You can appreciate that.'

Della impulsively leant forward and touched Fidelma's arm.

'Believe me, I am a mother, too. I would do the same were I in your place. I have not had a happy life. When I

161

was young, I had ambitions to marry and have children. That was denied me. My problem, if you like, was that I always fell in love with the wrong man. I gave love and trust, and those men took them from me and then left me with nothing but angry memories. That was how I was led into being a *bé-táide*, seeking to revenge myself on men.'

'I cannot see,' Fidelma replied with a frown, 'how prostitution is a form of revenge on men?'

Della chuckled, a sound without any humour.

'It makes men come cap in hand, seeking women's favours and having to pay for the privilege. That is revenge for all those women whom they force their attentions on, whom they claim mastery over, simply because they are their husbands.'

'Women do not have to put up with men's pretensions in that field,' admonished Fidelma. 'Under law, women have the right to separate and to divorce.'

Della was still bitter.

'Law is logical. Sometimes the law is only as good as human nature. What happens between a man and wife within the bedroom is often beyond the reach of the law.'

'A woman does not have to be afraid. If a man threatens or inflicts physical violence on his partner it is grounds for an immediate divorce. Likewise, if the man circulates lies about his partner and holds her up to ridicule—'

Della cut her short.

'You do not understand, lady. I know you have a perfect marriage and I wish you well in it. But the minds of men and women are not always logical. Sometimes a woman will bear ills that logic might dictate are easily curable in law because of her feelings for her partner. Not everything can be cured by logic.'

Fidelma felt a sudden overwhelming weariness. Then, she

could not help it, tears sprang into her eyes. She tried to blink them away.

Della gazed at her in surprise.

'Why, lady, what is amiss?' she asked, leaning forward, a hand on Fidelma's arm.

Fidelma found that she could not speak.

'Oh, forgive me, lady, I am too selfish.' Della seemed truly in distress. 'I forgot this was about your missing child. How can I be so unthinking?'

Fidelma tried to recover her poise. Then she sighed.

'Oh, Della, it is not just Alchú's loss that has cast me into an abyss I can see no way out of.'

The woman stared at her for a moment, lost in thought. Then she shook her head.

'The Saxon brother? Your husband? Is he the cause of this grief, lady?'

'It is more that I have been upsetting him by my vanity, Della,' she replied brokenly.

The woman regarded her with an appraising look.

'Tell me about it,' she instructed.

At first Fidelma hesitated and then, slowly at first, but with growing abandon, she began to tell Della about the situation that had evolved between herself and Eadulf. It flooded out. As she spoke, she began to realise that it was a long time since she had talked to a woman, someone she could trust. In fact, Fidelma had not had an *anam chara*, a soul friend, since the disgrace of her friend Liadin, who had once been as a sister to her. They had grown up together and when they had reached the 'age of choice', when they had become women under the law, they had become soul friends, sworn to be spiritual guides to one another as was the custom of the Faith in Ireland. Liadin had married a foreign chieftain, Scoriath of the Fir Morc, who had been driven from his own lands to dwell among the Uí Dróna of Laigin. Liadin had acquired a lover and become involved in the murder of her husband and son and betrayed her oath to Fidelma. Since then, Fidelma had not accepted anyone as a soul friend.

Now all her fears, her hopes and her worries, came out in a rush like a dam breaking and the waters gushing forth.

For some time after she had finished speaking, Della sat quietly.

'The one thing that I have learnt, lady, is never to advise someone on a course of action when it comes to a relationship between a man and a woman,' she said at last. 'From what you say, the pursuit was all on the Saxon's side. He must take the greater responsibility. Is there not an old saying among our people, lady, that a man who marries a woman from the glen marries the whole glen? Did your man not realise that when he married you he had to marry who you were, and that meant he had to accept you were of the Eóghanacht?'

'Perhaps he did not understand exactly what it entailed.'

'He cannot blame you for his lack of knowledge, lady.'

'He is not happy here, Della, nor could I be happy in his country.'

'There is always a compromise to be found between two extremes.'

'But what compromise?'

'That is for discussion between yourself and your man.'

'It is not that easy.'

'Perhaps it is because you are trying to find a route by logic. The shortest cut through emotional problems is often to let your feelings show you the road. When you have seen the choice before you then it is time to make a decision.'

Fidelma shook her head. 'Where the heart leads, logic must go also.'

'You may see the problem through logic, lady, but you will understand truth through your emotion. It is emotion that has taught people how to reason.'

Fidelma suddenly rose with a brief smile. 'You are a wise woman, Della.'

Della rose also. 'Wisdom has not made me rich.'

'Wisdom excels all riches, Della.'

'That is as may be, lady, but for now I am a former *bétáide* under suspicion of encompassing the death of Sárait.'

Fidelma looked Della straight in the eye.

'My instinct tells me that you are not involved. Yet it also tells me something else. It tells me that you are holding something back.'

Della flushed. 'I can assure you that I am innocent of any involvement in the killing of Sárait or the disappearance of your baby. You are the last person I would inflict hurt upon.'

Fidelma inclined her head for a moment.

'I will accept that until it is proved otherwise,' she said quietly, before turning towards the door. At the door she halted as a thought occurred to her. 'Promise me this, Della, that you will not mention anything to anyone about the garment that is missing or my interest in it.'

Della smiled wryly.

'That I can easily do. I did not even know it was missing until you asked me to look for it. The garment that you are interested in, and the fact that it is missing, will remain a matter strictly between the two of us.'

Fidelma smiled.

'Let it be so,' she said softly before she left.

Chapter Ten

Fidelma sat opposite Eadulf as they breakfasted together on goat's milk, freshly baked bread, cheese and apples. Fidelma had been reticent about the details of her meeting with Della on the previous evening. She had told him about the boy at the inn and went so far as to tell him that Della had once possessed the green and red silk cloak. She had also mentioned seeing Gormán, but little else, and Eadulf had not bothered to press her further. In fact, he had come late to their chamber, when she was almost asleep, for he had discovered in the library of Cashel a copy of *Historia Francorum*, a history of the Franks, by Bishop Gregory of Tours. Eadulf was always interested in the history of various peoples. The *scriptor* in the library had told him that this had been one of the last books to be copied at the great book-copying centre in Alexandria. The story was told with much verve and enthusiasm and Eadulf soon discovered that Gregory was no Frank but a Gaul, a Romanised Gaul it was true, but not above pointing out the error of Frankish ways and praising his own people. The time had passed quickly and so, returning to their chamber, he had found Fidelma already in bed. He re-emerged into the real world with a feeling of guilt that a mere book could provide him with escape from his problems for a few hours.

'So what can we do now?' Eadulf asked, as he poured a drink from the jug of goat's milk.

'There is little we can do but wait,' Fidelma replied. 'Let us hope we get a quick response to our demand for proof.'

'Do you think that we shall?'

'If Alchú has really been kidnapped and if his kidnappers are serious about the exchange – yes. But there is nothing to be done until we hear. Anyway, old Conchobar has asked me to go and play *brandubh* with him this morning. He probably knows that I need some distraction.'

Brandubh was 'black raven', an ancient board game which Eadulf prided himself on being rather good at. Before the coming of the Faith to the five kingdoms, it was said that the great god of arts and crafts, Lugh, had invented it and most of the kings and heroes were thought little of unless they were masters of the game.

Conchobar was an elderly apothecary and physician who dwelt at Cashel and had known Fidelma since she was born.

'You might ask him if he can discover where Alchú is,' Eadulf said with some bitterness in his voice.

Conchobar was not only a physician but also an adept at making speculations from the patterns of the stars. Indeed, medicine and astrology were often twins in the practice of the physician's lore and the study of the heavens, *nemgnacht*, was an ancient art in this land where most people who could afford to do so had a chart cast for the moment of their children's birth which was called *nemindithib*, a horoscope.

'That is nothing to joke about,' Fidelma replied sharply.

Eadulf sat back and gazed thoughtfully at her.

'Who said I was joking?' he countered. 'Your astrologers

claim to be able to answer all manner of questions and even find people, don't they?'

Fidelma rose abruptly, her mouth a thin disapproving line.

'I am going to join Conchobar for a game of *brandubh*!'

There was almost a flounce in her gait as she left the room and slammed the door shut behind her.

Eadulf sniffed in irritation and stretched in his seat, gazing at the closed door for a moment or two. Everything he said seemed to upset Fidelma. Yet he had been half serious in his suggestion, because he knew that Fidelma was not one to dismiss the ancient beliefs and customs of her people. Old Conchobar himself had often told him that Fidelma had shown a talent for casting star charts and several times her knowledge had come in handy to solve a particularly puzzling mystery. So he was not exactly being sarcastic when he suggested that the answer to Alchú's kidnapping might be found in some astrological map of the heavens.

He finished his meal slowly and rose reluctantly, wondering how he should occupy his day. He already felt guilty at wasting time reading when he should have been thinking about how to investigate further. He went to the window and stared out across the grey walls of the palace complex. The late autumnal day was bright. There did not seem to be a cloud in the clear blue of the sky and yet the weather was not unduly cold. At this time of year when the sky was clear, it usually meant the day was cold and frost would lie on the ground. Clouds often meant the day would not be so cold even though they might bring rain.

His view from the window gave access to the south where the forest stretched from the far side of the township down towards the distant River Suir.

It was then that the notion struck him. It would probably result in hearing the same information but to pursue the idea would be better than just sitting around doing nothing.

He hurried from his chambers and made his way down to the stables.

A stableboy obligingly saddled his horse for him. Eadulf was not the most expert horseman; when it came to horses he liked to leave matters in the hands of those with better knowledge. Once it was saddled, he led the beast across the courtyard to the gates.

Caol was on duty there and saluted Eadulf.

'I am going for a ride. I need some exercise,' Eadulf said before being asked.

'A good morning for it, Brother,' replied Caol. 'Though I had not thought of you as being one who rides for pleasure,' he added, with a wry grin.

'I mean to find a spot in the hills yonder,' he indicated southward, 'and then walk for a while.'

'Due south is a lake, Loch Ceann,' confirmed the warrior. 'You'll find good walking there.'

'Due south? Is that near where the woodsman Conchoille works?' Eadulf asked innocently.

'Fairly near. The place where he is felling trees is close by at Rath na Drínne. Did you wish to see him, Brother?'

'A few questions do occur to me now that you mention it. So I may take the opportunity to look for him.'

Eadulf thanked the warrior, mounted and trotted down the incline that led from the mound on which Cashel was built, twisting down to the start of the township below. But he avoided the edge of the town, keeping to the road that ran along its eastern border and then joined the track into the woods.

It was not Loch Ceann that he was heading for but Rath na Drínne, where the woodsman Conchoille was working. It did not take him long before the small hill rose before him and just before it was the old wooden inn with the sign swinging in the gentle morning breeze. He halted and dismounted.

There was no one inside as he entered the dark interior. It was too early in the day. However, only a few seconds passed after the door banged shut behind him before a short, rotund man, sleeves rolled up and wearing an apron, came from a side room and examined him with curious eyes for a moment before greeting him.

'Good day, Brother, and what can I do for you?'

'I'll take a mug of your mead,' replied Eadulf with a smile, 'and the answers to some questions.'

The innkeeper frowned as he spoke.

'A Saxon by your accent? Would you be Brother Eadulf, husband to our lady, Fidelma of Cashel?'

Eadulf gave an affirmative nod. 'And your name would be Ferloga?'

'I am he, and most sorry to hear of your troubles, Brother Eadulf. The lady Fidelma is well respected in these parts. I hear that the gossip is that it is our old enemies, the Uí Fidgente, who are behind this evil.'

'Where did you hear that?' asked Eadulf, moving to a chair near the log fire in the corner of the taproom.

Ferloga had poured a pottery mug of mead and brought it to him. He sat down opposite Eadulf.

'We are a small community, Brother. Many of my customers live or work in Cashel.'

'Like Conchoille?'

'Like Conchoille,' the innkeeper agreed. 'There is little that happens at Cashel that we do not hear about.'

Eadulf sipped thoughtfully at his mead. It was sweet with the honey.

'Conchoille was in here just before he found the body of

170

Sárait,' he said, making it a statement rather than a question, for he already knew the answer.

Ferloga looked reflectively into the fire.

'I remember that night well. I didn't hear the details until the next morning, you understand. But because of that, when Conchoille came here and told me, I went over the events of the evening.'

'Conchoille came to tell you the details?' asked Eadulf innocently.

'Of course.'

'How did he describe what happened?' asked Eadulf persuasively. 'You see, it is my experience that a story can often be distorted in the retelling of it. By the time that Fidelma and I came along and heard it from Conchoille's lips, he must have told it a hundred times. You would have been among the first to hear exactly what happened. You see? Your version may contain an important item that has been overlooked.'

Ferloga chuckled. 'I doubt that Conchoille would have overlooked anything. He is not only a woodsman but also a fine *senchaid*, one of the best in this area.'

Eadulf knew that a *senchaid* was a reciter of stories, keeper of an ancient and oral tradition. Stories were handed down from one generation to the next in word-perfect fashion. He knew, from experience in attending such storytelling gatherings, that the audience would often know a tale as well as the reciter and woe betide the *senchaid* who faltered or put a word in the wrong place. They would be severely corrected.

'Yet a *senchaid* is not infallible, Ferloga. Tell me what was said from your own memory.'

Ferloga leant back and closed his eyes for a moment as if to help him in the recollection.

'Conchoille usually comes here for an evening meal and

a drink when he is working in the district. He is a widower so has no woman to cook for him. So that evening, when the sky was darkening, he came in and had his meal and a few drinks, and stayed for some time exchanging a story or two. Then he left.'

'It was late?'

'It was so, for we had a few tales to tell each other.'

Eadulf looked at the innkeeper.

'Tales such as . . . what?'

'Local gossip, local news. That is an innkeeper's stock in trade. I had a tale to tell of the itinerants who had been in earlier with their baby, and I about to throw them out when my wife intervened and gave them food in exchange for a salve for an infection on her leg. Anyway, Conchoille lit his lantern and set off along the track to Cashel.'

'And what did he tell you happened then?'

Ferloga smiled. 'He said that he was nearly at the outskirts of Cashel when he tripped over a bloodstained shawl. That was when he discovered the body of the nurse Sárait. She was quite dead.'

'And then?'

'He left the body and went straight to Sárait's sister, Gobnat, who dwelt with her husband not far away. The husband, as well you will know, was Capa of the king's warrior guard. Capa went with Conchoille to recover the body and along the way they encountered a warrior on his way to the palace and told him to raise an alarm, for Sárait was known to be in service to our lady, Fidelma. But when Caol and his guards arrived it was realised that Sárait had left the palace with lady Fidelma's . . . with your baby. A search was mounted immediately without result.'

'And that was all?'

Ferloga shrugged. 'Only that the search was maintained

by torchlight for some time and then resumed again the next morning. Both village and woods were searched.'

Eadulf sat back in thought.

Ferloga's retelling of the tale had not materially added to his knowledge. He had not expected that it would. But there was something that was bothering him; something at the back of his mind which he could not quite place.

'Conchoille has not added anything to this account since he first told you?'

Ferloga was frowning now.

'Is it that you suspect Conchoille of something?' he demanded. 'He is a trustworthy man who fought in many battles against the Uí Fidgente.'

Eadulf turned thoughtful eyes upon him.

'Including Cnoc Áine?' he asked abruptly.

'Many of us were at Cnoc Áine,' confirmed Ferloga.

'Including Sárait's husband, Callada.'

Ferloga drew his brows together quickly. 'There is no denying that fact. He was killed there.'

'And you are saying that you and Conchoille were there? Forgive me, aren't you too old to be in battle? Cnoc Áine was scarcely two years ago.'

Ferloga raised his chin defensively. 'A man is as young as he feels.'

'Was the service compulsory?'

'Love of our leader is a better duress than compulsion under law.'

'Did you see how Callada was killed?'

Ferloga actually chuckled sarcastically.

'I think I know what you are getting at, Saxon. There is a story abroad that Callada was killed by one of our own and not by the enemy.'

'And have you a comment on that?'

173

Ferloga shrugged. 'It seems far-fetched. Anyway, Conchoille and I were not in the fore ranks of that charge at Cnoc Áine but held in reserve by Colgú lest the Uí Fidgente break through our lines. When we finally marched forward it was merely to take prisoners and pursue the disorganised rabble.'

'So, as far as you are concerned, the story of Callada's death was only a rumour?'

Ferloga gestured diffidently. 'Strange stories circulate after a battle, especially when it was as bloody and as vicious as that one. Whether there was truth in it, I cannot say.'

Eadulf decided to switch the topic.

'Did you take part in the search for Alchú?'

'By the time I was told, which was midday on the day following the finding of Sárait's body, there was little I could do. By then, the king's guard had been scouring the country-side for some time.'

'I see.'

Eadulf was disappointed, although he had known that little information would come of his visit to the inn. However, he had had just a small hope that Ferloga might have remembered some significant incident. He sat back with a sigh.

'Well, as I am here and it approaches noon, I will eat something light. Some cheese and bread, perhaps. Or did you say your wife cooks? Ah yes, you mentioned she had some infection. I trust the salve cured that. You see, I studied the art of the apothecary at Tuaim Drecain.'

Ferloga smiled.

'My wife is visiting her sister at the moment, Brother Eadulf. Thank you, the salve worked well. Perhaps it was a lucky thing that she came when she did to prevent me throwing out the itinerants.'

'I thought the law of hospitality would have prevented the refusal of hospitality, not your wife.'

Ferloga flushed at being reminded of his duties under law as an innkeeper.

'This is not a public inn, a *bruiden*, where everyone has to be accommodated. This is my own inn. I do not like itinerants. They are usually untrustworthy. Beggars. You know the sort.'

'I thought these beggars were selling salves.' Eadulf accented the word 'beggars'.

Ferloga sniffed in irritation.

'Salves, balms, herbs. They were selling things but they were itinerants nevertheless. Itinerants with their noisy, bawling child.'

'It sounds as though you have good reason to be thankful to them.'

Ferloga was obviously reluctant to give credit.

A sudden thought occurred to Eadulf.

'A man and wife and child, did you say?'

'Indeed, a couple with their baby. He said that he was a herbalist and en route to the abbey of Colmán.'

'When exactly did they pass by here?'

'That's easy. It was the same day that Sárait's murder took place, but the day had scarcely darkened when they left here. That was long before Conchoille arrived. That was why I was telling him the story about them.' Ferloga's eyes suddenly widened. 'You don't think that they killed Sárait, surely?'

Eadulf did not respond to the question.

'You say that they were itinerants. Could they have been Uí Fidgente?'

Ferloga immediately shook his head.

'Not Uí Fidgente, that's for sure. They had the accent of the people of Laigin. There is always a reason why people take to the road in the five kingdoms, Brother Eadulf. Usually it is because they have fallen foul of the law and cannot redeem themselves or their honour price. They cannot put down roots again and are doomed to wander.'

Eadulf drained his mug and stood up. He had made a decision.

'Thank you for your help, Ferloga. You have been most helpful.'

The innkeeper raised his brows in question.

'What of your food?'

'I realise that I must return to Cashel,' Eadulf excused himself. 'I have remembered something I must do.'

Eadulf had ridden not more than a hundred yards when he urged the horse into a canter. Anyone who knew Eadulf would realise that this was unusual behaviour. However, he was full of excitement. A thought was irritating him, sparked by the innkeeper's words. If he were correct, perhaps the mystery was not as insoluble as he had, at first, thought.

Fidelma was sitting frowning at the gaming board.

Conchobhar was winning the game of black raven. It was a difficult game, for the board was divided into forty-nine squares, seven by seven. In the centre of the board, the middle square stood for the royal palace of Tara and held the piece representing the High King. On the squares immediately next to the High King, north, south, east and west were pieces representing the four provincial kings whose task was to protect the High King. On the outside squares at the edge of the board were the attacking pieces representing the forces of chaos, each piece moved on the throw of the dice. The object of the game was to ensure the safety of the High King piece by allowing it to move, through the encircling pieces, to the side of the board or to one of the four squares allotted to the provincial kings.

Usually it was a challenge Fidelma enjoyed, but today her mind was not on the game. She had already lost two defending pieces.

Conchobar, the elderly religieux whose apothecary shop stood in the shadow of the royal chapel in the palace grounds, was regarding her with a concerned expression.

Fidelma caught his eye and shrugged.

'I am sorry, old friend,' she said, for she had known him all her life. 'I cannot concentrate.'

Conchobar regarded her with a sharp eye.

'It is understandable. It does not need my arts to tell me that. Yet I had hoped the game would be a means of distraction. We will continue another time.'

Fidelma sighed deeply. She had been thinking about Eadulf's suggestion about astrology and realised that he had simply voiced something in the back of her mind that she was trying to suppress. In her desperation she felt she should try anything within reason.

'I would use your arts to find my child, Brother Conchobar,' she said quietly.

The old man shook his head regretfully.

'You know that is not possible.'

'But you are the greatest adept in the field of making speculations from the patterns of the stars.'

'I would not claim as much. Though I did study under Mo Chuaróc mac Neth Sémon, the greatest astrologer that Cashel has ever produced, yet my skill is not beyond criticism.'

'I have heard that a good *réalt-eolach*, one who gathers knowledge from the stars, could cast a chart to trace the location of an object. Why not do so for my baby?'

Conchobar was sympathetic.

'Alas, Fidelma, I once tried to teach you the art of charting the heavens and, had you stuck to it, you might have made an excellent interpreter of the portents. The one thing that you should remember is that there is always a correct time to ask a question of the stars.'

'What if I ask now?'

'It would not work. Asking a question of the stars must be timed for the exact birth of the question. It is like drawing up a natal chart for a person. The chart must be timed for the exact moment and location otherwise it is useless. I do not mean just a day, or a specific day in a specific year, but the exact time of that day, for the stars move quickly through the heavens. What is correct for one person will be wrong for another born even ten minutes later in the same location.'

'I understand that. But what are you saying?'

'You have been asking yourself this very question for many days. How do I know the exact time when your question was born?'

Fidelma shrugged in a gesture of resignation.

'I feel so frustrated just waiting and not being in control.'

Conchobar nodded sympathetically.

'You have always been impatient, Fidelma.' He smiled softly. 'You were impatient to be out of the womb. I was in attendance at your birth and you came before the due time, screaming and bawling for attention. You were impatient to come into life, impatient to learn what you wanted to learn, impatient with all those you considered fools who were not as quick as you were.'

'Don't we have a saying that patience is the virtue of donkeys?' snapped Fidelma.

Conchobar's eyes narrowed slightly.

'I remember a great Brehon once said that whoever had no patience had no wisdom. That Brehon was—'

Fidelma grimaced as she interrupted.

'I know. It was my own mentor, Brehon Morann. He did not have to wait, feeling useless, while his child was prey to God only knows what dangers.'

'Fidelma, it is a saying that if you have patience, the bee will provide you with honey. Today is a day when you should undertake no precipitous action. For this is the time when An Bech dominates the sky.'

Fidelma knew that what the Irish called the Bee was the constellation known to the Romans as Scorpio – the Scorpion.

'Why?' she demanded.

'Because not only does the sun stand in Scorpio but so does Mars, the ruler of Scorpio, as do Venus and Jupiter. All at this same time. I see that this might result in a restriction of expression for you, Fidelma. You might, with strong character, make decisions that could be for the good but might also be for the bad. Also, and be prepared, Scorpio is the zodiacal house of death.'

Fidelma paled a little. Then she grimaced.

'You are supposed to be bringing cheer into my life, Conchobar.'

'I am supposed to be helping you tread the path that you must tread, Fidelma. Instead of sitting here playing *brandubh* with an old man like me you ought be with your husband.'

Fidelma sniffed deprecatingly. Again Brother Conchobar looked thoughtfully at her.

'Is there something wrong between you and our Saxon friend?'

'There is much wrong, Conchobar.'

'I am not your *anam chara*, but—'

'I don't have an *anam chara*. Not since Liadin.'

'Then if you have need of a soul friend, I am willing to listen to your inmost thoughts and give my opinion.'

Fidelma lowered her gaze to the *brandubh* board. 'This game is child's play to the thoughts that race around my head and I can find no sanctuary in the squares that make up the board game of my life.'

Conchobar stared at her for a moment.

'It is hard for Brother Eadulf not only to be in a foreign country but also to be married to an Eóghanacht princess.'

'It was his choice,' she replied defensively.

Conchobar smiled thinly. 'And you had nothing to do with it?'

She coloured quickly at his gentle sarcasm.

'I tried to dissuade him, tried to . . .'

Conchobar's smiled broadened.

'I see. You were unwillingly overwhelmed and there was nothing that you could do?'

'The year and a day of my marriage contract is almost up. It falls within the next week.'

'And you plan to formally reject him? Awkward in the current circumstances, is it not?'

Fidelma compressed her lips and said nothing. Conchobar was being as devastatingly logical as she would be in his place.

'Apart from Eadulf's sensibilities in adapting to this lifestyle, what are your feelings? Do not tell me that you are an unwilling partner in this. I know you too well. You have never done anything in life, Fidelma, that you did not want to do. You went into this partnership because you wanted to, not because Eadulf wanted it.'

Fidelma opened her mouth to protest and then snapped it shut. She frowned, trying to think how best she should answer the question.

At that moment the door burst open and one of the religieux came in, not even noticing Fidelma but looking straight at Brother Conchobar.

'Come quickly, Brother Apothecary,' he called. 'You are needed at once.'

Fidelma rose quickly.

'What is it?' she demanded, her heart beginning to race.

The religieux turned, as if seeing her for the first time.

'Sister Fidelma! It is the Bishop Petrán. I think he is near to death . . . if not dead.'

Chapter Eleven

Bishop Petrán was dead. He lay on his bed, his skin pale, like tightly stretched parchment, but with a curious blue tinge on his lips. There was nothing that Brother Conchobar could do except pronounce him dead.

Two of Bishop Petrán's attendants, young brothers of the Faith, were present in the chamber, obviously anguished by the death of their elderly mentor. Fidelma had accompanied Brother Conchobar to the bishop's room primarily out of curiosity. The previous day the bishop had seemed in remarkably good health and his argument with Eadulf had demonstrated his mental agility. She was about to ask Brother Conchobar what he thought the cause of death was, but as she framed the question the door suddenly opened and Brehon Dathal, the chief judge of Muman, came in followed by Finguine, the tanist.

Brehon Dathal glanced about him in an officious manner, frowning in annoyance when he saw Fidelma.

'I shall take over the investigation of this matter, Fidelma,' he said sharply, as if she would argue with him.

She smiled thinly. 'You are welcome to do so, Dathal, although there is no investigation as yet. I merely came along with Brother Conchobar for I was playing *brandubh* with him when he was called to attend the bishop by these young brothers.'

Brehon Dathal turned to Brother Conchobar. 'I see that Bishop Petrán is dead. What was the cause of death?'

Brother Conchobar simply shrugged. 'That I cannot tell you for certain at this moment. I have not begun a thorough examination.'

Brehon Dathal glanced down at the corpse.

'Blue lips, blue lips,' he muttered. 'Surely a sign of poison?'

'Not necessarily,' the old apothecary protested.

'Always in my experience,' Brehon Dathal replied testily.

'I had not realised that you are a qualified physician,' replied Brother Conchobar blandly.

Brehon Dathal was bending over the corpse and did not appear to hear him. Brother Conchobar coughed loudly to attract his attention.

'I need to do some further tests in my workroom.'

Brehon Dathal turned away from the bed and sniffed.

'Superfluous. Clearly poison but, if you want to waste time, I have no objection. I am proceeding with the fact that he was poisoned and that this is a case of murder.'

Astonished, Fidelma gazed at him. 'Isn't that a little . . . a little precipitate?' she said quietly.

Brehon Dathal stared at her in irritation.

'I thought you were not involved in this matter?'

'Neither am I.'

'Then I need not detain you.' He turned sharply to the two young religieux. 'When did you discover the bishop?'

'We came a short while ago to escort him to luncheon. We found him thus. I went to fetch Brother Conchobar while my companion stayed with him.'

'When did you last see him alive?'

'Shortly after he had performed the morning's dismissal. He said he was feeling tired for it was only the day before yesterday that we had returned from the west coast.'

'Apart from fatigue after his journey, he was in good health?'

'Bishop Petrán was always in good health. He was never tired and this morning was the first time I had ever heard him admit to fatigue.'

'Just so, just so,' muttered Brehon Dathal. 'So we can say that the poison was administered when he returned to his chamber . . .?'

Brother Conchobar let out a gasp of protest.

'I have not yet stated a cause of death. I need to examine—'

Brehon Dathal waved him aside.

'A formality, a formality that is all.' He was already looking at a couple of pottery mugs on a side table. He picked them up and sniffed suspiciously at them. Behind his back, Finguine glanced across to Fidelma and raised his eyes to the ceiling with a shrug. Brehon Dathal was stroking his chin. 'He came in, drank the poison in innocence and thus died.' Suddenly he swung back to the two religieux. 'Did the bishop have any enemies that you know of? Has he been in recent arguments?'

One of the two young men glanced at Fidelma before dropping his gaze. 'On our return to Cashel, he was seen to have a very fierce argument,' he said quietly.

'With whom?' pressed Brehon Dathal eagerly.

'With the Saxon. The same Saxon with whom he had a fierce argument nearly a month ago.'

'The Saxon?' demanded Brehon Dathal.

'He means Eadulf,' Fidelma said quietly. She had gone suddenly cold at the implied accusation.

'That's right. With Brother Eadulf,' confirmed the religieux.

'What were these arguments about?'

'I can tell you that . . .' began Fidelma but Brehon Dathal waved her into silence.

'Let an unbiased witness speak. You are the wife to this Saxon and therefore will present a bias in his favour.'

'I think it was on matters of religious disagreement,' said the brother. 'They argued with harsh words and I know that on both occasions, when I attended the bishop afterwards, he was upset and went so far as to say that Cashel was the poorer when the sister of the king consorted with a—'

'I cannot listen to this!' snapped Fidelma.

Brehon Dathal turned on her disapprovingly.

'I have already suggested that your presence here is not needed. You may go, and tell Brother Eadulf to hold himself ready to answer some questions.'

Finguine glanced sympathetically at her as she left. Behind her she heard old Brother Conchobar demanding permission to remove Bishop Petrán's body so that he could examine it properly.

Eadulf was not in their chambers when she glanced in. She hurried down the grey stone corridor, trying not to run. Crossing the yard she saw Caol, the warrior, grooming a horse.

'Have you seen my husband, Caol?' she asked him, slightly breathless.

The warrior smiled in greeting as he stood up, brush in hand.

'Not so long ago. I've just rubbed his horse down before he left again.'

She stared at him.

'Left *again*?' she said with emphasis.

The warrior nodded. 'He went out early this morning, after breakfast. He said he was going for a ride but I think he went to see Conchoille, the woodsman. Then he came back, apparently in a hurry, and asked me to prepare his horse to go out again. While I was doing so, he disappeared for a short while, returning with a filled saddle bag, and then was off.'

Fidelma was standing still in her astonishment. 'With a full saddle bag?'

'It looked as though it was packed for a long trip.'

'Did you see which way he went when he left Cashel?'

'I did not. I needed to start rubbing down my own horse.' He gestured to the horse that he had been attending to.

Fidelma paused for a moment before turning and making her way to the main buildings, again trying not to run. She returned to her chambers. Entering, she peered round more carefully this time. There was a note on the pillow of their bed, left in such a manner that it should have been immediately spotted. It was from Eadulf.

I could not wait. I have a lead, which I think it important that I should follow. I need to go to the abbey of Colmán in the west. I may be gone several days.

She sat down abruptly, head in hands, and groaned aloud.

For Fidelma, the rest of the day passed in a turmoil of thought. Her mind was not only filled with worry for Alchú but now for Eadulf as well. She even found herself thinking the unthinkable. Had Eadulf really left Cashel to follow a clue or was Brehon Dathal's suspicion correct? She had witnessed the verbal violence of his anger against old Petrán and she had seen his unusual explosive temper on several occasions now. Had he been involved in the killing of the elderly bishop? Surely Eadulf had not killed Petrán! That was a ridiculous idea. But why had he vanished from Cashel at this particular time?

When Brehon Dathal had come to their chambers to question Eadulf and she had shown him the note, a triumphant gleam had come into the judge's eye. She knew exactly what he was thinking. The old Brehon had left saying that he would have to send someone in search of Eadulf. That could have only one interpretation. Brehon Dathal believed in Eadulf's guilt. She had gone to her brother, who was discussing the matter with Finguine.

Colgú had regarded her anxious features sympathetically.

'I cannot interfere in the actions of a Brehon while pursuing an investigation, Fidelma. You know that well enough.'

Finguine had softened the blow a little by adding: 'Brehon Dathal should have waited for Brother Conchobar's report before making his mind up about poison.'

'Why hasn't Brother Conchobar finished his examination?' she demanded angrily.

'Brother Conchobar has just been called to Lios Mhór on some errand of mercy. The living require his medical skills as well as the dead,' Colgú replied. 'He told his assistant that he had completed his examination of Petrán's body, but no one seems to know what conclusion he had reached.' He glanced anxiously at his tanist. 'Finguine and I have been discussing this matter. We have become worried about Dathal's behaviour recently. I think it might be time to consider his retirement as Chief Brehon. It has been noticed that he is too fond of leaping to conclusions before he is apprised of all the facts. I think it is a sign of age. He and Bishop Ségdae are constantly at one another's throats. It is not good to have that conflict in government.'

Fidelma shook her head immediately. 'That must not happen until Eadulf's name is cleared of this accusation. You can imagine what stories will spread if you dismiss Dathal while this matter is outstanding.'

It was Finguine who answered.

'Yet it will be for the good of the kingdom that it is done, cousin.'

'But not for the good of Eadulf,' she replied.

'We were hoping to get your advice as a *dálaigh* about how to enforce Dathal's retirement,' Colgú said.

'I cannot advise you on that, brother, at a time when I have such vested interests. I do believe Brehon Dathal has acted precipitately in the case of Petrán's death but then I would have to say that, wouldn't I? You might imagine what a good *dálaigh* would make of the purpose behind my advice if I agreed with you.'

Colgú regarded his sister with an expression of sorrow.

'You are right. We should not have mentioned it,' he said. 'Nevertheless, it is on my mind and must soon be dealt with. Dathal was – is – a just man and has been a good guide for this kingdom. But, as I say, I have had several recent reports of bad judgements.'

'At the moment things rest with Brother Conchobar. When will we hear his report?'

'When he returns from Lios Mhór. Meanwhile, what news of Eadulf?'

'None except the note he left me.'

'What could have possibly sent him to the abbey of Colmán?' Her brother was puzzled. 'And alone? He has to cross Uí Fidgente territory to get to it and if it is true that we have to contend with some Uí Fidgente plot, then he could be in a great deal of danger.'

Fidelma shivered slightly. But she had not wanted to admit just how scared she was for Eadulf.

'He has been in danger before, and remember how he

survived Uí Fidgente when fate took me to the abbey of the Salmon of the Three Wells?'

Colgú smiled. 'That seems many lifetimes ago, Fidelma.'

'I feel it so,' agreed Fidelma.

'You had best have some supper and get to bed. Eadulf is capable of taking care of himself, but I do confess that I wish he had not left Cashel at this time.'

Fidelma had left him. She had no stomach to eat when the evening mealtime came. When she retired she found slumber difficult and it was only after many hours of wakeful agonising on the events of the day that she had finally fallen into a fitful sleep.

It was early the next morning when an attendant came to wake her.

'Lady, the king your brother has sent me. Would you attend him in his chambers as soon as you are ready?'

Fidelma rose to a sitting position and tried to focus on the woman from under heavy lids.

'What has happened?' she asked, rubbing her eyes.

'I am told that Gormán has come to the palace with something of importance connected with the baby, Alchú,' the attendant replied.

'Tell my brother I will join him directly,' she said, her heart beginning to beat faster.

As the woman left, Fidelma rose from the bed, shaking her head from side to side as if the action would clear it. She still felt exhausted. What new disaster did this portend? Gormán had news of Alchú – but what news?

When Fidelma entered her brother's chamber, she found Finguine and Gormán standing together talking with her brother. Before them, on the table, was a strip of birch bark and a single *cuarán*, a tiny baby shoe whose upper was of *lee-find*, undyed wool, mounted on a small sole of half-tanned hide, retaining its softness and pliability like rawhide. As her eyes fell on it, Fidelma gave an involuntary intake of breath.

She recognised the shoe as belonging to Alchú.

She snatched it up, holding it closely before her eyes, examining it to make sure. Colgú appeared a little embarrassed as he stood helplessly by.

'I have already identified it, Fidelma. The pair was a present from me. I can confirm that because I had it made by our local *cuaránaidhe*,' he said, almost apologetically. 'Indeed, I remember getting the shoemaker to make sure of the softness of the rawhide and I examined it myself. I know the patterning well.'

Fidelma straightened her shoulders. 'Only one shoe was sent?'

Colgú glanced across to Gormán. The big warrior coughed nervously and then spread his hands almost in a defensive gesture.

'I was the one brought it here, lady. It was found together with that note. Just the one little shoe.'

Fidelma's eyes travelled back to the table where the strip of birch bark lay. She put down the baby shoe and picked up the note. There were only a few words on it. She noticed that it was written in the same ill-formed hand as the first note had been.

Your proof, it said simply. *Now follow our previous instructions.*

Fidelma turned back to Gormán with a look of interrogation.

'Where exactly did you find this?'

'I was passing the inn in the township this morning when the innkeeper hailed me. He found the shoe hung in a little leather bag on his door – the same place where the first note was apparently found, lady,' the big warrior replied. 'The note was with it.'

Her eyes went to the small leather bag. She picked it up. It had no distinguishing marks on it, a small bag of worn kidskin that fastened, sack-like, with a leather thong round its top. It was barely big enough to cover a man's fist if pushed inside. Fidelma turned the bag inside out and peered into the creases caused by the seams. Seeds and bits of dried vegetable matter clung along them.

She made no comment but returned the bag to its original shape. Then she picked up the shoe again. It was clean. There was no sign of dirt on it at all.

'There is no question now, cousin,' Finguine was saying.

She turned her attention sharply to him with a frown.

'No question? Of what?'

Finguine raised his hands in an encompassing gesture.

'That this is some Uí Fidgente plot. They hold your son in return for the release of the three Uí Fidgente chieftains.'

Colgú was nodding in agreement.

'There is nothing for it, Fidelma. We will have to release the three chieftains. We have no other way of tracking down those who hold the baby.'

Finguine looked almost apologetically at her.

'Your brother is right. However, it is my task to point out that no guarantees have yet been offered about the return of Alchú. It seems that we now have to take the word of the Uí Fidgente that they will do so once the chieftains cross the border.'

'We have to trust them,' Colgú echoed in resignation.

'Once they have crossed into the territory of the Dál gCais,' Finguine reminded her, 'the first note said the baby would be returned.'

'Has Capa returned from the Uí Fidgente country yet?' Fidelma suddenly asked.

Finguine shook his head.

'From the swiftness of the response, we may presume that whoever holds the baby is hiding within proximity to Cashel,' said Colgú.

Fidelma inclined her head thoughtfully.

'It is a logical deduction,' she admitted.

'Well, we can follow the chieftains once they are released,' Finguine suggested. 'Follow them and see who contacts them and then we will know who holds the baby.'

'That would be pointless,' Fidelma replied. They regarded her in surprise.

'Pointless?' Colgú made the word into a question.

'The chieftains, on their release, will start presumably for the country of the Dál gCais. Those who hold the child will be watching them. Doubtless watching them from the very moment of their release. What do you think they would do if they saw anyone following them?'

Colgú immediately realised the implication.

'They would continue to hold the child. So, are you saying that we have to let the chieftains go without following them?'

Gormán had been looking thoughtful for some time. 'Forgive me, lady, but where is Brother Eadulf? Surely he should be here with us to make this decision?'

'Were you not in the palace yesterday?' she asked.

'No, lady.' He hesitated. 'Well, I stayed with a friend last night before returning this morning.'

Finguine looked a little embarrassed.

'Eadulf left the palace yesterday. He left a note saying that he had found something that might resolve the mystery.'

'Where has he gone?'

'He rode off to the abbey of Colmán.'

Gormán appeared surprised. 'Ridden off . . . without escort? That is across Uí Fidgente territory.'

Fidelma smiled tightly. 'I think Eadulf can find his way about without an escort.'

Gormán made a whistling sound between his teeth.

'Even so, he would have done better in these troubled times to take a warrior with him.'

Fidelma pursued her lips in annoyance.

'I have no worries. Eadulf is capable of finding his own way.'

'There is something else that Gormán should know,' added Finguine quietly. 'Bishop Petrán was found dead yesterday. Brehon Dathal thinks Eadulf poisoned him.'

Gormán burst out laughing. They looked at him in surprise.

'It is such a ridiculous idea,' he explained, controlling his mirth. 'I do not know Brother Eadulf well, but I know men. Poison is not how he would deal with anyone who irritated him in a discussion on theology.'

Fidelma appraised him quickly.

'You knew there was some antagonism between Eadulf and the bishop on matters of theology?'

'Several people heard of the argument he had with Petrán when we returned to the palace the other evening.'

Fidelma hesitated for a moment and then turned to Finguine.

'Has Brother Conchobar returned to Cashel as yet?'

Finguine shook his head.

'Do we know what it was that sent Brother Eadulf riding west?' pressed Gormán, returning to the subject. 'Any information should be shared.'

'I was not informed,' replied Fidelma. 'I did not see him before he left. He wrote me a note. All I know is that he was going to the abbey of Colmán.'

Gormán rubbed his chin thoughtfully. 'Beyond Cnoc Loinge it is not wise that he travel alone.'

Colgú was impatient. 'Well, let us return to the matter in hand. Are we all agreed to release the chieftains?'

'Reluctantly,' affirmed Finguine. 'But shouldn't the council meet and approve such a decision? Bishop Ségdae, Brehon Dathal . . . perhaps we should wait for Capa's return?'

Colgú shook his head. 'The response urges prompt action. If the deed is to be done, let us do it now. Capa might not return for several days. Bishop Ségdae has ridden to Imleach. Brehon Dathal is involved in the matter of Petrán and I am not sure that his advice . . .' He paused and shrugged. 'Let the rest of the council be told of our decision when they are available and they can question it when we all meet later.'

Fidelma said: 'But I want a word with the chieftains before they are released.'

'You want to speak with these Uí Fidgente?' Her brother raised his eyebrows in surprise.

'Do you have an objection?'

'Very well, Fidelma,' he replied. 'So be it. I shall send for the *giall-chométaide* to escort you. Unless you want me to come with you?' The *giall-chométaide* was the jailer in charge of the hostages. Fidelma replied in the negative, and Colgú turned to Gormán.

'I will want you to escort the chieftains to the northern road as soon as Fidelma has finished with them.'

The big warrior was looking thoughtfully at Fidelma. He suddenly frowned and turned to Colgú.

'To the northern road?'

'At least you can point them in the direction of their home,' the king explained patiently. 'We will not then have long to wait for a response.'

It was a while before the *giall-chométaide*, a wiry little man, with ferret features and a ready smile that Fidelma did not exactly trust, entered the room to receive his instructions from Colgú. When he was told that the three chieftains were to be released, he showed no sign of surprise but impassively acknowledged the order.

At the back of the palace complex was an area that was separated from the rest of the buildings by a high wall through which only someone with permission from the king or his tanist could enter. It was known by the ancient name Duma na nGiall – the mound of hostages. The old word *duma* once applied to a tumulus and then to a man-made mound often named Duma Dála for a place of assembly. Now, whether a mound of assembly or one of encampment, it was used in the context of a place where prisoners were held. On passing through the gates, preceded by the jailer, Fidelma found herself in a series of austere but well-appointed apartments.

The ferret-faced jailer chuckled at her expression as she looked round.

'This is where we keep the nobles taken prisoner in war who will not give their *gell* – their word of honour – to the king,' the jailer explained.

A *gellach* was one who took a pledge under law and by the Creator not to abuse any freedom he was given, as in the manner of a parole. Usually prisoners of war gave their pledge and were allowed the freedom of the clan area or even the kingdom. It had even been known for such prisoners to marry or be adopted by their captors and settle happily in the area. The fact that the Uí Fidgente chieftains preferred to retain their status as prisoners without freedom told Fidelma a lot about their characters.

She found them all together. They were seated in a chamber having finished their first meal of the day. The *giall-chométaide* announced her.

'The lady Fidelma of Cashel, daughter of Failbe Flann, sister to Colgú, king of Muman.'

The men hesitated and then one of them rose to his feet, followed somewhat reluctantly by his companions. They stared at her, their dislike mingled with curiosity.

Fidelma swept all three with a quick scrutiny. One was elderly with features she could only describe as cunning. A large nose and eyes close set, dark, speculative eyes which seemed to bore through her as if searching for a weakness. The lips were fleshy and the face carried a scar of battle, distorting one eyebrow. The other two were younger, swarthy and aggressive-looking – perhaps with a cast of arrogance in their features. One thing that they all held in common was the belligerence of their features as they greeted her.

'Who has not heard of Fidelma of Cashel,' the elderly man said slowly, 'who played such a distinctive role in the overthrow of our lord Eoganán?' His voice showed that her name was not pleasing to him.

'And you are?' Fidelma asked, seating herself and regarding him without expression.

'I am Cuirgí of Ciarraige. These are my cousins Cuán and Crond.'

'Sit down and we will talk,' Fidelma said, turning to the jailer and dismissing him. The Uí Fidgente glanced at one another in surprise.

'You do not fear to be left alone with the mortal enemies of your people?' sneered Cuirgí.

'Do I need to fear?' replied Fidelma.

They realised that they were still standing before her and Cuirgí promptly sat down, stretching arrogantly. He did not bother to reply to her question.

'And have you come to lecture us, Fidelma of Cashel?' he asked, still slightly sneering his words. 'And in what capacity do you come? As an Eóghanacht princess? As a religieuse? Or as a *dálaigh*?'

Fidelma folded her hands in her lap. 'I come as a mother.'

Cuán, one of the younger of the men, smiled bleakly.

'We have heard that you have decided to partner some foreigner and given birth to his brat.'

Fidelma's green eyes seemed to change into cold blue and her glance wiped the smile off the man's face.

'I am married to Eadulf of Seaxmund's Ham in the distant land beyond the seas which is called the land of the South Folk,' she said quietly. 'Our son is Alchú.'

'And what is your domestic arrangement to do with us, Fidelma of Cashel?' asked Cuirgí.

'Have you heard what has happened to my son?'

To her surprise the men looked blankly at her. Cuirgí said: 'We hear little talk in our palatial incarceration. What game is this that you are playing?'

Fidelma controlled her features.

'Are you saying no word has come to you, either by way of palace gossip or through other means, of what has taken place here during the last week?'

Cuirgí leant forward belligerently.

'You – an Eóghanacht – are now questioning the word of an Uí Fidgente? Say what it is you have come to say and then begone.'

'Very well. My son has been kidnapped. He is apparently being held by your supporters in exchange for your release.'

There was no faking the looks of astonishment on the faces of the men before her.

It was Cuirgí, who appeared to be their leader, who recovered first.

'You appear to be bringing us glad tidings, Fidelma of Cashel.'

'You will be released.'

The younger men let out gasps of pleasure.

'You will be released and allowed to ride north for your own lands. Once you have crossed the mountains your confederates have promised that they will release my son. You knew nothing of this plan?'

Cuirgí was smiling triumphantly and ignored the question.

'When do we depart from this place?'

'What guarantees do we have, do I have, that your confederates will keep their word?' demanded Fidelma.

'The word of the Uí Fidgente is as good as that of an Eóghanacht!' snapped the younger man, Cuán.

Fidelma snapped back: 'Then the value of the word of the Uí Fidgente has changed since your prince, Eoganán, swore an oath of service to my brother and within the year led the Uí Fidgente in an attempt to topple him from the throne of Muman. I am not here to argue the relative worth of the words of the Uí Fidgente and the Eóghanacht. I am here to find out whether the promise of your followers is good or not. It is my baby that is the pawn in this game.'

Cuirgí sat back and gazed at her thoughtfully, and then he shrugged.

'I have told you that we do not know these confederates. We did not have any knowledge of their plans. But it is good to hear that our defeat at Cnoc Áine has not utterly destroyed the manhood of the Uí Fidgente. If they have encompassed this means of having us released from the grey prison walls of Cashel, then my heart sings praises to them and I will say that whatever they do, I am for it.'

Fidelma's eyes narrowed into glowing points of ice.

'Very well. When you meet your deliverers, Cuirgí of Ciarraige, tell them this from me – they must keep their promise and Alchú must be delivered without harm into my arms. If they even contemplate not doing so, I swear, by all

I hold holy, to hunt them down. Each one of them, each one's son and each one's son's son, even to the last generation so not one of them shall have anyone to remember him.'

Her voice was quiet but so cold that her sincerity could not be questioned. Cuirgí was surprised by her vehemence.

'A religieuse, issuing curses?' He tried to put derision into his tone but failed.

'It is not the religieuse but the mother who issues the curse,' Fidelma replied softly. 'And lest you be in doubt, I am acquainted with the ancient ways as well as the new. I will have no compunction, no reservation at all, at pronouncing the *glam dicín*.'

Cuirgí's jaw dropped suddenly.

'But that is expressly forbidden by the New Faith.'

The three Uí Fidgente chieftains saw something in her eyes that caused an involuntary shiver to visit them.

'There any many things the New Faith disapproves of, Cuirgí,' she said softly. 'Disapproval does not cause them to evaporate into thin air nor does it stop their use. For a thousand years and even a thousand years before that, our druids knew the power of the *glam dicín* and passed it on, and who are we religious but the druids in new guise?'

The *glam dicín* was a potent incantation directed against a particular person or persons – a curse which was feared to the extent that it could put the recipients under a sense of shame powerful enough to result in sickness and death and even prevent their rebirth in the Otherworld. Those under the *glam dicín* were rejected by their families and all levels of society, and were doomed to remain outcasts without hope in this world or the next unless the curse was lifted. It was a curse that was ancient, ancient before time began.

'You could not do that,' Cuirgí muttered but his voice was not confident.

'You cannot know the pain of a mother whose child is threatened if you think I would refrain from any means to protect my baby,' replied Fidelma quietly.

Cuirgí examined her for a moment and then shrugged.

'When we meet our deliverers, I shall pass on your message.'

Fidelma stood up abruptly.

'Then gather what things you need to take. The jailer will take you to the gates shortly and you will be escorted to the northern road and set upon it.'

She left the chamber before they could stand or respond.

The ferret-faced jailer let her out of the Duma na nGiall back into the main complex of the palace. She went straight to her chamber and poured a beaker of *corma* and swallowed it in one draught. She felt weak and angry with herself, for she had not meant to go so far as to threaten anything so serious as the *glam dicín*. If that threat came to the ears of even Bishop Ségdae, who was a fair-minded and progressive member of the Faith, she could be excommunicated. It was a serious matter. Yet the primitive anger that welled within her as she thought of her baby had got the better of Fidelma's emotions. She could think of no other weapon to threaten the Uí Fidgente with.

She sat down on the bed and groaned aloud, holding her head in her hands.

'Oh, Eadulf! Where are you when I need your calm strength?' she whispered. She rocked to and fro on the edge of the bed for a few moments and then, with a sniff, she tried to draw herself together. What was he up to? Where had he gone?

She rose, hearing movement in the yard outside. Leaning from the window she looked down and saw horses being prepared. Colgú was even giving the chieftains mounts to allow them to make the journey back to their land at speed and in comfort.

She left her chamber and hurried along the corridor and down the stairs into the yard. She looked round for Gormán, who was to escort the Uí Fidgente chieftains. There seemed no sign of him but she spotted Caol leading a horse forward from the stables.

'Where is Gormán?' she asked curiously.

'Gone,' replied Caol laconically. It was clear that he was preparing his own mount for the escort of the chieftains.

'I thought he was going to escort the Uí Fidgente and put them on the northern road?'

Caol shrugged. 'All I know is that Gormán asked me to do this duty and said he had important matters that took him from Cashel.'

'Important matters?'

'He had his horse saddled.'

Caol mounted as the three Uí Fidgente were escorted forward. Fidelma hurried on to the gate where Finguine was waiting to watch the former hostages make their departure.

'Do you know what mission has sent Gormán from Cashel?' she asked without preamble.

Finguine looked at her blankly.

'No mission of mine, cousin, that's for sure. I thought he was escorting the chieftains.'

'Caol has been asked to undertake that task. He and the chieftains are leaving any moment.'

'Ah well, maybe it was some personal business that he had to deal with.' Finguine turned to one of the guards at the gates. 'Did Gormán tell you what business drew him from Cashel?'

The guard shook his head. 'No, lord Finguine. He rode past me a short time ago but said nothing.'

Fidelma was frowning.

'I don't suppose you happened to see what direction he took?' she asked on impulse.

'I watched him go down the hill then turn through the township. He took the west road.'

Fidelma suddenly felt a chill sensation. So Gormán had turned west, west along the road that Eadulf had said he was taking; west to the abbey of Colmán.

Chapter Twelve

❦

Eadulf had spent the night at a wayside inn a short way to the west of Cnoc Loinge. He had not really wanted to be beholden to the hospitality of Fiachrae the loquacious chieftain of the settlement and so he had skirted it and ridden on for a while. Aware of the oncoming dusk and a mist rolling down from the surrounding hills, he had started to wonder whether he had made the right decision when he saw the bobbing light in the distance, set by a crossroads. A moment later he had halted his horse under the lantern, which was swaying in the evening breeze whispering through the trees that towered on all sides. The sign said 'Bruden Slige Mudán'.

Eadulf never ceased to admire the concept of hospitality expressed in the five kingdoms by the establishment everywhere of public hostels for free lodging and entertainment of all who chose to claim them. Each clan appointed a public hostel manager or innkeeper called a *brugaid* whose duty was to keep an open house for travellers. The *brugaid* was allotted a tract of land and other allowances to defray the expenses of the inn. His office was held in high regard. Most public hostellers were of the rank of *bo-aire*, magistrate, and were empowered to give judgement on certain cases brought before them. In local terms, each was able to hold court in his course for the election of a chieftain of his clan. At least one *bruden* was maintained in its territory by each clan.

Not all inns were free, however. Ferloga's inn, like Aona's at Ara's Well, as Eadulf had discovered, was an independent inn at which guests had to pay.

Eadulf had spent a pleasant night in the hostel of Mudán's road, as it was called, at least so far as his physical wants were concerned. The food and drink were excellent and the bed very comfortable. The hosteller was friendly and answered Eadulf's questions as to the exact directions to the abbey of Colmán. There had been several travellers on the road recently, he said, but he could not recall anyone specifically during the period that Eadulf was concerned about. However, he did warn him that within a short distance the road would enter the country of the Uí Fidgente at its most southerly border. The hosteller had little respect for his neighbours and uttered some colourful curses which Eadulf was hard pressed to understand. His host several times expressed a desire that cats should eat the women of the Uí Fidgente, but the man had not been able to tell him the origin of such a curse.

Eadulf rode on. The day had turned out to be cold and there were one or two snow flurries from the greying sky but, thankfully, the snow had not lain and the flurries eventually ceased. In spite of the shortness of the day, Eadulf made good time. Although not an expert horseman, he seemed to hold his own when Fidelma was not there to criticise his efforts. The journey through the long stretches of forest which covered the broad plain that spread westward from Cnoc Loinge was without incident. It was an easy ride and there were no signs of hostility from the Uí Fidgente. On the contrary, the natives of the area, on the occasions when he encountered them, seemed as courteous as anyone else. It took some time to cross the broad tree-covered plain and now and then, when on a rise through the thickets of the trees, he could see mountains rising to the south which the road skirted across their foothills. A mist was hanging on the mountain tops when he rode through a pass between higher hills and came to a broad river.

Frustrated, he turned southward along its bank searching for a ford or a bridge. He had not gone far when he came across a woodcutter. The man instructed him as to the location of a ford and told him that the broad expanse of water was called Fial's River. Eadulf made the mistake of wondering aloud who Fial might be and the woodsman was nothing loath to tell him that she was the elder sister of Emer daughter of Forgall Manach. And when Eadulf made the further mistake of saying he did not know these personages, the man began to explain that the great hero of Ulaidh, Cúchulainn, had rejected Fial as his lover and turned to her young sister Emer. The lecture delayed him considerably. Darkness was already beginning to fall when he managed to find the ford across the river.

He sat hesitating for a moment, wondering if he should chance the crossing. But there was no shelter that he knew of on this side of the water and he could just make out a light in the gloom on the far side of the ford. One thing that Eadulf had learnt from Fidelma was that a horse was intelligent and left to its own devices would usually find a sure-footed crossing. He coaxed the animal forward into the dark waters, and sure enough the crossing was accomplished without mishap.

On the far side, Eadulf urged his mount in the direction of the light. He could just discern that he had joined a wide track, but with dusk now given way to darkness he could not make out what type of countryside he was riding through. All he knew was that he must be moving southward. He could see no stars nor moon. Heavy clouds hung low in the sky creating the blackness. Only the small light in the distance guided him.

After what seemed an eternity, and feeling that the track was beginning to ascend steeply, he arrived at the lantern that was the source of the light and knew that he had reached an inn. Thankfully, he slid from his horse and found a hitching rail lit by the lantern. He felt stiff and cold. He entered the inn and was immediately cosseted by the encompassing warmth of a roaring fire. Closing the door behind him, he stamped his feet to restore the circulation and glanced around. The inn was empty of guests, or so it seemed. Then a small, dark-featured and smiling woman appeared from another door. A tall, hook-nosed man with dark suspicious eyes followed her.

'Good evening, stranger. You are late on the road,' he said, without much warmth.

Eadulf took off his cloak and saw the couple exchange a glance as they perceived he was a religious.

'I am not sure of the road at all,' he confessed, moving unbidden closer to the fire. 'I have a horse outside,' he added.

The man nodded, frowning a little.

'I will attend to it, Brother. By your accent, I gather that you are a Saxon.'

'I am. I am journeying to the abbey of Colmán.'

The innkeeper shrugged. 'Of course. There is no other religious foundation near here. If you follow the road southwards through these mountains, and across the plain beyond, passing the mountain range that you will see to your right – that is, to the west – you will come upon the abbey. It stands at the head of a large inlet. It is an easy ride from here. If

206

you leave here after sunrise you will be there before midday.'

The innkeeper turned for the door while his wife offered food and drink. Eadulf stretched on a seat before the fire.

'What place is this?' he asked.

The woman continued to smile. It seemed her normal expression.

'We call this the Inn of the Hill of the Stone Forts.'

'Cnoc an gCaiseal?' repeated Eadulf. 'Has the name significance?'

The woman poured a beaker of *corma*.

'In the hills above us there are many ancient forts of stone that were used in the ancient times.'

'What are these mountains called?'

'Sléibhte Ghleann an Ridire.'

Eadulf frowned. 'Mountains of the Valley of the Warriors?' he repeated.

'In ancient times gods and warriors fought one another in these mountains,' she declared solemnly.

Eadulf decided not to pursue the matter.

'Do you have many travellers passing through here?'

'A fair number, Brother.'

'A week or so ago, would a herbalist with his wife and two babies in a wagon have passed this way?'

The door slammed as her husband returned. He was looking at Eadulf in suspicion.

'Why do you ask?' he demanded. There was a defensive tone in his voice.

Eadulf smiled easily. 'They passed through Cashel some days ago and I am interested in catching up.'

'As my wife says, many people pass through here and we cannot remember them all.'

There was little point in pursuing a conversation that was not welcome.

'No matter,' Eadulf said, dismissing the subject. 'I take it you have a bed for the night and are able to take care of my horse?'

'Your horse is already stabled and my son is giving the beast a rub down and will feed her. I have brought your saddle bag in, Brother.' He produced the bag and placed it beside Eadulf.

'Thank you, innkeeper. I will take another bowl of your wife's excellent stew and most certainly another beaker of *corma*.'

The man went to fetch the drink while his wife filled another dish with the stew and placed it before him. As she did so, bending down to set the plate on the table, she whispered: 'The people you seek did pass this way about a week ago. They told me that they planned to stay awhile at the abbey of Colmán so you might yet catch up with them there.' She grimaced apologetically. 'My husband is old-fashioned and thinks that a traveller's business is his own.'

The innkeeper came across with the *corma* and looked suspiciously at them.

'I was just complimenting your wife on this stew,' Eadulf assured him. 'I was trying to pry her secret from her.'

The innkeeper sniffed in disapproval as he put down the drink.

'You are kind to us, Brother. However, we would soon be out of business if we told passing strangers all our secrets.'

'Then I shall not trouble you further except for a bed after I have eaten,' replied Eadulf solemnly.

It was the waiting that irritated Fidelma. She could hear the voice of her old mentor, the Brehon Morann, intoning, 'The person who prevails is the person who is patient, Fidelma.' It had always been her major fault, if fault it were.

'Impatience,' she had once told the old judge, 'is a sign that we have not resigned ourselves to mere hope of a solution but to its pursuit. To say, let us wait and see what fate provides, is no virtue. I would rather be doing something than sitting in inactive expectation.' Brehon Morann had shaken his head sadly. 'Learn patience, Fidelma, when patience is needed. Be impetuous and restless when that is needed. Above all, learn to differentiate between the need for either, for it is said that those who do not understand when patience is a virtue have no wisdom.'

The morning after Eadulf's departure, Fidelma had risen with a thousand thoughts cascading through her mind. For the rest of the day, following the departure of the Uí Fidgente chieftains, she had wandered the palace, pacing nervously, unable to settle to anything. Nothing distracted her from the worries that flooded her mind. Even old Brother Conchobar had not returned and Brehon Dathal was growing impossible. She found herself moving irritably from one room to another, from one place to the next. Now, as she rose to face a new day, she realised she could not go through yet another period of inactive frustration.

She went to the chapel and was relieved that there was no one about. Taking a seat in a dark corner, she closed her eyes, feeling the silence encompassing her.

She tried to concentrate, to clear her mind, seeking refuge in the art of the *dercad*, the action of meditation by which countless generations of the ascetics of her people had achieved the state of *sitchán*, or peace, quelling extraneous thoughts and mental irritations. She tried to relax and calm the riot of thoughts that troubled her mind. Fidelma had been a regular practitioner of the ancient art in times of stress. Yet it was a practice which many leading religious in the churches of the five kingdoms were now denouncing. Even the Blessed

Patrick, a Briton who had been prominent in establishing the Faith here, had expressly forbidden some of the meditative forms of self-enlightenment. However, the *dercad*, while frowned upon, was not as yet proscribed.

It was no use. The one time when she needed patience, she could not engage the ancient techniques. She surprised herself, for she had thought herself an adept in the method.

She rose abruptly and left the chapel.

Almost without knowing it she found herself at the stables. There was no one about, and she uttered a prayer of thanks for it. She wanted to be alone. To face the fears that dwelt in her mind. She found her horse, her favourite black mare, and after a short time she was leading it out through the gates of the palace complex.

The guards were standing around awkwardly.

'Lady,' one saluted her, 'we have a duty to ask you not to go out alone. Not with the possibility of Uí Fidgente about.'

'And your duty is therefore done,' Fidelma replied curtly. 'Have no concern. I am only going out for a ride.'

Before the man could protest, she had mounted and was urging the horse down the slope from the gates. The township which had grown up around the ancient fortress of the Eóghanacht, the capital of their great kingdom of Muman, lay to the south of the limestone rocky hill on which the palace rose, towering nearly two hundred feet above the plain which surrounded it. Instead of making for the township, she turned along the track that led round the rock and northward across the plain. Once out of the shadow of the palace complex, she dug in her heels and gave her mount its head.

Fidelma had learnt to ride almost before she could walk. She loved the experience of being at one with such a powerful beast, rider and horse working together in unison, speeding across the plain. Leaning forward, close to the mare's neck, she cried words of encouragement as it thundered forward, and sensed the animal's enjoyment at the lack of restriction, the freedom of movement, being able to fly like the wind without constraint.

It was only when she felt the sweat on the beast's neck, and began to hear a slightly stertorous note enter its breathing, that she started to draw rein, to slow its pace and ease it to a trot, so that the sudden deceleration would not harm it. She finally reined it to a halt where the River Suir was joined by the Clodaigh, rushing down from the distant peak of Cnoc an Loig. She glanced up at the sun and realised it was well after noon and that her early morning ride had taken her many kilometres north of Cashel. Indeed, she realised to her surprise that she had come so far that, at this time of year, it would be dark by the time she had ridden back, and her horse was already tired from the exertion.

She sat undecided. Her brother kept a hunting lodge a few kilometres to the south-east at a vale called the Well of the Oak Grove, beside a little stream whose spring gave the spot its name. She could, at least, get a meal there before heading back to Cashel. The lodge was used as a hostel for those her brother chose to send there. There was no reason to ruin a good horse by riding it when it was so exhausted. She felt cheered by her decision.

She leant forward and patted the beast's neck reassuringly, and then turned its head in the direction of the woods that surrounded the hunting lodge.

The way was, at least, across flat ground, for the great plain that spread north of Cashel stretched almost undisturbed as far as the eye could see from the top of the great rock on which the Eóghanacht palace stood. She walked her horse carefully along the track, which she knew led to her destination, moving slightly eastward through the forest.

Now that she had slowed her pace, and her mind was not preoccupied with the thrill of the gallop, her thoughts turned again to Eadulf and she felt both guilt and anxiety. Guilt for her own attitude and anxiety about the matter of Bishop Petrán. And why had Gormán ridden to the west? She was sure that he had gone after Eadulf – but why? Did Gormán believe that Eadulf was guilty? Brehon Dathal had said he would send someone after Eadulf. Had he instructed Gormán to go? And there was Gormán's relationship with Della. He claimed that he had loved Sárait. But he appeared intimate with Della and Della was surely twice his age. She shook her head in confusion.

What it came down to in the end was her attitude to Eadulf. Why did she not take him into her confidence and discuss things with him as she had in the early days? Why did she find herself indulging in constant contention with him? She knew deep within her that she had many faults – she did not like to share, not even confidences; she liked to work things out on her own without discussion with others. It was not just Eadulf she did not confide in. She was too self-centred.

She did not like revealing her emotions. Showing passion had hurt her when she was a young student. That was what made her reticent with Eadulf, or so she told herself. There were moments when she felt warm and tender towards him. And then a word, a look, and she felt the bitter words tumbling out and his responses causing more bitter words until she felt such anger that she could hardly control herself. Was there something wrong with her? Or was it simply a wrong chemistry between them? Or was it something simple – as simple as Eadulf's being a foreigner? He wanted to return to his own land where he had status and she wanted to remain in her country where *she* had status and, moreover, where she could practise the occupation she loved most – the pursuit of the law. If there was to be some compromise, she could not make it. A trip to Rome, a trip to the Saxon kingdoms, had been enough for her. She could never live anywhere but Muman. This was her country, her life. There could be no concessions on her part, but would Eadulf ever compromise? He would surely see it as submission.

Could there be any future for them as man and wife?

It was the one time she felt that the ascetics were right. The religious should not marry but lead a life of celibacy. Once again she was starting thinking about the fact that the end of the trial marriage was approaching, when, under the law, without renewing their vows, she and Eadulf could claim incompatibility and go their separate ways.

It happened without warning and she momentarily cursed her lack of those senses that should have warned her.

Suddenly, two mounted warriors emerged on to the track, blocking the path before her. There was a sound behind her and glancing swiftly over her shoulder she saw a dozen or so more gathering on the path at her back. She did not need a close examination of the banner and arms they carried to realise they were Uí Fidgente.

She turned back to face their leader.

He was a tall, well-muscled man, with a shock of black hair, grey eyes and the livid white of a scar across his left cheek.

Her eyes widened in surprise.

'Conrí!'

Conrí, warlord of the Uí Fidgente, smiled complacently as he came forward.

When Eadulf awoke, the morning was bright but cold. A frost lay on the ground and only a few wispy clouds, high up, stood out against the soft blue of the sky, hardly moving at all. There was no wind to speak of. Eadulf set out early from the inn and crossed into the valley beyond. Within a few hours he began to smell the salt tang of the open sea. He could just see a strip of blue slightly to the south-west.

The road was easy and before long he spotted the grey buildings of an abbey complex standing where a river emptied into a bay. Around the abbey were several buildings, a small settlement which stretched on both sides of the river. To the north-west of these he saw foothills rising swiftly into tall and spectacular mountains.

He rode towards the complex. Before the abbey's walls was a broad green. His heart beat faster when he saw a covered wagon drawn up nearby, away from the buildings of the little settlement. Two horses were grazing nearby. There was a fire lit close to the wagon, and a man was stirring something in a small cauldron that hung on a tripod over it. Seated on the step of the wagon was a woman feeding a baby from her ample bosom. Under an awning Eadulf saw a table on which various herbs and plants were arrayed, and strips of dried plants were hanging from poles. It was clearly the stall of a herbalist. Scarcely daring to believe his luck at tracking down those he sought, Eadulf guided his horse towards the wagon and dismounted.

The man straightened from where he had been stirring the cauldron. He was of middle age, with thin, dark features. He smiled as he surveyed Eadulf's attire.

'God be with you, Brother.'

'Jesus, Mary and Joseph be your guides,' replied Eadulf solemnly. 'I am called Eadulf.'

He watched for any hint that the name might mean something to the man, but it did not appear to carry any significance. Instead, he was waved to a seat by the fire.

'Come, join us, for the day is chill, Brother Eadulf. I perceive that you are a Saxon. I am called Corb and that is my wife Corbnait. What manner of potion or balm do you seek, my friend?'

Eadulf regarded the herbalist for a moment. He glanced at the woman with the baby, who smiled in greeting to him. Then he decided not to prevaricate.

'In truth, Corb, I came in search of you and your wife. I have followed you from Cashel.'

The woman's smile changed into an anxious look and it seemed she held the baby more tightly to her breast.

'We have done nothing wrong,' she said at once. The man threw her what was clearly a warning glance.

'I did not say you had,' replied Eadulf mildly. 'Is there any reason why I should think so?'

'What do you want with us?' demanded the man called Corb, slightly belligerently. 'Have you followed us in search of cures?'

'You have come from Cashel.' Eadulf made it a statement.

'We are from the kingdom of Laigin. It is true that our route here lay through Cashel.'

'I see you have a fine, bouncing baby there.'

Corbnait blinked nervously.

'God was good to me,' she muttered. 'I am blessed with my son.'

Eadulf tried not to sound excited.

'So this is your only child?'

'It is. We call him Corbach.'

'Yet you have been seen travelling on the road with two babies.' Eadulf's voice was suddenly sharp.

The woman gave an audible gasp and her features went pale. Corb tried to sound defensive.

'Who says so?' he demanded.

215

Eadulf smiled up at him. 'Come, herbalist. Do you remember travelling through Cashel?'

Corb hesitated. 'We did not travel *through* Cashel.' He placed an accent on the word.

'By Cashel, round Cashel. Do not play semantics with me. Do you remember going into an inn for food – Ferloga's inn, just south of Cashel?'

The herbalist's lips thinned. 'If you check with the innkeeper's wife at that place, she will tell you that we only had one baby.'

'Exactly so.' Eadulf's voice was tight. 'That is what brought me all this way after you. You only had one baby when you were at Ferloga's inn. Yet witnesses along the road saw that your wife carried two babies. How did this miracle come about?' He sat back and stared interrogatively at the herbalist and then at his wife.

Corbnait was clearly confused.

'We cannot be accused of anything,' she suddenly said. 'The child was unwanted.'

Eadulf sighed deeply. He hid the smile of satisfaction.

'I think that you should start to explain,' he said softly. 'Where did you pick up this "unwanted" child?'

The man seemed about to protest but the woman shook her head.

'The Saxon brother has followed us from Cashel, husband. We must tell the truth.' She turned to Eadulf. 'My husband, Corb, is a herbalist and we are poor. We rely on what we sell by way of cures and potions. My husband was expelled from his clan several years ago, as was I. You see, we eloped. We were both married to others at the time but we could not help our love for one another. So our union was forbidden and our child born of this union is outcast. That is why we have taken to the roads, selling where we can without hope of settling down in one place.'

She paused. The herbalist was nodding in agreement with her account.

'Go on,' Eadulf said. 'What happened in Cashel?'

Corb took up the story.

'We wanted to stay at the inn for it was a cold night. Ferloga's inn, that is. But while the innkeeper's wife would have been happy to accommodate us in exchange for a medicine that I had given her, a salve for a lesion on her leg, the innkeeper was still hostile. He would have none of us. So we left the inn and drove our wagon further along the road towards Cashel. Night was upon us but we found a small track by a stream and turned along it, coming to a clearing. We decided to stay in our wagon for the night.'

'You lit no fire? Surely that is unusual?' Eadulf asked.

'Perhaps,' replied the man. 'But I was uneasy about attracting attention. Some people, like the innkeeper, dislike those who take to the roads. I did not even unharness the horses but threw a blanket over them as they stood in the shafts. I meant only to sleep for an hour or so and then move to the north-east so that we might avoid passing through Cashel. I wanted to avoid any hostility.

'It was well before midnight when I was awoken. It was a clear night and I could see from the position of the moon and stars that it was still fairly early. Something had disturbed me. A hound was howling nearby.'

His wife, Corbnait, nodded in agreement. 'The hound also awakened me. Then I heard someone shouting.'

'I thought someone might be in trouble,' continued Corb, 'and so I took my staff and, leaving my wife in the wagon with our young one, I decided to walk back along the track. I could hear no further noise from the hound or the shouting voice. But I was no more than a hundred and fifty metres from the wagon when I heard a sound to my right. I stopped. I know enough about babies to recognise the sound of a baby's cry, though, in honesty, this infant was not crying as such. It was more or less gurgling – the sort of noise babies make, not unhappy, not distressed. I peered round. There seemed to be no one about, for the moon was high and bright in spite of the time of year. I began to move forward and almost immediately I saw the light covering of a shawl.'

Eadulf was leaning forward now. 'And?' he pressed eagerly.

'There it was – an abandoned baby.'

'What makes you think it was abandoned?'

The herbalist laughed harshly. 'The baby was alone in the middle of a wood. There was no one else around. What was worse was that it was placed well away from the main road-way to Cashel, even well off the woodland path that I had turned my wagon down. Had I not been disturbed, the child would never have been discovered. It would have died of the chill or worse . . . for there are wolves and other animals wandering the woods.'

'So what did you do?'

'What could I do? I picked it up and took it back to my wife. It seemed well nourished and its clothing bore the signs of wealth. Why it had been abandoned, I do not know. It worried us. Clearly there were evil people about. So we decided to move on right away and continued along the path round Cashel, crossing northwards. At dawn we stopped and slept again.'

'And you say this happened before midnight? The sound of the hound, the shouting and the discovering of the baby?'

'It did.'

'It was a fine, healthy baby,' the woman added. 'No more than six months of age with fine strands of red hair across its forehead. He was wrapped in woollens that indicated wealth.'

The herbalist was suddenly firm.

'Now, Saxon, what is your interest in this?' he demanded. 'We have told you much but you have told us nothing. We will say no more until you have told us what you want with the child.'

Eadulf regarded them both gravely.

'The baby is Alchú, son of the lady Fidelma of Cashel. Its nurse was murdered close to where you say you were in your wagon. The child disappeared after her death. I have tracked it to you.'

The woman gave a little scream, and lifted a hand to her mouth to smother it. The herbalist blinked, his determination faltering.

'And . . . and what is this matter to you, Saxon?' he said hesitantly, still trying to sound defensive.

'I am Eadulf of Seaxmund's Ham. I am the child's father.'

There was a shocked silence. Then the woman started sobbing.

'We swear that we had no hand in this matter other than what we have told you,' she managed to utter between the choking sounds of her distress.

'It is as my wife says; the story we told you is true,' added her husband. 'We know of no murder.'

'Then I suggest you now produce my son.'

There was a silence.

'We cannot,' cried the woman.

Eadulf went cold.

'Cannot?' His voice grated.

'We no longer have the child,' said the herbalist in a flat tone.

*   *   *

Fidelma had frozen in her saddle as Conrí, war chief of the Uí Fidgente, approached her.

'We are well met again, Fidelma of Cashel. We were riding to Cashel when one of my men spotted you entering the woods and we thought that we would come to meet you. In truth, it was you I sought.'

Fidelma tried to still her pounding heart, recovering from her shock and forcing herself to appear nonchalant.

'What business have you at Cashel, Conrí? Or, indeed, with me?'

The warlord's face was serious. 'To put an end to a lie,' he replied sharply.

'A lie?'

'The other day your brother sent a *techtaire* to the land of the Uí Fidgente with a message that was posted at every wayside inn. It told my people that we must prove that we hold your child, a babe called Alchú, and show that he was safe and well, before you released three of the chieftains of the Uí Fidgente whom your brother has held as hostages since our defeat at Cnoc Áine.'

Fidelma controlled her expression as she met the warlord's gaze.

'My brother, Colgú of Cashel, did send such a message. Do you come in response to it?'

Conrí's eyes narrowed in anger. 'I do.'

Fidelma's mouth was dry. 'And will you return my child?'

'I will not, for the simple reason that we are not guilty of any kidnapping.'

'But . . .' Fidelma began in a surge of emotion, but the Uí Fidgente warlord held up a hand.

'Listen to me, Fidelma of Cashel. I had barely returned to my people when your herald arrived. No Uí Fidgente knows of this matter. You may think the worst of us, for we have long been in enmity, but we are not beasts that take children as hostages. As children are sacred to you, they are equally sacred and dear to us. I have made inquiries among the clans. No one, I repeat, not even those who have suffered in the recent war at your brother's hands, would use the innocence of a child to cause you suffering. I pledge this is the truth by the innocence of my own two sons.'

His voice was low but intense and Fidelma stared at him, trying to comprehend what he was saying.

'But the demand for the release of the Uí Fidgente chieftains to secure the release of my son . . .? After our herald's demand for proof, we were sent Alchú's little shoe. The three chieftains were released and given horses to ride back to their country. We now await the release of my child.'

Conrí was frowning.

'You have already released the three chieftains? You mean Cuirgí, Cuán and Crond are free?'

'They were released yesterday at midday,' Fidelma confirmed.

The warlord was shaking his head as if in disbelief.

'There is something very wrong here, Fidelma. Let me be honest with you. Some of my people have been led into wars against the Eóghanacht that have brought death and destruction on them. Eoganán and his family, who plotted to overthrow your brother and seize the kingdom, have led them. Eoganán paid with his life for that ambition at Cnoc Áine, as did many of his clan. Indeed, for every member of his family that died, one hundred of the Uí Fidgente died by their folly. We are a decimated people, Fidelma. The three chieftains whom your brother captured at Cnoc Áine were fanatical followers of their kinsman, Eoganán. Cuirgí, Cuán and Crond are no loss to my people.'

Fidelma was frowning, following his words and trying to understand what he was saying.

'What do you mean, Conrí? You are warlord of the Uí Fidgente.'

Conrí smiled quickly. 'I was elected to lead the remnants of my people after our great defeat. But cannot a warlord have wisdom? Is it not a saying of the ancients that peace is better than even an easy war?'

'Go on. I still do not follow you.'

'We do not want the release of the old chieftains. We do not want them to start stirring enmities and hatreds. We want a time of peace. We want to build up our crops, our herds and flocks and start to live again. For those reasons, it was not the Uí Fidgente who kidnapped your son to secure the release of those who have led us so badly in the past.'

Fidelma was silent for a while.

'Perhaps there are some among you who have taken this means to secure their release without your knowing?'

Conrí shook his head. 'While I can accept that as a possibility, I do not think it is probable. I came here, with a few of my men, at the request of my people to tell you the truth, and to offer our help. If it is shown that anyone of the Uí Fidgente are involved in such a plot, then we will punish them.'

Fidelma exhaled sharply.

'The punishment is enacted by law,' she said automatically, 'and prescribed by law.'

Conrí frowned, glancing up through the trees as if searching for something.

'It must be well after noon,' he muttered. 'Do you know what route the chieftains took?'

Fidelma hesitated a moment or two before replying.

'They were supposed to ride north from Cashel to join

222

the Suir. I think that they were crossing at the ford by what is called the High Hill, Ard Mael, and heading through the mountains of Slieve Felim.'

'Once through those mountains, they will be within an easy ride of our country,' the Uí Fidgente war chief muttered reflectively. 'I think they'll have skirted the mountains to the south and headed up through the valley of the Bilboa.' He suddenly snapped his fingers. 'If my men and I took the route across the shoulder of Cnoc an Loig and along the road past Cnoc an Báinsí, we could intercept them at Crois na Rae before dawn tomorrow.'

Fidelma looked at him in surprise. 'Then what?'

'If there is some evil plan and they and their accomplices are responsible for the kidnapping of your child, we shall discover it. Whatever befalls, if your child has not been returned by tomorrow, you will know that whoever was responsible did not intend to keep their word. There was to be no exchange.'

Fidelma's face became a taut mask hiding her anguish. What Conrí was saying was correct.

Conrí reached forward a hand and touched her lightly on the arm.

'I am sorry for your troubles, Fidelma of Cashel. Believe me. But this matter must be resolved. When we find the chieftains and those responsible, where may we find you? At Cashel?'

Fidelma was about to confirm it but then changed her mind. 'It is not exactly safe for Uí Fidgente warriors to be seen near Cashel at the moment. My horse is exhausted and I was going to seek rest at my brother's hunting lodge, which is not far from here, at a place called the Well of the Oak Grove. It is only a few miles in that direction.' She indicated with a wave of her hand. 'The keeper of the lodge has a son whom I can send back to Cashel with a message that I am resting there for two nights. When you have discovered your quarry you will find me there. But the day after tomorrow I must start back for Cashel.'

Conrí gave her a quick smile of reassurance.

'With God's grace, lady, we will find you at the Well of the Oak Grove before tomorrow evening.'

He raised his hand in salute to her and then urged his horse along the path towards the west, followed by his companions.

She felt a curious pang of isolation after they had departed. Now her thoughts were even uneasier than before as she turned the events over in her mind. There were only two possibilities. Conrí was lying to her. Or, if he spoke the truth, there was some plot among the Uí Fidgente to overturn Conrí and the new chiefly house by reinstating the three hostage chiefs, which would mean a return to war between the Uí Fidgente and the Eóghanacht. Her lips thinned as she contemplated the prospect. She sat thinking for a few moments. Then she sighed when she realised that she could come to no conclusions. She eased her tired horse into motion.

Eadulf was aghast as he regarded the herbalist and his wife.

'You no longer have Alchú? What did you do with him?'

The woman looked nervously at her husband.

'Speak!' demanded Eadulf in a tone of anger as he rose from his seat, almost in a threatening manner.

'Had we known what you have just told us, we would have come directly to the palace of Cashel, believe me,' muttered the herbalist.

'Speak!' demanded Eadulf again. 'What happened?'

The man raised a shoulder as if to indicate helplessness.

'Believe me, Brother, we thought the baby had been abandoned. We sold the child to a worthy protector.'

'Sold . . .?'

Eadulf sat back down abruptly. The shock took all animation from him. He looked wordlessly from one to the other of them.

'You see, we had our son,' went on the herbalist. 'Our own flesh and blood. We thought that we had been the instrument of saving the other baby for a reason . . . to help us, as it is a hard life travelling from settlement to settlement in the hope of selling cures and potions and salves. When we fell in with the lord of . . . you see, it was a means of obtaining some money so that we might settle in one place.'

'The lord of where?' Eadulf spoke coldly. 'What lord?'

'During our journey here we camped further up the valley near those mountains you see to the north. Well, we were encamped within the shadow of them. We were sitting before our fire and my wife had fed our son and the baby with red hair. We were resting when we heard a bell sound . . .'

'A bell?'

'Into the light of our lantern and campfire came a grey-cloaked figure. He was clad from poll to foot in his robes so that we could see nothing of him, but he rang a bell to announce his approach. Behind him, in the shadows, stood a tall warrior, dark and menacing. The figure seated himself on a log on the far side of the fire and asked for a drink and food.'

The herbalist paused a moment before continuing.

'I gave him food and like any passing traveller he asked who we were, where we had come from and about the two babies. Now I reflect, he asked us if we had come from Cashel.'

'Did you tell him of the story of finding Alchú?' demanded Eadulf.

'I saw no harm in that, although I did not know the baby was called Alchú, nor anything other than what I told you.'

'The man said that we had been good servants of the Faith by performing the act of charity in saving the baby,' the woman said hastily.

'What then?'

'He suggested that if we wished to disburden ourselves of the child, he was lord of the territory and he would take the child to his church to be brought up in comfort and in the service of the Christ.'

'And you agreed?' gasped Eadulf.

'The man placed three silver *screpall*s on the log to compensate us for our trouble.'

'We thought that we were doing the right thing,' added the woman.

'So you handed the baby to a total stranger . . .?'

'Not exactly. He told us that he was a lord of that area. Lord of the passes, he said. A warrior attended him, the one who waited silently in the shadows. On our agreement, the tall warrior picked up the child. I am unsure whether this lord had the use of both arms. He certainly had a dragging foot. I found it curious that he carried a hand bell.'

'What name did you say this man gave you?' Eadulf asked.

'We do not know. The warrior simply called him lord.'

'You know no more? What direction did he ride in? Those mountains are tall and spread widely.' There was now an anguished helplessness in Eadulf's voice.

'There can be few lords in this region of his description,' offered the herbalist. 'For myself, I have no wish to know who he was, nor do I wish to encounter him again.'

'Why so?'

'In truth, Brother, I felt there was something evil about him.'

'Yet you handed an innocent baby to his care?' Eadulf was aghast.

The herbalist and his wife exchanged another look. The woman grimaced towards Eadulf.

'We did not know for certain that there was anything ill about the man. It was a feeling. The warrior treated him with respect and the man promised to take the child to a sanctuary. We thought that we were doing it for the best. For the sake of the baby. We thought that he had been abandoned.'

Eadulf gestured to the walls of the abbey behind them.

'I am told that this is the biggest abbey in these parts. The only sanctuary. Have you spoken with the steward? Perhaps this lord brought the child here?'

Again the herbalist looked at his wife.

'Corbnait insisted that I make an inquiry. She became worried later. No, the man did not bring the child here. But those mountain passes are the gateway to a great peninsula which is the land of the Corco Duibhne. Perhaps the man took the child there.'

Eadulf suppressed a deep sigh. Then a thought occurred to him, and he stood up with an impatient gesture. His next step was clear. Perhaps the steward at the abbey of Colmán would be able to identify the leper who was a lord in this territory. Eadulf stared sternly at the herbalist and his wife.

'Let me tell both of you this fact. I have no authority in this kingdom, although I am husband to the lady Fidelma of Cashel. You may know that she is a *dálaigh* and highly respected by the Brehons of the five kingdoms of Éireann. We speak not only of my child but of hers, and she is sister to Colgú who rules this kingdom. Whereas I accept your story and believe that you acted in all innocence, it may be that you also acted in greed. You say you thought you were giving the baby up for its own future well-being. I shall say

227

this to you . . . it is a matter that still has to be argued before the Brehons of Cashel. I cannot compel you to do anything. But if you were to ask my advice as to what you should do now, I would tell you this. Return to Cashel, ask for Fidelma, and if she is not there ask for Colgú the king himself and tell either one your story. Tell them neither lies nor embellishments. The truth must be told. You will not lose by telling that truth.'

The herbalist looked nervous. 'Will you be there to speak for us?'

'God willing, I shall be,' answered Eadulf determinedly. 'But first I have to find this leper lord and retrieve my son.'

He turned, and taking his horse he walked slowly to the gates of the abbey.

It was but a few moments before he was admitted to the chambers of the *rechtaire*, the steward of the abbey. He was a pleasant man, anxious to help once he knew Eadulf's status and influence.

'We are loyal to the primacy of Imleach, Brother. Bishop Ségdae, who holds the *pallium* of the Blessed Ailbe, patron of all Muman, is our guide. How can we help you?'

'Evil has befallen Cashel,' Eadulf began, but to his surprise the steward nodded.

'News travels quickly, and bad news travels faster than a plague. We have known of the disappearance of the lady Fidelma's child – your child,' he hastened to add, 'for over a week.'

'Did the herbalist and his wife bring you this news?' asked Eadulf thoughtfully.

The steward made a negative gesture.

'Some messenger from Cnoc Loinge brought it, I think. But you refer to the travelling herbalist and his wife who camp outside the abbey? They seem to take no interest in anything, although the man recently asked me if a baby had been brought into the safe care of this abbey, at which I told him no.'

'Did he mention anything else?'

The steward was looking thoughtful.

'Do you suspect them of abducting the child?' he asked. 'Why, I . . .'

Eadulf shook his head. 'They were the engine by which the child was brought into this part of the country, Brother Steward,' he said, 'but it was, I believe, by accident. I do not think that they knew the identity of the child.'

The steward was shaking his head. 'Well, they have kept their own counsel, whatever it is.'

'The herbalist did not ask about a lord in this land, one who called himself "lord of the passes" and seemed physically impaired to some extent?'

The reaction was surprising. The steward reared back in his seat and actually crossed himself.

'You obviously know this person,' Eadulf observed sharply.

The steward swallowed hard.

'There is only one who fits that description. Uaman the Leper. Uaman, son to Eoganán. Eoganán was the prince of the Uí Fidgente who was slain at Cnoc Áine a few years ago.'

Eadulf groaned aloud.

Chapter Thirteen

❧

The Well of the Oak Grove was a pleasant little vale that Fidelma had known from childhood. It was a spot where she and her best friend Liadin, who had grown up to be her *anam chara*, used to play. Fidelma felt a quick pang of anguish as she thought about her soul friend. If only Liadin had not tried to involve her in her murderous plot against her husband and child. The law was supposed to be about rehabilitation of the wrongdoer, about forgiveness, for was it not said that everyone has some means of redemption in them? Yet Fidelma could find no way of forgiving her friend for her betrayal of her.

Some centuries before in the five kingdoms, when somebody was thought beyond redemption and refused to work for the welfare of the clan to restore his honour and pay the necessary reparation to his victims, then, reluctantly, the old Brehons were left with no other course than to put the wrongdoer in a boat, give him water and food for one day, and tow him out of sight of land, casting him adrift to be left to the mercy of the wind and the waves.

The old storytellers told that such a wrongdoer had been named MacCuill, an unrepentant thief and murderer who dwelt in the land of Ulaidh. The Brehons had duly cast him adrift. But the wind and tide washed him ashore on an island sacred to the old ocean god, Mannánan Mac Lir. Having survived, he saw the error of his ways, converted to the New Faith and ended his days as a bishop on the island. And the people of the island had since called him 'blessed' and prayed for his spiritual intercession in their affairs. In Fidelma's eyes, the story was told merely to demonstrate that even in those who were perceived as the worst of criminals there existed a hope of rehabilitation even when they were thought to be beyond redemption.

She returned her mind to her surroundings.

It was an idyllic spot. A thick oak wood spread itself through the vale and a tiny stream sang its way through the centre of the trees and crossed a clearing. To one side of this clearing rose a log-built hunting lodge, constructed for the kings of Muman so long ago that it was not recorded exactly when. The woods around were the habitation of good game, of wild deer, boar, pigs and other animals, and the stream carried trout as well as princely salmon.

It had become a tradition for the kings of Muman to place a *brugaid*, a lodge keeper, there for such times as the king and his friends decided to use its facilities. In winter no one would be using the place, but Fidelma knew that Duach, the lodge keeper, would be there anyway. She could send his son Tulcha to Cashel with her message. She crossed the stream and halted before the lodge.

'Duach! Tulcha!' she called.

The buildings looked deserted. No one came out.

Could Duach have deserted the hostel? One heard many things in Cashel and she knew that Duach had been here just a few months ago. She had known him since she was a little girl; surely someone would have mentioned if Duach had left her brother's service. She slid from her horse and stared up at the shuttered windows and closed doors.

She called again.

This time she caught the soft sound of the blowing of a horse in the stable building, impatiently expelling air through its nostrils. Her own mount caught the sound, twitching its ears and stamping a forefoot.

Frowning, she walked to the stable door and tried it. It swung open and she glanced inside. There were four horses there and she noticed, curiously, that three of them looked strangely familiar to her.

'Duach? Tulcha?' she called again.

One of the horses appeared skittish, a little nervous. It moved backward, kicking up the straw. As the stalks fell away, she caught sight of a human foot and lower leg. Eyes wide, she moved forward.

There was a body concealed in the horse's stall.

She bent to examine it, and her hand came automatically up to her mouth in a gesture of astonishment and horror. The body of Duach lay there, his eyes wide and staring in death. Someone had cut his throat. Then she saw the second body. It was young Tulcha. She gasped, suddenly remembering why the three horses were familiar.

At the stable door the shadowy forms of three men stood, blocking the entrance.

'Well, now,' came the sneering tones of Cuirgí of Ciarraige, who had recently been the hostage of her brother. 'Well, now, it seems, my friends, that we have our own hostage now. We have a female whelp of the Eóganacht delivered into our hands. Now, indeed, have the fates been kind to us. Now, indeed, can we make our way safely back to our homeland so that we can pursue our path of vengeance against Cashel.'

*   *   *

232

Eadulf was peering at the shocked features of the steward of the abbey of Colmán.

'Where might I find this Uaman the Leper?' he repeated.

'What business do you have with that spawn of Satan?' whispered the steward. 'I would rather give you directions to the gates of Hell itself.' Then he gasped again. His eyes widened as he guessed the reason for Eadulf's inquiry. 'You cannot mean that the herbalist has given the baby into Uaman's custody?'

'I do mean that. And now I must retrieve my son. So where can I find this man? He seems well known to you.'

The steward's face was pale.

'He is well known to most people in this area, Brother Eadulf. Even in the days when Eoganán ruled the Uí Fidgente, Uaman, his son, was lord of the passes of Sliabh Mis. He was not yet a leper in those times but a warrior son of Eoganán, who, as you may know, was a ruthless tyrant who tried to overthrow the Eóghanacht of Cashel. Eoganán met his end at Cnoc Áine . . .'

'I know.' Eadulf nodded impatiently. 'But what of Uaman?'

'He was Eoganán's youngest son and adviser and withal even worse than the despot himself. He made life unbearable among the abbeys and religious houses of the kingdom. He would come against us with warriors and demand tribute from us. But God punishes debauchery.'

Eadulf frowned momentarily.

'Ah, you mean the leprosy?'

'Just so. Even before Cnoc Áine, he had contracted the scourge. Yet he somehow retained his power, and, until the Uí Fidgente were overthrown, he remained lord of the passes here. After the defeat of his ill-fated father, he retreated into this corner of the kingdom where he still remains a tyrant and is followed by a small band of warriors. Thank God, not so many as he could command before. Now he has hardly six to guard him – poor, demented souls. They follow him because their souls and flesh are rotten as well as his. His soul is evil and decayed on the inside as his skin is decayed on the outside.'

'Does he still raid the area?'

'We are too strong for him now. But with only a few warriors he still controls the roads along the great peninsula to the north of us where the lands of the Corco Duibhne lie. The peninsula stretches nearly fifty kilometres into the wild western sea, mountainous and bleak, with tracks so narrow that he can force travellers to pay tribute to him for the privilege of passing through.'

'Surely the chieftain of the Corco Duibhne can challenge him? If he has only six men to guard him, then he can surely be overthrown with ease.'

'Not so easily, my friend. Uaman dwells in an impregnable fortress. It is a great stone stronghold whose walls rise like a round tower on a small island and is built in such a way that even great armies could not gain entry.'

'Tell me more about this place.'

'The Tower of Uaman?'

'Where does it lie?'

'Not far from here, Brother Saxon. You take the track north of our abbey, round the great bay you see before you, passing before the mountain range you find rising to your right. The road runs westwards and is straight and narrow. At high tide, on your left, you will see an island. It has no name but Inse.' Eadulf knew this was the word signifying an island. 'It is cut off at high tide but at low tide it becomes almost a peninsula, for the sand dunes stretch all the way to the grassy knoll on which the Tower of Uaman rises.' The steward suddenly grasped Eadulf by the sleeve, tugging at it. 'Come to our watchtower, Brother Saxon. Then you may see the Tower of Uaman in the distance.'

'It is so near?' asked Eadulf in surprise and some relief.

'We may see it across the bay,' replied the steward, 'but it is a lengthy ride round the coast.'

Sure enough, from the top of the abbey's tower, Eadulf could see across the grey waters of the bay what seemed to be a black tower in the distance, just visible against the darkness of the mountains behind. From that angle, it looked as if the tower was set on the mainland on the northern side of the bay.

'It doesn't look so impregnable to me,' he remarked.

The steward shook his head quickly.

'Do not be misled, Brother Saxon. The stretch of sand that links it to the mainland appears to be firm enough when the tide is out but there are *beo-gainneamh* to beware of. An entire army can disappear.'

Eadulf did not understand and said so. 'Do you mean reeds?'

The steward shook his head. '*Gainneamh*,' he repeated.

'Ah, sand,' Eadulf corrected himself, now recognising the word. 'But *beo-gainneamh*? That means living sand?'

The steward nodded. It took Eadulf a few moments to realise this must mean quicksand. He shivered slightly.

'Even with the tide out, the tower is dangerous to approach. It is a natural fortification. And when the tide comes in, it comes in so rapidly that treacherous waters can cover the entire sandy link from mainland to island in moments. Indeed, the chief of the Corco Duibhne tried to assault the tower once and lost a dozen men in one attempt.'

'Well, I don't intend to attack him, only seek him out to demand information leading to the return of my child.'

The steward raised his eyebrows.

'You do not demand from Uaman. You avoid him. You say that you want to ask him to return your child? In that case, get Colgú to raise a massive army – that is the only way that Uaman will return anything that is not his.'

Eadulf shook his head. 'I appreciate your warning, Brother Steward. But perhaps he does not realise whose child it is? Why would such a man want to keep a baby? And sometimes a single man speaking with the tongue of logic can encompass what an army will fail to do.'

'I will pray for you, Brother Saxon, as I have prayed for the other brothers of the Faith who have preceded you.'

Eadulf raised his brows in surprise.

'Other brothers of the Faith? What do you mean?'

'A week or so ago there was a brother from Ulaidh travelling with a strange brother from some distant land. I think he was a Greek. They came here asking, as you have done, for Uaman. I told them where they could find him and they went on their way. They promised to return within a few days. They have not.'

Eadulf rubbed his temple. 'I have heard of these brothers upon the road. What would they want with Uaman?'

The steward shrugged expressively. 'The stranger did not speak our language well but his companion told me that he was a healer from the east who had been visiting our shores and specialised in the scourge under which Uaman suffered. A message had been sent to him to bring this healer to Uaman and a reward was promised should he alleviate his suffering.'

'Perhaps they left by some other route?'

The steward smiled sadly. 'They promised to come back this way for the stranger promised to instruct us in the ways of the Faith as practised in his country. I fear for them, truly I do.'

Eadulf thought for a moment and then smiled without humour.

'Well, it seems that I shall have to be careful with this lord of the passes, this Uaman. I thank you for the information, Brother Steward. As a good friend of mine would say – *praemonitus, praemunitus*.'

'Forewarned is forearmed,' translated the steward, still serious. 'Be so, Brother Saxon. Be forearmed and above all be careful.'

Fidelma stared at the three armed Uí Fidgente, disguising her growing horror as she realised that they must have killed the hostel keeper and his son. She tried to maintain a commanding demeanour.

'What are you doing here?' she demanded. 'You are supposed to be heading for your own country so that your friends will release my son.'

Cuirgí gave a short bark of laughter. 'You don't think we fell for that trick, do you?'

Fidelma was genuinely puzzled. 'Trick?'

'Ransom notes and the like. A ruse, that's all, to get us out of your brother's protection so that some of his supporters can waylay us on the road and slaughter us. That would solve a problem for your brother, wouldn't it?'

Fidelma's eyes widened at the fanciful suspicion.

'But . . . but it is no trick. My son really has—'

Cuirgí cut her short.

'Then what are you doing following us? We purposely took the path away from the Suir and the road to the land of the Uí Fidgente so that we would avoid ambush. We thought that we would conceal ourselves here until it was safe . . . but you must have been following us closely. Who else is with you?'

237

Fidelma was shaking her head in bewilderment.

'I came here by accident. I did not follow you,' she protested. 'And the ransom demand is genuine. If you do not go back to the land of the Uí Fidgente, if you do not cross the border, your confederates will kill my son.'

'Do you think we are fools? If this exchange – us for your son – were genuine then we would have been informed. It would have been easy enough to smuggle messages into our prison. This is some trick to lure us away and kill us.'

'But, I tell you . . .' She paused. Was there some other force at work here? Conrí had said he had been sent on behalf of the Uí Fidgente to disclaim all knowledge of the kidnap. She fell silent as she tried to reason out the possibilities.

Cuirgí glanced at his companions with triumph on his features.

'I thought so. Her silence admits the plot. Crond, scout the paths here and see if there is any sign of anyone accompanying this Eóghanacht bitch. Cuán, help me tie her up. At least her presence will provide us with a safe passage to our own country.'

'But—' Fidelma began to protest.

Cuirgí suddenly reached forward and slapped her across the cheek. It was a hard, stinging slap and made her dizzy.

'Silence! No more words from you!'

Fidelma stumbled back and, before she could recover her senses, Cuán had expertly tied her hands with cord. He began to drag her out of the stable and towards the main building.

'Put her above stairs for the time being and make sure she is secured,' came Cuirgí's instruction.

'What if she has companions?' demanded Cuán as he half pushed, half dragged her across the main room of the lodge.

'Then they will be given a choice. To withdraw and let us proceed in safety, or else be given her body.' Cuirgí laughed without humour. 'I think even Colgú will make the right choice.'

'Listen to me. You are making a mistake . . .' Fidelma cried once more but a rough hand was clamped across her mouth. Cuirgí looked on with an approving sneer.

'Make sure she is secured and cannot cry out to alarm her friends.'

She was dragged up the staircase to the top floor of the lodge and pushed into one of the sleeping chambers. She could not help feeling it a strange irony that she was put into the very room where she had slept as a child and felt so safe and protected. Now she was a trussed and helpless prisoner.

Cuán was no amateur when it came to ensuring that his victim was bound so as to be completely helpless. He secured her hands behind her and trussed her at the ankles. Then he tore a strip of linen from the cover of the *adart*, or pillow, and tied it firmly across her open mouth.

'Comfortable?' he grinned viciously, and then he pushed her helplessly back on the *lepad*, the wooden bed. She gazed back coldly.

What if Cuirgí and Conrí were both wrong? What if there was some new Uí Fidgente plot to have the chieftains released and neither knew about it? What if her son was going to be sacrificed to their mistrust and lack of knowledge?

She waited until Cuán went downstairs and then she gently tried the bonds. They were very tight. She exhaled in frustration. She felt no movement against them in her feet or wrists. Resigned, she lay back on the bed and closed her eyes, her mind racing as she tried to think of some plan of escape.

Some time later, she was not sure how long, there was a shout from downstairs.

'Crond is coming back!'

She heard the sound of a horse arriving outside the building, and identified Cuirgí's voice.

'What news?'

'No sign of anyone,' replied another voice that she supposed was Crond's. 'I went up to the hill yonder, where you can see the approaches through the woods into this vale. There is no movement. I would take my oath that the woman was on her own.'

'It is not your oath that will be taken if she is not,' sneered Cuirgí.

'So I would not be making a mistake when my own life is what I should lose,' snapped back the other, apparently not intimidated. 'We are secure here for the moment. Perhaps the woman spoke the truth, that she was alone and stumbled on us by accident.'

'More fool her if she did,' a third voice joined in. That was Cuán, the man who had tied her up.

'Very well.' Cuirgí's assertive tone showed that he was in command. 'If we accept that the Eóghanacht bitch came here by accident, then the fates have been on our side. All we have to do is wait awhile and then continue our journey back to our homeland.'

'But what if some of our supporters have truly kidnapped this woman's child?' It was Crond who voiced Fidelma's thought.

Cuirgí laughed. 'You believe that tale? We would have known about it.'

'I grant you that you have put up a good argument against it, but . . . but what if it were true?'

'What if it is so? There will be one less Eóghanacht in Muman and we are still free.'

'If it is true, Cuirgí, and the child dies, by tomorrow all the warriors of Cashel will be searching for us to

240

redden their weapons with our blood,' Crond argued.

'And does that frighten you?' sneered Cuirgí. 'We have fought the Eóghanacht before.'

'I am an Uí Fidgente of the same proud lineage as you, Cuirgí!' Crond replied angrily. 'I am prepared to shed my blood in our cause. But I am not prepared to shed it wastefully. If I am to be hunted down and killed, I do not wish to be remembered as someone who died in reparation for a child's death. Do you?'

'That is a point, Cuirgí.' This time it was Cuán. 'While we wait here, the entire countryside might be roused against us and our journey home become impossible.'

There came a chuckle from the older chieftain.

'You forget that we have the sister of Colgú to secure us a safe passage. Anyway, I have told you before . . . if there was such a plot to free us we have friends who could have bribed someone to get a message to us. That old jailer used to take bribes to pass messages in and out and even bring us luxuries. We would have heard something. This is an Eóghanacht plot. I am sure of it.'

Listening to them, Fidelma groaned inwardly. She had to admit that Cuirgí was making a good point. If someone had gone to all those pains to construct the kidnapping then it would have been an obvious move to inform those involved about what was happening. But if this was not a means of releasing the Uí Fidgente, what was it? Who was behind it?

The three men had removed themselves to the room below and their voices had become muffled. Fidelma was aware that darkness was spreading across the window. The hour was growing late.

She had intended to send poor Tulcha to Cashel to inform them where she was staying. When she did not show up, and no message from her was received, she wondered what her brother would do. Might he guess that she could be at the hunting lodge? She tried to move into a more comfortable position. The gag was making her feel sick.

She must have dozed in her exhausted state for the next thing she knew the room was lit with an oil lamp. Someone was removing her gag. She coughed and gasped for breath. Powerful hands reached under her arms and pulled her into a sitting position with her back against the wooden head-board of the *tolg*, or bedstead.

Crond was sitting on the edge of the bed looking down at her with a humourless smile on his lips.

'What time is it?' she finally gasped when she had cleared her throat.

Crond chuckled in amusement.

'Not very late, lady. It is well before midnight. I thought that you might like some food. We wouldn't want you getting weak. There is a long journey to the land of the Uí Fidgente before us.'

Fidelma blinked rapidly. 'When are you starting out?'

Crond shrugged. 'Whenever Cuirgí thinks it safe enough. Perhaps tomorrow; perhaps the next day.'

Fidelma glanced at the bowl of stew and drinking mug that he had placed on the side table.

'If I am to remain bound, you will have to help me eat and drink. If not, then release my hands so that I can feed myself,' she said.

Again Crond chuckled.

'Oh, I shall feed you, lady. I have little else to do and we would not want you to get any foolish ideas, would we?'

'The cords are cutting into my flesh,' she protested.

'I don't doubt it,' Crond assured her. 'Cuán has a remark-able talent for binding people so that they stay bound.' He

242

reached forward and took the mug, raising it against her lips. 'I presume you would like to drink first?'

The drink was mead. It was slightly sour but her throat was dry and irritated after the hours that the linen gag had been tied across her mouth. She sipped eagerly.

When he put down the mug she licked her lips and regarded the Uí Fidgente with speculation, wondering if she could persuade him to help her.

'I think you are more intelligent than your companions, Crond,' she began.

The man raised his eyebrows in mock surprise.

'I think so too, lady. But what makes you say so?'

'I heard you arguing with Cuirgí. Truly, my brother made no plot to lure you out of Cashel to kill you. My nurse Sárait was murdered and my child stolen. We did receive a ransom note demanding your release and saying that once you crossed the border then my son would be returned.'

Crond's face was impassive. 'Why should I believe you?'

'Because I think you know that I am speaking the truth. Whoever holds my son is going to kill him if you do not do as they have instructed. They will believe that my brother still holds you prisoners. I do not want my son to die.'

Crond shrugged. He leant to the side and took the bowl of stew and a spoon. He held out a spoonful.

'Cuirgí makes a good point, lady, that if this were genuine, we would have been informed. I can confess to you that we have had messages smuggled in to us before now. It was simple. Your old jailer is easy enough to bribe.'

'And he will be brought to account for that,' Fidelma snapped in irritation, forgetting her position for a moment.

Crond smiled in admiration.

'You have spirit, lady, I'll say that.'

'My son's life is at stake.'

243

'Our lives are at stake,' he pointed out bluntly. 'We are not going to squander them without cause.'

There was a movement at the door. It was Cuirgí. He stood leaning against the door jamb with folded arms.

'You seem to be getting along well with the prisoner, Crond,' he observed coldly.

Crond looked up in amusement.

'Is it forbidden to talk as I feed our prisoner, then?'

'That depends on the subject of conversation,' returned Cuirgí. 'It is well known that this woman has a tongue of silver. She is a *dálaigh* and is it not said that a good lawyer will turn black into white and white into black? Pay no attention to her words, Crond.'

Crond grimaced cynically. 'After two years in an Eóghanacht prison, I am not liable to be beguiled by the words of this woman, Cuirgí. However, the sooner we reach our homeland, the better I shall like it.'

Cuirgí nodded thoughtfully, his sharp eyes on Fidelma.

'Finish feeding her and come down. We need to discuss our route. Cuán knows the lands north of here and has an idea.'

'When do we leave here? Tomorrow?'

Cuirgí shook his head. 'If we wait a further day, they will think we have already reached—' He cut himself short as he glanced at Fidelma. 'We will talk about this below. Be quick finishing here.'

He stayed for a second or two more and then disappeared. Fidelma heard him going down the stairs. Crond returned to feeding her. He winked at her and whispered softly: 'So, lady, it looks as if you'll be spending a little more time in this cramped condition.'

'My hands and feet are numb, Crond,' she said. 'Can't you loosen these bindings? If I am left like this, I won't be able to walk or ride when the time comes. Surely you can see that I can't escape?'

Crond hesitated, and then he realised that she was right. He put down the bowl and bent to her ankles to release the bindings a fraction, so that they were still secure but no longer biting tightly into her flesh. She could feel the blood flowing into her limbs and an almost painful sensation as if pins and needles were coursing through her flesh. Crond turned her over and repeated the exercise with her wrists. She sighed as her cramped arms began to tingle. Setting her back against the bed frame, he finished feeding her the stew and then gave her another drink. Then he stood up.

He looked at the discarded gag for a moment and she saw his glance.

'Who am I going to call out to?' she asked sarcastically.

He hesitated and then smiled.

'It will be a long night, lady. Sleep well.'

Then he was gone. She lay on the bed for a long time listening to the noise of their voices drifting up from below before she started to wriggle her bonds. Although Crond had loosened them, they were still secure. Try as she might, she could make no headway in making them slack enough to enable her to manipulate her hands out of them. It was some time before she gave up and found herself dozing again. The next thing she knew, the grey light of dawn was seeping into the room.

Chapter Fourteen

Eadulf had left his horse tethered loosely to a bush in a copse. He had spent the night at the abbey and at first light had taken the track in the direction of the Tower of Uaman. He had found the crossing point without trouble and decided to leave his horse hidden among the trees and approach on foot. He tethered his horse loosely as he had learnt from Fidelma. If he did not return before the beast started to fret, he was confident that the animal would be able to pull free, but he knew the horse was a patient steed and would only leave the spot when hunger or danger threatened.

Eadulf hid himself behind the trees that overhung the shoreline and gazed out across the bay towards the little island on which the tower rose. Cold restless waters separated it from him. It seemed incredible that there was any prospect of the grey sea's receding and leaving a land passage for one to walk across to the island. On the island, a grey stone tower rose, its circular walls both dark and menacing. Around them was a high wall encompassing the central tower itself. Eadulf tried to estimate its circumference but gave up, although he guessed the diameter to be a hundred feet across. It was large.

The entire atmosphere of the place was one of threatening evil.

Eadulf tried to tell himself that it was merely his imagination. Both the herbalist and his wife as well as the steward at the abbey of Colmán had conjured an image in his mind. Had he not talked to the steward, he asked himself what his attitude might be. In the first place, he thought that he might have ridden directly to the abode of Uaman and stated why he had come there. That the baby had been taken by mistake and was not the property of the travelling herbalist to sell. That was still his ultimate intention. The more he thought about it, the more firmly he believed that this was the only course of action he could adopt. He was being foolish in giving way to the sinister thoughts implanted by others. He had even imagined, after he had left the abbey, that someone was following him. He could not shake off the feeling and kept looking round for some unseen danger. He gave a sigh of exasperation.

He had ridden over the mountain road, keeping away from any habitation. The way seemed bleak and covered with threatening shadows. At the point where he had moved down to the wooded shore of the bay, he had seen a number of dwellings further up the mountain, and presumed it was a settlement. A settlement so near to this stronghold probably indicated that the inhabitants were supporters of the chieftain or that he could rely on them for service. He bypassed the settlement and led his horse deep within the forest to avoid it.

Now he would wait until the tide was on the ebb and then walk to the island as there seemed no other way to cross. He would simply tell this Uaman the reason for his visit. Logic would prevail. The chieftain was surely not as evil as people made out. No one was that evil. He felt satisfied at this reasoning and felt a sudden surge of excitement. He would bring Alchú home to Cashel. Perhaps, then, he would be able to reason with Fidelma about how to tackle the problems of their life together. He felt a peace spreading within himself at the thought. There would be an answer; a resolution to the problems that had beset them during this last year.

It was an hour or so later when he noticed that the tide had begun to turn. He presumed that it would not be at its flood again until early evening. He stood up and walked down to the shore to examine the sandy link that was being uncovered with a critical eye. The dunes that stood revealed by the receding sea looked firm enough. He saw crabs scuttling over them, following the waters, and here and there a sea bass or pollock caught unawares in a pool, splashing in search of its vanishing environment. He looked from the shore across to the dark island. The sandy way seemed quite wide, but if there were soft patches of quicksand, as the steward had warned him, then it would be best to keep to the highest point of the dunes.

Eadulf hesitated a moment, then left the shore and started to hunt through the trees and bushes until he found what he was looking for. A low branch of a yew tree had been snapped off. He took out his knife and began to strip the bough of its excess growth and twigs until he had a passable staff of six feet in length. Then he returned to the sandy crossing and stepped gingerly forward. The sand sank a little under his feet and water ran from where it was compacted but his foot only went in to a depth of the first joint of his little finger. The sand seemed firm enough. Ever cautious, however, Eadulf thrust the staff in front of him before each forward step.

It was some time before he had traversed the sand link to the island, and when he looked back he was somewhat reassured by the line of his footsteps stretching away behind him. It would be easier on the return trip, he told himself.

He made his way up some stone-flagged steps to the grassy knoll of the island and across to the forbidding grey stone wall surrounding the round tower. It was deceptively large, as big as many abbeys he had seen. There was no sign of life. Great wooden double doors rose to a height of ten feet but stood shut, the thick oak reinforced by iron. A series of windows was placed round the stone walls at a height just above that of the gates. They appeared to ring the structure.

Eadulf stood for a moment examining the building. There seemed to be no bell for visitors to ring such as usually hung outside an abbey. He walked across to the doors and was about to raise his makeshift staff to bang on them to announce his presence when they suddenly swung inwards. Just inside stood a man draped from poll to toe in grey robes, a cowl hiding his head and features.

'Welcome, Brother. Welcome to the Tower of Uaman.' He spoke in a high-pitched, almost sing-song voice.

Eadulf started at the unexpected apparition. The movement was not lost on the grey-robed figure. A thin chuckle issued from behind the robes.

'Do not be surprised, Brother. I have watched your approach from the shore yonder. I have noticed that you have been cautious in your progress across the dunes.'

'I was told that the crossing was treacherous.'

'Yet you have chanced the perils of the sea and sands. There must be some great purpose in your coming here.'

'I have come to see Uaman . . . Uaman who is chieftain of this place.'

The figure raised an unusually white hand, almost claw-like in its skeletal structure, and beckoned him to enter.

'I am Uaman, lord of the passes of Sliabh Mis,' came the

voice. 'Welcome to my fortress. Come freely in, and may your stay be as pleasing to you as it will doubtless be to me.'

Eadulf hesitated but a moment, trying to rid himself of the fears that rose again in his mind. Then he entered between the heavy oak gates. He was aware of the great wooden structures swinging shut behind him and he glanced round. They seemed to be closing of themselves and then he realised that the mechanism must be in the thick walls. Iron bolts had appeared from apertures in the stone and snaked directly across to secure the doors in place.

Uaman gave his thin mirthless chuckle as he saw Eadulf start nervously.

'There are many beyond my walls who wish me harm, my friend.' He paused. 'You bear the tonsure of Rome, not of the brethren of the Church of the Five Kingdoms. What name is given to you?'

'I am Eadulf of Seaxmund's Ham.'

There was a silence. Eadulf knew the name meant something to the bent figure. A long, low hiss of breath came from the folds of the cowl and Eadulf had a feeling that cold eyes were staring at him.

'Eadulf!' The voice was suddenly soft and almost threatening in its sibilance. 'Of course. Eadulf of Seaxmund's Ham. You are husband to an Eóghanacht of Cashel.'

'I come here with peaceful intent,' Eadulf explained hurriedly. 'I am not interested in your quarrels with Colgú of Cashel.'

'If you come with peaceful intent, Brother Eadulf, then you are received with peaceful intent. Yet you seem, by implication, to know that I am of the Uí Fidgente. What do you seek from me?'

'I have come west on a quest in which I think you are unwittingly involved.'

The figure chuckled again. 'Unwittingly involved?' he said, as if this was some matter of amusement. 'Now that is an interesting phrase. Then, Brother Eadulf of Seaxmund's Ham, come to my chamber where we will talk of this quest and its purpose.'

Eadulf made to move forward towards the figure but the white skeleton hand suddenly drew a small bell out of the folds of the robe and shook it with a warning note.

'*Salach! Salach!* Unclean!' came the high-pitched voice. Eadulf halted abruptly. 'A little distance, if you please, Brother Saxon.' Uaman's voice was more controlled now. 'I suffer the affliction which decays and putrefies the flesh.'

'A leper?' gasped Eadulf. Until this moment he had not fully appreciated the enormity of the curse under which Uaman suffered.

The bent figure gave his spine-tingling laugh. Then the leper hobbled forward and Eadulf noticed that he was dragging one foot as if it were useless. Uaman entered a tiny doorway in the wall and climbed a stone-flagged stairway which rose to another level which, Eadulf judged, was at the height of the windows he had seen. The stairway gave on to a walkway that was, indeed, on a level with the windows. Eadulf suddenly realised that there were several dark-clad warriors lurking in the shadows by the windows, obviously keeping a watch. He glimpsed ugly and scarred faces, one man lacking an eye.

The leper began to lead him confidently round the walkway, following the great walls.

'Do not bother to count the windows, Brother Saxon. There are twenty-seven, that I might look out on the star clusters from which knowledge and power are gained.'

Eadulf frowned. He recalled that this was some pagan doctrine and wasn't sure what it implied.

'Are you not of the Faith?' he queried.

The leper chuckled. 'Is there only one Faith then, my friend? Faith in the singular means that we must disbelieve all other faiths.'

'Faith is Truth,' countered Eadulf.

'Ah, when reality and hope are dead, then Faith is born. Believe in all things, Brother Saxon, and you will not be disappointed.'

Uaman halted before a door and opened it, beckoning Eadulf to follow him through a corridor into an inner chamber. It was a well-appointed apartment, the walls lined with polished red yew and hung with tapestries of sumptuous colours. The leper pointed to a couch.

'Be seated, Brother Saxon, and tell me the purpose of your coming hither. What is this quest of which you speak?'

Uaman seated himself across the room by the open hearth in which logs glowed hotly. He kept his cowl on and Eadulf could not discern his features. All he was aware of was the dead white flesh of the single claw-like hand that remained uncovered.

'I have come in search of my child, Uaman. I am here in search of Alchú.'

'Why do you think I can help in that matter?'

Eadulf leant forward. 'The baby was left at Cashel in the charge of a nurse named Sárait. She was murdered. She, or some other, had left the baby by itself and a wandering herbalist and his wife found the child and thought it was abandoned. They took it and brought it with them to this country where you fell in with them. And you paid them money for it. I accept that you could not know the identity of the child and your desire was simply to help it. Where is Alchú? I will recompense you for what you paid the herbalist but I must take the infant back to Cashel.'

The leper's shoulders moved. At first Eadulf thought the man was having a fit, but then a high-pitched sound came from beneath the cowl. He realised that Uaman was laughing again.

'So far as you are concerned, Eadulf of Seaxmund's Ham, the baby is dead,' Uaman finally said in a flat tone. 'Dead to you and your Eóghanacht whore.'

Eadulf made to rise from his seat but became aware of sharp, cold steel at his neck. One of Uaman's guards must have entered unseen behind him and now stood with knife or sword at his throat.

'What does this mean?' he asked through clenched teeth. He realised that the question was a silly one for now his suspicions were tumbling into certainties. Deep within him he knew that he had been taking a naive approach to Uaman the Leper.

'It means that the fates have been kind to me, Eadulf of Seaxmund's Ham. In the last two years you and your Eóghanacht whore have gained quite a reputation in the five kingdoms. It was a bad day when you were taken from that Gaulish ship and made to work in the mines of Beara as our prisoner, before our intended rising against Colgú.'

Eadulf cursed himself for a fool. So Uaman had known about even that.

'Have we met before?' he asked.

'You knew Torcán of the Uí Fidgente.'

'He tried to kill me but he was slain by Adnár, the local chieftain, who was loyal to Cashel.'

'Torcán was my brother,' Uaman replied icily.

Eadulf blinked rapidly. He should have worked that out before. Torcán was also a son of Eoganán.

'Exactly,' Uaman said as he watched the realisation dawn in the other's eyes. 'A son of Eoganán who was slaughtered at Cnoc Áine by Colgú.'

Eadulf grimaced. 'If truth is to be served, it was Eoganán, your father, who raised his clan in rebellion against Colgú and met the fate of one who unlawfully rebels. He who draws his sword against a prince might as well throw away the scabbard.'

'A Saxon axiom?' sneered Uaman.

'How could you have known the baby with the herbalist and his wife was the child of Fidelma and me? Even I was not entirely sure they had taken him until I followed them to the abbey of Colmán.'

'News travels swiftly in this land. The Uí Fidgente still have loyal followers. Minds that are obviously quicker than that of the great *dálaigh*, your wife. Someone close to Cashel told one of my messengers that the child was missing and likely to be in the possession of the itinerant herbalist and his wife.'

Eadulf look amazed. 'A traitor? In Cashel?'

'No, my Saxon friend, not a traitor but an Uí Fidgente patriot,' Uaman said in satisfaction.

'Where is my son?' Eadulf demanded harshly.

'You mean the son of the Eóghanacht whore who thwarted our plan to take power? Well, he will never grow up to become an Eóghanacht prince.'

Eadulf started forward but the sharp steel at his throat kept him in the chair.

'You swine! You have killed him!' he cried helplessly.

Again Uaman chuckled in his high-pitched tone.

'Oh no, my poor friend. He is not killed. Far worse.'

Eadulf looked at him in bewilderment and the leper chuckled again.

'He will live, be sure. But he will grow up never knowing his father and mother, or the bloodline to which he is heir. He will, if he lives so long, become a simple shepherd, herding his sheep on the mountains haunted by the daughter of Dáire Donn. And your son will bear a name that will symbolise my revenge against his people. That is his fate. Already he is being nursed by peasant folk who do not know his origin but think of him as my gift to fill the void in their pointless, childless lives.'

'You decaying son of a . . .' Eadulf snarled and this time the blade drew blood from his neck.

Uaman seemed even more amused.

'Indeed, I am *iobaid*, one who decays and rots because of this evil sickness that has been laid on me. It was not always so. I was my father's right hand, his adviser, while my brother Torcán was his tanist, his heir apparent. Many blows were struck at Cnoc Áine. I fled the field after my father's death and soon the sores began to show on my body. I realised then that the ancients had cursed me for my failure and that only cold vengeance would remove the curse.'

Eadulf gasped. 'That's nonsense!'

'First, Cashel will suffer. I will make it suffer. The suffering has already begun.'

'So you arranged the murder of Sárait?'

To Eadulf's surprise Uaman shook his head.

'That was purely fortuitous. I heard the news of her death and the disappearance of Fidelma's child. But it was purely by chance that one who was sympathetic worked out that the herbalist and his wife had found the child. He sent me a message to that effect and I could not believe my luck. Nor could I believe their greed. They did not even question me when I offered money for the baby. Ah, human frailty. That is my faith, my Saxon friend. I believe in the frailty of human beings.'

Eadulf sat glowering at him.

'You are telling me that you had no hand in Sárait's

murder? That you did not intend this . . .' he made an encompassing gesture with his hand, 'from the start?'

The leper's shoulders were moving again in the indication of his mirth.

'You may dwell on all these things in the time that is left to you, Brother Eadulf of Seaxmund's Ham,' he said. 'And that, alas, is not very long. You have until high tide and then your earthly span is ended.'

The white claw-like hand gestured in dismissal and Eadulf found powerful fingers gripping his arms. He was dragged from his seat and realised that there were two men behind him. It was useless to struggle. He was dragged through a side door and along the dark grey corridors, his mind whirling as he tried to understand what he had been told. Once more he found himself being half pushed, half dragged round the circular walkway in the outer wall of the rounded fortress. Then he was propelled through another straight corridor that seemed to jut out at an angle from the rest into a square structure that stood apart from the tower. He was being pushed down a circular flight of stone steps to where a flagstone was raised. A wooden ladder led into the dark aperture. One of the warriors pushed him towards it.

'Get down there, Saxon,' he said, indicating the aperture with his sword.

A smell of sea and dankness rose up. It reminded Eadulf of the odour of sea caves.

'You might as well kill me here,' he told them defiantly. 'I can see nothing below that ladder, so if you want me to go into some subterranean cave full of water I should tell you that I prefer the sword to drowning.'

The guard laughed uproariously.

'Didn't Uaman tell you that you had until the high tide?

He wants you to dwell on your fate for a while. So we must not kill you yet, my friend.'

His companion grinned eagerly.

'I'll tell you what . . . we'll give you this oil lamp. The light should last you until the high tide. Don't worry. See how solicitous we are about your needs?' He shoved a lighted oil lamp at Eadulf.

'Now get down the ladder or we might reconsider,' snapped the guard with the drawn sword.

Eadulf hesitated only a moment. At least he had light and he had freedom of movement. While he had those, he had hope. The alternative was dying from a sword wound at once.

He turned and began to climb down the ladder.

As he descended he found that he was moving into a chamber whose sandy floor was four metres from the stone aperture in the ceiling above. It was square in shape, some two metres by two. It was chill and had an overpowering smell of sea about it. Yet he saw that the walls were not those of a cave but made of great blocks of stone even though the floor consisted of wet sand.

He stepped off the bottom rung, holding his lamp high, and peered round.

Almost at once, the ladder was pulled swiftly up.

Laughter came from above him.

'Until high tide, Saxon,' called one of the men. 'Pleasant dreams!'

The stone thudded into place above him and he was alone.

Fidelma later regarded it as the longest and worst day of her life. She lay on the bed in the upper room of the hunting lodge, securely bound. Now and again one of the Uí Fidgente would look in and check on her, ensuring that the bonds still held. During the day, Crond came in twice to

257

give her food and drink, this time freeing her hands but standing over her in case she made any attempt to escape. The most embarrassing moment came when she was forced to answer nature's demands. Crond rigged a blanket round a pail in a corner and actually stood in the room during the proceedings. For the most part, she was alone with her thoughts.

She had tried once again to seek refuge in the *dercad*, the act of meditation, but a strange thing happened. She began to question even that as a means of escape from the present. She realised that she must start facing reality – perhaps for the first time. She was confronting a question that she had always tried to avoid. She could admit that now, as she lay alone and unable to act. She began to think about her relationship with Eadulf and her child – their child. Suddenly, tears were streaming from her eyes, although she did not yet understand why she had begun to feel this uncontrollable emotion. She had always been in control before. She had, perhaps, been too controlled.

Once she had tried to take refuge in the idea that, after her youthful experience with the warrior Cian, it was a rational decision not to get too close to any man. It was a good excuse, an easy excuse. But it was merely an excuse. Had she been deceiving herself? What did she want? She had wanted independence, to rely on no one except herself. She wanted to be a good *dálaigh*. She had an exceptional ability for solving puzzles, and that was her motivation in life. If it was taken away from her she could not fulfil her ambition and live contentedly. She realised that she regretted that her cousin, Abbot Laisran of Durrow, had persuaded her to enter the religious. It was true that most people in the professions in the five kingdoms had done so, because it was the custom. But her time at Kildare had not been happy, for institutions implied restriction of freedom and what Fidelma desired most of all was personal freedom.

That was it! Freedom. That was the heart of the problem between her and Eadulf. She was unwilling to be restricted. She did not want to be bound. Suddenly, she could hear the sage tones of her mentor, the Brehon Morann, asking: 'What is it that binds you, Fidelma?' Indeed, what bonds was she afraid of? She had left Kildare, and her ability and qualification as a lawyer had caused her to be sought after. If she admitted it, she was also lucky. She had been born a daughter of Failbe Flann, king of Muman, and her brother was now king. She did not want for security. So, once again, she found herself asking what bound her.

Her mind returned to Eadulf and little Alchú.

Was she living just for herself? Her favourite philosopher was Publilius Syrus. He had been brought to Rome as a slave from Antioch and finally given his freedom. He had written many moral maxims that Fidelma had learned by heart, for in Brehon Morann's law school he had often been referred to. His maxim *iudex damnatur ubi nocens absolvitur* – when the guilty man is let off, the judge stands condemned – was almost a slogan. Fidelma had objected to the interpretation and as a youthful student argued that it was better a guilty man be let off than an innocent man be condemned. She claimed that the pressure placed on judges by this maxim would encourage them to condemn a man simply out of fear lest they themselves should be condemned.

She was vehemently supportive of the Irish system in which the law wisely accepted *cach brithemoin a báegul* – to every judge his error. But a judge had to give a pledge of five ounces of silver in support of his judgement, and pay a fine if they left a case undecided. All judgements could be appealed and judges had to pay compensation if they were found to be false.

She had let her mind wander. She caught herself with a frown. What had she been thinking about? Publilius Syrus? Was she living just for herself? That was it. That was what she had been asking herself. Publilius Syrus had said that they who live only for themselves are truly dead to others. She shivered slightly.

Why was she pushing Eadulf and little Alchú away? That was what she had been doing. She groaned inwardly. Eadulf was not creating the bonds which held her. She was. Her ideal of life was in her mind and the impediment to the ideal was there also. It was not external; it was within her.

Eadulf! She suddenly realised that he had been so patient, accepting her faults and acknowledging her abilities. What had made her long for his company after she had left him in Rome? What had brought her in haste from the Shrine of St James, sailing back to the five kingdoms when she heard that he had been charged with murder? She was not in love with him but something infinitely more real – she loved him and needed his companionship, wisdom and support. She had been looking for an *anam chara*, a soul friend, and she suddenly realised that there had been no need to look. What a fool she had been.

Where was Eadulf now? And little Alchú?

She groaned again. Tears were still welling in her eyes when merciful sleep overcame her again.

Holding the oil lamp high, Eadulf peered around his prison.

The sand beneath his feet was wet and a few strands of seaweed lay discarded on it, along with some broken shells. A movement in a corner caught his eye. It was a crab cowering in the shadows. A cold chill caught Eadulf as he continued his examination. The stone walls were dark with water stains and a tiny green moss clung to the blocks. The water-line stretched almost up to the ceiling. He turned to exam-ine the base of the walls. There were three apertures in one of them, but they were tiny – a man's head might be placed in them but there was no way anyone could crawl through. As he peered into these holes, he became aware of a strange sighing sound. He bent to listen. It did not take him long to realise that he was listening to the sighing of the sea some way beyond the apertures. Peering along the tiny tunnels, he thought he could see some reflected light.

He swallowed hard.

Beyond the small tunnels was the restless, brooding sea. That's what Uaman meant! High tide! At high tide the sea would come rushing in through these holes and into this prison chamber. There was no escape. He would be drowned, for there was no way out.

Eadulf became aware of a new noise: a muffled sound. It seemed to come from high above him. It sounded like a knocking. Masonry began to fall into the confined space from a point high in one corner. Concerned, Eadulf moved to the opposite corner. Was there some new torture in store for him? A heavy block of stone suddenly plummeted down on to the sandy floor with a thud.

A faint light showed above him, not the light of a lamp but a dull white glow. Something moved in the aperture. It was someone's head and shoulders.

'*Kairongnothi!*' came a cry of triumph.

Eadulf stood still, peering upwards. There was a scrab-bling as the head and shoulders emerged a little further through the aperture.

'*Dos moi pou sto kai ten gen kineso!*' grunted a male voice in satisfaction.

Eadulf recognised the phrase from Archimedes. Give me a place to stand and I will move the earth! The voice was speaking in Greek.

'Stay there!' he cried out. 'Don't come any further or you'll fall!'

He realised he was calling out in his own tongue. Then, trying to summon up his knowledge but realising it was confined to the Greek of the sacred texts, he tried again, but by this time the person above him had seen the danger as the oil lamp Eadulf held illuminated the four-metre drop into the cell below. There came a stream of Greek that Eadulf could only presume was the owner of the voice expressing his disappointment in voluble terms. Then there was a pause.

'Do you speak this language?' came the voice at length.

'I have only few words. Do you speak the language of the Éireannach?'

'No.'

There was another pause. The man above must have been examining Eadulf in the gloomy light of the oil lamp.

'I see that you wear a Roman tonsure. What of the Latin language?' asked the voice in that language.

'I speak it well enough,' Eadulf replied, feeling relief.

'Are you a prisoner too?'

Eadulf caught the emphasis of the word 'too'.

'So you are a prisoner? Indeed, I am a prisoner of Uaman, and if I am not mistaken, I am a prisoner not long destined for this world. I have been put in this place to die.'

'How so?' demanded the voice.

'I was told that I had until high tide. From the look of this cell, I believe that when high tide comes, it floods up to roof level. The walls are damp and thick with moss and seaweed.'

The voice muttered something in Greek that he took to be an expression of surprise. Then the man spoke again.

'I thought that by removing a few stone blocks in my cell, I would be tunnelling out to a place from where I might escape.'

'You were escaping from your cell, then?'

'I was.'

'And where is your cell?'

'Just behind me. The floor of my cell is just above what appears to be the level of this roof.'

'Where is the light behind you coming from?'

'Ah, I have a small barred window that looks out on the sea.'

'Are you sure that you are above the sea level?'

'I have watched the tides,' came the response. 'At high tide, I am just above sea level. Certainly the stone walls and floor of the cell that I am in keep out the waters.'

Eadulf felt a sudden surge of hope.

'Then if I could somehow climb up to you and into your cell, I would avoid being trapped and drowned down here.'

'You would be merely exchanging one cell for another. I have been trying to escape these last few days. I thought I had when I forced a way through into your cell.'

'Well, better your cell than mine.' Eadulf smiled in the gloom. 'At least, from what you say, I won't drown there.'

He peered up, trying to figure out distances by the light of his lamp. If the aperture was four metres from the floor, as he estimated, then it might as well be a million. The stone was too wet to climb and clammy with seaweed and lichen. There was no hope of even attempting to scale it. It would be far too slippery.

'Perhaps when the water starts to flood in, I might be able to rise up with it,' he suggested.

'Dangerous, my friend,' warned the voice above him. 'Wait.'

Eadulf was about to rejoin that he would not be going anywhere, but the head and shoulders had disappeared.

An interminable time passed. He heard strange sounds, a tearing noise. Then the head and shoulders appeared again.

'Stand by!'

Something came snaking down. It was a series of strips of torn linen knotted together. It came to just above his head.

'Can you reach the end, my friend?'

'If I put down my lamp and jump.'

'In that case, do so. I think it will be strong enough. I have tied the end to the wooden cot here so I think it should hold.'

Eadulf put down the lamp. At his second jump his hands closed over the end of the strip and for a moment he swayed, crashing into the side of the cell and grazing himself on the stone blocks. He hung for a moment and then, slowly, he began to haul himself up hand over hand. The man above encouraged him and it did not seem very long until his head drew level with the aperture high in the wall. It was not large, but big enough to thrust his head and shoulders through.

His companion had started to back through the space before him. Eadulf realised that the mouth of the aperture gave on to a small tunnel-like hole which stretched upwards at an angle for a little more than a metre. The man backed upwards and out of the hole while Eadulf managed the difficult task of heaving himself over the edge into the inclining tunnel. A few moments later he was through and lying on the stone-flagged floor of his new-found companion's cell, recovering from his exertion.

After a few moments he glanced round. His rescuer was

hauling in the makeshift 'rope' which had been tied to a wooden *imda*, a bed frame. In fact, this was the only piece of furniture in a stone-walled, stone-floored cell. There was a thick wooden door at one end and in one wall a small barred window which, when he later examined the view, looked out on to the seaward side of the island.

Eadulf turned to his companion and grinned.

'At least I am given a respite from a watery grave.'

The man facing him was older than he was. He was tall, and fairly muscular, with black hair that receded from his forehead and an abundant beard. He had sallow, olive skin, and his brows and eyes were almost as black as his hair, which he wore without a tonsure. He met Eadulf's grin with an equally humorous expression and shrugged.

'A respite only, my friend. That is, unless we can make a new tunnel and find a means of escape.'

Eadulf went to look at the hole his fellow prisoner had made. A large block had been lifted to one side immediately under the bed, which disguised it from anyone making a quick examination from the doorway. The man shrugged.

'I saw the stone was loose and prised it away. Then I saw the tunnel beyond. Well, not tunnel exactly. You saw that it was scarcely a metre long. I think it must have been an air vent when they first constructed it. However, I had hoped it would lead into another room or give me some means of egress. I little dreamt that I would be entering a cell far worse than mine. Had you not been there, I might have attempted to climb down, broken my leg or worse and then wound up drowning myself.'

Eadulf gave an affirmative nod. 'You have my thanks for your intervention, for what my thanks are worth. It seems that they may not be worth much. Once our captors discover they have not drowned me, they will come here. But my thanks for this moment of respite.' He reached out a hand. The dark man took it. His grip was warm and firm. 'My name is Eadulf of Seaxmund's Ham.'

The man raised his eyebrows a fraction. 'A Saxon?'

'From the land of the South Folk?' Eadulf nodded.

'Truly, my friend, you are far from home.' His companion smiled.

'I would say that you must be even farther from home,' Eadulf pointed out with an answering grin.

The man responded with a chuckle.

'Forgive me, my friend. I am called Basil Nestorios.'

'A Greek?'

'A healer, but from Jundi-Shapur.'

Eadulf shook his head. 'I do not know of that land.'

'Ah, it is a city, my friend, in the kingdom of Persia. The hospital and college of Jundi-Shapur hold first place in the world of medicine and science. Do you not know that all the great courts of the kings of the world recruit their physicians from Jundi-Shapur? Pupils from all the nations of the world gather there.'

Eadulf smiled softly at the pride in the other's voice.

'Persia is a long way from this land, Basil Nestorios.'

'I do not doubt it, for have I not travelled every metre of the path here? A long journey only to end in this fashion . . .' He gestured disdainfully to the stone walls. Then he looked at Eadulf. 'What are you doing here, and why have you been imprisoned by the Evil One?'

'The Evil One?' Eadulf frowned.

'The leper with the unpronounceable name.'

'Uaman?'

'That is he.'

Briefly, Eadulf told him the story. The healer from

266

Jundi-Shapur nodded sadly. 'He is, indeed, the Evil One.'

Eadulf saw beyond his immediate problems as a memory came back.

'You were travelling with a brother from Ard Macha and you passed through Cashel a short time ago? A Brother Tanaide? I heard your names at the abbey of Imleach.'

'That is so,' agreed Basil Nestorios. 'I came to this land to discover what cultures and beliefs lay on the western rim of the world. Through intercession from a bishop in the country of Gaul I was put in touch with a bishop in Fearna, the capital city of the land called Laigin.'

Eadulf knew Fearna well and had nearly lost his life there. He sighed as he thought of how Fidelma had saved him.

'What then?' he said, thrusting the memory from his mind.

'It was the bishop who gave me Brother Tanaide as my guide and interpreter. When it was discovered that I was a physician, the bishop and the king of Laigin begged me to stay awhile and practise my arts.' He shrugged. 'I suppose it was news of my cures that reached the Evil One . . .'

'Uaman?'

'The name is difficult for my tongue and lips. Ooo-er-mon? Is that how it is pronounced?'

Eadulf smiled encouragement. 'Good enough,' he acknowledged. 'But are you saying that Uaman heard of you in Laigin?'

'Truly, my friend. He sent word to me there that he would pay a large sum if I came to his palace to try my skill at curing him of the disease that had struck him down. In Jundi-Shapur we know much of this disease that causes disfigurement, skin lesions and sensory loss. We have several means of treating it and I had brought with me a box of the cures we use.'

Eadulf was interested in spite of the surroundings and the

dire straits they were in. 'I have studied some of the healing arts but do not pretend to be a healer. Here, it is usual to pound burdock leaves in wine and cause the sufferer to drink it as a way of treating the disease.'

Basil Nestorios grimaced. 'Where I come from we have a herb called gotu kala . . . it can be taken both internally and externally. It is an ancient cure for healing wounds and curing leprosy. I brought some with me.'

'So you arrived here with Brother Tanaide at Uaman's request?'

Basil Nestorios inclined his head. 'Cursed be the day when I crossed the mountains to this place.'

'Where is Brother Tanaide? In another cell?'

Basil Nestorios shook his head. His expression was a mixture of anger and sadness.

'The Evil One had him killed.'

Eadulf felt a chill run through him, but he was not shocked, knowing the extent of Uaman's treacherous soul.

'What happened?'

'He was run through by one of the Evil One's swordsmen and thrown from the tower into the sea. He was dead before he fell into the water.'

'But why? Why, if you had come to cure him? Why did he kill your companion and imprison you? I do not understand it.'

'Understand this, my friend. The disease of his skin is reflected in the disease of his mind. He is evil. There is no redeeming quality in him.'

'So he has saved your life only for you to tend to him? Are you treating him?'

'I am prolonging my life, that is all. Twice a day I am taken from this cell to mix and prepare my medicines and then treat the man. So far as I can see, he is beyond cure, either physically or in the darkness of his mind, which seems to nurse dreams of revenge on all who challenge him.'

Eadulf rubbed his chin thoughtfully. 'Twice a day? At what times?'

'Something crosses your mind, my friend. What is it?'

'Have you never thought to use your skills to escape?'

The physician frowned. 'I am not sure what you mean.'

'Simple. What can cure can also kill.'

Basil Nestorios looked shocked. 'In my culture, my friend, a physician must do no harm. Many centuries ago there lived on the island of Cos a physician named Hippocrates who is regarded as the father of the physician's art. He imposed an oath on his pupils which says that we cannot use our knowledge to inflict harm on people. We of Jundi-Shapur swear that oath even today.'

Eadulf smiled wanly. 'So you would rather suffer from his evil, and allow him to inflict it on many other innocent people, than prevent it?'

Basil Nestorios raised his hands in a helpless gesture.

'What can I do? The oath is absolute.'

Eadulf was thinking furiously.

'When will you be called to treat him next?' he repeated.

The physician glanced through the window, trying to estimate the hour. The sky was already darkening. At this time of year that implied that it was mid-afternoon.

'The tide will be on the flow soon. Any time now the guard will come for me. I have watched their time-keeping for several days now.'

'Then if you will not poison Uaman, surely you can make a brew that will render him unconscious?'

'I could. But it would take some time for such an infusion to work. I will be brought back here and locked in. What then?'

'I'll be waiting behind the door when the guard brings you back. Get him to come into the cell on some pretext . . . I know . . . I'll leave the stone out by the bed and if he doesn't see it, draw his attention to it. Then I can jump him from behind.' Eadulf began to get enthusiastic as he considered the idea.

'But it would still take some time for the infusion to work on Uaman,' Basil Nestorios pointed out again. Then he paused and said reluctantly, 'I could increase the dose. On reflection, the sooner we take our departure the better.' Then he sighed in irritation. 'But when the guard comes to fetch me for the treatment, you will be found here.'

Eadulf shook his head and pointed to the tunnel.

'I will slip into there and you will push the stone slab before it, not blocking it off, but allowing me to hang on with my hands, for my legs will be over the edge dangling into the next cell. As the bed covers your tunnel, with luck the guard will not notice that the slab is not quite in place.'

Basil Nestorios was looking thoughtful.

'It might work. But even so, if we can deal with one guard, when we escape then there are still five others.'

'Let us deal with one thing at a time,' replied Eadulf. 'How do you propose to render Uaman unconscious? Do you have any *gafann*?'

The physician looked puzzled as Eadulf, momentarily, could only think of the word used by the people of the five kingdoms.

'Henbane,' he said, trying to think of the Latin word. '*Mandragora*,' he added, knowing that the plant was related to the mandrake. 'That is what I would use. In infusions it yields a potion which, if given in undiluted form, will cause a loss of speech and physical paralysis.'

Basil Nestorios smiled agreement.

'You have some knowledge, my friend. Left with no alternative, I would say that it is a good choice. Yet I have, among my medicines, a distillation of a plant that grows in parts of my country which is called *papaver* and which will be far stronger and quicker in its effect. It is a white poppy that we use at Jundi-Shapur which is a powerful narcotic and sometimes relieves pain, sometimes stimulates the mind. But it can also be dangerous in large doses.'

'A white poppy?' Eadulf frowned. It was a new plant in his experience.

'We make an incision in the seed head that ripens once the plant has flowered. The cuts secrete a thick juice, which we scrape off and leave to dry. From this we take our medicinal potion. It will dull the Evil One's brain and induce a deep sleep. That I am prepared to do, but I will inflict on him no more than sleep.'

Eadulf shrugged. 'Well, sleep is better than nothing. If he is not able to order and co-ordinate his warriors, perhaps we have a chance. Are you sure there are no more than six guards in this fortress?'

'I am sure. I have seen only six men who look after the Evil One.'

Eadulf glanced round. 'So where is your chest of medicines?'

'The Evil One looks after it. He does not trust me. He keeps the chest in the chamber where I treat him.'

Eadulf glanced through the window to judge the sky and the tide.

'We had better get prepared, Basil Nestorios,' he said.

The physician nodded. 'Let us hope we are not beloved of the gods,' he muttered.

Eadulf glanced at him curiously.

The physician replied with a smile. 'In my land we have

a saying – *hon hoi theoi philousi npothneskei neos* – those whom the gods love, die young.'

Eadulf grinned as he prepared to crawl back under the bed.

'Let us hope that we are considered to be well past our youth, then,' he replied before pushing himself backwards into the hole.

The physician waited a few moments to allow him to settle himself and then pushed the stone block before the entrance, using his hands to sweep away the rubble. He then sat on the edge of the bed facing the door.

'Are you all right, my friend?' he whispered.

'My arms are beginning to ache,' Eadulf replied. 'A pity this space is at such an acute angle. If it was level, then perhaps I would not need to put my weight on my hands.'

'Let us hope the guard comes soon.'

'Sssh . . . I think . . .'

Eadulf could hear bolts being drawn back. Metal rasped on metal as the door swung inwards. A voice called: 'Come!' He heard Basil Nestorios standing up and moving to the door. A moment or two later he heard the door bang closed and the bolts being pushed back.

Eadulf waited a short time before he began to haul himself from the hole, pushing at the stone block, which, fortunately, was not heavy. It was but a few moments before he was crawling under the bed and back into the cell again. His first thought was to try the door. As he expected, it had been secured from the outside. He had wondered whether, if the door had been left open, he might have found an opportunity to ambush the guard from the outside rather than wait inside the cell.

Now there was nothing to do but wait.

Chapter Fifteen

❧

Eadulf was dozing. He had almost fallen asleep when a noise startled him into wakefulness. There was a movement outside the door. He sprang up, back against the wall, behind the door. He glanced to where the stone lay. It should be well visible from the doorway. Then he heard the bolts being drawn back. He wished he had a weapon of some sort, but there was nothing to hand.

The door swung inward. A guttural voice said: 'In you go. You will get your food later.'

Eadulf waited for the warrior to come forward into the cell. Was he blind? Why didn't he see the stone? He heard Basil Nestorios begin talking in voluble Greek.

'Silence!' grunted the guard. 'I don't understand your heathen gibberish, and . . .'

The voice fell quiet. It seemed that Basil Nestorios was pointing to the stone in an attempt to make the warrior move forward into the cell. It finally worked. Eadulf heard a gasp and then the bulk of the warrior was inside the cell, beyond the door. Eadulf was on the man like a cat springing on its prey, his hands fastening round the warrior's neck, clenching tight. The man was muscular and large; his big hands

273

came up to tear at Eadulf's grip. He swung this way and that as Eadulf clung on in desperation, refusing to let go and trying to constrict the man's breath.

It seemed hopeless. The man was strong and struggled violently to dislodge Eadulf. Just when Eadulf was almost giving up, the man suddenly relaxed and crumpled to the floor. Eadulf went down with him and remained with tightened grip until he was sure the warrior was not faking. He kept a tight hold on the man's neck for a few seconds more, then suddenly released his hold and sprang for the door, where Basil Nestorios stood. He slammed it shut and shot the bolts before the guard could stir. He leant against the door, panting for breath. A few minutes passed and then he looked at the physician.

'How did it go with Uaman?' he whispered urgently.

'I am not sure,' replied the man. 'I mixed the potion and told the Evil One it was a new part of the treatment which he must drink. If he does, I would say it should be working already.'

Eadulf looked aghast. 'You mean that you didn't wait to ensure that he drank the mixture?'

Basil Nestorios shook his head. 'The Evil One simply told the guard to take me back to the cell. I left the potion by his side in his chamber.'

Eadulf groaned softly. 'Then we cannot rely on Uaman's being incapacitated. We must get away from here immediately.'

'But my medicine chest, my saddle bags . . . they are still in his chamber.'

Eadulf snorted in annoyance.

'Abandon them for the time being. I am not going to waste time going to Uaman's chamber to see if he is asleep in order to retrieve them. They'll slow us down anyway.'

Basil Nestorios looked as if he would argue, but then he realised the logic of what Eadulf was saying.

'Where now, then, Saxon friend?'

Eadulf looked about. He realised that the corridor they were in, like the others he had seen, ran around the outer wall in a circular fashion. There must be another level above this one where the windows were. He estimated, therefore, that they were on ground level.

'If we follow round, this must lead out to the inner courtyard by the gates. If we can get there without being observed, and then through the gates, the tide should not be so far advanced as to prevent us getting to the mainland.'

Basil Nestorios pursed his lips. 'It is already getting dark, though, and I think the tide comes soon after.'

'Then let us not waste time debating,' snapped Eadulf. 'Follow me.'

He began to move through the narrow stone corridor, watching carefully for any means of exit or sign of movement from the guards. After a while he halted.

'There is a small door in the inner wall just ahead. I think it must lead into the courtyard. There are neither bolts nor locks on it. Are you ready?'

The physician nodded quickly.

Eadulf moved to the door. There was a circle of metal that raised the latch by which the door was fixed. Eadulf reached out a hand and gave it a tentative twist. The latch lifted without any noise. He pushed it cautiously so that a crack to the outside appeared between the door and the jamb. He applied his eye and let loose a soft sigh.

The door did open into the inner courtyard. In fact, he could see the tall wooden gates that led to the exterior of the tower stronghold. Then he moved back and closed the door quickly and without noise, glancing to the puzzled Basil Nestorios.

'There is a guard going round lighting the brand torches for the evening,' he whispered in explanation.

The physician said nothing. Eadulf stood mentally counting the minutes until he felt the guard would have completed his task. There could be no more than half a dozen torches lighting the inner courtyard.

Carefully, he opened the door again and peered round.

The courtyard appeared deserted. The torchlight lit the area with an eerie glow. If the guards were patrolling it, the fugitives would be seen as soon as they emerged from the door. They would have to take that chance. Eadulf hoped that the guards would not be bothered about the interior of what appeared to be an impregnable fortress. After all, in their eyes, their prisoners were safe in the cells and there was no way out – unless the guard who had been escorting the physician was missed. They had to move now, for the longer they delayed the slimmer their chances of escape became.

Abruptly, there came the jangle of a distant bell.

Eadulf froze.

He heard Basil Nestorios exclaiming something in his own tongue that did not sound happy.

'It's Uaman's bell,' hissed the physician. 'He cannot have taken the potion.'

'Then it's too late to do anything other than make for the gates. There are two iron bolts on them – see? I'll take the top one, you take the bottom one, and don't stop for anything.'

The bell was jangling urgently now.

Eadulf opened the door quickly and dashed across the courtyard to the gates. He felt rather than saw Basil Nestorios behind him. He grabbed at the top iron bolt and wrenched it back with a thud. The physician was almost in time with him. Eadulf pulled on the tall wooden doors just as a shout sounded behind him.

Eadulf hurried through the gap between the doors, closely

followed by his companion. Then he skidded to a halt, eyes wide in dismay.

Outside, directly in front of him, stood a tall, broad-shoul-dered warrior, his sword already raised as if to strike. Eadulf stood frozen, petrified with shock as he recognised the features of the man in the torchlight from the brands in their holders on either side of the entrance.

'Gormán!' he gasped.

The warrior of Cashel's eyes flickered over Eadulf's shoul-der and narrowed slightly.

'Move, Brother Eadulf!' he cried, his sword already begin-ning to swing.

Eadulf plunged forward, ducking in an automatic reaction to the shouted command. Then he swung round on his heel, nearly tripping himself in the movement. Behind him, as Basil Nestorios had also leapt aside, two of Uaman's men had come through the gates, swords in hand.

Gormán's slash caught one in the neck, either killing or disabling him. As the man fell sideways, his weapon dropped from nerveless fingers. The second warrior met Gormán's next cut with a parry, and for a few moments blade clashed against blade. But the second warrior was no great swords-man, and the singing sword of Cashel's élite golden-torqued warrior swept under his guard and caught him beneath the rib cage. With a grunt the man, still grasping his weapon, dropped to his knees, staring wildly before him. Then his eyes seemed to glaze and he fell forward on his face, drop-ping his blade.

'Are there more behind you?' cried Gormán.

Eadulf tried to find his voice. 'Two or three,' he croaked.

Gormán glanced at the physician. 'Who is this?'

'A fellow prisoner.'

They could still hear the jangling bell.

Gormán turned in the darkness and pointed to the shadows that denoted the shoreline.

'The tide is coming in. We must get back. Do you know the way, Brother? The sand link to the shore is treacherous.'

The bell had suddenly stopped and an unearthly wail was sounding within the dark tower. It was scarcely human. Eadulf shivered. It was Uaman's cry of rage.

'That will bring his remaining warriors,' Eadulf cried. 'Let's get to the shore where we will be safer.' He turned and peered into the darkness. He was aware of the sibilant whispering of the sea on either side. 'Straight ahead. Follow me.'

He walked forward, trying not to hurry and making sure each foot came down on firm sand before moving on. It took time. Halfway across, they could still hear the noise of shouting, a bell intermixed with screams. At one point, Eadulf dared to glance behind.

The burning brand torches, in their braziers hanging either side of the great doors of the tower, cast a light on the porch where they had left the two fallen warriors of Uaman. Another warrior, perhaps two – even three – were moving there, and he saw the crooked figure of Uaman himself, a thin, dark shadow, with his bell, standing framed in the doorway, screaming abuse.

'They are coming after us,' muttered Basil Nestorios, also glancing round.

Eadulf saw that Uaman was now leading the three warriors after them along the sandbank. All four carried torches to light their way and they thus had an advantage over their quarry. In spite of his dragging foot, Uaman was moving at an astonishing pace. It was clear that he had not taken the potion prepared by Basil Nestorios. Indeed, he appeared to be moving more quickly than his warriors. Eadulf increased his pace.

'At this rate, we might make the shore but we will have to stand and fight,' grunted Gormán, glancing behind.

'Then we will stand and fight,' replied Eadulf.

He realised that the incoming tide was now lapping at his feet. The water was coming in rapidly, but not rapidly enough, he thought bitterly.

A moment or so later, they were scrambling up on the firm bank before the dark trees. There they turned, preparing for the worst.

It was a curious, eerie sight that met their eyes. In the background the tall round Tower of Uaman rose on the island, dark and sullen, although its doors now stood open, still lit by the burning torches on either side. A shaft of silvery moonlight had somehow escaped between the low-lying clouds and danced with a thousand pinpricks of light on the sea. By this, they could see how quickly the tide was coming in. There was now little to be seen of the sand link to the island.

Uaman was not far from the shoreline now. Surprisingly, he was about ten metres ahead of his three warrior companions. His torch was raised in one dead white claw-like hand. It seemed his rage had taken the better of him, for he had no other weapon.

'Look!' Gormán suddenly whispered.

Eadulf followed the warrior's seaward-pointing finger. Something dark was moving on the silvery waters of the sea, moving towards the strip of water that separated the island from the shore.

At first Eadulf did not understand what it was.

'*Tonn taide!*' whispered Gormán.

A tidal wave, higher than the average man, came pouring through the narrows. Within a second the three warriors behind Uaman, taking the full force of the water, were swept into the darkness, vanishing as their torches were extinguished. Uaman was closer to the shore and escaped the full force of the wave but he, too, was swept off his feet, though he managed by some miracle to cling tightly to his torch, keeping it above the waves. They saw, by its light, the waters recede for a moment or two; long enough for Uaman to clamber to his feet and start towards the shore. But the leper had been swept away from the main path, and as he moved forward, he began to sink rapidly into the sand.

'The quicksand!' muttered Gormán.

Already the clawing sand had reached Uaman's waist and he was flailing about in panic. Eadulf began to move towards him but Gormán held him back.

'You cannot help,' the tall warrior muttered.

Eadulf was beside himself with anxiety.

'Don't you see, don't you see . . .? He is the only one who knows what he has done with Alchú. The only one who can lead me to my baby.'

He started forward again, but the relentless sea was coming in once more and the sand was already up to Uaman's chest.

'Uaman!' Eadulf yelled, moving as close as he dared. 'Where is my baby? Where is Alchú?'

Uaman's cowl had fallen from his white, bald skull of a head. In the flickering torchlight, they could see where the disease had eaten into his flesh.

'My curse on you and the Eóghanacht! May you all never see the cuckoo or the corncrake. May you die screaming. May the cats eat your flesh. May you fester in your grave . . .'

The tidal wave returned a second time. The torch was extinguished. Uaman's voice was silenced. Only whispering black waters could be seen at the spot where they covered his quicksand grave.

'*Es korakes!*' grunted Basil Nestorios with satisfaction in his voice. 'To the ravens with him.'

Eadulf suddenly sat down in the darkness and cradled his head in his hands.

The nightmare was vivid.

The slow procession of religious emerged from the brass-studded oak doors of the chapel and into the cold, grey light of the central courtyard of the abbey. It was a large court-yard, flagged in dark limestone, yet on all four sides there towered the cheerless stone walls of the abbey buildings, giving the illusion that the central space was smaller than it actually was.

The line of cowled monks, preceded by a single religieux bearing an ornate metal cross, moved slowly, almost sedately. Heads bowed, hands hidden in the folds of their robes, they were chanting a psalm in Latin. Behind them, at a short distance, came a similar number of cowled nuns, also with heads bowed, joining in the chant on a higher note and harmonising with the air to make a descant. The effect was eerie, echoing in the confined space.

They moved to take positions on either side of the court-yard, standing facing a wooden platform on which stood a strange construction of three upright poles supporting a trian-gle of beams. A single rope hung from one of the beams, knotted into a noose. Just below the noose, a three-legged stool had been placed. Next to this grim apparatus, feet splayed apart, stood a tall man. He was stripped to the waist, his heavy, muscular arms folded across a broad, hairy chest. He watched the religious procession without emotion; unmoved and unashamed of the task that he was to perform on that macabre platform.

Fidelma was on her knees before the platform, held down by two viciously grinning women. One she knew by instinct was Abbess Ita of Kildare, who had caused her to leave that religious house, while the other was Abbess Fainder, the evil head of the abbey of Fearna. They held her in a strong grip, and even though she tried to struggle Fidelma found herself unable to move. She was forced to look up at the grim apparatus and executioner.

Then two strong religieux came forward, dragging a young man between them. He, too, was forced to his knees before the platform.

'Eadulf!' she cried as she recognised him. But his escort also held him tight so that he could not look at her.

Then a third man came forward holding a baby in his arms. It was handed up to the waiting executioner, who began to move forward towards the noose.

'Help us, Eadulf! For God's sake, help us!'

In her dream, Fidelma knew that she was screaming, but suddenly she came awake, moaning and struggling against the bonds that still tied her hands and feet. She was bathed in sweat.

There was a grey light seeping in at the window. She lay still for a moment, trying to gather her thoughts and rationalise the dream. She wished she could wipe her face of the perspiration that stood there.

The faint whinny of a horse came to her ears. She presumed it came from the stables but she heard movement below and voices were whispering. She rolled over to try to listen. Why would the Uí Fidgente be whispering? Suddenly, her heart began to beat faster. Could Colgú have worked out that she was being held somewhere and tracked her down to the hunting lodge at the Well of Oaks? Was there someone out there intent on her rescue? She uttered a quick prayer that it might be true.

Then there was a noise outside and the door opened. The harsh voice of Cuán came to her ears.

'It must have been some wild animal making the horses restless. I can see no one.'

She felt a sudden black despair. For a moment she had been full of hope. There was some laughter downstairs.

'Then we'd best be off. No one is looking for us now. Let's take the woman and get back to our own country.'

'I'll saddle the horses,' replied another voice. 'Crond can bring the woman.'

Something else caught Fidelma's ear now; there was a soft sound of scrabbling on the roof above her. Below she heard the door of the lodge open and then an agonised yell as something fell.

Cuirgí's voice yelled: 'Crond, get the woman. Quickly!'

Footsteps began to ascend the stairs rapidly just as a dark figure swung in through the shattered glass of the window and dropped on to the floor.

Crond burst in through the door, his sword ready. The figure rose, a sword appearing in his hand as if by magic. Fidelma gasped as she recognised him.

'Conrí!' she gasped, but the name went unheard as the blades of the two men clashed in a noisy exchange. The room was too confined for a sword fight but the blows were deadly as the two men sought to kill or injure each other. Crond made a series of rapid thrusts at his opponent's torso. Had any blow landed, it must have been mortal. But Conrí was obviously not war chief of the Uí Fidgente for nothing. He parried each thrust and then pressed his own attack while Crond paused to rethink his strategy.

A swift thrust drew blood from Crond's upper arm and seemed to anger him. In his fury he dropped his defence, for he raised his weapon for a blow leaving his right side unguarded. He looked almost comical in his surprise as Conrí's sword sank deep between his ribs. He dropped his

283

weapon, staggered back and then slowly collapsed on to the floor.

There was a brief silence. Then, down below, Fidelma became aware of shouting. A strange voice called up: 'The lodge is ours, Conrí!' Then Conrí had sheathed his sword and was cutting her bonds with a knife.

'Fidelma! Are you injured? Are you all right?'

Fidelma could, at first, only nod as she massaged her wrists. The bonds had cut deep into the flesh, leaving harsh marks around them and her ankles.

'How came you here, Conrí?' she managed to ask at last.

The war chieftain gave her a grin. 'Have you forgotten that we planned to meet here, lady?'

She smiled at his bantering tone. 'But not in these circumstances,' she returned in kind.

'True indeed,' he agreed. 'Our story is simple. We did as I told you we would and went through the valley of Bilboa and waited for the chieftains at Crois na Rae. When they didn't turn up, I decided to post half my men to cover the mountain passes, in case they went that way, and then to come back to make our rendezvous with you here. Because we waited a while, we could not reach here last evening, but came on through the night to arrive at dawn.'

'How were you warned of the presence of the chieftains?'

Conrí shrugged. 'I was more concerned with encountering your brother's warriors, seeing that Colgú's whole kingdom could be raised against us. So we approached the hunting lodge cautiously, leaving our mounts behind in a copse at some little distance. I was about to reconnoitre the stables when I spotted Cuán. I knew something was wrong.'

'So how did you know where to find me?'

'I told my men to cover the main door and then I climbed up to the roof. I saw you through the window. One of the chieftains went out through the main door and I think one of my men shot him. So I had to come through the window. I barely had time to regain my balance before Crond came bursting in.'

'You knew him?' queried Fidelma.

'He was an Uí Fidgente chieftain. Am I not warlord of the Uí Fidgente? I know them all.'

'Is he dead?' Fidelma asked, coming slowly to her feet and looking down at Crond.

'He is dead,' confirmed Conrí, 'but for the harm he has done, I shall not weep at his graveside.'

One of Conrí's men came up the stairs to see if all was well, and informed them that Cuán had taken an arrow in the shoulder but would recover while Cuirgí had been captured without a struggle.

'And your baby, lady, where is he?' asked Conrí.

Fidelma shook her head. 'That I do not know, my friend. They denied any knowledge of abduction or involvement in abduction. If this was not a plot by some Uí Fidgente to have these chieftains released, then I am at a loss to understand it.'

'It is as I said, lady,' Conrí replied. 'Unless there is some rebellious group that we do not know of, the Uí Fidgente disclaim all knowledge of this matter. We have made our peace with your brother and we will remain at peace with him.'

Fidelma stamped her feet a little to restore her circulation. She looked up at Conrí.

'Are you prepared to come with me back to Cashel and make that statement? To return these chieftains to my brother's authority as a sign of good faith?'

'Will we be under your protection? The Eóghanacht will not take kindly to Uí Fidgente in Cashel.'

Fidelma nodded. 'You will be under my protection,' she said gravely.

'Then we shall come and gladly.'

'Then let us break our fast and prepare for the journey back,' she replied. Her brother would be thinking the worst about her disappearance. Fidelma's relief at her rescue and the recapture of the Uí Fidgente chiefs was tempered by her frustration that the only apparent reason for Alchú's disappearance and the killing of Sárait had ended in a blank wall through which she was unable to see further. The relief at her rescue was nullified by her feeling of fear for her baby and for Eadulf. She closed her eyes for a moment to hide her inward pain. Eadulf! Where was Eadulf now?

Chapter Sixteen

❧

Eadulf awoke from a fitful doze. It was still night. He became aware that Gormán was putting wood on the campfire that they had made earlier. He raised his hand to massage his forehead and looked round. He dimly recalled how in the darkness they had organised a makeshift camp in the forest clearing near the water's edge. His own horse as well as Gormán's mount had been tethered nearby. He turned. On the other side of the campfire, lying on his back with his eyes still closed in slumber, was Basil Nestorios.

Eadulf realised that he had sunk into such despair that he had not been able to concentrate on anything. Much of the organising of the fire had been done without his assistance.

Gormán, spotting that he was awake, turned and handed him a drinking horn.

'*Corma,*' the warrior explained. 'How do you feel, Brother Eadulf?'

Eadulf grimaced before he took a swallow of the fiery liquid and wiped his mouth with the back of his hand. Then he shook his head.

'I have lost the only chance I had of finding my baby,' he said simply. 'How should I feel?'

The tall warrior was reassuring.

'You are a clever man, Brother Eadulf. You have traced the baby thus far, and you will trace it further.'

'How did you get here, anyway?' Eadulf demanded. 'Were you following me?'

Gormán shrugged. 'I was a full day behind you. As soon as I learnt from the lady Fidelma that you had ridden west to the abbey of Colmán, I knew that your path would take you through the land of the Uí Fidgente and, that being so, you might need a strong sword-arm. So I saddled my horse and tracked you. When I came through the mountain pass near the Hill of the Stone Forts, I encountered a herbalist named Corb and his wife. They confessed that they had taken the child—'

'You did not harm them?' Eadulf asked quickly. 'I believe that the part they played was an unwitting one.'

'They were returning to Cashel at your behest. I did not harm them. I followed you first to the abbey of Colmán and thence to the Tower of Uaman. I arrived there at dusk and made my way across the sand link to the gates. I was about to demand entrance when the gates opened and, lo and behold, you and your taciturn friend there came running out. The rest you know.'

Eadulf leant forward and laid a hand on the warrior's arm.

'Thank the fates for that,' he said reverently. 'Had you not been there, we would not have made it this far. Uaman had marked me down for an early grave while our Persian friend was only allowed to live so long as he treated Uaman for his ailment. However,' he examined Gormán with a side glance, 'I find it hard to believe that you thought me so important that you chased me across Muman simply in order to protect me.'

Gormán hesitated, then spread his hands expressively.

'You are a perceptive man, Brother Eadulf. It is no wonder that you and the lady Fidelma have garnered the reputation that you have. When I heard that you had gone to the abbey of Colmán, I knew that it must be for a specific purpose. You had gained some knowledge that sent you hurrying there. I wanted to be on hand in case you needed help in achieving that purpose.'

'Are you so devoted to the service of Cashel?' Eadulf could not help sounding a little cynical.

The big warrior smiled softly.

'I am devoted to the service of Cashel, that is true, Brother. But you may recall the personal reason that brought me hither.'

'Ah.' Eadulf's eyes lightened as he remembered Gormán's confession of his feelings for Sárait.

'I will make no attempt to disguise it.' Gormán saw that Eadulf had remembered. 'I want to be present when the person who murdered Sárait is caught. I have a score to settle with them. Did Uaman kill her?'

'No. But he bought my baby from the herbalist and his wife who had picked up the child thinking it was abandoned. Therein is a mystery. Someone, soon after the child went missing, had worked out that the herbalist and his wife had taken it without knowing its identity. That person sent a message to Uaman to tell him. That much I learnt in the Tower of Uaman.'

Surprisingly, Gormán did not look astonished at this information.

'I do not think one will have to look far for the culprit. There have been rumours about Fiachrae of Cnoc Loinge for some time. He believes that he should be of the rightful line of the Eóghanacht kings. He also dwells too close to the border of the Uí Fidgente country.'

'Fiachrae?'

Eadulf suddenly sat bolt upright and let out a curse in Saxon. While Gormán did not understand the meaning of the words he recognised the tone and looked at Eadulf in mild surprise.

'The clues were facing me the whole time,' groaned Eadulf. 'Capa told us during the council meeting that riders had ridden as far west as Cnoc Loinge with the news the morning after Sárait was found. Then, when we were at Cnoc Loinge, Fiachrae pretended he knew nothing of our missing baby until I told him. Yet his manner did not suggest undue surprise. Also, he told me that no itinerants had passed through the place. I had not even raised the matter. He knew. He knew, and is the man who betrayed Alchú to Uaman! And didn't the steward of the abbey of Colmán tell me that a messenger from Cnoc Loinge had brought the news about the missing baby? It must have been Fiachrae . . . but no. That can't be. How would he know that Corb and Corbnait had picked up Alchú? Not even they knew the identity of the child.'

'You should have spoken more closely with the herbalist Corb,' said Gormán. 'He told me that when they passed through Cnoc Loinge on their way here, they told one of the women of Fiachrae's house about their discovery of the child in the hope of having the baby adopted there.'

'Fiachrae will be tried and punished for his betrayal,' Eadulf vowed. 'But it doesn't help us to find my child now, or the person who killed Sárait.'

'I pray God I will be there when we do find the murderer,' Gormán said with vehemence. 'I will do what I have to do and I will have no regrets.'

'Well, I regret that Uaman perished with his foul secret still within him.'

'Uaman must have said something that might lead you

further?' pressed Gormán. He suddenly started forward. 'Perhaps the baby is still in the Tower of Uaman?'

Eadulf shook his head. 'He has given the baby to some shepherd and his wife to raise without knowledge of his origins. The child will be raised herding sheep on some mountainside . . . but where? I could spend a lifetime searching the mountains of this land. Those raising him know only that Uaman provided them with a child. There will be no way of identifying him. He will bear another name.'

'How did you learn this?'

'From what Uaman told me.'

'I once heard the lady Fidelma say that if you study carefully the exact words that someone says, then clues may be found there.'

Eadulf stared at the warrior in surprise. The man was right. That was precisely what Fidelma would say.

'Think, Brother,' urged Gormán quietly. 'Think of the words.'

Eadulf closed his eyes and tried to recall what Uaman had said.

'He did not mention any names of places. There were no clues. Just that Alchú would be raised by a shepherd and his wife, herding sheep in the mountains. And . . .' He paused.

'Have you thought of something?'

'He said something about the mountains being haunted.'

Gormán gave a cynical grimace. 'What mountain in the five kingdoms is not haunted by some wraith or other? Mountains are old and have seen countless great kings rise to lead their people and then be blown away like chaff from the wheat. They have memories, the mountains. They are haunted, right enough.'

Eadulf was shaking his head. 'He said the daughter of someone haunted them.'

Gormán leant forward eagerly. 'That is more promising, Brother. Whose daughter?'

The name came in a flash.

'Dáire Donn.' Eadulf was triumphant. He looked expectantly at Gormán but the warrior only shook his head.

'We will have to make inquiries,' he said. 'Meanwhile, we must sleep. In the morning, if I have understood your friend Basil Nestorios, he has a horse and some precious objects that he left in the tower yonder. We will wait until the low tide and then go to fetch these.'

Eadulf agreed. Then another thought occurred to him.

'We imprisoned one of Uaman's warriors in the stranger's cell. He might be a means of leading us to Alchú.'

Gormán was cheerful. 'In the morning, while we are awaiting the change of the tides, I can ride up to the little settlement that I saw up in the mountains behind us. They should be pleased to hear that Uaman is no longer chieftain over them. Moreover, they might be able to help identify this Dáire Donn.'

'Agreed.'

Eadulf realised, however, that the rest of the night was going to be cold in spite of the wood that Gormán was throwing on to the fire.

The night passed in fitful sleep. It was too cold to rest for any long periods and, as each wakened, they helped to keep the fire well fuelled. As well as the cold there were the cries of nocturnal animals, the howl of wolves and the cry of a wild cat to disturb their slumber. Eadulf was almost thankful when the sky began to lighten and grim, grey streaks started to appear from the east.

'Tonight we find an inn,' he announced, as Gormán set about making breakfast. 'I will perish if I have to pass another night in the open.'

Basil Nestorios was already up and stamping his feet to restore some circulation. He seemed to guess what Eadulf was talking about.

'I swear that I never knew it could be so cold,' he said, reverting to Latin as their common language. 'In my country, the icy hands of night may clutch you but as soon as the sun rises you will be warm again.'

Eadulf gestured to the thick grey clouds above them.

'Here we do not always have a sunrise, my friend. The clouds always seem to cheat us by hiding it from us.'

Gormán had taken some salted slices of pork from his saddle bag and was turning them above the fire on the end of his sword. Basil Nestorios sniffed suspiciously and frowned.

'I have noticed that you eat a lot of pig meat in this land. Pig is regarded as an unclean animal in our country.'

'A strange land, this Jundi-Shapur,' muttered Eadulf, helping himself to the drinking horn of *corma* and taking a sip of the fiery liquid before passing it to the physician. At least the alcohol gave him warmth.

Basil Nestorios sniffed in irritation.

'I told you that Jundi-Shapur was simply a city in the land of Persia. It is also called Genta Shapirta, which means "of the beautiful garden". It was the king of Persia, Shapur the second of his name, who first allowed the Nestorians to teach medicine in the city.'

'Nestorians? Your own name is Nestorios,' Eadulf pointed out. 'What is signified by this?'

Basil Nestorios raised his brows in surprise. 'You have not heard of the Nestorians and yet you are a brother of the Faith?'

Eadulf admitted his ignorance.

'Nestorios was a monk of the east. He taught the Faith in

Antioch. He was a learned and wise man and was appointed patriarch of the great city of Constantinople.'

'When was this?' queried Eadulf, who never missed an opportunity to expand his knowledge of the Faith, even when his thoughts were only half engaged.

'About two centuries ago. Nestorios was condemned by what the Church called a heresy. He denied the complete emergence of the divine and human natures in Christ.'

Eadulf smiled tiredly. 'I thought that the great council at Chalcedon had agreed that Christ was born of a mortal woman but possessed two natures – that divine and human united in one person without losing any of their properties.'

Basil Nestorios sniffed as if dismissing the matter.

'That is the dogma of both Rome and Constantinople. They even go further to talk of three divine natures apart from the human one – that God, Christ and the Holy Spirit are one.'

Eadulf shrugged. 'Well, the people in this land have no problem with believing in triune gods and goddesses, so they can easily accept a Holy Trinity.'

Basil Nestorios shook his head sadly. 'We believe that Christ was only one person who had two natures – one human and one divine.'

'Old arguments,' countered Eadulf. 'Didn't Arius claim that Christ was not fully divine but created by God to accomplish our salvation? And are there not Gnostics who claim that Christ was never human at all, and his human appearance was merely an illusion to enable him to live among men? Then there are those who say that Christ was born a human male and became God's adopted son only when he was baptised in the Jordan. There are many such arguments.'

Basil Nestorios was unimpressed.

'Mary could not be the mother of a god because she was

of human flesh and thus could not give birth to divinity. However, men, being what they are – frail and human – objected to the logic of what Nestorios said.'

'So what happened?'

'There was a synod at the city of Ephesus when the Bishop Cyril excommunicated Nestorios and his followers. The eastern emperor Theodosius exiled Nestorios and so our church, all those who follow Nestorian teachings, went its own way and flourished. We have taken the word far into the east, beyond the great mountain ranges that guard the strange, exotic lands that shelter behind them. We have spread the teaching through the deserts and Jundi-Shapur is one of our great centres of learning.'

Eadulf was fascinated. 'I have never heard of this church from which you take your name.'

Basil Nestorios made a wry grimace. 'But, then, dear friend, I did not know that the church in this country was so different from that which follows the rules dictated by Rome. We cannot know everything in the world. But we must keep our minds open and be receptive to what we can know.'

'In that I would agree with you.'

Gormán had finished preparing the breakfast.

'I did not follow all you said,' he confessed. 'My Latin is confined to just a few words. I gather that you were discussing religion.'

Eadulf smiled. 'You do not sound enthusiastic.'

Gormán reached for the *corma*. 'Religion has its place, Brother Eadulf.'

'Which is?'

'There is a time for religion. Usually when there is adversity. Is it not an old saying that when there is prosperity, no altar is seen to be smoking? I turn to religion like everyone else – when there is a need for it.'

Eadulf grimaced in disapproval. 'A pragmatic approach, I suppose.'

Gormán looked across the waters to where the tower still stood dark and brooding on the island.

'The torches are smouldering,' he observed. 'They have burnt out. The doors are still open. That seems to indicate that there is no one moving inside. When the waters go down, we can go across and retrieve the property of the stranger.' He motioned to Basil Nestorios.

'Very well. What of the settlement you mentioned last night? If they can supply some information about this Dáire Donn it might help resolve our next course of action.'

'I'll ride up now while you break camp,' the young warrior agreed.

It was some time before he returned, urging his horse forward as if he was being pursued. He came to an abrupt halt before them and almost leapt from his mount.

'What is it?' demanded Eadulf, peering along the track in concern.

'I thought I should return quickly,' Gormán replied, dismounting. 'The people are determined to sack and burn Uaman's tower now that they know he cannot harm them. They are working themselves up with drink and celebration. We need to get across and retrieve whatever it is you need from there before they arrive.'

Eadulf glanced at Basil Nestorios and swiftly interpreted.

'And also release the guard we imprisoned in my former cell before they reach him,' Basil Nestorios added. 'I had almost forgotten him. He can do us no harm now. I would dislike to be the cause of further death. Of more value is my chest of medicines, which I would hate to see fall into the hands of people who do not appreciate its value.'

Gormán had tethered his horse alongside Eadulf's.

'Let us go. Uaman ruled this area with an iron fist,' he said, turning. 'When I told the people of the settlement that he was dead, they went wild with joy which soon began to turn to anger, so let us move quickly. The tide is low enough now to allow us to cross.'

'Should we take the horses over?'

'It is better to leave them here. We have to bring other animals from the tower. And the sand link may be difficult for them to negotiate. It will take the people from the settlement only a short while to muster and march down here.'

As they began to walk to the tower across the sand dunes, abandoned by the reluctant sea for a short while, Eadulf could not help thinking of Uaman's end. He felt a chill as he thought of the leper's body being dragged down into the soft sands nearby. He shivered involuntarily, and glanced at Gormán, who was leading the way.

'Were you able to mention that business of the ghost to the people of the settlement before they went wild?'

The big warrior smiled broadly.

'Have no fear, Brother. I made that my first duty. And have had some success.'

Eadulf's heart lurched in expectation.

'And?' he almost snapped.

'They knew of Dáire Donn. He was, according to an ancient story, the King of the World and he landed on this very peninsula with his great army. He was opposed by the High King's general Fionn Mac Cumhail and they fought a bloody battle at a place called Fionntragha, the white strand, towards the end of the peninsula.'

'How does this help us?' Eadulf interrupted impatiently.

'Well, Dáire Donn was defeated and he and his army were slain. But he had a daughter who, finding her slaughtered father on the battlefield, went insane and fled in her dementia into the mountains. It is said that it is her ghost that haunts them.'

'Go on,' urged Eadulf.

'The name of the daughter was Mis.' Gormán, with a smile, jerked his thumb behind them. 'The peaks that rise there take their name from the highest of them, which is Sliabh Mis – the mountain of Mis. Your son is in those mountains.'

Eadulf halted and looked round, his eyes rising to the peaks behind, some, he guessed, as high as a thousand metres.

'Somewhere there, somewhere among those peaks, is Alchú,' he whispered. 'But where? How can we find one shepherd in such a country?'

'There seems to be a way,' Gormán assured him. 'There is a valley behind us to the north, whose entrance is marked by an old standing stone. We follow the river that courses this valley – it is called the river of the borderland, I think – until we find another menhir inscribed in the ancient ogham, standing by a ford. I am told we will find an old man dwelling nearby, called Ganicca. He is supposed to know the mountains well. We should make inquiries there.'

Eadulf gave a shout of exuberance. Then he explained to the physician.

'What road will you take when we leave here?' he asked.

Basil Nestorios thought for a moment.

'Without poor Brother Tanaide, I have no guide. By your leave, friend, I will remain with you and this tall warrior, and perhaps be of help in your quest for your child. Eventually, I can return eastward with you to this great capital you call Cashel and perhaps see what the future brings.'

Eadulf clapped him on the shoulder.

'It will be good to have your company.'

They had reached the doors of the tower now, still standing open, with the bodies of the slain warriors lying where they had fallen. Gormán glanced around.

'I would leave them to the disposal of the villagers, Brother,' he said, as he saw Eadulf about to make a move to shift them. 'Let us do what we have come to do first.'

'I will go to the Evil One's apartment and gather my medicine chest,' the physician said immediately.

'I will take Gormán and release the warrior we left in your cell. We will meet by the stables – there.' Eadulf thrust out his hand towards the wooden structure at the side of the courtyard that was obviously a stable. Basil Nestorios agreed and disappeared on his task, while Eadulf led Gormán along the narrow corridor until they came to the wooden door of the cell. He banged on the door.

'Do you hear me in there?' he cried.

A muffled voice answered in surprise. 'I hear you. Let me out.'

'We will do so. But do not try to resist. Your master is dead. Do you understand? Uaman is dead. Your comrades are all slain. Do you wish to escape with your life?'

There was a silence.

'Do you hear?'

'I hear,' came the muffled voice.

'The people from the settlement that stands on the mountainside are coming here soon. They mean to destroy this evil place. We will let you out, give you horse, and the rest is up to you. Do you understand?'

'I understand.'

Eadulf glanced at Gormán, who had drawn his sword and stood ready. Then he threw the bolts back and pushed the door open.

A moment later, the warrior emerged. He looked drawn and tired, and his weapons were sheathed. Eadulf addressed him sternly.

'Precede us to the stables and do not attempt anything, for there is nothing to be gained.'

'You have my word,' muttered the man.

They were first to arrive at the stable. There were eight horses in the stalls. Eadulf gestured towards them.

'Take the one which belongs to you and begone before the people arrive.'

The warrior said no more. He went to an animal, saddled it, and led it into the courtyard. Then he turned hesitantly to Eadulf.

'You have my thanks, Brother.'

'You could give me better thanks if you knew aught of the baby that your master took and how he disposed of him,' Eadulf said, not expecting to receive any useful information. The Uí Fidgente warrior grimaced.

'I was not with Uaman when that happened. I heard that he had bought some baby from a travelling herbalist and his wife a week or so ago and then took it by himself up into the mountains. He returned a day later without the baby. I did not ask what he had done with it. No one would dare question Uaman. May I go now, Brother?'

Eadulf waved him away. 'As you go, remember that your life is spared by the grace of the Eóghanacht, to whom you should owe your thanks and allegiance.'

The warrior swung up on his horse, raised a hand in acknowledgement and then rode out fast through the gates and across the sand.

A moment later, Basil Nestorios rejoined them. He carried large saddle bags of a strange design in one of which, Eadulf saw by the hastily fixed straps, was a small wooden chest. The physician grinned.

'I have my belongings.' He held out his hand to reveal several gold pieces. 'And I have taken these as payment for my services. Exactly what I am owed. There is plenty more, if you want. But it is cursed gold. I would rather leave it for the people this Evil One has wronged.'

Eadulf glanced at Gormán. 'I would agree with that sentiment,' he said.

'Let us saddle the stranger's horse,' Gormán said to Eadulf. 'We can release the rest.'

Basil Nestorios pointed to two of the beasts.

'That one is mine, the other belonged to poor Brother Tanaide. I should return it to Laigin.'

They were harnessed in a moment with Gormán's expert help. They released the other animals and saw them galloping across the sands towards the distant shore.

They were halfway to the shore themselves, with Basil Nestorios leading both horses, when a crowd of people came bursting through the trees, carrying scythes, billhooks and staffs, and crying like hunters after their prey. Gormán moved forward to intercept them, his hand held up.

'Peace, my friends. You remember that it was I who brought you the news of Uaman's death? These are my companions, who have been his prisoners.'

A burly man, whose manner of dress proclaimed him to be a blacksmith, glanced quickly at them.

'I recognise you, warrior. You and your companions have no need to fear us. Pass on your way and peace follow you on your road.' Then, turning to his rowdy comrades, the burly smith waved them on towards the tower.

Having collected their own mounts from their makeshift camp, Gormán and Eadulf led their companion up through the forest and along the track towards the mouth of the high valley that led into the tall, dark mountains.

Once beyond the tree line, where the woods gave way to more open shrub land, and long stretches of heather, Gormán paused, resting easily on his horse. The others followed his gaze as he looked back. From the higher elevation they could look down on the quiet blue seas, so different from this distance from the turbulent tides that had borne their enemies away. Even the island, with its grey stone tower, looked peaceful from here . . . except already plumes of black smoke were rising from it. The people of the settlement were wreaking their vengeance on the stronghold of Uaman the Leper, the Evil One, as Basil Nestorios still insisted on calling him.

It was dusk by the time they reached the small hamlet round the ford on the river. It was too dark to see the standing stone by which they would know they were in the right place, but Gormán stopped before a small forge at which a solitary blacksmith was still working, bending horseshoes on his anvil with hammer and tongs.

'We are looking for a man called Ganicca. Is this where he dwells?'

The blacksmith gave them an encompassing glance.

'You are strangers in this country.' It was a statement, not a question.

'We are.'

'Ganicca is to be found in the last dwelling over there.' The smith gestured with his hammer towards three buildings on the river bank.

Gormán thanked him and they moved towards the house that he had indicated. As they halted before it, Gormán called out. A thin, reed-like voice invited them in and so they dismounted.

It was light and warm within the dwelling. A fire blazed in the hearth and oil lamps provided the light. An elderly man sat in a chair by the fire, over which a small pot simmered with the aromatic smell of meat and vegetables arising from it. The man had a shock of white hair and parchment-like skin. His eyes were bright, and of an indeterminable colour.

'Welcome, strangers,' he said.

'Blessings on this house and those who dwell within it,' Eadulf answered formally.

The man chuckled appreciatively. 'We do not often have strangers in these parts. You are a religieux, I see.'

'I am. We are come in search of one called Ganicca.'

'And who would be searching for Ganicca?' queried the old man.

'My name is Brother Eadulf . . .'

'Ah, the husband to the lady Fidelma of Cashel, sister to Colgú, king of Muman. I have heard of Eadulf. A Saxon. And you say that you are this man?'

'I am. This is Gormán, a warrior of the bodyguard of King Colgú. This other is Brother Basil Nestorios from faraway Persia. I presume that you are Ganicca who, it is reported, knows all that is worth knowing in these parts?'

The old man gave another wheezy chuckle.

'To the illiterate, a man who can write his name is the king of literature,' he responded. 'Come, my friends, be seated before my fire, for it grows cold outside. Have you given thought to where you will stay this night? You will not be able to travel further among the mountains in the dark.'

'We meant to find some inn or hostel. Is there one close by?'

Ganicca shook his head. 'We are an isolated community and we have no call to keep a hostel for travellers, for no one comes through these mountains, at least not while our current lord is master of the passes.'

A grim smile played on Eadulf's lips. 'You mean Uaman?'

The old man blinked rapidly. 'It is a name which is not to be mentioned lightly.'

'Have no fear. Uaman the Leper perished last night. His

stronghold was in flames when we left it this morning. Uaman will no longer haunt the passes of these mountains.'

The old man stared at him long and hard.

'I believe you speak the truth, Eadulf, husband of Fidelma. It is a story that I did not think to hear before I passed on to the Otherworld. You must spend this evening in the telling of it. There is a small stable by the house where you may tether your horses and there is barley and hay to feed them. I have a stew simmering upon the fire and you may make yourselves comfortable in my home this night. It is poor, but it is warm, and better than sleeping in the chill air of the mountains.'

Gormán went off to attend to their animals while Eadulf discussed with the old man the real nature of his business.

'I knew that you did not come seeking me out to tell me of Uaman the Leper's death,' chuckled Ganicca.

'Uaman has done Fidelma and me a most grievous wrong and it might be that you are the means to resolve it.'

After Eadulf had explained, Ganicca rubbed his chin thoughtfully.

'We are at the centre of a pass through the mountains,' he said. 'It is an isolated spot, but mountain folk come to it now and then, when the itinerant priest visits to conduct marriages and bless the progeny of those unions and conduct our lamentations over the dead. No regular priest would dare stay here while Uaman was lord of the passes. Therefore I know a lot of what goes on even in the places where not many dare tread, high up in the dark peaks above us.'

'So is there a shepherd in this vicinity?'

Ganicca laughed, though with little humour in his tone.

'My friend, there are a dozen shepherds in this area alone.' He saw Eadulf's disappointment and reached forward, touching him lightly on the arm. 'But do not be disheartened. Most of them are wedded with children. A few live on their own, isolated and solitary. However, there is one couple who have been wedded for a time and yet remain childless. The wife had a stillborn child less than one moon ago. She was distraught, and I heard that she and her husband would barter their souls to resurrect that child. It might be that you would do well to visit this couple. Uaman could well have chosen them, for in their desperation they might not ask too closely where the child had come from.'

Again Eadulf felt a surge of excitement.

'How may we find this shepherd and his wife?' he asked.

'In the morning, follow the river further up the valley to the end where it comes down from the mountains. To your north on the hill there are a number of ancient graves, so old that no one can recall who built them; to the south the mountains climb to a great height. Continue due east over the hills. There is a pass that will take you to another valley beyond. It is criss-crossed with rivulets and streams and a large river called An Fhionnglaise. Keeping due east, you will find two dwellings on a rise. The place is called Gabhlán. At Gabhlán you will ask for Nessán, the shepherd, and his wife Muirgen.'

'And if the baby is not there?' queried Eadulf, ever the pessimist.

'Then, my friend, all you have heard of my knowledge can be set at naught,' replied the old man. 'Now, tell me . . . tell me all in detail . . . how did Uaman the Leper come by his end? This is a story that will be told and retold through the mountains here long after the child you seek has had children and they have had children.'

The evening passed pleasantly enough in storytelling, and at dawn the little company rode onwards up the mountain valley.

Had the road been straight, then the distance to their

destination would have been no more than four miles. But the track twisted even as the river twisted and then there was the climb over the shoulders of the mountains, twisting again, turning and dipping. It was just before midday when they came to the rising hill in the valley of streams, exactly as Ganicca had directed. On the slope before them, they could see a group of buildings. Two huts appeared to be the main dwellings, which were separated by several outhouses and a sheep pen. Eadulf led Gormán and Basil Nestorios along the track towards them. Dogs started barking at their approach.

A large man came out of one of the huts. A man from the other dwelling quickly joined him. As Eadulf and his companions drew nearer, they stood watching them. One of them, the large man, held a crook in his left hand which proclaimed his occupation as a shepherd, although he seemed to carry it as if it were a defensive weapon. The three riders halted and dismounted. The shepherd's keen eyes examined first Eadulf, then Nestorios, and finally Gormán.

'What do you seek here, strangers?'

'Is this place called Gabhlán?' asked Eadulf.

'It is.'

'Then we are looking for Nessán.'

The shepherd frowned and glanced quickly at his neighbour.

'How do you know my name? What do you want with me?'

Eadulf smiled grimly. He decided to try the direct approach.

'Uaman the Leper is dead. We have come for the child.'

There was a silence, and then there was a feminine gasp. A moment later a woman of middle years emerged from Nessán's hut. It was obvious from the body language between them that she was his wife. She came to grasp his arm as if for support.

'Do you tell us truly?' she whispered. 'Is the leper dead?'

The second man, at a further glance from Nessán, had reluctantly returned to his own business.

'I speak the truth,' Eadulf confirmed solemnly. 'My companions here will testify to that.'

The shepherd's wife gave a long sigh. Her shoulders seemed to drop in resignation.

'I am Muirgen. All this week, I knew that this day would come, though I selfishly prayed it would come later rather than sooner. But I have known it would come from the moment my man came back from the hill to say that Uaman had given us this child.'

Nessán placed a protective arm round her. 'Have a care, woman. These strangers could be anyone, even servants of Uaman, testing our loyalty. My neighbour is within call, so be warned, strangers. His dogs are fierce.'

Eadulf smiled sorrowfully. 'You have a right to be suspicious, my friend. I assure you that we are not any servants of Uaman and he is truly dead.'

Muirgen examined him with a deep, penetrating gaze. 'In your eyes,' she said suddenly, 'I see the eyes of the child reflected back at me.' She turned to the others and nodded slowly. 'They do not have the faces of those who would consort with the leper. Even the one who has the look of a stranger to this land has something kindly in his eyes.'

'You are perceptive, Muirgen,' Eadulf said. 'I am Eadulf. I am he whose child has been stolen by Uaman.'

Muirgen moved close to him and peered again into his eyes.

'I knew that Uaman must have stolen the child from somewhere. I have looked after him well; looked after him

307

as if he were my own. He thrives, I promise you that, Brother.'

Eadulf nodded, feeling, in spite of himself, sympathy for the woman in her plight.

'Then bring him to me.'

Muirgen nodded slowly. 'Tell me, before you take him, what name does the child bear?'

Eadulf hesitated. 'His name is Alchú and, as I have said, he is my son. My son and the son of Fidelma of Cashel, sister to Colgú, king of Muman.'

Nessán made a whistling sound through his teeth in reaction to the news. His wife was nodding thoughtfully.

'That explains much. Uaman was of the Uí Fidgente and that was why he insisted on our calling the baby Díoltas.'

'Vengeance?' Eadulf said grimly. 'That certainly suited his twisted, cruel mind. Come, let me see the child.'

He made to move to the hut but Nessán laid a strong restraining hand on his arm.

'What will happen to us, Brother Eadulf? What will happen to my wife and me? Will Colgú of Cashel punish us?'

Eadulf regarded them both with sympathy and shook his head.

'I cannot see a crime here for which you should be punished. Uaman, who claimed chieftainship in these mountains, gave you the baby. He asked you to look after the child and you have done so. Where is the crime?'

Nessán sighed deeply, raising a hand almost in supplication.

'It is just that we wanted a child so much and our prayers have never been answered.'

'Are there no orphans that need fostering?' Gormán asked rhetorically. 'I would have thought that your chieftain would have been able to assist in that. There is always some *dilechta* or orphan that needs a home.'

'No one wants to give a child to a shepherd. I am but a

lowly *sen-cleithe*, a herdsman who does not even possess his own herd. There is no one lower than I am except those who have lost their rights by transgressing the law, the cowards and the hostages. I cannot bear arms or have a say at the clan assembly.'

'We have never been able to appeal to the chieftain of the Corco Duibhne, for Uaman has dominated the passes on this peninsula for many years. Is he truly dead?' Muirgen added again.

'Uaman is truly dead,' Eadulf repeated solemnly, aware that the couple needed reassurance. Gormán, standing behind him, coughed impatiently.

'We are wasting time, Brother Eadulf,' he muttered.

The woman turned immediately and darted into the hut. When she reappeared, she had Alchú in her arms. There were tears in her eyes as she smiled down at the sleeping child before handing it to Eadulf.

Eadulf looked down at the baby, tears rimming his own eyes for a moment. He felt a constriction in his throat as he looked upon the son he had once thought never to see alive again. He sniffed, and grinned fiercely to fight back the tears.

'You have looked after him well, Muirgen,' he conceded.

The woman inclined her head. 'I have done my best.'

'When I return to Cashel, I will talk to the Chief Brehon about your situation. Perhaps your prayers may be answered. There must be something that can be done for you.'

It was clear from their expressions that they did not believe he meant a word of what he was saying, but they smiled politely. He told the woman that he would allow her a few moments to say her farewells to the sleeping baby. It was then that Basil Nestorios drew him aside.

'I believe that this is your first child, Brother Saxon?'

Eadulf looked puzzled but answered in the affirmative. The physician smiled gently.

'I thought so. How far is it to Cashel? A few days' ride?'

'What are you saying?'

'You are meaning to carry the child on a horse? A baby of that age will not find such a means of transportation comfortable. It never does to shake a baby too much.'

'We will take it slowly. We can probably pick up a wagon at the abbey of Colmán. That will be easier on him.'

The physician continued to smile. 'And how is the child to take nourishment?' he asked. 'Don't you require a *trophos*?'

Eadulf had not heard the Greek word before. 'Take nourishment . . .?' Then it dawned on him. On the journey from Cashel to the abbey of Colmán, the herbalist's wife had acted as wet nurse to the child. Of course, the baby needed a wet nurse for the journey back. He glanced to where Muirgen was saying her farewells to the child. The solution appeared simple. Then another thought struck him. He stood in contemplation a moment or two before turning to Gormán.

'You said that you were at Cnoc Áine, didn't you? Callada, Sárait's husband, was killed there, wasn't he?'

The tall warrior nodded impatiently. 'I did, and Callada was slain during the battle. Now,' he glanced at the sky, 'if we want to get back to the village by the ford before dark, we should start soon, Brother Eadulf.'

'When was that battle?' insisted Eadulf. 'Remind me.'

'It took place in the month of Dubh-Luacran, the darkest time of the year,' replied Gormán, puzzled by his excitement.

Eadulf waved an impatient hand. 'But when? How long ago?'

'We lack but two months before it will be exactly two years since the battle.'

Eadulf exhaled slowly.

'We should be on our way, Brother,' Gormán chided again.

Eadulf brought himself back to the present and smiled at Basil Nestorios. He suddenly felt in buoyant mood.

'Thank you for your good advice, my friend. *Trophos*, eh?' He turned to the shepherd's wife. 'Muirgen, I have been reminded of the child's care. Will you be his wet nurse on the journey back to Cashel? You will be well paid for your trouble.'

The woman was startled by the abruptness of the offer. She glanced at her husband.

'I have never left these mountains in my life,' she began.

'Your husband can accompany you, and I will ensure that you are both rewarded and escorted on your return to ensure your safe passage,' Eadulf said to pre-empt any further debate.

'And we will receive compensation?' Nessán wore a thoughtful expression.

'And I will argue your case before the Brehon Dathal,' Eadulf conceded.

The shepherd and his wife exchanged another glance and then a silent agreement passed between them.

'My sheep are in the lower pasture for the winter. I need only inform my neighbour that we shall be gone awhile and that he will be compensated for looking after them. I can be away for a few weeks before I need to return.'

Eadulf thrust his hand into the leather purse he wore at his belt and drew forth two *screpalls*.

'Give him this on account.'

Nessán hurried off. The neighbour and his wife had already come out of their hut to watch what the strangers were doing, and the business was soon concluded. It was not long before the procession set off on the first leg of their journey back to Cashel. Muirgen, with the baby slung in a shawl in front of her, was seated on Basil Nestorios's spare horse, which the physician led with a rein from his own mount. Nessán rode pillion behind Gormán, and Eadulf led the way.

Eadulf felt a real sense of elation. A sense of achievement. He had retrieved Alchú – his child – entirely through his own efforts and powers of deduction. It was his achievement and no other's. He smiled as he recalled a saying of his father, who had been hereditary *gerefa* of the South Folk before him. 'Remember, my son, that when you raise your sword, it is not enough merely to aim it. You must hit your target.' He had ridden away from Cashel with only a suspicion of the target. Now he was returning thither having accomplished what all Cashel had been trying to achieve for well over a week. He could quote Fidelma's favourite philosopher at her – what was it Publilius Syrus had written? Great rivers can be leapt at the source. He had found the source and leapt the great river and would return in triumph.

Chapter Seventeen

❧

Since returning to Cashel two days before, the time had passed for Fidelma with incredible slowness. There was no word of Eadulf and Brother Conchobar was still in Lios Mhór. Gormán had been missing for some days, while Capa had only just returned from his mission to the borders of the Uí Fidgente country. The two surviving Uí Fidgente chieftains had been returned to their prison and would be tried for the killing of old Duach, the king's lodge keeper, and his son Tulcha. Conrí, the warlord of the Uí Fidgente, and his men had been given hospitality at Cashel and started talks with Colgú on the rebuilding of relationships between the two peoples. But apart from that, for Fidelma, it seemed that there had been no progress at all. If anything, things had regressed. Now there was no clue to the whereabouts of either Alchú or Eadulf.

Fidelma decided that the only thing to do was try to retrace the steps that had led Eadulf to leave Cashel. He had gone to see the woodsman Conchoille and, having done so, he had come back to the palace, taken a full saddle bag and made off to the abbey of Colmán. That is what she would have to do. But first she would see Conchoille and find out what passed between them.

Caol was on duty at the gates of the palace and he raised his hand in salute as she walked towards him leading her horse.

'What news, lady?'

'I was about to ask the same question of you, Caol.'

The warrior shrugged. 'Rumours in plenty but little news.'

'I am going to see Conchoille the woodsman. I want to ask what he said to Eadulf which made him go westward,' she said.

'In that case, lady, you will not have far to go. As I came up from the town a short time ago, I saw Conchoille entering Capa's house.'

'Capa's house?'

'He often delivers logs there as well as to other houses. He is paid for that service.'

Fidelma thanked the warrior for his information and made her way down the road into the township.

Capa, the guard commander, opened his door to her knock and stared at her in surprise.

'What brings you here, lady?' he asked, and when she told him her purpose he stood aside and motioned her into the small but warm room. Capa's wife, Gobnat, came forward almost nervously with an offer of hospitality, a mug of mead, but Fidelma politely declined. Conchoille the woodsman had risen from a seat by the fire. He stood awkwardly.

'You came in search of me, lady?' His hands twisted nervously round the pottery mug he had been drinking from.

'I did, Conchoille, but I will not delay you long,' she replied. 'I believe that Brother Eadulf came to see you on the day he left Cashel.'

The woodsman turned owlish eyes on her.

'He did not, lady,' he replied.

Fidelma was not expecting this response.

'He did not come to see you at Rath na Drínne?' she asked in surprise.

Conchoille shook his head. 'I never spoke to the noble brother after the council met in the palace. I was told that he had left Cashel but I never saw him on that day. He went to see Ferloga, though. Maybe he was looking for me.'

'Ferloga the innkeeper?'

There came the distracting howl of a dog outside the house. From where she stood, Fidelma could see Capa's brown, wire-haired hound digging furiously for something in the yard.

Gobnat looked angrily at her husband.

'Go and control your hound, man!' she said in a vicious tone. 'We will have no yard left at this rate.'

The warrior glanced apologetically at Fidelma.

'It is my dog, lady. He's probably after some old bones.'

He went outside and grabbed the animal roughly by the collar and secured him, whimpering, to a tree. Fidelma turned back to Conchoille for clarification, and accidentally kicked a small metal cauldron by the fire. Looking down, she noticed a large dent in it.

'Did I do that?' she queried, in surprise, bending to examine it. Gobnat almost snatched it up.

'It is nothing. An old cauldron, lady. An old dent.'

Capa, coming in, was frowning as he glanced at Gobnat holding the cauldron.

'I heard that your husband was in trouble, lady. Is there anything I can do?'

Fidelma had the impression that he was diverting the conversation for some reason. She shook her head. Her next move would be to see Ferloga. If it was not Conchoille who had sent Eadulf riding towards the abbey of Colmán, then it

315

was something Ferloga had said. She was not going down Brehon Dathal's path of reasoning, she thought angrily. Eadulf had left because he had heard something about Alchú. Of that much she was certain.

She suddenly saw that Gobnat was regarding her with a concerned expression.

'Are you worried for your man, lady? That is the curse of all women, for there is little constancy in men. They come and they go and do not give heed to the grief that they leave behind.'

Capa frowned in annoyance at his wife.

'Still your tongue, woman. The king's sister does not want to hear your philosophy.' He went on hurriedly, 'I am told that the *crossan*, the players we encountered at Cnoc Loinge, have arrived this morning and are setting up their camp behind the township.'

'The company was due to perform in Cashel,' Fidelma explained.

'It is sad that the dwarf who dressed as a leper was killed,' went on Capa. 'He might have been able to identify the woman who pretended to be my wife and sent him with the message to Sárait.'

Fidelma was still thinking about Eadulf. Gobnat mistook the meaning of her thoughtful features.

'Perhaps some other person will be able to identify the woman who pretended to be me. It should be easy to find someone who wears such a distinctive cloak.'

Fidelma nodded absently. 'Let us hope so, for if the Uí Fidgente are not involved in this matter, then we have to find . . .'

The noise of a galloping horse caused her to pause. A moment later a voice cried out: 'Sister Fidelma! Lady!'

Capa reached the door first, followed by Fidelma.

A messenger from the palace sat outside on horseback.

'What is the matter?' demanded Capa, annoyed that one of his warriors should seem so undisciplined.

'I was told the lady Fidelma would be here,' the messenger cried. Then he spotted Fidelma behind Capa. 'Brother Eadulf, lady! It is reported that he is at the bridge across the Suir and on his way to Cashel . . . and he has Alchú with him. Safe and well, according to one of our sentries who rode here immediately to alert us.'

Fidelma stared at him without speaking.

'It is true, lady,' the man confirmed. 'He will be at the palace shortly if not already. Caol and some warriors have been sent to greet him. Your baby is safe home again, lady. Safe!'

Fidelma was already running for her horse.

Eadulf and his party had crossed the bridge over the River Suir and seen one of the guards on it despatched at a gallop towards the distant Rock of Cashel. Eadulf and Basil Nestorios rode ahead with Gormán just behind, and a light wagon driven by Nessán the shepherd, with Muirgen at his side carrying the baby, brought up the rear. They had proceeded a fair distance when Gormán raised his arm and called to Eadulf.

'Here comes our escort, Brother.'

A group of horsemen came trotting along the road towards them, and Eadulf immediately recognised Caol at their head. The warrior raised his hand in greeting as they came up. His expression was serious.

'Is it true?' he demanded, looking curiously from Eadulf and Gormán to Basil Nestorios and then to the couple on the wagon. His eyes fell on the baby in Muirgen's arms. Eadulf nodded towards the infant with a smile.

'Alchú is safe and well and we are bringing him home. Does Fidelma know?'

'Someone has gone to tell her. Much has happened since you left, Brother Eadulf.'

Eadulf frowned when he saw no lightening of the serious expression on the other's face.

'This should be a moment of joy, Caol. Yet you seem unhappy.'

'Everyone has been wondering why you left Cashel so quickly.'

'Haven't an itinerant herbalist and his wife arrived in Cashel?'

Caol stared at him a moment as if he did not understand. Then he shrugged.

'I am told that travelling players and a herbalist are encamped outside the town, ready for the forthcoming fair day.'

'And they have not spoken to anyone yet?'

Caol shook his head.

'Well, I'll explain when we get to the palace,' said Eadulf. 'Meanwhile, we can rejoice at the safe return of Alchú.'

'There are many questions to be answered first.' Caol turned to Gormán. 'And I suppose that you have a good excuse for deserting Cashel at this time?'

Gormán flushed. 'I felt my duty was to go in support of Brother Eadulf.' There was a slight note of defiance in his voice at the censure implied by his comrade's words.

'And were it not for Gormán,' added Eadulf, 'I and my good friend Basil Nestorios,' he nodded to his companion, who was looking bewildered, 'would not be here at all.'

'And who are these others?' asked Caol.

'They are a shepherd and his wife, who have come to look after Alchú on our journey back to Cashel.' There was anger in Eadulf's voice now. 'What is wrong? Why this strange greeting when you should be filled with joy for Fidelma and myself?'

Caol looked at him apologetically.

'Eadulf of Seaxmund's Ham, I am acting on the orders of the Brehon Dathal, Chief Brehon of the kingdom. I have no other choice but to make you my prisoner. You have been charged with murder.'

Eadulf gasped in astonishment.

'Murder? Of whom?' he demanded.

'Of Bishop Petrán.'

Eadulf sat on the single cot in his cell-like chamber in the section of the palace given over to prisoners and hostages. The final leg of the journey to Cashel had been a curious experience. Fidelma had arrived soon after Caol. After fussing over the baby, she, too, appeared shocked when Caol told her that Eadulf was formally a prisoner. She demanded on whose authority Caol was acting and, when told that it was on the specific order of Brehon Dathal, had told Eadulf not to worry and gone riding off like a mad thing towards the palace.

Caol had been correct in his behaviour and during the time he rode as escort with Eadulf he sought to bring him up to date on all that had happened during his absence. When they arrived at Cashel, Eadulf was led immediately to the area where prisoners were kept and told he must wait for Brehon Dathal to question him. Caol promised to take Muirgen and Nessán directly to Fidelma and also to look after Basil Nestorios. Capa, he was told, would probably reprimand Gormán, as he was commander of the guard. With little more ado, Eadulf had been left to his own devices in the small stone chamber. He felt a black despair. He had endured so much, and now to be falsely accused of killing the old bishop . . . His mind went back to his false imprisonment in the abbey of Fearna. Fidelma had come to his rescue then, but now he was imprisoned in the palace of Fidelma's own brother and charged by his chief judge. Despair and anger fought within him but despair had the upper hand.

Several hours seemed to pass before the door opened abruptly and Fidelma appeared.

He sprang towards her and for a few moments they held each other tight.

'How is the boy?' he asked.

Fidelma smiled. There were tears in her eyes.

'He is fine. Muirgen and her husband Nessán are still looking after him. They have Sárait's old chamber next to ours. They have told me their part in the story. I have also been talking to Basil Nestorios. I can't wait to hear the full tale from you. But first we must deal with this matter. This is all Brehon Dathal's doing.'

'You must know that I would not harm old Bishop Petrán.'

'I know that. The trouble is that Dathal is Chief Brehon. He has authority, even over my brother to some extent. I am waiting to see Colgú. He does not know what has happened yet as he is in council with Conrí, the Uí Fidgente warlord.'

'I heard that Conrí was here. I must hear all about that from you.'

'It is a long story. But let me ask you first what it was that took you to the abbey of Colmán? In other words, why did you leave Cashel? Brehon Dathal is claiming it was because you killed the old man.'

'That is sheer nonsense. I went to find Conchoille, the woodsman—'

'Who says you never saw him.'

320

Eadulf nodded quickly. 'That is true. I went to the inn where Conchoille said he had supper on the night he found Sárait—'

'Ferloga's inn at Rath na Drínne?'

'The same. Ferloga told me of itinerants who were encamped in the wood. But they only had one baby with them . . .'

Fidelma's eyes brightened with excitement.

'And when we went to Ara's Well we were told these itinerants had two babies?' she said.

'Exactly! I knew that they were heading towards the abbey of Colmán, so I left the note for you and hurried after them. It was a desperate lead, but our only one. It turned out that I was correct. They were innocent in their intent and they are now here at the camping ground with the *crossan* to explain matters. Their names are Corb and Corbnait.'

'I will go to see them.'

'One other thing. Gormán will give you the details . . . but Fiachrae of Cnoc Loinge is a traitor to your brother.'

Fidelma looked shocked, and then she said quickly: 'I want to hear it all in detail. But first we must secure your release.'

'How am I supposed to have killed Petrán?'

'By poison. I am told that Brehon Dathal is coming to question you. Do not worry. We shall have you free soon.'

Eadulf sighed deeply. 'In the short time that I have been here in this cell, Fidelma, I have thought much. On the ride back from the bridge Caol told me roughly what had happened with you and Conrí. Is it true?'

'That Conrí rescued me? It is true.'

'And if Sárait was not murdered during the kidnapping of our child and Alchú was simply left to perish in the woods, as the travellers claimed, why was Sárait lured out of the palace to her death in the first place? Who killed her?' Eadulf leant forward and laid a hand on her arm. 'Think about this, Fidelma. We employed Sárait to be a wet nurse to young Alchú, didn't we?'

Fidelma made an impatient gesture. 'You know we did.'

'But when?'

'From the time he was born. Six months ago. What is there to think about on that matter?'

Eadulf regarded her with an intent look for a moment.

'I had overlooked the point until it was proposed to me that I needed a wet nurse to look after the baby on the journey to Cashel,' he said quietly. 'When we employed Sárait her own child was very recently dead. It was stillborn, according to her account. Alchú was born six months ago and she was able to feed him.'

Fidelma was trying to follow his thoughts. 'And?'

'Who was the father of Sárait's baby?'

'Why, Callada, of course, who was . . .' She paused and stared back.

Eadulf gave a small smile of triumph. 'Who was killed at Cnoc Áine,' he said softly. 'Exactly so.'

Fidelma exhaled slowly. 'Gormán? You think he was the father?'

'I have not asked him yet.'

'I see,' she said softly. Then she shook herself, almost like a dog shaking itself after being immersed in water. 'But the first task I must set myself is to find out why Brehon Dathal has had you incarcerated. Don't worry, I shall get you released soon.'

She made a move towards the door and then turned back, impulsively taking both his hands in her own.

'Eadulf, I regret all the things I did or said, and any actions of my people, that have made you feel a stranger and inferior to us.'

322

Eadulf grinned awkwardly. 'No one can make another feel inferior without his or her consent. If a person thinks others are deeming him inferior it is because *he* feels it. I may have felt unwelcome at times, but that is because I am a stranger to this land and, as such, *not* welcome to some. But that is the nature of people. We are always more comfortable with the things we know.'

'Will you forgive us . . . will you forgive me?'

'You cannot forgive the golden eagle for being a golden eagle,' he replied gently. 'There is nothing to forgive you for because you have acted in accordance with your nature.'

Fidelma pouted. 'Eadulf, at times you make me despair. You are too nice and forgiving,' she admonished him.

He shrugged with a whimsical smile. 'And that is *my* nature.'

Fidelma was crossing the courtyard when she became aware of a disturbance at the gates. She crossed to them and found Caol with a man and a woman. The latter held a baby in her arms.

'What is it?' Fidelma demanded.

Caol grimaced in annoyance. 'An itinerant herbalist and his wife demanding entrance. I have told them to be on their way.'

'But the Saxon brother—' began the man.

'Silence. You are speaking in the presence of the sister of the king,' snapped Caol.

'Wait!' instructed Fidelma. 'You are the herbalist Corb and you are his wife Corbnait?'

'We are. Brother Eadulf told us to come here and we promised we would even though it might bring down punishment upon us. I am a man of my word. I was not always an itinerant.'

Fidelma's face softened. 'You are most welcome. I do not blame either of you for the role you have played. Indeed, you were the means of saving my son's life when he was abandoned in the forest. Come, we will take a drink together and over it you may tell me the story that you told to Brother Eadulf.'

She was turning away when Caol called after her. She glanced back.

'You asked me to tell you when Brother Conchobar returned to Cashel,' the warrior reminded her. 'He has done so.'

The door of the cell opened and Brehon Dathal came in. He stood looking sourly at Eadulf.

Eadulf sprang up from the single cot that furnished the cell.

'What is this nonsense?' he demanded.

Brehon Dathal motioned to someone who stood outside the door and a warrior handed him a three-legged stool.

'Sit down,' the old man ordered sharply.

Eadulf reluctantly obeyed. 'I say again, what is this nonsense, Dathal? Who has made up this preposterous story that I killed Bishop Petrán?'

'Do you deny that you have often argued with Bishop Petrán?'

Eadulf almost laughed. 'I do not. We disagreed fundamentally about matters relating to the conduct of the church. And most people in the five kingdoms would also disagree with his teachings. While I have supported the authority of Rome, for we are told it is where Peter, into whose hands the Christ gave the building of his church, began that task, I cannot support Petrán's other more ascetic arguments.'

'So you killed him?'

Eadulf snorted in indignation.

Brehon Dathal regarded him sourly.

'You would do well to take me seriously, Saxon. Do you think that because I am old I cannot any longer judge the facts?'

Eadulf stared at him for a moment or two.

'I do not care whether you are young or old. When a false accusation is made, I do not take it kindly. I could similarly ask you whether it is because I am a stranger to this land that you think I must be guilty of murder?'

'I abide by the law,' snapped Brehon Dathal. 'I am not prejudiced against you.'

'I abide by facts.'

'The facts are simple. Bishop Petrán was found dead in his chamber. He was poisoned. You fled from Cashel on that very day. On the previous evening you were seen to have had a violent row with the bishop. Do you deny these facts?'

'I do not deny that I had a row with Petrán but I deny it was violent. I deny that I fled from Cashel. I left Cashel, leaving a note for Fidelma, after I had discovered something that led me to believe that I might find my son. And find him I did. I had no idea that Petrán was dead until Caol told me on my return.'

'And you expect me to believe that?'

'I do not expect anything except the courtesy of being heard without bias.'

Brehon Dathal coloured. 'You dare accuse me, the Chief Brehon of Muman, of being biased?'

'I do not accuse you. I merely comment on what I see,' snapped Eadulf.

'Things will go badly for you, stranger, unless you confess your misdeed now.'

'You threaten me?' Eadulf sprang up.

A warrior appeared in the doorway. He looked apologetic.

'Brother Eadulf, it would be wise if you remained seated and answered the Brehon's questions with respect,' he said quietly.

Eadulf realised that he was doing himself no good by giving vent to anger. He returned to his seat on the bed.

'I refuse to answer any questions from someone who seems to have prejudged my guilt and does not offer me the slightest evidence to back his accusation apart from the fact that I was seen to have an argument with the bishop.'

Brehon Dathal, the skin stretched tight around his mouth in anger, rose and strode from the room. The warrior picked up the abandoned stool. The cell door slammed shut.

Eadulf began to feel rage overtaking his sense of despair and he fought to control it.

Fidelma, having confirmed the story of Corb and Corbnait and ensured that they were receiving proper hospitality as witnesses, hurried to Brother Conchobar's apothecary shop.

'You should have warned me,' she said immediately on entering, irritation and disapproval in her voice.

The elderly apothecary glanced up in surprise from the herbs he was pounding in a pestle with a mortar.

'Warned you, lady?' he asked blankly.

'About the results of your tests on Bishop Petrán,' she snapped.

The man's face was blank. 'Why would I warn you about that?'

'Because Brehon Dathal has had Eadulf arrested and charged him with the killing. Eadulf is in serious trouble and I need to know from you how this poison was administered and anything you can tell me about its nature.'

Brother Conchobar looked utterly confused.

'Poison? Killing? What are you talking about, lady?'

Fidelma tried to contain her impatience.

'I am talking about Bishop Petrán. Eadulf is charged with administering the poison that killed him.'

Brother Conchobar raised his arms helplessly.

'Bishop Petrán was not poisoned.'

It was now Fidelma's turn to look utterly bewildered.

'Then how was he killed?'

The old apothecary ran a frail hand through his thinning grey hair.

'I do not know how you came by this information, lady. Petrán was not killed. He died, true. He died of failure of his heart to continue to beat. It happens and no one is to blame. I have seen the signs before but I wanted to conduct a few tests to make sure. If death is ever deemed natural, he died a natural death. I told that old fool Dathal as much before I left for Lios Mhór. Didn't he . . .?'

Fidelma stared at him in astonishment.

'Lady . . .?' he prompted nervously.

'Who told Brother Dathal that it was poison?' she finally whispered. 'Who said that it was murder?'

'Not I,' the apothecary replied firmly. 'In fact, I explained clearly to Brehon Dathal that Petrán's heart had simply failed. It was before I left for Lios Mhór, as I told you. I said that I would make a formal statement to that effect after my return but he has not sent for it.'

'Not sent . . .?' Fidelma was silent for a moment. 'Thank you, old friend,' she said softly. 'Your statement may well be wanted soon.'

Brother Conchobar shrugged. 'I am getting used to Brehon Dathal's not taking formal statements on matters relating to the cause of death,' he said irritably.

'What do you mean?' Fidelma inquired, turning back from the door.

'Sárait's manner of death, for example.'

'You examined the body?'

'I did, and should have been required to give evidence. No one asked me for a statement.'

Fidelma stared at him in surprise. In the initial confusion about who was investigating the case, the fact that Conchoille and Capa had mentioned the blood about the head and the stab wounds, she had neglected to ask who had made a formal pronouncement of death.

'What evidence would you have given?' she asked softly. 'That she died from a heavy blow to the head?'

Brother Conchobar made a negative gesture.

'That Sárait was already dead when the blow was struck. She had been the subject of a frenzied knife attack. There were five stab wounds in her chest and lacerations on her arms where she had tried to protect herself from the descending knife. She was facing her attacker when it happened. The blow to the head looks to me as if she fell during the attack and hit her head on something.'

There was a silence. Then Fidelma nodded slowly. 'You have been a great help this day, my old friend,' she said in thoughtful satisfaction.

A few minutes later she was in her brother's reception chamber. The king's conference had just broken up but he was still discussing what had been said with his tanist Finguine. They both glanced up in surprise as she entered without being announced.

With a quick wave of her hand to still their questions, she told them what she had discovered about Brother Conchobar's report on Bishop Petrán.

Colgú sat in silence for a moment or two before turning to Finguine. 'Go and release Brother Eadulf at once and bring him here.' When he had gone, Colgú glanced uncomfortably towards his sister. 'The duties of a king are arduous, Fidelma. Brehon Dathal is elderly.'

'He is Chief Brehon of the kingdom. He cannot act like this.'

'I agree. I do not mean to excuse him but I think age and pressure are telling on him. You know I have been trying to think of a way of asking him to stand down from his position. He is making increasingly erroneous judgements. Some time ago he made a really bad misjudgement at a hearing in Lios Mhór and it went to appeal. The appeal was successful and Dathal has had to pay several fines and compensation.'

Fidelma regarded her brother silently for a moment.

'I recall being told that it was Brehon Dathal who was asked to hear the claims that Sárait's husband, Callada, was killed by one of his men at Cnoc Áine. He found no case to answer. I wonder . . .?'

'Too much time has passed to speculate on that judgement, Fidelma. However, Dathal has recently been getting ideas which become fixed in his mind and he has often pursued them without sufficient reflection on the evidence. He no longer has the sharp mind that is needed to be a Brehon, let alone Chief Brehon. But I need to allow him to leave with some dignity, Fidelma. You will appreciate that.'

Fidelma tried to put aside her personal feelings and view the matter objectively.

'I can understand there are politics to be played here, but he must be made to stand aside and you have the responsibility for making him do so.'

Colgú nodded unhappily. 'I would rather persuade him than force him.'

'You are the king,' she said grimly.

There was a knock on the door and Finguine came in. Eadulf was behind him.

Fidelma hurried towards Eadulf, catching him by the

hands. 'Everything is all right. It was all a mistake on Brehon Dathal's part.'

Eadulf grimaced cynically. 'I could have told you that,' he said with an attempt at humour. 'Finguine has just told me the news.'

Colgú came forward and embraced him.

'My friend, husband of my sister, you must forgive us. Brehon Dathal leapt to conclusions with an impatience he should not have indulged. You should never have been put through such an experience, coming so soon after your own travails. At least our family is once again united.'

Eadulf felt awkward. He was embarrassed at the warmth exhibited by Fidelma's brother and, in truth, a little unsure of the affection that Fidelma was displaying towards him.

Then he found Finguine holding out his hand and grinning. 'Am I forgiven as well?'

Eadulf's glance encompassed them all.

'Well,' he said, unable to banish all the sarcasm from his tone, 'it is difficult to keep an equilibrium when first having one's life threatened, then being incarcerated and finally being welcomed into a family again . . .'

Fidelma squeezed his arm hard. 'We have much to apologise to you for, Eadulf. We will try to compensate you for the way you have been treated.'

Eadulf shrugged expressively. 'You cannot say fairer than that,' he sighed.

Colgú clapped him on the shoulder. 'Then we shall feast tonight, and—'

Fidelma shook her head quickly. 'Eadulf and I have a lot of work to do. There is still a mystery to be resolved and the killer of Sárait to be brought to justice. And you, my brother, have to deal with Brehon Dathal. When all this is done, then there shall be feasting.'

Some time later, the Chief Brehon of Muman was ushered into the king's chamber.

Colgú motioned the old man to be seated. He had known Dathal since he was a boy. Indeed, Brehon Dathal had been a young judge at the court of his father, Failbe Flann, nearly thirty years ago now. Brehon Dathal looked grave. He had already been informed of Eadulf's release on Brother Conchobar's evidence. Colgú wondered how he should approach the delicate matter at hand.

'Dathal, you have served this kingdom as Chief Brehon for a long time,' he began gently.

Brehon Dathal, with a quick frown, picked up on the nuance.

'Do you imply that it is too long?' he retorted sharply.

'Everyone reaches a point where they are not as youthful, not as active, as they were. My day will also come. I hope that I may have the good sense to acknowledge it when it does so that I can abdicate into a comfortable restfulness.'

'Restfulness is a quality that cows have, my prince. It is not for people.'

Colgú smiled. 'Didn't Horace write that one should dismiss an old horse in good time lest it falter in the harness and become an object of pity or scorn to spectators?'

Brehon Dathal sniffed in irritation.

'I made a mistake, that is all. Is not a judge entitled to a mistake? There is no harm done and the Saxon is free.'

'The Saxon is my sister's husband, Brehon Dathal,' Colgú pointed out. 'And compensation must be paid to him.'

'I know the laws of compensation.'

'I do not doubt you do,' Colgú returned. 'Remember that Eadulf of Seaxmund's Ham might be a stranger, but he had status in his own land. He was a hereditary *gerefa*, a sort of judge among his people.'

331

'Hereditary!' sneered Brehon Dathal. 'How can one inherit the competence of a judge without learning?'

'The ways of the Saxons are not our ways,' murmured the young king. 'However, the point I am making is that Eadulf is deserving of respect if not for his own sake, then for my sake and that of my sister.'

Brehon Dathal said nothing.

'Brehon Dathal, we have known each other a long time. Consider your position carefully now. You have made more than one error in recent times.'

Brehon Dathal's chin came up aggressively.

'Are you suggesting that I am no longer capable?'

'I am suggesting that it is now time to rest and watch others work. Stay in Cashel, if you will. Be an adviser to me. But now is the time to cease the arduous task of holding courts.'

'Who will you promote in my place . . . your sister?' The words were spoken challengingly.

Colgú shook his head quickly. 'Fidelma is not qualified for the position, nor would she want the task. She has studied only to the level of *anruth*, as well you know. To become a Brehon of standing she would need two – even four – more years of study to become a *rosai* or an *ollamh*.' These were the highest qualifications anyone could aspire to. 'You are a man of great experience and wisdom. In this appointment, friend Dathal, I would appreciate your advice. Who would you choose as my new Chief Brehon?'

Brehon Dathal began to look slightly mollified. Colgú waited patiently while the old man sat hesitating. Then it seemed that the old judge became reconciled to the inevitability of the decision that had to be made.

'Well, there is a *rosai* named Baithen whom I would think well qualified.'

Colgú smiled in satisfaction. He spared the old man's feelings by neglecting to say that he had already sent for Brehon Baithen, who had been conducting hearings at Lios Mhór. It had been Baithen who had thrice heard appeals against Dathal's judgements and overturned them.

'I have heard of this Brehon. It is a good choice.'

'He has a growing reputation,' Brehon Dathal agreed reluctantly. 'He is talented.'

'Then he will be asked here to judge of the matter of Sárait's death and apportion blame and compensation.'

Brehon Dathal frowned slightly at this news.

'So your sister believes that the Uí Fidgente are innocent of Sárait's death and the abduction of the baby, does she?'

'I believe that she has learnt new facts and prepared fresh arguments. Eadulf has brought us interesting evidence. But the case will be argued before Baithen.'

The old man's shoulders sagged slightly.

'Your sister does not take kindly to me over this matter of Bishop Petrán.'

'I am sure that she will agree that you acted according to your conscience, my old friend. You were simply not in possession of the facts. That is all.'

He knew he was bending the truth of Brother Conchobar's evidence to save the old man's dignity.

There was another silence, and Colgú felt somewhat relieved when the old man rose slowly from his seat.

'With your permission, my king, I shall retire to my chamber and rest.'

Colgú gestured with his hand in agreement.

The old judge, head bent to his shoulders, left the chamber, shutting the door behind him.

For some time Colgú sat looking at the closed door and then he sighed sadly. It was no more than two years since he had been confirmed in the kingship and for several years before that he had been heir apparent to his cousin Cathal, who had died of the Yellow Fever. This was the first time that he had been forced to dismiss one of his closest advisers, one who had served his father and his cousin, and now . . . Colgú turned to a side table and poured himself a drink of *corma*. It was the duty of a king to realise that time had to move on. People had to move on. It was inevitable. With the office of a ruler came the duty. If a king did not act he would not be regarded; if he was too hard, he would be broken; if he was too feeble, he would be crushed. Above all, he had to move with wisdom and subtlety, for if he showed himself more wise than others too much would be expected of him, and if more foolish he would find people deceiving him. There was always a middle way. That was the nature of kingship.

Chapter Eighteen

❧

Eadulf lay on the bed, hands folded over a well-filled stomach, and gave a deep sigh.

'There were times, Fidelma, during the last few days when I did not expect to be in this bed or this chamber again.'

Fidelma was pouring some mulled wine into a goblet as she knelt by the fire in the hearth. She rose and went across to the cot where Alchú lay peacefully asleep.

'Nor I, Eadulf. Nor did I expect to see this young one again.' She glanced anxiously at him. 'It is only when you lose something that you realise just how valuable it is to you.'

Eadulf eased himself into a sitting position. For a moment he wondered whether Fidelma's face was red from the heat of the fire or from the mulled wine that she was sipping. Before he could say anything Fidelma went hurriedly on as if drowning out her own thoughts: 'I have listened now to everything the witnesses have to say. The abduction of Alchú does not seem to be the issue. It was a matter of accident that Corb and Corbnait mistook him for an abandoned baby.'

'Uaman's involvement was no accident.'

She inclined her head thoughtfully. 'I spoke to Gormán. Colgú has already sent some of his guard to bring Fiachrae back to Cashel for a hearing of his conduct. We may get some of the Uí Fidgente to confess to Fiachrae's involvement with them. But the main mystery remains. Who killed Sárait and precipitated this evil series of events?'

Eadulf rubbed his chin pensively. 'Have you spoken to Della further about the cloak you recognised as hers?'

'Not yet.'

'Do you think she had lost it on purpose, or had someone taken it?'

'I don't think Della was lying. Why would she want to kill Sárait?'

'There is an answer. Gormán told us both that he was in love with Sárait. You believe that Della is more than fond of Gormán. And we know that Sárait's husband was not the father of her stillborn child. It seems logical that Gormán might have been the father and that Della . . .' He paused and shrugged.

'It sounds far-fetched,' muttered Fidelma. 'Della is not so blind in her emotions that—' She stopped short. Where emotions were concerned, all beings could become blind.

Eadulf was silent for a while. Then he sat up and rose from the bed, going to the fire and pouring himself another goblet of the warm, mulled wine.

'I meant to ask you, what made everyone so certain that the ransom note was genuine? Before I left, it was agreed that proof was to be demanded from the kidnappers. So why were the three Uí Fidgente chieftains released?'

Fidelma stretched in a chair before the fire. 'Throw another log on,' she instructed as Eadulf was bending before it. He selected one and placed it on the flames. Fidelma continued: 'Didn't Gormán tell you?'

'Gormán? What has he to do with that?'

'The innkeeper in the town handed him the response to

our demand. It was attached to the door of the local tavern.'

Eadulf whistled sharply. 'So the person responsible was in the vicinity of Cashel the whole time?'

'I wonder why Gormán didn't mention it?' Fidelma pondered.

'There was a lot going on at the Tower of Uaman,' Eadulf said, with a grimace of dismissal. 'But what was the evidence that was presented?'

'One of Alchú's baby shoes . . . the ones that my brother gave him for a present. I nearly died when I saw it returned to confirm that the kidnappers held him.'

Eadulf stared at her for a moment. 'But I brought back the baby shoes that he was wearing. Muirgen still had all his clothes.'

Fidelma started to shake her head and then a frown creased her brow. She went to the drawer of her chest and fetched the birch bark note and the shoe that had been sent back.

'Were these not what he was wearing on his feet?' she said, holding the latter out to Eadulf. He shook his head.

'No. He was wearing little woollen booties. Muirgen will testify to that. They are a bit soiled after all this time but they were the only pair missing from the chest. Don't you remember that your brother asked me to look through his clothing so that a description of what he was wearing could be given when the men went out to search?'

Fidelma was staring at him blankly. 'I don't understand.'

Eadulf was patient. 'Do you recall that Colgú wanted us to check the chest of clothes so that we could identify what clothes and footwear Alchú must have been wearing on the night Sárait took him out?'

Fidelma pursed her lips. 'Vaguely.'

'Vaguely would be right, for you were too upset to do it and asked me to check the chest.'

337

'The chest?' Fidelma cast a thoughtful glance at it, then gave an impatient gesture. 'And so? What are you saying?'

'Well, the shoe that you are now holding was in the chest when I looked. I mean the pair of shoes was there.'

'Are you sure?'

Eadulf sniffed indignantly. 'Perfectly sure. I would know them anywhere. Your brother had a cobbler make them especially for the little one.' He pointed to the shoe that Fidelma was holding. 'See the rawhide soles which I thought were too advanced for a baby of his age.'

A curious expression gathered on Fidelma's face.

'Do you remember when we returned to our chamber after it had been decided to demand proof from Alchú's so-called abductors? Wasn't Gormán lurking in the corridor by our chamber? He would have had an opportunity to take the shoes then.'

Eadulf cast his mind back, recalling the incident. 'You believe Gormán to be involved?'

Fidelma's features began to relax. 'I think that I am beginning to see a light in this curious business, Eadulf,' she said quietly. 'I need to see Della again.'

Eadulf shook his head. 'It is midnight. Not exactly the right time to go visiting.'

Fidelma hesitated, and then laughed, with a deprecating shrug.

'You are right. It's been a tiring day, a tiring two weeks. I'll go tomorrow. I don't think the quarry we hunt will have fled.'

It was mid-morning when Fidelma rode down to Della's house. With Eadulf's agreement, she had decided to approach the woman on her own.

Della gazed uncertainly at Fidelma when she opened the door to her.

'There is a purpose in your expression, lady. You look like a hunter who has sensed the quarry and is now moving in for the kill.'

Fidelma remembered her words to Eadulf on the previous night.

'That is a good analogy, Della. I have sensed the quarry but not yet driven it into the snare.'

'How may I help?' The former *bé-táide* stood aside and motioned her inside the warm little house. In the main chamber, where a fire smouldered, Fidelma sat down and indicated that Della should do likewise.

'Let me return to the conversation I had with you.'

'About the missing cloak?'

'That as well. I presume that you have told no one about it?'

'Of course not. You asked me not to.'

'I would ask you to keep this information quiet also. The dwarf who was sent with a false message to lure Sárait from the palace to her death has arrived in Cashel.'

Della frowned. 'But you told me he could not identify the woman?'

'There may be other ways of identification.'

Della compressed her lips for a moment but said nothing.

'You mentioned when we last spoke about Sárait that she had told you that she had been raped?'

Della nodded. 'But she never told me who it was.'

'I remember. Although I think we could deduce from what she said that the man was a warrior who had been at Cnoc Áine. Was it Gormán? Did he rape her?'

Della flushed. 'Never Gormán!' she snapped. 'He was in love with her.'

'And he told you that?' Fidelma said swiftly.

Della opened her mouth and realised she had said more than she had meant to.

'You might as well tell me everything,' Fidelma said. 'A warrior raped her. Did Sárait ever mention Gormán to you?'

At once spots of colour rose on Della's cheeks. 'It could not have been Gormán.'

'Are you in love with Gormán?'

To Fidelma's surprise Della started to laugh. 'Of course I love Gormán,' she said in amusement. 'Is that forbidden?'

Fidelma was taken aback. She had not been prepared for the honesty of the reply. There was a long silence.

'Let us move forward to something that is not in contention,' she said at last. 'Sárait had a stillborn child. It was born so long after Cnoc Áine that it could not have been the child of her husband Callada.'

Della sat back, watching Fidelma carefully, but said nothing.

'Clearly, the baby was conceived after her husband met his death. Was the child born of the rape?'

Della hesitated.

'It is important, Della,' Fidelma pressed. 'I do not ask with frivolous intent. I believe that the father of her child was her killer.'

Della stared in horror. 'What about the Uí Fidgente and the ransom?'

'A cunning ruse to set people on the wrong track. Linked with an accident of fate by which wandering strangers found the baby when it had been left to die in the woods, it did indeed lead me down the wrong path for a while.'

Della was quiet for a few moments and then she shrugged.

'You have presumed correctly, lady. The stillborn child was the result of the rape and Sárait was thankful that it died.'

340

Fidelma exhaled slowly. 'It is sad that one gives thanks for the extinguishing of life. But I can understand her feelings. When did you know about this?'

'I told you that Sárait first came to me within days of the rape to seek my advice – or rather she needed to talk to someone who would understand and not condemn her.'

'Why not discuss this with her sister, Gobnat?'

'Gobnat, as I have already said, was prudish. She would not have been the best of people to confide in. Sárait felt easier speaking to me. It was two months later that she came to me and said she was with child.'

'And she told you her condition resulted from the rape? But she did not tell you who the father was?'

Della nodded. 'She could not stand it. She wanted to know how she might get rid of it before it was born.'

'And you advised her?'

'Do you mean that I, as a *bé-táide*, would naturally know of these things?' There was some bitterness in Della's voice.

'I do not mean that,' snapped Fidelma. 'I have looked at the *Pharmacopoeia* of Dioscorides and could probably name the eight herbs that he maintains induce a state whereby the unwanted pregnancy is aborted. I am simply asking whether you advised her.'

Della blinked. 'I advised her and I gave her some of the plants that I have used, those which are diuretics and laxatives. I used to buy rue from the merchants of Gaul and take it as an infusion, mixing it with water.'

'But these remedies did not work.'

'Obviously. And I advised Sárait against going to the physicians who would butcher her body. So she had the child.'

Fidelma was frowning. 'Yet surely someone at Cashel would have known, would have suspected.'

Della shook her head quickly. 'She did not look pregnant.

341

And when she realised that soon she would not be able to disguise it, I sent her to a cousin of mine who lived up in the mountains at Araglin. She stayed there some months.'

Fidelma raised her head slightly. 'Araglin? I know that place.'

'Well, she stayed there for a while, had the child and, as you know, it was stillborn. It was buried there in the mountains, and when she was well Sárait returned to Cashel. She was still lactating for her child. I heard that you were in search of a wet nurse and sent her to you.'

'She never told me that you had sent her.'

'I did not want to embarrass you, lady. I told her to present herself to you as the widow of Callada the warrior, which I considered was recommendation enough.'

'It was. And that was why I assumed that her dead child was his. I had not realised what time had passed . . . Ah! Well, too late to dwell on past mistakes. Things become clearer.'

'I don't understand.'

'You may have to come to the palace, Della, and give your evidence before the Brehon. Will you do that?'

'If it helps to identify who killed Sárait and who was behind your baby's going missing all this time.'

Fidelma rose and smiled. 'If my suspicions are correct, we will soon identify that person. The question will be whether we can convict them.'

She suddenly frowned, holding her head to one side. There was a snuffling outside, and the whimpering of a dog. Both she and Della went to the door. A brown wire-haired hound was digging away in a corner. Fidelma had seen it before.

Della opened her mouth to shout to scare it away but Fidelma stayed her. The hound was throwing up earth in a feverish attempt to dig something up. Then with a yelp of triumph its muzzle went down and it drew something from the hole. It described a crazy circle and then, as if in a gesture of victory, it threw the object up in the air and caught it again.

Fidelma went into a crouching position and called in coaxing fashion to the dog, stretching out her hands. The animal bounded over and dropped the item at her feet, then backed away, head down, paws splayed, obviously expecting her to throw it for it to retrieve again. Instead, she rose to her feet and turned the earth-soiled object over in her hands.

It was a baby's shoe, the companion of the one that had been brought to her by Gormán. It was Alchú's missing shoe.

Fidelma had seen something else in the hole and she walked over to it, accompanied by the yapping dog, and stared down. Then she bent and began to pull some material out of the earth. It was green and red silk and was obviously a cloak with hood attached. She glanced back to where Della stood.

Della was staring at it, her face seeming to drain of blood.

Fidelma stared at her long and hard.

'I think that you had better walk back with me to the palace, Della. We have much to talk over.'

Chapter Nineteen

❧

The great hall of the palace of Cashel was thronged with people. The Brehon Baithen had arrived from Lios Mhór and Colgú, in agreement with Fidelma, had announced that a special court would be held which would clarify the abduction of Alchú and the murder of Sárait. It seemed that the whole of Cashel and the surrounding countryside had come to hear the new Chief Brehon of Muman give judgement in the matter.

The witnesses had been gathered and seated. Forindain the dwarf, Corb and Corbnait, Nessán and Muirgen, Conchoille the woodsman; everyone who had been connected with the events was packed into the great hall. Della was there, sitting grim-faced, and next to her, looking equally grim, was Gormán. Gobnat, Sárait's sister, was also there, glowering at Della. Her husband Capa, as guard commander, was in charge of the warriors, with Caol at his side. Even the old apothecary, Conchobar, who never attended such hearings unless absolutely necessary, had come to see the proceedings.

The guards had also led in Fiachrae of Cnoc Loinge, now a prisoner, who would later have to answer charges of betraying the Eóghanacht and working with the Uí Fidgente to overthrow Colgú. Enough witnesses had now come forward to make the case against him certain.

By special invitation of the king, Conrí was there with his Uí Fidgente warriors, towards whom many dirty looks were cast and muttering threats made. Even the old Brehon Dathal had entered the hall and made for the seat of the Chief Brehon before an embarrassed *rechtaire* or steward had guided him to a side chair.

Fidelma and Eadulf had already taken their seats just to the left of the chairs of office that the king, the tanist and the Chief Brehon would occupy. Cerball the bard and Bishop Ségdae had taken their seats. Then the *rechtaire* banged his staff of office and everyone rose as Colgú, Finguine and Brehon Baithen entered and seated themselves.

A ripple of expectation ran through the hall before Colgú raised his hand for silence. He waited until the hush descended.

'There is no need for me to explain why we are gathered nor what has happened these last two weeks. It is my duty to welcome the Brehon Baithen to my court and proclaim his office as the new Chief Brehon of the kingdom. Brehon Dathal, who has held that office since my father's day, has decided that it is now time to give way to a new and younger judge, having served us long and well in that position. We wish him prosperity in his new life and assure him that we will call upon him when appropriate to share with us his wisdom and advise us in our future affairs.'

Rumours about Brehon Dathal's retirement had already spread and the announcement was not new to those present.

The king then deferred to his new Chief Brehon.

While Baithen was of middle age, he had an almost ageless face. His skin was fresh and unblemished and his hair was of a golden corn colour. He was a fleshy, jocular-looking man, whose bright eyes twinkled as if he found the proceedings humorous.

'This hearing is a legal one and I will tolerate no demonstrations. Nor will I tolerate disrespect for the law, its officers or the solemnity of the occasion.' His features seemed to belie that very solemnity. 'So let us to the business of the day. Fidelma of Cashel will be our guide.'

Fidelma rose quickly and with a quick bow of her head towards the Brehon and her brother, in acknowledgement of their office, she turned to the gathering in the great hall.

'You all know that my nurse Sárait was murdered and that my baby son Alchú vanished for nearly two weeks. It was thought that he had been abducted and Sárait had been killed during the course of his abduction. Rumours circulated that it was a plot of the Uí Fidgente. This was not so. You all know Brother Eadulf, my dear companion and father of my child. He will now tell you the first part of the story, to demonstrate that our child was not abducted, but taken by accident. He will, I know, be modest, but he put his own life at risk in following our child to the Tower of Uaman and bringing him safely back to Cashel. Should proof of his adventures be demanded, witnesses sit in this very hall to confirm the facts.'

She turned to Eadulf who rose with some embarrassment and swiftly explained how he had discovered Alchú and brought the child back to Cashel. Fidelma smiled faintly in satisfaction as murmurs of approval echoed round the hall. When he reseated himself, she rose again.

'Should any point of the story be challenged, we have gathered witnesses to confirm it,' she said to Brehon Baithen. 'Gormán sits there, as does Brother Basil Nestorios, who needs must give his statements in Latin; also the itinerant

346

herbalist Corb and his wife, and the shepherd Nessán and his wife. All will confirm Eadulf's tale.'

Brehon Baithen asked if anyone would challenge the story but no one did, and so the judge urged Fidelma to continue.

'Now, those among you who have followed the proceedings may realise that this leaves a mystery. If Alchú was not abducted, if his intended abduction was not the cause of Sárait's being enticed out of the palace, then *she* was the victim. It was her death that was the object of the plot. Why and who plotted it, those are the questions we must answer today.'

She paused, sweeping her gaze across the expectant faces before her.

'It will be simplest if I take everyone through a sad story from the beginning. There were two sisters. I shall name them – Gobnat and Sárait. Sárait was the younger of the two. Both had married warriors of the élite bodyguard of the kings of Cashel. As you will know, one married Capa, our current commander of the guard who stands there. One married Callada who was killed at Cnoc Áine. Someone looked upon Sárait's marriage to Callada with jealousy for they were filled with lust for her. She rejected his advances, for she was happy with Callada.'

Gormán groaned in his seat and hunched forward. Della reached to lay her hand on his.

'I loved her,' the young warrior muttered, his voice audible to the hall.

Fidelma glanced at him without expression. 'As you made clear to me when we first met, and later repeated to Eadulf.' She paused, and then went on addressing the hall. 'The warrior who lusted after Sárait began to hate Callada to the extent that his hatred knew no bounds. Then came the day when in the heat of the battle of Cnoc Áine he found and took the opportunity to kill his rival. Rumours went round, as rumours do. Rumours that Callada had been slain by one of his own side. I do not have to bring forward such famous warriors as Cathalán to attest to the story, nor Capa, who was commanding the troop in which Callada served that day. Gormán, too, was in that troop. So was Caol. Many among you were at Cnoc Áine, like Ferloga there, and Conchoille. No one will deny the rumours . . .' she paused, 'and they were true.'

There was a silence as people digested her words.

'Some time later,' she went on, 'the killer of Callada began to pay attention to Sárait once more. Sárait had begun to suspect and distrust the man. She had turned for solace to another and that infuriated the killer almost to the point of madness.

'Time went by until the killer could no longer hold his passion in check and he raped Sárait. I think it was then that he probably boasted of what he had done for lust of her – he would, of course, claim it was for love of her, but I would say for lust. Sárait was disgusted. The word is too mild to convey the revulsion she felt. She was revolted when she found she was carrying the result of that rape – a child. She went to Della, for Della is known to be wise in these matters. She told Della what had happened but withheld the name of the man who had done the deed.

'Further, she told Della that she did not wish to bear a child conceived in rape and lust. She tried many things but the child was born, although no doubt in answer to her prayers and efforts that poor life was snuffed out at birth. When Sárait came to the palace in search of work, I employed her as wet nurse to my son Alchú. Here I must admit an error . . . I thoughtlessly assumed the child she had been carrying was Callada her husband's.

'It was Eadulf who first pointed out to me the fact that the time between Callada's death at Cnoc Áine and the baby's birth did not add up. She had conceived several months after her husband's death. It was then that I began to realise the extent of the problem we faced.' She looked without emotion at Della. 'Sárait was not Della's only confidant. Gormán also made a confession to her – that he was in love with Sárait.'

Della was pale and swayed a little in her seat, still clutching on to Gormán's hand.

'I saw Gormán leave her house one night, saw him embrace her intimately. Do not actions speak just as clearly as words?'

Della drew herself together. 'Gormán did not kill Sárait. He was in love with her and she told me that she responded to his kindness. He was not the one who raped her.'

Gobnat was glaring with hatred at Della.

'The whore should not be present!' she shouted. 'Disgusting! She is twice the age Gormán is. I wager she put him up to killing my sister.'

Fidelma ignored her.

'Indeed, a plot was evolved to kill Sárait. Not a simple plot, because the person who wished to kill her also wished to do it in such a way that they would not be suspected. The motive for the murder lay in hatred of Sárait because she was unwittingly the object of the warrior's lust and the murderer's jealousy.' She glanced quickly at Della. 'A woman was behind this plot.'

Della stared back, pale to the lips. Gormán groaned again. There was a deathly silence in the hall.

'The idea was to draw Sárait out of the palace one night and kill her. But how to do it without drawing attention to the killer? The woman who concocted this plot placed herself in the shadows near the inn so that she would not be

349

identified. She asked a child to go to the palace with a message saying that Sárait's sister wanted to see her urgently. Only such a message would draw Sárait from the comfort of the palace at night. But the child could not take the message because his father left the inn at that very moment and, having over-indulged in *corma*, needed the child's help to guide him home. Oh yes,' Fidelma smiled quickly at the assembly, 'I met and had a word with that child.'

She paused for a moment, but no sound was heard in the great hall.

'Now the woman had a piece of luck,' Fidelma continued. 'A traveller came to the inn. He was a travelling player – a *crossan* – wanting to check out the aspect of the township for his company. He was a dwarf whose name was Forindain. The woman offered him a *screpall* to take the message to the palace. Forindain was nothing loath to do it. But the woman knew the guards at the palace well and was aware they might ask questions. So she told the dwarf to act as if he were mute. She took from her *marsupium* a piece of birch bark on which she had already written the words "I am sent to see Sárait". Therefore he would be asked no questions. This action, however, caused some light to be shed on the woman and while her hood hid her features Forindain saw that she was wearing a very distinctive cloak. He described it to me.'

Caol suddenly raised his voice.

'That is not so, Fidelma,' he protested. 'The dwarf was killed at Cnoc Loinge before anyone could question him. You cannot put words into the mouth of the dead.'

Fidelma paused to let the murmurs die down.

'The poor dwarf who was killed at Cnoc Loinge was Forindain's brother, Iubdán, who just happened to be wearing Forindain's costume. He was mistaken for his brother and thereby lost his life.'

Capa was frowning, and glanced to the dwarf sitting nearby.

'Are you saying that this . . .?' he began.

'There sits the real Forindain,' Fidelma pointed to where the small *crossan* sat, 'who was in Cashel that evening, and who took the message to Sárait. He is the one who described the distinctive cloak to me. It was a description I immediately recognised, having seen the cloak worn by someone I knew. However, it was obvious that Iubdán had been killed in mistake for Forindain in order to still his tongue as a witness.'

Capa turned, pointing in accusation at Gormán. 'Gormán was the one who found the dwarf when we were at Cnoc Loinge.'

'I did find the body,' Gormán muttered, 'but I immediately sent word to Capa.'

'I remember,' said Fidelma solemnly. 'Let us turn to the matter of the cloak.' She bent to a bundle and extracted the red and green silk garment and held it up. A murmur rippled through the hall.

'That is the whore's cloak!' Gobnat suddenly yelled and for a moment everyone was in confusion until the Brehon Baithen brought them all to silence again.

'You recognise it, Gobnat?' asked Fidelma.

'I can attest to having seen that whore wearing it. So they are both in this together. They killed my sister!'

Fidelma nodded and laid the cloak down. She then picked up two baby shoes.

'When we asked for proof of Alchú's abduction, we were sent a baby shoe that belonged to him. The other I found with the green and red cloak. Both were buried in Della's yard.'

There were now angry shouts and threatening gestures,

351

directed at Gormán and the former *bé-táide*. Again the Brehon Baithen called sternly for silence and when the noise died away Fidelma continued once more.

'It was a dog that finally solved this murder,' Fidelma said evenly, and then turned to Della and Gormán. 'Della, I am sorry to have put you through this ordeal. You also, Gormán. Della and Gormán were not involved in this affair although several actions of theirs made me suspicious of them, my distrust being compounded by the fact that the real culprits – or one of them at least – did their best to lay a false trail to Della out of spite and hatred. Della and Gormán share a love . . . but it is the love of mother for son and son for mother. Is it not so?'

There was no need to ask the question. The faces of mother and son affirmed the truth. The silence that descended was almost unearthly. Everyone seemed to be holding their collective breath while awaiting any new revelation Fidelma might make.

Brehon Baithen leant forward from his chair. 'Are you going to eventually name the guilty one, Fidelma?' he asked softly, a faint note of sarcasm in his voice.

She swung round with raised brows. 'Is it not obvious? Gobnat killed her own sister because it was her husband, Capa, who was enamoured of Sárait. It was Capa who killed Callada and who raped Sárait. Having then discovered that his wife had killed Sárait, Capa did everything to lead suspicion away from her, even to the point of killing the dwarf Iubdán whom he had mistaken for Forindain.'

Gobnat began to protest shrilly, calling Fidelma worse than a whore to protect her whoring friend. It needed firmness to restore order, as well as some of the guards, who now took their orders from Caol. Brehon Baithen was looking baffled.

'For those who do not possess the quickness of your mind, Fidelma, perhaps you would share those of its processes that have led you to make this accusation?'

'I am prepared to do so. I said in my opening that there were two sisters, Gobnáit and Sárait. They were very different in character, although both married warriors. But while Capa was married to Gobnat he lusted after her younger sister. He felt that the only thing that stood in the way of a consummation of that lust was Callada. He killed Callada at Cnoc Áine. Then, having thought that his path was clear, he found Sárait revolted by him. He raped her. The rest of her story I have told you.

'Sárait had not only confided in Della – without naming Capa, of course – but had made the mistake of confiding in her sister, from whom one might have expected a close sympathy and understanding. Gobnat, to whom Capa had not been able to resist boasting of his subjection of her sister, became enraged. Despising Della as she did, she decided to strike down Sárait in such a way that guilt and punishment might be laid at Della's door. The object of Capa's jealousy, Gormán, whom Gobnat suspected of being Della's lover, would therefore also be implicated.'

Brehon Baithen rubbed his chin. 'What made you suspect that Gormán was Della's son?'

'From the first Gormán told Eadulf and me that he was the son of a prostitute. When I went to see Della, she mentioned that she was a mother. The connection became easy to work out. In fact, Gormán told us that he thought Capa disliked him because his mother was a prostitute. That was only partially true. Capa also knew that Sárait had become fond of Gormán while she rejected his own attentions. So he tried to implicate Gormán in the killing of the dwarf. Capa felt he had to kill Forindain, by the way, because

353

he thought the dwarf might have been able to identify his wife. He could not be sure that the dwarf had not seen her face in the lantern light of the inn.'

'What I can't understand is why did Gobnat go to the trouble that you have described when she must have had countless opportunities to kill her sister without evolving such an ingenious plot?' Baithen pondered.

'As I say, she wanted to absolve herself of any implication in it, and to implicate Della. To that end, she stole Della's cloak, a distinctive garment. Then came the charade of sending the message to the palace. If anyone saw her, she could be sure that it was not Gobnat who would be described. Someone in rich silk, indeed, when Gobnat dressed so austerely.'

'This is madness!' cried Gobnat.

'We will see,' replied Brehon Baithen.

Old Brehon Dathal coughed and stood up.

'I have listened to these accusations. In my opinion, were I still Chief Brehon, I would stop you now, Fidelma, and dismiss the case at once. There are too many suppositions, and questions pile up for you to answer.'

It was clear that Brehon Baithen was irritated by this intervention, but before he could remonstrate Fidelma replied: 'Then let me continue and I will answer them.'

'Indeed,' Brehon Baithen said quickly. 'We will hear what the learned *dálaigh* has to say, as is custom in *my* court, Dathal.'

'Like all plans,' Fidelma went on, 'Gobnat's plan went awry. First, Sárait came to her sister's dwelling with Alchú. She thought that while she carried the child with her, Capa would not attack her again. She knew that even in his perverted lust he would never endanger an Eóghanacht baby. He was, strangely, a loyal servant of my family. Gobnat had no such loyalty – only hatred.

'Although Gobnat planned to kill her sister in cold blood, the murder was done in a fit of rage. The number of knife wounds demonstrates that. How she must have hated Sárait. She struck her again and again in her fury. The head wound occurred when Sárait fell, striking her head against a small cauldron by the fireplace that I noticed had been dented. At least that is my guess. The murder, I believe, was done in Gobnat's house. Where else would Sárait go in response to an urgent message from her sister but to her sister's house? Gobnat's aim was to hide the body at Della's house so that it would be found with the cloak. But before she could do so, Capa, her husband, came home. Capa was no angel and he knew what would happen to him if Gobnat was caught and told her reasons. He now had to get rid of Sárait's body and little Alchú.

'Something prevented him from taking the body to Della's house, and hence the first flaw in the plot. The other thing was that by some strange morality he could not bring himself to kill the baby. Sárait had been right. He could not do it directly, but he left the child in the woods to die.'

Capa was standing up to protest. His face was pale and the muscles were twitching around his mouth.

'This is a fantasy! Where is your proof?'

'When we first start on the path of deceit we have to weave through many side paths. We keep having to cover the original lie by more lies. And more actions. You took the body of Sárait into the woods where Conchoille, the woodsman, later found her. When you simply left the baby elsewhere for the beasts to devour, you did not realise that Corb and Corbnait were nearby. They took the child away with them, believing it to be simply abandoned.

'You had probably not long returned to your home when Conchoille, who knew Sárait, came running to say he had found her body. You then went through the motions of being an outraged brother-in-law. Gobnat, meanwhile, had to bury the cloak in her own yard for the time being because the discovery of the murder and Alchú's being missing made it difficult to do anything else.

'This is where Capa began to act on his own to cover up this terrible affair. He feared the dwarf Forindain could identify Gobnat, and while we were searching for the dwarf in Cnoc Loinge he came across the person he thought was Forindain and killed him. That was a mistake.

'Gobnat also made a mistake. She had succumbed to Capa's insistence that they lay another false trail. He had her write a ransom note that would point to Uí Fidgente involvement. The three Uí Fidgente chiefs were to be released in return for Alchú. It was a good idea to do it while Capa was away at Imleach and Cnoc Loinge. But Capa had not realised that we would demand evidence that the person who wrote the note held Alchú. After the meeting when we decided to ask for evidence, he was sent to get a herald's standard from a room near our chamber and took the opportunity to snatch a pair of baby shoes from our chest. When the shoe was presented as evidence I did not realise that Eadulf had seen it in the chest of clothes well after the abduction. Alchú had not been wearing them. They had been taken long afterwards.

'I was confused at first by the fact that we found Gormán outside our chamber door at that time. So when Eadulf pointed out that Gormán could not have had the opportunity to take the baby shoes, I asked him how could he be sure.' She glanced at Eadulf, who took up the story.

'A servant was inside our chamber preparing it for the evening. If Gormán had just emerged from the chamber she would have seen him. But there had been time for Capa to slip inside and grab the shoes before she entered the room.

He did so hurriedly, leaving a piece of clothing trailing out under the lid. Which we wrongly blamed the servant for doing. That was another mistake.'

'It is still all surmise,' Brehon Baithen pointed out.

'Yet this surmise fell into place when Gobnat made a major slip,' replied Fidelma. She turned towards Capa's wife with a soft smile of triumph.

Gobnat was concentrating with a frown, trying to remember what she had said.

'I was in your house the other night looking for Conchoille. You and Capa seemed worried by your dog's digging in the yard.'

'Why shouldn't we be annoyed at the dog?'

'No one had mentioned or described the cloak worn by the woman who sent the message to the palace that night. Only Forindain, whom you thought dead, had seen it and described it. Only Della and myself knew the description of the cloak, and only we two knew that it was missing from her trunk . . . and, of course, one other person – the person who stole it and was wearing it when she gave the false message to Forindain.

'Thinking that Forindain had been killed, you turned to me and said: "Perhaps some other person will be able to identify the woman who pretended to be me. It should be easy to find someone who wears such a distinctive cloak." Those were your exact words.'

Gobnat shrugged. 'So what? Forindain, as you say, was not killed. He described to you the cloak that the woman who sent him to the palace had been wearing and it was a cloak belonging to that whore . . .' She was indicating Della when she stopped. She blinked as she realised what she had said.

Fidelma continued calmly. 'No one, at that time, had

mentioned anything about a woman in a distinctive cloak. How could Gobnat know, unless . . .?' She left the question hanging in the air.

There was a moment's silence and then Capa rose. His voice came out in a scream of rage.

'It was her . . . her . . .' he yelled, pointing to his wife. 'She did it and what could I do but protect her? I am not responsible for the deed. I am innocent of it. My role was to protect her . . .'

Gobnat collapsed as the realisation of her situation dawned on her.

When some order had been restored, Brehon Baithen turned to Fidelma.

'You said, however, that a dog had solved the puzzle. How was this?'

'It was Capa's hound that brought it all together,' Fidelma agreed solemnly.

Brehon Baithen raised his eyebrows in query. 'I do not see . . .'

'First, when Forindain was called by the woman standing in the shadows, a hound had leapt, probably in play, at him. But the woman called it away. That of itself was nothing. Then, what woke Corb and Corbnait in the wood and led them to find Alchú abandoned there? It was the howling of a hound and the sound of someone calling it away. When I saw Capa's hound digging in the yard, I was surprised that it seemed to upset both Capa and Gobnat. I suspect that it was where Gobnat initially hid the cloak and the remaining baby shoe. That night, Gobnat dug them up and did what she had initially intended – she waited until dark and reburied them in Della's yard. She could not have planned it better, for I was there when the hound came along and dug them up again. But why would a hound dig up these particular clothes? The answer was that Gobnat had worn them and her scent, which the hound recognised, was on them. That is what attracted the dog to them.'

'A most complicated business, Fidelma,' mused Brehon Baithen. 'You, and of course Brother Eadulf, are to be congratulated on bringing this matter to a successful conclusion.'

Fidelma suddenly grinned; it was her mischievous grin. It had been a long time since she had been able to grin.

'I think the hound deserves the congratulations. Sometimes dogs are more intelligent than humans.'

Two days later, Fidelma and Eadulf sat stretched before the hearth in their chamber. A fire crackled, keeping out the winter chills. They both sipped mulled wine from goblets replenished from a pottery jug, which stood warming by the fire. Little Alchú was peacefully asleep in a corner of the room. Suddenly, Fidelma uttered a deep sigh.

'*Si finis bonus est, totum bonum erit,*' she said quietly. 'I remember saying that to Gormán before we started out to Imleach.'

'If the end is good, everything will be good. What is happening with Gormán and Della?'

'Gormán will overcome his sorrow, for that is the way of things. He has no reason to be ashamed of Della for she is a good mother and a good friend.'

'*Haec olim meminisse iuvabit,*' muttered Eadulf. Time, indeed, was a great healer and most wounds could be healed by its passage. 'But there is still something that I do not understand. Do you remember when we discussed matters with the council I said that the first mystery was why Sárait took our baby with her that night when she could have left him with one of several women in the palace? And you agreed with me. Yet you said at the hearing that she thought Alchú would protect her from harm. How did you know that?'

'Like most things, the answer was simple,' replied Fidelma. 'Della confirmed that after Sárait had been raped – by Capa, as we now know – she feared further harm. She believed that no harm would come to her while she was looking after the king's nephew. Mistakenly she thought the rank of the child would protect her. Hatred is a great leveller. Gobnat hated her too much to let that stand in the way.'

'And Conrí and his men have departed for their home?' Eadulf said, after a moment or so of reflection.

Fidelma confirmed it with a nod of her head.

'Let us hope that some period of peace may now begin between our peoples. And your friend Brehon Dathal has now officially retired to his little rath by the River Suir,' she added mischievously. Eadulf pulled a face that set her laughing. 'Anyway, Brehon Baithen is a good man. He will serve my brother well. And so will Caol as new commander of his guard. And tomorrow we are invited to the fair on the green below to see Forindain and his company of *crossan* play the story of the Faylinn. If there is someone who deserves our sympathy it is the little dwarf who lost his brother. Capa has much to answer for.'

'Yet slaughter is a warrior's philosophy and art,' pointed out Eadulf. 'We train warriors to kill on our behalf in order to protect our society and us. But in creating the killing instinct in the warrior, surely we create something that is not easily controlled. A warrior can as easily kill on his own behalf, when he feels there is cause, as he can kill for his chief's cause. Telling a man raised in the philosophy of slaughter not to kill is like telling a bird not to fly. It becomes his first choice as a reaction and not his last. That was Capa's way of trying to protect himself and Gobnat.'

Fidelma was not convinced.

'Not all warriors are like that. I have known many who are honourable.'

'Perhaps. But are they exceptions or the rule? Many are not so honourable and we should not be surprised when they show their nature.'

'In that case perhaps my brother should not have handed over Cuirgí and Cuán to Conrí. They are certainly trained killers. Of all of them, I felt only Crond had some saving grace, but in the end even he would have killed me.'

'Which proves my point. Anyway, Conrí is going to have them tried by the Brehon of the Uí Fidgente so that they can be stripped of their chieftainships. He feels that it is a way to heal the wounds between his people and yours.'

'Let us hope so.'

'And what of Muirgen and Nessán?' demanded Eadulf. 'When do they head back to Sliabh Mis?'

'If you agree, they will not. I was going to bring this up later. Muirgen will make a very good nurse to young Alchú and my brother has herds on the slopes of Maoldomhnach's Hill that need a good pastor.'

Eadulf's eyes widened in surprise.

'Have they agreed to this?'

Fidelma gave a gesture of affirmation.

'We now await your approval of the idea. If so, Nessán can head back to Sliabh Mis to make the necessary arrangements for closing their homestead and dispersing their flock before rejoining his wife. Muirgen seems to have taken to life in Cashel with some enthusiasm. And perhaps we can find an orphan for them to foster as their own as well. Perhaps someone for Alchú to go into fosterage with.'

'Fosterage?' Eadulf frowned.

'You know our laws now, Eadulf. When Alchú reaches

the age of seven we must send him to fosterage until he is seventeen. Under the law, we must send him to some chieftain or learned person who will tend to his welfare and education. This is our custom, intended to make our people strong by creating bonds between families.'

'Have I nothing to say in the matter?' Eadulf felt a pang of his old frustration.

'Not under our law,' she replied gently. 'Alchú is the son of a *cú glas*, a foreign father, and therefore it is up to me as mother to make the arrangements for fosterage. It is our custom and our law.'

'Which raises a point . . .' began Eadulf.

'It does,' said Fidelma, looking suddenly serious. 'In a few days' time, our trial marriage comes to an end. The year and a day is up and I shall no longer be a *ben charrthach* and you will cease to be my *fer comtha*.'

Eadulf knew the terms well. He waited silently. He had known for some time that this day would come.

'Well, Eadulf, we must make a decision. Do you want me to become a *cétmuintir*?'

Eadulf looked at her. He realised that she was smiling. A *cétmuintir* was the first contracted wife. The partner of a permanent relationship. Eadulf put down his goblet of wine and reached out both his hands to her with a growing look of amazement.

'Let's talk about it,' he said softly.

Historical Afterword

⌘

In the previous fourteen books of the Sister Fidelma series, it has been my custom to include a historical note at the beginning as I have felt that for most readers the setting of the series, in seventh-century Ireland, would be unfamiliar. By now, I think that most people who pick up a Fidelma book will know the general background and that a weighty historical foreword now gets in the way of the story. The forewords remain in the previous editions and may also be found on the website of The International Sister Fidelma Society at *www.sisterfidelma.com* Further information may be found in the Society's thrice-yearly magazine *The Brehon*, distributed free to all members of the Society wherever they may be.

Suffice to say that the books accurately reflect the society, the law system, and the Celtic Church of seventh-century Ireland, and while some matters may still come as a surprise to readers, nevertheless this was the system that existed, as supported by the evidence of the surviving Irish law manuscripts and an extensive early medieval literature.

In deference to continued requests, the pronouncing guide, the list of principal characters and the map of Fidelma's world remain part of the present volume.

The action of *The Leper's Bell* takes place immediately following the events in *Badger's Moon*, during the month of Cet Gaimred, the first of the winter moons, which approximates to the modern month of November, in the year AD 667.

Pronunciation Guide

ℰ𝒟

As the Fidelma series has become increasingly popular, many English-speaking fans have written wanting assurance about the way to pronounce the Irish names and words.

Irish belongs to the Celtic branch of the Indo-European family of languages. It is closely related to Manx and Scottish Gaelic and a cousin of Welsh, Cornish and Breton. It is a very old European literary language. Professor Calvert Watkins of Harvard maintained it contains Europe's oldest *vernacular* literature, Greek and Latin both being a *lingua franca*. Surviving texts date from the seventh century AD.

The Irish of Fidelma's period is classed as Old Irish; after AD 950 the language entered a period known as Middle Irish. Therefore, in the Fidelma books, Old Irish forms are generally adhered to, whenever possible, in both names and words. This is like using Chaucer's English compared to modern English. For example, a word such as *aidche* ('night') in Old Irish is now rendered *oiche* in modern Irish.

There are only eighteen letters in the Irish alphabet. From earliest times there has been a literary standard but today four distinct spoken dialects are recognised. For our purposes, we will keep to Fidelma's dialect of Munster.

It is a general rule that stress is placed on the first syllable but, as in all languages, there are exceptions. In Munster the exceptions to the rule of initial stress are a) if the second syllable is long then it bears the stress; b) if the first two syllables are short and the third is long then the third syllable is stressed – such as in the word for fool, *amadán*, pronounced amad-awn; and c) where the second syllable contains ach and there is no long syllable, the second syllable bears the stress.

There are five short vowels – a, e, i, o, u – and five long vowels – á, é, í, ó, ú. On the long vowels note the accent, like the French acute, which is called a *fada* (literally, 'long'), and this is the only accent in Irish. It occurs on capitals as well as lower case.

The accent is important for, depending on where it is placed, it changes the entire word. *Seán* (Shawn) = John. But *sean* (shan) = old and *séan* (she-an) = an omen. By leaving out the accent on his name, the actor Sean Connery has become 'Old' Connery!

These short and long vowels are either 'broad' or 'slender'. The six broad vowels are:

a pronounced 'o' as in cot   á pronounced 'aw' as in law
o pronounced 'u' as in cut   ó pronounced 'o' as in low
u pronounced 'u' as in run   ú pronounced 'u' as in rule

The four slender vowels are:

i pronounced 'i' as in hit   í pronounced 'ee' as in see
e pronounced 'e' as in let   é pronounced 'ay' as in say

There are double vowels, some of which are fairly easy because they compare to English pronunciation – such as 'ae' as *say* or 'ui' as in *quit*. However, some double and even triple vowels in Irish need to be learnt.

ái pronounced like 'aw' in law (*dálaigh* = daw-lee)
ia pronounced like 'ea' in near
io pronounced like 'o' in come
éa pronounced like 'ea' in bear
ei pronounced like 'e' in let
aoi pronounced like the 'ea' in mean
uai pronounced like the 'ue' in blue
eoi pronounced like the 'eo' in yeoman
iai pronounced like the 'ee' in see

Hidden vowels

Most people will have noticed that many Irish people pronounce the word film as fil-um. This is actually a transference of Irish pronunciation rules. When **l**, **n** or **r** is followed by **b**, **bh**, **ch**, **g** (not after **n**), **m** or **mh**, and is preceded by a short stressed vowel, an additional vowel is heard between them. So *bolg* (stomach) is pronounced bol-ag; *garbh* (rough) is gar-ev; *dorcha* (dark) is dor-ach-a; *gorm* (blue) is gor-um and *ainm* (name) is an-im.

The consonants

b, **d**, **f**, **h**, **l**, **m**, **n**, **p**, **r** and **t** are said more or less as in English

g is always hard like the 'g' in gate

c is always hard like the 'c' in cat

s is pronounced like the 's' in said except before a slender vowel when it is pronounced 'sh' as in shin

In Irish the letters **j**, **k**, **q**, **w**, **x**, **y** or **z** do not exist and **v** is formed by the combination of **bh**.

Consonants can change their sound by aspiration or eclipse. Aspiration is caused by using the letter **h** after them.

bh is like the 'v' in voice

ch is a soft breath as in loch (not pronounced as lock!) or as in Ba*ch*

dh before a broad vowel is like the 'g' in gap

dh before a slender vowel is like the 'y' in year

fh is totally silent

gh before a slender vowel can sound like 'y' as in yet

mh is pronounced like the 'w' in wall

ph is like the 'f' in fall

th is like the 'h' in ham

sh is also like the 'h' in ham

Consonants can also change their sound by being eclipsed, or silenced, by another consonant placed before it. For example *na mBan* (of women) is pronounced nah *m*'on; *i bpaipéar* (in the paper) i *b*'ap'er and *i gcathair* (in the city) i *g*'a'har.

p can be eclipsed by **b, t**

t can be eclipsed by **d**

c can be eclipsed by **g**

f can be eclipsed by **bh**

b can be eclipsed by **m**

d and **g** can be eclipsed by **n**

For those interested in learning more about the language, it is worth remembering that, after centuries of suppression during the colonial period, Irish became the first official language of the Irish state on independence in 1922. The last published census of 1991 showed one third of the population returning themselves as Irish-speaking. In Northern Ireland, where the language continued to be openly discouraged after Partition in 1922, only 10.5 per cent of the population were able to speak the language in 1991, the first time an enumeration of speakers was allowed since Partition.

Language courses are now available on video and audio-cassette from a range of producers from Linguaphone to RTÉ and BBC. There are some sixty summer schools and special intensive courses available. Teilifís na Gaeilge is a television station broadcasting entirely in Irish and there are several Irish-language radio stations and newspapers. Information can be obtained from Comhdháil Náisiúnta na Gaeilge, 46 Sráid Chill Dara, Baile Atha Cliath 2, Éire.

Readers might also like to know that *Valley of the Shadow*, in the Fidelma series, was produced on audio-cassette, read by Marie McCarthy, from Magna Story Sound (SS391 – ISBN 1-85903-313-X).

Smoke in the Wind

Peter Tremayne

En route from Ireland to visit the new Archbishop of Canterbury, Sister Fidelma and her faithful Saxon companion, Brother Eadulf, find themselves on the coast of the Welsh kingdom of Dyfed when their ship is blown off course by a storm. The elderly King Gwlyddien is quick to offer hospitality, not least because the famous Irish *dálaigh* may be the only person capable of solving the mystery which has baffled the wisest of men – the entire monastic community of nearby Llanpadern, to which Gwlyddien's eldest son belongs, has vanished into thin air.

Who, or what, is behind the disappearance of the monks? Is it sorcery or some sinister plot – and what does the perpetrator hope to achieve? But before Fidelma and Eadulf can begin to answer these questions, they must contend with the shocking and seemingly unrelated murder of a local girl – a death whose consequences will be more tragic and more far-reaching than anyone can imagine.

Peter Tremayne's ten previous Sister Fidelma books are also available from Headline.

'The background detail is brilliantly defined . . . Wonderfully evocative' *The Times*

'Sister Fidelma is fast becoming a world ambassador for ancient Irish culture' *Irish Post*

0 7472 6434 1

headline

The Haunted Abbot

Peter Tremayne

Their business with the Archbishop of Canterbury now complete, Sister Fidelma and Brother Eadulf are preparing to return to Ireland when they receive a mysterious message. Eadulf's childhood friend, Brother Botulf, has requested their presence at Aldred's Abbey at midnight on the old pagan feast of Yule. Puzzled and intrigued by their summons, Fidelma and Eadulf battle against the harsh winter storms to make their appointment, only to find they are too late. Botulf is dead – killed by an unknown hand.

And as they struggle to comprehend this staggering news, it soon becomes clear that the murder of this young monk is not the only trouble facing the abbey. Another, less tangible danger threatens – the ghost of a young woman haunts the cloister shadows – a woman some say bears a startling likeness to the Abbot Cild's dead wife. But can Fidelma and Eadulf discover the truth before they themselves fall victim to the danger which pervades the abbey walls?

Peter Tremayne's eleven previous Sister Fidelma books are also available from Headline.

'The background detail is brilliantly defined . . . Wonderfully evocative' *The Times*

'This is masterly storytelling from an author who breathes fascinating life into the world he is writing about' *Belfast Telegraph*

0 7472 6435 X

headline

Now you can buy any of these other bestselling books by **Peter Tremayne** from your bookshop or *direct from his publisher*.

FREE P&P AND UK DELIVERY
(Overseas and Ireland £3.50 per book)

Absolution By Murder	£6.99
Shroud for the Archbishop	£6.99
Suffer Little Children	£6.99
The Subtle Serpent	£6.99
The Spider's Web	£6.99
Valley of the Shadow	£6.99
The Monk Who Vanished	£6.99
Act of Mercy	£6.99
Hemlock at Vespers	£6.99
Our Lady of Darkness	£6.99
Smoke in the Wind	£6.99
The Haunted Abbot	£6.99
Badger's Moon	£6.99
Whispers of the Dead	£6.99

TO ORDER SIMPLY CALL THIS NUMBER

01235 400 414

or visit our website: www.madaboutbooks.com

Prices and availability subject to change without notice.